A RAGING DAWN

Fatal Insomnia, Book Two

CJ Lyons

PRAISE FOR *NEW YORK TIMES* BESTSELLER CJ LYONS' THRILLERS WITH HEART:

"Everything a great thriller should be—action packed, authentic, and intense." ~*New York Times bestselling author Lee Child*

"A compelling voice in thriller writing...I love how the characters come alive on every page." ~*New York Times bestselling author Jeffery Deaver*

"Top Pick! A fascinating and intense thriller." ~*RT Book Reviews*

"An intense, emotional thriller...(that) climbs to the edge of intensity." ~*National Examiner*

"A perfect blend of romance and suspense. My kind of read." ~*New York Times Bestselling author Sandra Brown*

"Highly engaging characters, heart-stopping scenes...one great rollercoaster ride." ~*Bookreporter.com*

"Adrenalin pumping." ~*The Mystery Gazette*

"Riveting." ~*Publishers Weekly*

Lyons "is a master within the genre." ~*Pittsburgh Magazine*

"A great fast-paced read....Not to be missed." ~*Book Addict*

"Characters with beating hearts and three dimensions." ~*Newsday*

"A pulse-pounding adrenalin rush!" ~*New York Times bestselling author Lisa Gardner*

"...Harrowing, emotional, action-packed and brilliantly realized." ~*New York Times bestselling author Susan Wiggs*

"Explodes on the page...I absolutely could not put it down." ~*Romance Readers' Connection*

A RAGING DAWN

A Novel of Fatal Insomnia

CJ Lyons

EDGY READS

To fear love is to fear life,
and those who fear life
are already three parts dead.
~Bertrand Russell

CHAPTER ONE

LIVING WITH LIES means sleeping with fear. Or in my case, *not* sleeping and running away like a thief racing the dawn.

The December moonlight eased its way through the sheer curtains of Ryder's bedroom, as I scanned his dresser. I wanted to make certain I hadn't left anything behind. It wasn't as if I could never come back if I forgot something, but I didn't want to make assumptions. Or promises I couldn't keep.

Ozzie, the service dog who'd adopted me, looked up from where he lay in front of the door, blocking my escape. A sigh heaved through his body in the way only fat, pampered, well-loved Labs can sigh.

"Hush," I whispered, mindful of Ryder still asleep in the bed I'd just left. "I have to go."

He thumped his tail and looked at me with mournful eyes.

"I know you miss her," I said as I bent to tie my Reeboks. Ozzie's owner, a ten-year-old girl named Esme, was away at school and had entrusted me with his care. It's a long, complicated story involving a tragic love affair, a ruthless billionaire, a vicious gang leader, and a serial killer stalking the city.

My life used to be so simple: go to work in the ER, play my fiddle, eat a little humble pie at family meals, repeat. But in the last three weeks, my existence had spiraled from one complicated story into another to the point where it was becoming difficult to remember which were lies and which were secrets.

Not after today. My shoulders slumped as I turned back to the bed one last time. Today was the day the truth would come out and I could walk away from my life. Maybe to Tahiti. Probably to Tahiti. Most certainly alone. I told myself that's always been the way I wanted it: no strings, no debts, no heartbreak.

Well, maybe this time, a little heartbreak.

My gaze fell on the sleeping man I'd left behind. I wanted…I wished…

The numbers on the nightstand clock blinked. Three twenty-one. I spotted my cell phone beside it. Instead of reaching out to Ryder, sleeping deeply, as any sane person would be this hour, I grabbed my phone. No assumptions, no promises. Not today, when I'd be learning for sure if there'd be any tomorrows for Ryder and me.

He's a detective, assigned to Good Samaritan's Advocacy Center where I used to be an ER physician. We met only three weeks ago, but you'd be amazed at how much you can pack into three weeks when you agree to not talk about the past or the future, and one of you is recovering from a minor bullet wound, while the other is hiding from a death sentence.

A tremor shook my free hand, and I clenched it into a fist, smothering it inside the pocket of my hoodie. At least I had Tahiti…

Tahiti wasn't me giving up. I was going to fight for every moment I could. Rather, it was a promise. I might be dying, but death would not define me. I was going out when I decided and how I decided, disease be damned.

Except…Ryder. A complication almost as unexpected as my one-in-a-hundred-million diagnosis. I couldn't allow myself to want or need Ryder more than I already did. Sex was something we could both walk away from without getting hurt.

I stood there, staring, phone in my hand, watching him sleep, yearning to reach out and comb his hair back from his eyes. Ryder doesn't snore; the sound he makes is more a constant rumble like a furnace running hot. After I left his warm embrace, he'd curled up on his side, one fist tucked under his chin like a baby.

Not that I'd ever tell him that. In addition to being a detective, facing the worst the streets of Cambria City have to offer, Ryder had been to war in the early days in Afghanistan. Yet, he still projects an aura of untarnished innocence. Not naïveté, definitely not. More like he's seen it all—the good, the bad, and the ugly—and has somehow risen above.

It took all my strength to turn away from him now. Ozzie raised his head, shaking it, the fairytale wise man warning me to turn back before it was too late. Except this was no fairytale.

The phone in my hand rang. A cheerful ring tone crashing through the night like a battering ram. I didn't have to look to know Ryder was awake. Fully alert, the way cops and soldiers and ER doctors woke, instantly and ready for anything.

I also didn't have to look to know who was calling. "Are you okay?" I answered.

"There are footsteps. In the hall. They keep coming and going." Tymara Nelson's voice stretched tight with fear, ready to break.

I sagged onto the bed, my back to Ryder, but I felt his warmth as he shifted to sit up behind me. He settled one hand on my shoulder, a gift of encouragement and understanding.

"Did you actually see anyone? Did they stop at your door?" The first four times Tymara had called like this, I'd sent the cops to check on her. The next, I'd called Devon Price, the owner of the Kingston Tower apartments where she lived, and he'd ordered his men to watch over her. But Devon's former gang members had made her too nervous, and so she'd sent them away. Not that I blamed her for being nervous about testifying, but there wasn't much more I could do to help.

"No. When I look, there's no one there." A strangled cry emerged with her words. "But I know it's them."

Seven months ago, Tymara had been viciously attacked. A man she barely knew had raped her at knifepoint. Then, he'd blindfolded and bound her and invited others into her apartment to do worse. They'd left her for dead after a night filled with degradations that were unimaginable—unless you were the ER doc performing her forensic exam and taking her history after she miraculously survived.

Tymara didn't sleep much anymore. If I hadn't convinced her that the conviction of the one man the police had caught would be our best chance to get him to reveal the names of his partners in crime, she wouldn't even be testifying today. In the six months since he'd been arrested and placed behind bars, there'd been no actual threats against her, but that didn't stop her middle-of-the-night phone calls to me.

"It's going to be all right, Tymara." I kept my tone soothing and gentle as I lied to her. I'd dealt with enough victims to know it would never be all right, but things would—could—get better. "I'll come over."

"No. No." She blew out her breath. "I'm fine. It's all in my head, I know. I just needed—"

"I don't mind. Whatever you need. I can come to your place, or I can call the police—"

Cambria City barely had enough funds to keep the police department functional, much less provide anything extravagant like witness protection, but Ryder had friends who owed him. He'd offered to watch over Tymara himself, even though he didn't start his new position at the Advocacy Center until today and technically, this wasn't his case. He still felt a sense of ownership. Tymara was one of our victims, which meant we'd do whatever it took to bring her the justice she deserved.

"No." Her tone was firmer now, filled with hope that this would all soon be over and she could reclaim her life. "I'll be all right. It's only for a few more hours."

"I'll be there by eight thirty to pick you up." Today was the second day of the trial; administrative issues and the testimony of police officers and lab techs had consumed the first.

"I go after you, right?"

"No. I think Manny decided to start with you before lunch. And then me after." Manny Cruz was the ADA prosecuting Tymara's rapist, Eugene Littleton.

"Right, right. I remember. He'll be there? In the same room?" She meant Littleton.

"Yes. But you don't have to look at him. You've met Manny, just focus on him."

"You won't be there?" She was twenty-three, but the uptick in her voice made her sound like a little girl.

We'd gone through this dozens of times. I'd walk her through it a dozen more if it helped to ease her fears. "I'll be waiting outside. I can't come in, not until after I've testified."

"Right. Sequestered. That's what Mr. Cruz said. He's nice, don't you think?"

Actually, I didn't. Manny Cruz was one of those competitive types who measure every encounter as a win or loss—and he liked to win, no matter the cost. Which made him the perfect prosecutor for this case. Once he won and Littleton was convicted, Manny would go after everyone else involved, knowing that with Littleton's testimony in exchange for a lighter sentence, they'd all be easy wins.

Whatever it took. "Sure you don't want me to come over?" Ryder squeezed my shoulder, offering his own services. It scared me that in only three weeks we didn't need words. It had never been that way with my ex, Jacob, and he and I had been married two years.

Tymara's voice drifted drowsily. "No. Really. I'm fine now. I'm going to go back to bed. Thanks, Dr. Rossi."

"No problem at all. Let me know if you change your mind. See you soon." I hung up.

"Coming or going?" Ryder asked from behind me, his breath stirring the small hairs on my neck. His tone wasn't judgmental. Ryder never judged me, not even at times like this, when he had every right to.

I slid free of his warmth, stood, and steeled myself against the cold. "What do you mean?"

"Where do you go after I fall asleep? Even if I wake up in the morning and you're still beside me, I can tell you've been gone during the night."

It was a valid question. What kind of woman used a man for sex and every pleasure imaginable, but couldn't remain in his bed for a full night?

Answer: the kind of woman whose brain is half-rotted by warped proteins known as prions.

Whatever my final diagnosis turned out to be, my brain was literally burning itself out. Which scared the hell out of me. And yet, during my time with Ryder, waiting for my lab results, I couldn't help but convince myself that at any moment I'd get a call from the hospital telling me that they'd made a dreadful mistake, that everything was going to be just fine.

This is why doctors make the worst patients. Our knowledge leaves us powerless. Forces us to lie to ourselves, to those around us. To deny the truth and seek the impossible. But my lies were swiftly crumbling to dust.

"Going." I somehow found the strength to tell him.

He glanced at the clock. "There's plenty of time." Another lie, but he didn't know it. He patted the empty pillow beside him. "Come back to bed."

God, how I wanted to.

"I can't."

He blinked, nodded. "Your appointment with your doctor. That's today, isn't it?"

I stepped back, away from him, from everything he had to offer. He was breaking the rules and he knew it—my illness was off-limits. Here, in his house, in his arms, it did not exist.

Anger flooded over me. He didn't deserve it. They were my ridiculous rules, and he'd been patient for three long weeks, but still, I couldn't help it. I wasn't angry with him. I was angry with the entire universe. Heaven and Hell. From the farthest celestial body to the microscopic proteins ravaging my life. So damn angry. All the time.

One more reason to leave. Before my rage poisoned what we had together.

So I did. I'm not proud of it. I ran. From his questions, from his half-hidden glances of concern, from everything he offered without asking for a single thing in return except the one thing I couldn't give him, not without destroying us: the truth.

What comes after dread? Fear.

I'm not used to feeling like this. Afraid. Usually, I'm the one people turn to when they're afraid and need saving.

Except this time, I'm the one who needs saving.

I'm Angela Rossi. I'm thirty-four years old, and this is the story of how I die.

I'm a lover and ex-wife and sister and daughter and friend, and this is the story of how I betray them all.

Most of all, it's a story of redemption.

And hope.

Guess it all depends on your point of view…

CHAPTER TWO

GLISTENING WHITE-SAND beaches, gleaming ruby-turquoise sunsets, graceful arching palm trees…the Tahiti travel brochures duct taped to my refrigerator promised escape.

Sodden Pennsylvania December skies, diamond-edged sleet, wind chill hovering a few degrees above freezing…that was the reality outside my apartment windows. A cold front had moved in after I returned from Ryder's house with Ozzie a few hours ago.

I downed my handful of morning meds and drank a stringy, green antioxidant shake straight from the blender before it had a chance to congeal. The stuff tasted as foul as it looked. But when you're down to last chances, you learn to swallow your pride.

Since I'd arrived home, while Ozzie snored on the couch, I'd pounded away the miles on my treadmill, trying to force my body to produce the endorphins I'd need to keep me functional in court today. Endorphins that a brush of Ryder's gaze and a single touch of his lips could produce effortlessly. I hated how I'd left Ryder, wished I were able to go back and invite him to stand with me when I went to the hospital today to learn my fate.

Hated myself even more for wanting that. Selfish. Cowardly. Leaning on Ryder, letting him get closer…that path led to heartache for both of us.

When the running didn't work, I turned to my fiddle, my lifelong refuge from reality. But after my shaking hands produced an off-tempo, discordant symphony of missed notes, the strings escaping my fingers, I threw it down in frustration.

As the clock ticked down to when I'd have to leave for my appointment, I made a mental list—I couldn't bear to write it down—of everything I'd need to take care of after today: telling my family, helping them mourn, making final arrangements. Death strikes in an instant. You're there, then gone. But dying…dying is a logistical nightmare.

My mood turned as leaden as the sky outside. Not that Cambria City is known for its sunshine, but it seemed as if we were getting more than our fair share of gray and dreary this winter. Ozzie looked up from where he lay on my couch. I finished my shake and sat on the arm, idly scratching between his ears with one hand while I turned on the TV with the other. Animal Planet, his favorite. He thumped his tail in thanks.

I looked around my loft as if I might never return, already missing the old-brick walls, heart-of-pine floors, jumbled books, scattered medical journals, and dirty laundry. I lived in the same apartment I grew up in, above my Uncle Jimmy's bar. It's the closest I've ever come to a home.

Leaving the TV on for Ozzie, I grabbed my bag and left. I didn't want to be late. The thought stopped me. Didn't want to be late? I was headed to my neurologist's office to see how long I had left to live.

I shook my head, torn between laughing and crying and settling on neither. Instead, I wrapped myself in the numb limbo I'd worked so hard to create these past three weeks. A calm before the storm. Or maybe simply a calm. Wouldn't that be nice? Escaping the anger and bitterness and regret by embracing denial.

Denial. It was so unlike me, the rebel, the fighter; I felt like a stranger to myself. I hadn't felt this way, this weird, almost out-of-body disconnect with reality, since I was twelve and my father died. God, how I missed him, even twenty-two years later. He gave me my first fiddle, taught me how to play, his foot keeping time, his smile bringing the notes to life.

Not even that memory could break through the brick wall my emotions hid behind. I clutched the doorknob to my apartment. It took all of my energy not to turn tail and run back inside and hide under the covers.

No. I would not stop fighting. Could not give up hope.

But first, I needed to know who the enemy was.

Clattering down the stairs, I made the mistake of leaving by the front door, which meant crossing through my uncle's bar. It's a traditional dark-paneled, working-class Irish pub with high-backed booths, large tables scarred with cigarette burns and knife marks, and a stage for live music. Music is a family affair, going back to the ceili band my father founded decades ago. Dad was Italian, but with his love of traditional music no matter the nationality, he fit right in with the Kielys, my mom's boisterous Irish clan.

My hopes of escaping undetected were shattered when I ran into Uncle Jimmy. He's a Kiely, my mom's older brother, and like all Kielys, except me, has strawberry-blond hair and a complexion prone to flushing when he drinks too much, which all Kielys except me are prone to do. Me, I'm a Rossi through and through with my dark curls, high cheekbones, and deep-set eyes that mirror my dad's so much that after his death, my mom couldn't bear to look at me without breaking into tears. Thankfully my sister, Evie, two years younger than I am, takes after Mom's side of the family and never makes Mom cry or look away or sigh.

Jimmy was taking inventory after the weekend festivities. He glanced up from his clipboard and frowned at me. "Didn't you just get home a few hours ago? Where are you off to now?"

I was used to his prying. No one in my family ever minded their own business, at least not when it came to my life. It was the price I paid for being the prodigal returned home. "I have an appointment. Will you keep an eye on Ozzie for me?"

"It's not even seven in the morning. What kind of appointment has you dressed like you're going to Mass? Not that we ever see you there."

I'd changed into my court outfit: my best slacks, an ivory blouse, and a red blazer. Last thing I'd admit to was a visit with a doctor. "I'm picking up a rape victim and taking her to court."

I moved to rush past him, but he stepped into my path.

"Well, you can spare me a minute, young lady. We're all worried about you, the way you've been acting these past few weeks. Out all hours, barely home at all, not bothering to visit your mom, only dropping by to play a few sets and then vanishing again." He set his clipboard on the bar to give me his full attention. "Not to mention that new guy who keeps coming around. The cop."

Ryder loved hearing me play my fiddle with the ceili band and would drop by the bar to listen. He understood that I needed our relationship to remain private. I couldn't even fully explain why. It somehow made my time with him feel special, divorced from the ugly reality I faced every day. Last thing I wanted was him pulled into the drama my family generated as effortlessly as breathing.

Jimmy squinted at me when I didn't answer. "Haven't seen you take a drop, not here at any rate, but if I didn't know better—"

I held back my impulse to tell him to look in a mirror. "I'm not an alcoholic."

"Must be drugs then. Your playing is off. I've seen the shakes hit when you think no one's looking. I've seen how cops drink. Cleaned up after their other vices. What's that man gotten you into?"

"Nothing," I snapped, hating that he blamed Ryder.

His face creased with concern, and I reined in my temper. I might be an adult, a physician used to making life-and-death decisions, but to my family, I would always be the twelve-year-old girl whose poor judgment got her father killed.

I placed a hand—non-trembling, thanks to the meds I'd just

taken—on his arm. "I'm fine. Really."

He clapped his hand, large enough to swallow mine twice over, on top of mine and squeezed. "Then why did the ER let you go?"

"They didn't." From his expression, he didn't believe me. "I wasn't fired. I resigned. Thinking of moving. Trying something, someplace, new."

There. I'd lit the fuse. The explosion would come after he passed the word down the family grapevine and it reached my mom, Patsy.

"Move?" His hand fell away from mine. "What nonsense is that? You can't leave—you'll break your mother's heart." The "again" remained unspoken.

The bar's front door blew open, a gust of cold wind and a spark of sunshine casting aside the gloom. My younger sister, Evie, was carrying a cardboard box. Jimmy ran to help her while I shut the door against the December cold.

"Good, you're both here," she said, shaking her strawberry curls. "I was hoping to catch you."

"I'm on my way to court," I said. It was much too early to deal with Evie's eternal cheeriness.

"This won't take long," she said. Jimmy set the box on the bar, and she opened the top. "Mom wants twinkle lights for the Christmas party."

Our family celebrates Christmas Eve with an all-night party in the bar, open to everyone, filled with nonstop music, drink—and apparently this year, twinkle lights. Jimmy picked up a handful and grimaced. "I've already hung the evergreens she wanted, decked the halls with boughs of holly, even replaced the Christmas tree when she decided against the blue spruce," he protested. "But I draw the line at fairy lights. Next thing you know, she'll be wanting glitter on the damn taps."

My mom, Patsy, was the youngest Kiely sister, but she ruled the clan. She always got what she wanted—but that didn't mean she got it without a fight. Sometimes I think the Kielys lived for bickering, reconciling, and beginning the cycle all over again. I never understood it or learned how to play the game.

Now Evie? She was a master. She beamed at Jimmy, stood on her tiptoes, and kissed his cheek. "Do it for me, Jimmy? They'll look so pretty hanging from the rafters."

He blushed and nodded. Then she turned to me, handing me a piece of stationery with Patsy's elegant printing. "Here's the playlist Mom wants to start the party. She thought you could give it to Jacob."

Jacob is my ex. We were married two years, divorced for almost four. My family conveniently refuses to acknowledge the divorced part, as Jacob is an integral member of the family ceili band. Can't say I blame them. There have been plenty of times when Jacob and I also conveniently forgot we were divorced.

I dutifully pocketed the playlist. Jacob worked for the public defender's office, so we'd be on opposite sides today as he defended Tymara's rapist. Maybe I'd wait until tomorrow to give him Patsy's list.

I turned to leave. "What time will you be home?" Evie called after me.

"Not sure."

"But you *are* coming home?" With my back to her, it was impossible to tell Evie's voice from my mom's, they sounded so much alike. "Angela, you aren't in trouble, are you? We're worried."

"I'm fine," I lied and walked out the door, closing it on their suspicions and unvoiced accusations. Jimmy and Evie were only the first hurdle and by far the easiest. But sooner or later, I would have to face my mom.

Tahiti never looked so good.

CHAPTER THREE

LOUISE MEHTA IS my neurologist. She's also my best friend. Used to be, any time the two of us got together, it involved good wine and bad jokes. You have not heard a dirty joke until you've heard it told by a middle-aged, meticulously dressed Indian woman with a faint upper-crust British accent.

Only, it's been weeks since I've heard Louise joke about anything. Telling your friend she probably has a one-in-a-hundred-million, rare, always-fatal disease pretty much kills any punch line.

Louise loves routine, likes everything to follow a precise order. Her favorite thing is to check items off her many lists—lists of questions to ask patients, lists of articles to read, lists of groceries to buy. She's governed by bullet points.

I'm not. As an ER doc, chaos is my constant companion. Lists and practice guidelines, standard operating procedures, paperwork in triplicate—they all give me hives. I like being flexible, juggling a bunch of ideas—many contradictory—all at once, playing devil's advocate.

"Good morning. How are you feeling?" Louise's gaze was fixed on my chart as she entered the exam room where I waited. Trailing after her was a dark-haired man in his early thirties, his white coat brimming with tools, including the longest reflex hammer I'd ever seen. The tablet computer clutched in his hands was a match to the one in Louise's pocket.

"Resident," was my diagnosis. I restrained an eye roll. Amazing. I'd gone from attending physician to lab rat in a matter of days. Guess I knew what my tests were going to show if Louise was putting me on display for her neurology residents.

She glanced up, surprised I hadn't returned her greeting. Never mind that it was the kind of greeting you gave a patient, not a friend. She saw me staring at the man. "Oh, sorry. This is Tommaso Lazaretto, a visiting neurofellow from Penn. Tommaso, this is Dr. Angela Rossi. Tommaso has done some work in prion diseases, so he's very interested in your case."

I transferred my stare to her and arched one eyebrow. I felt an illicit rush of satisfaction when she flushed. "Tommaso, why don't you wait outside? Angela and I have a few things to discuss."

To his credit, Tommaso stepped forward and took my hand. "I'm so pleased to meet you, Dr. Rossi." He had the faintest of Italian accents. "I'm sorry it's under such unfortunate circumstances. I look forward to working with you."

I gave him a lukewarm handshake, having no patience for niceties. Not when Louise held my future in that file in her hands. Tommaso left, carefully closing the door behind him. Leaving me and Louise and my unnamed diagnosis trapped inside the tiny room.

Louise leaned against the closed door, looking down at where I sat on the swivel stool traditionally reserved for the physician. I'd taken it by habit and, once on it, couldn't bring myself to move to the patient exam table.

I drew in my breath, steeling myself. Didn't even give her time to take the other chair and sit down. "What did the DNA results show?"

Her face told me everything I needed to know. "We were able to isolate your father's DNA from the sample you brought in." I'd stolen my dad's old straight razor from my mom's stash of his keepsakes. "The results confirmed my suspicions. Although there are some abnormal genetic markers, your father tested positive for Fatal Familial Insomnia."

Her voice was steady, clinical. I was glad. If she'd shown emotion, I don't think I could have handled that.

She sank into the chair beside me as I processed this new reality. A strange fog of relief swirled through me, leaving me with goose bumps in its wake. "Do you think—could he have had symptoms already? Back then? I mean…" My voice trailed off, a breathless sigh of hope.

Could twenty-two years of family lore be wrong? Because if fatal insomnia, with its muscle spasms, hallucinations, and sudden fugue states—episodes that left a person catatonic for a period of time—had caused my dad's accident, then I wasn't to blame. For the first time in my life, I could forgive myself for being the reason why he was out on the road that stormy night, coming to pick me up after yet another afterschool detention. Maybe the rest of the family would finally forgive me as well.

Louise didn't have to check her notes. "Yes. It's definitely possible that he already had symptoms. I'd love to learn more about his family, especially anyone else who died young."

"Sorry, there's no one. His mother brought him here from Italy after his father died, and she died—cancer—before I was born." The facts helped distance me from the emotional tug-of-war raging in my mind. If Dad had fatal insomnia, then the odds I had it were fifty-fifty. Not just me, but my little sister as well. How the hell was I going to break it to Mom and Evie that she was at risk?

"And me?" I asked, sucking in my gut, preparing for the one-two punch.

She hesitated. "Indeterminate." That was the problem with testing for a disease that only hit one in one hundred million people. "We'll repeat it, of course. But given your symptoms, with him testing positive, I don't see any other possibility for a diagnosis."

Louise was the smartest person I knew. And the best doctor. If she had ruled out every other possibility, then that was that. The disease that had killed my father and let me off the hook for his death was also the disease that would kill me.

Okay. *Okay.* Now I knew what the enemy was—a microscopic protein known as a prion—the same thing that caused mad cow disease. A nasty, traitorous, crumbled clump of tissue had contaminated my brain, turning it into Swiss cheese.

She reached a hand toward my shoulder. Toddler that I was at times, I pushed hard with my feet, propelling the stool out of range of Louise's comfort so fast I ricocheted off the exam table and knocked over the empty metal waste can with a clatter. It rolled across the floor, landing at Louise's feet. She looked at me. At the can. Then she tilted her face toward me, a quirky half smile creasing her eyes. She gave me a quick nod as if agreeing to an unspoken conspiracy and kicked it soccer-style.

Her aim was perfection, careening it against the corner and back to me. I raised my foot and stomped down so hard the empty metal can caved in with a satisfying crunch. The perfect explosion of petulant, childish rage.

It felt good. Damn good. If not for the fact that the stupid, cheap tin can crumpled around my foot and I had to balance against the exam bed to shake free of it. Flushed, I turned to Louise. She waited for my response as I wavered between tears and laughter. Laughter won out.

I sat again on the stool, wheeled my way around the crushed can, and rejoined her at the desk. "Put that on my bill."

"You know they'll mark up that piece of essential medical equipment until the insurance company thinks you destroyed an MRI machine."

"Not like I'll be around to pay for it," I shot back. That sobered us both. But it was the truth, no sense in avoiding it. I released my breath, my stomach caving in. "So…Tahiti it is."

"Tahiti?" she asked, confused. I let it hang. Louise was smart enough to figure it out for herself. It only took a beat, and her expression turned fierce. "Angela Rossi. Are you that selfish? To

26

abandon your friends, your family—"

"I'm trying to spare them, and you damn well know it."

"You're a control freak. Brassed off that finally there is something beyond your control," she retorted.

"What do you want me to do? Lie there, helpless, awake and aware of everything, while the people I love wipe my ass for me? How's that for a final memory to haunt them the rest of their lives?"

Louise crossed her arms, hugging the chart to her chest. Inhaled and blew out her breath, lipstick feathering into the creases around her mouth. "It doesn't have to come to that. I can help."

I stared at her, surprised. She'd lose her job, her license, maybe even go to jail. "I can't ask you—"

"You didn't." She released the chart from her grip and set it between us. "I'm offering. It can be here or...Tahiti. But promise me, whatever you decide, you'll say good-bye first. Your friends and family deserve that at least."

Images of the band filled me. Of Jimmy's bar, music soaring, spinning out of control, as laughter filled the air and people danced: Mom, Evie, Uncle Jimmy, my two obnoxious cousins, Jacob—my ex—Louise and her family, my colleagues from the Advocacy Center and ER. And Ryder. It was the last that made me nod my agreement. The way Ryder looked at me when I played my fiddle, as if I were the only woman in the entire universe. Who could resist the chance to see that one last time?

Except...I looked away. "Ryder. It's not fair. He never signed up for this."

"Don't you think that's his choice?" Louise's infamous *you're screwing up again* glare said it all. It was the one she gave me every time I hooked up with Jacob for one of our on-again, off-again flings. Of course, she needn't worry. Jacob and I were never going to happen again. Not after Ryder. He'd be my last. And, in so many ways, my first. First time I ever needed, ever wanted a man in my life—no, that was wrong—first time I ever wanted to be part of a man's life, instead of solely living my own.

"Ryder deserves to know," she said.

"He deserves a lot more than that. Which is why I can't drag him into this." My words hung between us. Then I dared to ask the question I'd been avoiding. "How long?"

"There's been speculation that some alternative therapies may—"

"Do I have time for speculation?"

"Maybe." She hesitated, her mind scouring a hundred checklists of variables.

There are four stages to FFI. Stage one, your episodes of insomnia last a few days, resulting in muscle tremors, confusion, mood swings, anxiety, and irritability. All of which I had in spades. Which was why I'd finally quit the ER last month. I could no longer hide the muscle spasms that increased with stress. Plus, I'd experienced a few symptoms that weren't listed in any textbook—things that might have put patients at risk. So, good-bye, career. Hello to the sheer hell of the absolute boredom of the unemployable.

Most people with FFI die within nine months of exhibiting symptoms. My symptoms began five months ago. We'd already wasted three weeks waiting on the lab results. But I'd found a case report of a patient who had lived twenty-seven months by using a combination of stimulants, antioxidant supplements, sensory deprivation, and intense aerobic exercise.

A single case, one man. But it was enough to give me hope. Silly me. You'd think anyone who'd spent her adult life working on the front lines of the ER would know better.

"Angela?" Louise tapped my shoulder. I'd zoned out. I was doing that a lot lately. "Are you okay?" Frown lines born of concern crossed her brow.

"I'm fine," I lied. Last month I'd told Louise about my hallucinations—the echoes of color, the strange movements no one else saw, coupled with music so intense and soulful it would have made Mozart weep. They were a prelude to my fugue states, catatonic episodes in which my senses became hyperacute, while my body remained frozen and unresponsive. I'd even mentioned the symptom not found in any journal article or textbook: my newfound ability to communicate with patients who were in a certain type of coma.

"Any more seizures?" Louise and her multitude of tests had decided my symptoms were variations of the unique seizures patients with fatal insomnia were prone to. Nothing to worry about because they weren't real, merely hallucinations born of a brain riddled with holes. Especially that last, the talking with not-quite-dead people.

All the science said she was right. That what was happening to me was impossible. I couldn't bring myself to burst her cozy bubble of medical certainty and reveal the true extent of my symptoms. From a scientific standpoint, we'd already gone way past stage one right into the Twilight Zone.

"No," I lied. "The meds seem to be helping."

Louise scribbled refills for my prescriptions. Powerful stimulants. They were enough to make an elephant tap-dance, but they barely managed to keep me functional as my body burned through dosages designed for someone three times my size.

"Do you want me to tell your sister, arrange for her to be tested?"

Oh God. Evie. My stomach clenched so hard I felt my belly button slam against my spine. I never should have sniped at her this morning. I fought to keep my voice steady. "No. I'll do it."

She tapped her pen against the prescription pad. "There is something else we could try. Totally experimental, but after what you told me happened last month—"

"You mean PXA. No." I pushed the stool back, putting distance between myself and the thought of using the drug the street had nicknamed Death Head. Paramethoxamine destabilized the chemical process the brain used to create pain. A fact that sadistic serial killer Leo Kingston had taken advantage of, using the tunnels beneath the city as a lair for torturing his victims with PXA. His unique formulation of the drug created pain so intense and unrelenting his victims would do anything to stop it. Anything he commanded of them.

He'd used it on me before I killed him. I'd felt that pain. It was as if I was burning alive from the inside out. A pain that made you beg for death.

Louise was busy continuing down her checklist on her tablet, stylus in hand. "There's a research facility in Italy that specializes in Fatal Familial Insomnia. Tommaso knows the people there. I'm going to have them review your case, see if there are any treatment options. In the meantime, I want to see you in a week, after Christmas."

The air felt heavy, dragging down my lungs, as it if were already too late. I had a sudden vision: myself, lying on a remote beach, breathing my last, wide awake, feeling everything. Alone. It was as tempting as it was terrifying.

I slid the tablet from her, glanced at her checklist. It covered the entire screen, but highlighted at the top was *Have Tommaso double-check Angie's results.*

No way in hell Louise hadn't already checked and rechecked a dozen times over before coming in here. She didn't need some neurofellow to tell her what she knew was true. Yet she refused to give up hope.

If someone as smart as Louise still had hope, how could I not?

Ryder's face filled my mind. The Death Head, horrible as it had been, had tempered some of my symptoms, including my bizarre fugues. In a weird way, it was the combination of the Death Head and my fatal insomnia that had allowed me to save Ryder from Leo Kingston.

Could I really say no to what might be our final hope?

Pulling one of the ubiquitous drug-company notepads and pens across the table, I sketched a small box with sharp, bold strokes. Gold and blue flames flared from the edges of the paper, invisible except to me, and I studiously ignored them. In three weeks, I'd learned to tell the difference between hallucinations brought on by my Swiss-cheesed brain and reality.

"What are you doing?" she asked, leaning forward to look down on my handiwork.

"Making you a new list." In block letters, I wrote *Tell Angie she's dying.*

Louise made a guttural noise, filled with dismay, as I drew a large X in the box beside the words.

"I'm not done yet," I muttered as the flames grew, morphing into a deep purple and ruby. No music, so I had time before the fugue hit.

Another box scratched into the paper, one corner tearing at the page. Then I printed: *Help Angie find a way to FIGHT back.*

I pushed the paper, flames and all, across the table to her. As soon as she took it into her hand, the fire vanished. Her frown tightened her round face into a narrow heart shape. "There's nothing—not with prions—"

"Not yet." I pushed back my stool and stood. "Doesn't mean we can't be the first."

She glanced up at me, her mouth twisted in a strange combination of a smile and a sad grimace. "Does that mean you're staying?"

I couldn't make that promise. "It means I'm not giving up." I held out my hand, gesturing at her prescription pad. "Go ahead. Give me the PXA."

CHAPTER FOUR

DEVON PRICE SAT in a Louis XIV chair beside his biological father's handcrafted, black walnut bed and read the *Financial Times* aloud. The soft pulsating of a heart monitor kept pace with Devon's words as a feeding tube dripped sustenance into his father.

He and his father, Daniel Kingston, had nothing in common. Devon's skin was as dark as the coffee he sipped, while Daniel was paler than milk. Devon had been raised by his mother in Kingston Tower, the low-income housing complex that was a crucible of blood and violence. Daniel had lived all his life here in the Kingston family mansion, affectionately known as "the brownstone." Daniel hadn't even christened his bastard son with the family name; he'd reserved that honor for his "real" son, Leo.

Yet, it wasn't Leo here at his comatose father's bedside. It wasn't Leo taking control of the multinational family company. No, Leo, dear Leo, was dead. And Devon had played a large role in ending the sadistic son of a bitch.

As he tormented his dear, not-quite-departed father with news of impending economic doom—Devon shared only bad news with

Daniel—his gaze glided over the Kingston family crest carved into the headboard: Omnes nominis defendere. "Above all, defend the family name."

Too bad his half-brother hadn't taken those words to heart. Leo had poisoned Daniel with a dangerous designer drug, PXA, leaving him in a coma after Daniel discovered that Leo, the brilliant scientist, the good son, had been abducting girls. Leo had imprisoned them in a secret lab built in the tunnels beneath the city, injected them with his chemical cocktails, and then raped, tortured, and killed them.

So much for Kingston family values.

Devon turned the page. The prognostications all sounded so certain, as if money was what ruled the world. Idiots. He glanced at Daniel, being fed by a tube, eyes staring, unseeing, at the only son he had left.

Devon was only twenty-eight, but he'd seen a lot in this world. He had studied philosophers who lived above it in ivory towers as well as street poets who ran in gutters flowing with blood, racing to their own tragic deaths. Despite what the classicists said, the world did not revolve around logic, nor was your fate predetermined. The romantics had it all wrong as well: Passion and love weren't the answer.

No. What this world ran on was irony. Embodied by karma, kismet, payback…whatever you called it, it was a bitch.

His phone rang. Flynn.

"What did the doctor say?" he asked. Flynn was with Devon's daughter, Esme, at her new school up in Vermont. Esme was having a hard time adjusting. No surprise: it'd been less than a month since she'd seen her mother, Jess, killed.

"Same as the others," she answered. "Post-traumatic stress, normal for a girl her age who has been through what she has. This one wanted to give her medicine, but I looked it up. It's an anti-psychotic and has side effects."

Sometimes talking to her, he forgot Flynn was still a teenager. She had the uncanny ability to morph into whomever the situation called for—from protective nanny of a traumatized ten-year-old to stone-cold killer.

"Send me the info. I'll decide." He almost felt her flinch with his reminder that not only was he Flynn's boss, he was also Esme's father. Some father. First abandoning Jess, the love of his life, eleven years ago, and leaving the only home he'd known. He'd done it to protect her and their unborn child. And then last month, he'd returned home to find Jess murdered, but had reunited with the daughter he'd never known and the father he'd never cared to know.

Except now, he, the bastard son exiled and returned, the son who held his father's life and fortune in his hands, couldn't keep his own daughter safe. He'd been forced to send her far away, out of the line of fire from both his and Daniel's enemies. Relying on Flynn to protect the only person in this world Devon truly cared about.

Flynn was still on the line. Silent. Forcing Devon to ask. She didn't mean to be cruel; it simply was not in her nature to volunteer.

"How is she?" He tried and failed to keep the longing from his voice.

"Having a rough time of it. Not just the nightmares. The kids at school—"

"I pay that school enough they should elect her prom queen. Get me names, and I'll—"

"You'll what? Send me to take care of them? That's what Daniel would do." Her tone was flat, and he wondered if Daniel had ever actually used Flynn as an assassin. He wouldn't put it past his father.

"No. Of course not." He sighed, cut it short, but too late. Flynn already knew his weakness. "I just wish—"

"Give it time. That's what all the doctors and counselors are saying. Of course," her tone ticked up, and he knew he was not going to like what came next, "it might help if she came home for Christmas. Instead of spending it up here alone with a stranger."

"I'm just as much a stranger to Esme as you are. Besides, it's not safe here. People wouldn't think twice about using Esme against me to try to gain control of Kingston Enterprises."

There was silence on the line, and for a moment, he thought they'd been disconnected. Then Flynn's voice returned. "Guess that's the price you pay for having people you love."

She hung up before he could respond.

All Devon had ever dreamed of was a family: him, Jess, Esme.

Jess was dead, Esme gone, and he was alone. Except for his bastard of a father. If that wasn't the definition of irony, he didn't know what was.

Daniel gurgled, a stream of saliva escaping his lax lips. Not for the first time, Devon imagined how easy it would be to wrap his hands around Daniel's scrawny neck and squeeze the life from him, to finish what Leo had started.

Instead, he slid the newspaper aside, leaned forward, and gently wiped the spittle away with one of the Egyptian cotton washcloths stacked on the nightstand.

"Not yet, you son of a bitch," he said in a cheerful tone. He tossed the cloth into the hamper and stood, shaking the wrinkles from his Armani slacks. "You don't get off that easy."

CHAPTER FIVE

AFTER I LEFT Louise, I refilled my meds, gulping down a double dose of methylphenidate. As I was leaving the pharmacy and walking through the hospital's main lobby, I heard my name called.

"Angela, Angela." It was Tommaso, Louise's new neurofellow, jogging across the lobby, waving a hand at me. "I'm so glad I caught you, Angela." His Italian accent turned my name into something magical, filled with promise. "Good, good, you got your medications. Including the PXA, yes?"

I nodded, and he rushed on before I could say anything. "Since the PXA is experimental, you should take your first dose under supervision." He gestured back to the elevator bank, the white sleeve of his coat billowing. "I have time now to take care of you."

As charming as his offer was, I wasn't going to allow a total stranger dose me with a drug affectionately known as Death Head. For the first time in three weeks, I could honestly say, "Thanks, but we'll have to reschedule. I have somewhere I need to be."

Damn, such a little thing, but it felt so good. So normal. I wasn't the unemployed invalid who'd just spent three weeks trying to learn how to do nothing and failing spectacularly. No. I was a busy woman with important places to go, people to see. "I'm on my way to escort a victim from the Advocacy Center to court."

Tommaso didn't need to know the last, but it massaged my ego to tell him. For all of about half a millisecond. Then I remembered Tymara's voice, broken with terror, from last night.

"Later, then," he said, pressing his card into my palm. "Call me. When you're free today. I am at your disposal."

I slid the card into my pocket without looking at it. "I'll do that."

As I walked the three blocks from Good Samaritan to the Kingston Tower, I wondered about Tommaso. Was he the greatest suck-up in the world, or was it simply natural Italian charm? As a neurofellow, he'd be applying for real jobs soon, probably wanted to make a good impression on Louise—not to mention needing me to be his lab rat for his research.

The Tower came into view, its seven stories with two long wings stretching out from its main entrance on the corner shadowing even the massive Gothic cathedral that stood on the opposite end of the block. During most of my time working Good Sam's ER and Advocacy Center, the Tower had been the main source of much of the blood and tears I'd seen.

It had been built by Daniel Kingston in the seventies. A high-rise, low-income housing unit designed to enhance the community rather than segregate, it featured revolutionary rooftop gardens and a greenhouse, an expansive playground nestled next to St. Timothy's cathedral, and modern amenities. At least, that's what the plans had promised.

The reality had fallen short of Daniel's design. Nothing had ever been planted in the rooftop greenhouse except marijuana. The playground was quickly overrun by drug dealers. And the Tower became gang territory, with its residents, mainly women and children, enduring a siege behind locked doors that did little to protect them. The reign of terror had climaxed last month when Leo Kingston used his father's Tower as his stalking ground.

As I reached the block, I ignored the stout, soot-stained walls of St. Tim's to stare past the cathedral to the roof of the Tower. It was there that I'd killed Leo. He'd been poised to kill me, Ryder, and Esme, so I had no regrets.

But that didn't stop the nightmares. I guess the extra meds hadn't quite kicked in yet because Leo's final screams, heard only by me, echoed so strongly through my mind I had to stop and close my eyes, terrified I'd open them to see his face. A car honking brought me back to life. I licked my lips, trying to erase the taste of bile and stench of ashes. I shook myself free of the memory, and continued past the playground between the church and the Tower.

Empty of children, a lone man rocked on one of the swings. Despite his designer suit and overcoat, Devon Price looked at home there on the playground where he'd grown up—as if he owned the space. Which, I guess he did now that he controlled the Kingston family fortune.

"Good morning," Devon called. He gave me a wave then leaned back, pushing in a circle, twisting the chains, as he turned his face to the pale morning sky. I remembered the game, and couldn't help but smile as he raised his feet and spun like a top set free. His face filled with a joyful grin, unleashing the child in the man. That was Devon: a unique mix of sinner and saint, killer and protector, aged before his time, yet still able to experience innocent joy.

The chains finished unraveling, and he sat up straight. "Come on, try it."

The concrete path through the playground had been shoveled, leaving a mound of snow between where I stood and the cleared area around the swing set. I glanced at my shoes—plain black leather flats, more suitable for court than my usual hiking boots. Devon leapt from the swing, stretching to take my arm, and guided me in a less-than-graceful jump to clear the snow.

We sat on the swings, basking in the faint rays of winter sun and the crisp blue sky. It was December twenty-second, one of the shortest days of the year, yet the sky radiated hope that it could hold back the coming dark.

"Isn't it early for you to be out?" I asked as we swayed, chains squeaking above us. Devon wasn't exactly a morning person.

"Promised you I'd look after Tymara. Least I could do is escort her to court. Nothing like what happened to her is ever going to happen again, not while I own the Tower."

I glanced at him. He meant what he said, despite the fact we both knew it was a promise he was powerless to keep. "Thanks."

"What did Louise say?" he asked as he glided back and forth.

Instead of answering, I swung in a semicircle, facing away from him. Devon knew all my secrets and more about my disease and symptoms than anyone. Even Louise. It helped, having one person who understood, but it also left me feeling strangely vulnerable.

After a long moment, he touched my arm. "How long?"

I shrugged, the swing spinning me back toward him. "You know how you told me about your plans for the Tower?"

His face lit up as he twisted away from St. Tim's oppressive Gothic stone to face the yellow brick of the Tower behind us. He tilted his gaze up to the roof where the sun glinted from the glass of the greenhouse. "We'll be planting the community garden come spring, and work's already begun on the seventh floor. A full-sized gymnasium, art and music studios, a small theater, job training center, and if I can get the city and state approvals, a day care. This time next year, we should be up and running."

His voice dropped suddenly. He lowered his face to stare at me, his expression filled with regret. "That soon? I'm so sorry. You deserve better."

We sat in silence, the chill breeze rocking us until he stood, took my hand, helped me off the swing, and once again over the mound of snow at the edge of the sidewalk. We turned toward the Tower. "I'm going to ask the lead researchers at Kingston Enterprises to put everything into fatal insomnia. After all, what good is it inheriting a multinational, multibillion-dollar corporation, if you can't help a friend?"

I shook my head. "It's a one-in-a-hundred-million diagnosis, Devon. Never going to make you any money. Besides, research takes time." Time I no longer had.

He took my hand again, gave it a squeeze. "You know me better than that. I don't give a shit about money. If I did, I would have given up on this place long ago."

I knew what he really cared about, even if he'd never admit it. He wanted to create a legacy worthy of his daughter. "How is Esme?"

He hung his head. "Not so good. Flynn says she's still having night terrors. She hates it there—turns out a class of ten-year-old girls is more vicious than the Russian mob. If Flynn had her way, she'd take them all out."

"I'm sure Flynn is trying her best, but, Devon, don't forget she was trained by your father." Daniel Kingston had thought it amusing to take a street kid like Flynn and turn her into a killing machine. I wasn't sure if Flynn ever actually killed anyone, but Daniel had brainwashed her into thinking she was some kind of invincible, lethal, stealth weapon, untethered by morals, answering only to his command. Thankfully, she was absolutely devoted to Esme.

"Speaking of friends, I could use your help on something else."

That piqued my interest. It wasn't like Devon to be so circumspect with a request. "Not anything illegal?"

He chuckled. "God, no. Medical. I think. Can you meet me tonight?"

"You know I'm not practicing—" I raised my hands, let them fall again.

"Don't need your hands, just your opinion. My best chef is worried about his grandson, doesn't believe what the doctors are telling them. Thought you'd be a good translator since you speak medicalese. I'll pick you up after court."

We reached the front steps to the Tower. A pair of teenage boys—former Royales, I could tell by the gang's crown-shaped brand on the backs of their hands—slouched against the front wall of the building. They straightened as soon as they saw Devon.

"Shouldn't you two be in school?" Devon asked.

"Christmas break. No school," one answered, while the other nervously adjusted the drawstring on his hoodie, sawing it back and forth.

"You're not corner boys anymore. You got time on your hands, fill it with honest work." Devon glanced over his shoulder back the way we came. "Going to snow again. Grab some of the others, make sure all the paths and sidewalks are clear from here to St. Tim's and then around the rest of the block. People are going to want to get to the store, get their holiday groceries—you help the old ones. Do that, and I'll have Little Mike open the arcade for you."

"Yes, sir." And they took off, a blur of red and black nylon.

Devon opened the door and held it for me. "Should I be worried that the next generation would rather be paid with empty hours of video games than cash?"

"Quite a change from the reception I got last time I was here." Then, I'd been greeted by Royales pointing guns at me.

"What are the social workers always saying? They aren't bad kids, they just need direction? Turns out, there's some truth in that."

We crossed through the lobby to the elevators. The gang graffiti was gone, the walls freshly painted. The elevators were working as well. The doors dinged open, and a woman with a baby in a stroller emerged, smiling and nodding at Devon. In a few weeks' time, Devon had managed to turn the Tower from a place in which its residents felt like prisoners, trapped inside their own homes, to a place where a woman felt safe enough to ride an elevator without fearing for her life.

"You know," he said as he pressed the button for Tymara's floor and the doors closed, "wouldn't be the worst thing in the world if Eugene got off today."

How like Devon to address even a rapist like Eugene Littleton by his first name. Ryder was the only man I'd ever heard Devon use a last name with. As if Ryder was the only man Devon felt any respect for.

Devon's lack of respect extended to the justice system as well. He trusted himself to take care of matters more than he trusted the law.

And here, in the Tower, he *was* the law. Didn't matter to him that Tymara's rape had occurred long before Devon returned home. He couldn't risk anyone thinking they could get away with attacking someone under his protection. "If Eugene went free, I'd make certain he and his partners paid the price for their actions."

"I can't do that, and you know it."

"All it would take is a few slips of the tongue, a few forgotten facts, and he'd walk." His smile had a hint of the devil in it. "Don't worry. I wouldn't kill him. I—I need him alive and talking, telling me all about his friends."

"And once you had them, then you'd kill them all."

He shrugged one shoulder, tried a different tactic. "Do you know what the people of the Tower call the men Eugene was working with? The Brotherhood. It's like they're demons or devils, hiding in the shadows. Folks here are frightened that Tymara was only their first victim. They worry they might be the next."

"I haven't heard of any more rapes like hers." Using a proxy like Eugene Littleton was an unusual method of sexual assault, especially for an attack with such overwhelming violence. They could have easily grabbed any woman off the street without involving Littleton, but instead carefully orchestrated Tymara's rape as if following an elaborate script. In fact, that was Littleton's main defense: "They made me do it." If you believed him, he was a hapless pawn taken advantage of by the real criminals. Of course, that hadn't stopped him from protecting them with his silence while he was in jail awaiting trial.

"I think she was their first—or the first anyone paid any attention to," Devon said. "Unless we stop them, she won't be the last."

The elevator stopped, and we emerged into a small lobby with a miniature Christmas tree sparking colors against the bare white wall. Devon really had done a great job of rejuvenating the place in just three short weeks. Two long corridors stretched in opposite directions, and the smells of bacon and waffles wafting through the air mingled with the sounds of children excited by their first day of Christmas break and the competing rhythms of hip-hop and gospel music. I even spotted a few garlands of tinsel and evergreen wreaths hung from doors.

I hesitated. Tymara was terrified to testify, which was why I'd promised to escort her to the courthouse. After her attack, I wasn't sure how comfortable she'd be with a man's presence.

Devon understood. "I'll wait here."

I continued down the hall to Tymara's door. To my surprise, it was slightly ajar. She was expecting me. Still, I knocked. The door swung open.

Every light was on to ensure that whoever opened the door wouldn't miss a single horrific detail. It was the smell that hit me first, even as my brain tried to negotiate what my vision ruthlessly recorded.

Tymara. Her naked body displayed in the space in front of the doorway, skin flayed open like a bearskin rug, her organs spilling out. Her eyes were wide open, her palms nailed to the floor, her legs spread wide.

I must have made a noise. Whatever it was, I didn't hear it. All I could hear were Devon's footsteps as he pounded down the hall, racing in time with my heart beating in my ears. Gagging, I turned away and came face-to-face with one last atrocity.

Her severed tongue nailed to the wall beside the door.

Devon hauled me back, out into the hallway. His arms squeezed the breath from me when he saw what was left of Tymara. My mind filled with blurred sounds, as if in a tunnel: Devon's curses, voices of neighbors, Devon shouting at them to get back inside, call 911, and my heart roaring, howling that this could not be happening.

I'm not sure how much time passed before he released me. I slumped against the wall, sweat pouring from me, swallowing hard to keep from vomiting.

"I'll kill the sons of bitches," Devon muttered as he turned his back on the sight of Tymara's body. His voice was hoarse, tight. Which made it all the more deadly. "They're going to wish they'd never been born."

"It's my fault," I whispered, gagging on my tears. "She didn't want to testify. I talked her into it. Told her it was the right thing to do, that it would keep her safe."

I slapped my palm against the wall, the sting burning through my shock, the violent motion pushing me upright.

"Did you see?" I asked him, although I knew the answer. "Did you see what those animals did to her?"

Devon had a good poker face, but he wasn't using it now, not with me. The honesty of his rage burned in his eyes. "I saw."

"They won't get away with it," I said, spacing my words, taking care with each one. "I'm not going to let them."

"Leave them to me." He leaned in close, so close his face blocked the rest of the world from my view. "Get Eugene Littleton off. I'll get him to talk. No one comes into my Tower and does this to my people."

Vigilante justice. Street justice. Surely Tymara deserved more. Hadn't I promised her more?

"No. We do this my way. She came to the Advocacy Center for justice, and I'll get it for her." It wasn't Devon I was making my vow to, not any unseen deity either. It was Tymara. "I promise."

He opened his mouth, ready to argue, but the elevator doors chimed. He glanced down the hall, saw the shine of uniforms and badges, and frowned. Time wasted with the police was time better served hunting Tymara's killers.

"You got this?"

I nodded, and he vanished down the hall.

Leaving me to wrestle with my conscience and what my good intentions had brought Tymara.

CHAPTER SIX

IT DIDN'T TAKE long for the police to finish with me once the detectives arrived. The first officers had escorted me away from the crime scene to the empty manager's office on the first floor. The room was small, windowless, overcrowded with men, and stifling.

Shivering with shock, I sat on a cheap office chair, unable to resist a compulsion to pick at a wad of foam that had escaped through a split in the vinyl arm. Anything to avoid thinking of Tymara.

It didn't work.

At least eight uniformed and suited policemen asked me questions.

Did you touch anything?

Nothing but the doorknob.

Did you go inside the apartment?

No.

Is there anyone she was fearful of? Did she mention anything unusual?

And so it went. My answers emerged by rote, mechanical. My teeth chattered. Until, finally, it was my turn to ask a question: *What time did she die?*

I didn't get an answer. Not that I needed one. The math was

painfully obvious.

After I was dismissed, I pushed through the throng of curious onlookers, mainly kids off from school who crowded the Tower's front stoop, squinting at the Medical Examiner's van.

Once I was released from the confines of the Tower, my chills turned into a fever sweat.

Not sure where to go next, I stumbled back to the swings where Devon and I had sat earlier.

This time, I walked through the snow bank, inviting the wet chill that came with it. I shed my coat and held it in my lap. I felt queasy, sick. I'd seen my fair share of violence, but nothing like what I'd just witnessed.

No. That was wrong. I *had* seen something like this before.

Last month, when Leo Kingston was close to death, I'd entered his mind via the bizarre symptom-gift-curse of my fatal insomnia. Despite what Louise said, there was no way in hell—and I mean that literally—I could ever create any delusion or hallucination as warped as what Leo had done to the women he'd tortured and killed.

The memory overwhelmed what little control I had left. My body went slack, sending the swing spinning, only my arms wrapped around the chains preventing me from falling.

A dissonant chorus of women screaming filled my entire body, every cell shrinking from the noise; blood painting my vision.

One of my fugues.

As blood raged around me, my body frozen, I was unable to halt the awful visions that played out in exquisite, horrifying detail. Not delusions or hallucinations. *Memories.* Not mine. Leo Kingston's.

My eyes stared, unblinking, at the snow, and drool slid from my mouth as my fugue forced me to relive Leo's memories. I tried to fight them, shove them behind a locked door in my brain, better yet, bury them sixty feet deep, but they were too overwhelming. And vivid, so very vivid.

Not the victims' pain. I think I could have handled that, or at least comprehended it. But these were Leo's memories, so what I felt wasn't pain but…*glee* was the best word to describe it. The glee of a child pulling wings off a butterfly coupled with an insatiable thirst for more, more, more…

I fought to banish Leo and his horrors. Desperate to escape, I turned to my own life, to the people and times when I'd felt comfort: my dad launching me into the air before catching me in his arms; practicing my fiddle with him, my fingers so small they fumbled across the strings; playing in the band with Jacob, the music filling me with confidence; being in Ryder's arms, so warm, so strong…

All of it ammunition against a madman's memories.

Finally, I was able to break free of the fugue, my body slowly returning to my control. I wiped my mouth, tasting bile and wishing I could vomit, simply to purge myself of what I'd just lived through.

Because that was the thing. When I touch the mind of someone not-quite-dead, I don't simply visit and have a chat like in real life. Rather, I experience what they experience. Everything. A lifetime's worth of memories, dumped into my mind.

Every time I've done it, the person died soon after. They were all dying anyway, but I couldn't help but wonder if my touching their minds hastened their deaths.

Not to mention the healthy dose of fear for my own sanity. How many memories could I hold in my own brain without losing myself?

I wrapped my arms around the swing's chains, embracing the bite of the cold metal. Shoving my emotions behind sealed mental doors, I focused on the sunbeams glinting across the snow, the bruised shadows stretching out from the buildings surrounding me. I'd failed Tymara. I couldn't change that. But could I still see Eugene Littleton brought to justice?

"Hear you've had a rough morning," a friendly voice called from the sidewalk. Ryder. My knight in tarnished armor. As usual, his timing was impeccable.

He was tall enough that he could have easily stepped over the snow bank. Instead, he tramped down a path anyone could follow, ignoring the snow gathering in his pant cuffs. He joined me on the swings. I'd chosen to sit with my back to St. Tim's, facing the Tower. Ryder sat so he faced the church.

Of course he did. He still believed, had faith. Not me. I'd left the church and the capricious God who ruled it after my father died. Turned my back on it, just as I had so many things during that time. As painful as it was to have my family treat me as a scapegoat for their grief—after all, they couldn't blame God, right?—I'd accepted the role with the sullen fury of a twelve-year-old.

"I'm sorry about Tymara," Ryder said, his voice so gentle it made me blink. Thankfully, it was too cold for tears. Unlike Devon, he didn't twist and spin or play on the swings. Instead, he closed the space between us and took my hand in his.

"Are you okay?" he asked. The question had many layers, like the man himself. He'd been a detective with the Major Case squad before being demoted to work Advocacy Center cases. Only, Ryder didn't consider it a demotion.

"I need—" I broke off, no words to encompass all I needed.

He filled the void my silence left in its wake. "How about if I drive you home?"

Without me answering, Ryder guided me to my feet and helped me into my coat. Good thing, because now that my fugue had passed, I was suddenly shivering.

"Not home," I said as we walked toward his car, a city-owned gray Taurus parked in front of St. Timothy's, where it wouldn't block the official vehicles clustered at the opposite end of the block around the Tower. I stared at the Tower, counting down from the rooftop where I'd killed Leo last month, to the floor where Tymara lived. My insides twisted, and my mouth went dry. Where Tymara died. "To court."

"Court? The case is over without your witness."

"Maybe not. I need to talk to Manny Cruz. He's the assistant district attorney prosecuting the case." I could have called Manny, but I had a feeling he wouldn't approve of the faint inkling of a plan that I was formulating. Maybe I should go straight to the judge? I wasn't sure if that was against the rules or not; honestly I didn't have enough energy to care.

We arrived at Ryder's car. He opened the door for me. For a moment as I settled into the seat, I was looking up at his face, his eyes a shade darker than the sky behind him, his expression one of warm concern. "Sure you're okay?"

My jaw clenched, and I couldn't answer. Everything hit me at once. Louise's diagnosis; seeing Tymara, so young, her life full of promise, turned into a thing, an object, something less than human. Anger shook through me, an invisible earthquake, fierce and hot, unstable.

Ryder surprised me. I thought I was so good at containing my emotions, locking them into invisible Pandora's boxes, showing the world only what I wanted it to see. But I couldn't hide from Ryder. He crouched inside the open car door and bundled me into his arms, holding me so tightly that the strangled feeling in my chest finally eased and I could breathe again.

He knew better than to offer empty platitudes or promises destined to be broken. Instead, he simply held me, shielding me from any prying eyes, giving me time to glue together the pieces of my shattered facade.

"I'm here," he whispered. "Just tell me what you need."

I needed him. A desperate need that shamed me with its intensity. But as my plan crystallized, I pulled away, took a deep breath to prove to myself that I could, that I was in control. Of something. Anything.

"I need to see Eugene Littleton and his partners fry in Hell," I told him.

Ryder squinted at me, assessing more than my words, then nodded. "Okay, then. Let's see what we can do about that."

CHAPTER SEVEN

Jacob Voorsanger glanced at his watch. Ten thirteen. Something was wrong.

He and his client, Eugene Littleton, waited at the defense table in Judge Shaw's courtroom. The courtroom, with its high-arched ceiling crisscrossed by thick wooden beams, lit from overhead by a century-old, cobwebbed chandelier and from the sides by stained-glass windows depicting Justice in all her glory, reminded him of a European cathedral.

Cathedral of justice. Jacob liked that. Liked the way the air, despite the many drafts, felt different inside the courtroom. Not just this courtroom, any courtroom. Heavier, filled with gravitas. Life-and-death decisions weighed in the balance.

Sometimes, when the reality of the law with its wheeling and dealing and hairsplitting grew too stressful, Jacob liked to come into an empty courtroom like this one and simply sit in silence, breathe the air, and watch the dust motes glint as they settled to the ground. Justice was blind, but she also carried a sword, skewering deceit as she fought for truth.

Jacob glanced at his client. Little chance for any truth from him.

Eugene Littleton was relaxed, lounging in his seat, fiddling with his ill-fitting suit as he ogled the others in the courtroom: a bailiff standing in front of the door to the judge's chambers; the court stenographer; and the judge's clerk, a woman in her thirties upon whom Eugene fixed his gaze.

Jacob nudged his client and shook his head. Eugene rolled his eyes and pouted. Jacob glanced over at the empty prosecution table, the table that had been his until last month. That was when he'd been transferred to the public defender's office after crying foul about corruption in the DA's office.

Justice was justice, Jacob told himself. The system worked only if both sides fought with vigor and might. Anything less, and they'd have chaos.

Ten fourteen. For Judge Shaw, being fourteen minutes late was the equivalent of chaos. While she prided herself on being a legal maverick, someone who loved teasing out new interpretations of the law and finding its edges, she also was a martinet when it came to her schedule. Her court began on time, did not run late, and God help the lawyer who dawdled in presenting their case.

Where was Manny? Jacob wondered, staring at the door to the judge's chambers. Judge Shaw would never condone any *ex parte* communication.

As if on cue, the door opened. The bailiff listened to something, then nodded and jerked his chin at Jacob. "They need you in chambers, Mr. Voorsanger."

Jacob was surprised to see Eugene grinning. He didn't seem at all curious about what had stalled his trial. Instead, he seemed…satisfied. Like opening a present and getting exactly what he'd wanted.

Inside the judge's chambers, prosecutor Manny Cruz waited in front of Judge Shaw.

It was the other person standing before the judge who surprised Jacob. "Angie, what are you doing here?"

She wasn't scheduled to testify until this afternoon, after the victim,

Tymara Nelson. She looked exhausted, worn thin, yet was flushed as if a fever burned within her. For weeks she'd been avoiding Jacob, and now he wondered what was wrong. Her uncle and mother whispered theories—drinking, drugs—but he'd dismissed them all. Until now. "Is everything all right?"

"We have a problem." Judge Shaw leaned forward.

"Tymara's dead," Angie said. Her tone was flat, divorced from the emotion that crossed her face. More than emotion, he noted. Pain. "I found her this morning when I went to pick her up. She was murdered."

Shock froze Jacob where he stood. His first thought was, *Eugene knew.* No wonder his client had been so relaxed. He never expected the trial to continue.

Then a second thought collided with his first. *Angie.* She'd found the body. He turned to her, torn between wanting to offer her comfort, and needing to regroup and press his client's new advantage.

She made it easy, averting her gaze from his and stepping away from his outstretched hand. Barely holding it together, he saw. Compartmentalizing was Angie's gift, even if it made things difficult at times like this.

He used the hand instead to make an emphatic motion, drawing the judge's attention. "I don't see any problem. Dismiss the charges and release my client."

"Hold on now," Manny protested. "We have a jury empaneled. Judge, if you dismiss now—"

"My client has already served six months in jail awaiting his day in court," Jacob interrupted. "You cannot in good conscience keep him locked up indefinitely while the prosecution tries to rebuild its case without a victim. It's a violation of his Sixth Amendment rights."

The judge held her hands up. "We have an alternative I think is acceptable, although unconventional. It's never been tried in this jurisdiction."

So of course Judge Shaw was all for it. Jacob saw the judge give Angie a tiny nod of acknowledgment and realized where this was heading. "A victimless prosecution?"

"There was a case I read about," Angie said. "*Giles*—"

"*Verses California*. Right. But—"

"Your Honor," Manny chimed in, "we'd still need more time to prepare. A victimless prosecution creates an entirely new strategy. There's no way—"

"Why not?" the judge asked, folding her hands together like Solomon. "My understanding is that you were going to have the victim testify next, followed by Dr. Rossi, correct?"

"Yes, ma'am."

"Then it seems to me that you lose nothing by proceeding. Dr. Rossi can testify to the victim's statements she recorded as part of her medical history. She can also testify to her forensic findings, but solely in regard to Mr. Littleton as previously discussed."

It had been a hard-fought ruling that Jacob had won earlier, that the other men who had brutalized Tymara Nelson could not be mentioned, nor evidence of their attack included in the case against his client. At the time he'd doubted the ruling would be much help. As prejudicial as the evidence of the second attack against Tymara was, it was nowhere near as damning as the victim herself testifying to what Eugene Littleton had done to her.

Jacob glanced back toward the door he'd just come through. Without Tymara's testimony or the evidence of the second attack, there was a very good chance Eugene would leave a free man.

"Your Honor," Angie said. "There's another complication. I'm leaving on a sabbatical. I'll be out of the country and unable to testify in any future trial if we don't move forward today."

Jacob stared at her. Leaving? The country? When had this happened? He knew she was taking a break from the ER, but leaving Cambria City? Something was definitely wrong. She'd been acting strange. And her playing was off, as if her music, always her refuge, had suddenly abandoned her.

He brought his focus back to his client. "Your Honor, if word of Ms. Nelson's demise reaches the jury, it will prejudice them against my client. They could falsely assume he had something to do with orchestrating her death."

"Which he did," Manny countered. "Dr. Rossi and I both have documented multiple occasions during which the victim was the subject of intimidation—"

The judge waved a hand for silence. "The jury is already here, shielded from any news. If we proceed now and finish today, I'll order them sequestered during their deliberations. It's the best way to ensure a fair trial for your client. I'm sure you'll agree, Mr. Voorsanger."

Which meant he had no choice but to agree. Better than facing a judge's wrath. "That's acceptable with the defense, Your Honor."

She glanced at Manny. "What say you, Mr. Cruz?"

Manny stared at Angie as if this was all her fault. "The prosecution agrees with moving forward, Your Honor," he replied in a grudging tone. "If I could just have a word with Dr. Rossi before we begin?"

The judge nodded, and Manny hustled Angie out the door to the hallway beyond the judge's chambers. Jacob saw Angie's glare as Manny grabbed her by the elbow and was glad he wasn't on the receiving end. He felt a gleam of pride—she'd actually been listening when he'd expounded on the possibilities of a victimless prosecution. Of course, that had been back when he was working for the DA's office instead of the public defender's, but still.

The concept was intriguing. He could have pushed for a dismissal, but if the judge refused, his client would be facing more jail time or be forced to accept a plea bargain. This was the best chance Eugene Littleton would ever have for a fair trial.

Jacob pushed through the door into the courtroom. Eugene was bent over the desk, head resting on his folded arms, asleep. Sure sign of guilt, the psychologists would say. Or maybe just sleep deprivation from after six months in the county jail.

He frowned and glanced back over his shoulder at the judge's chambers once again. Rumor had it that if Eugene walked, Devon Price would try to exact street justice, make an example out of him. Rumor also had it that Eugene's partners in crime might silence

Eugene as well.

Seemed like everyone wanted a piece of Eugene Littleton. Even the DA was hoping that if this trial went his way, Eugene would turn on his accomplices, provide their names, and testify against them.

Jacob sighed. He half-wondered if maybe the safest place for his client would be to remain behind bars.

CHAPTER EIGHT

"WHAT THE HELL was that?" Manny whirled on me as soon as we were in the hallway, out of the judge's earshot, the door to her chambers closed behind us. A clerk signing people in for jury duty the next courtroom over glowered at him. He pulled me across to the high-arched windows facing the street, narrowing his eyes at me.

He had chiseled South American good looks that drew the attention of most women, but I'd never been interested in him. His machismo attitude, always focused on the win, the conquest, left me cold. Tymara had liked him, as did many of the victims he worked with. They mistook his passion for their cases as passion for justice, but I knew better. It was passion for winning. Period.

Unfortunately, he wasn't alone in that attitude over at the DA's office. Jacob was the exception—at least among the prosecutors I'd worked with. Of course, Jacob now worked for the other side. It had been so infuriating, watching him coolly calculate how best to push the new advantage Tymara's death had given him and his client.

Manny continued, "I don't know what kind of game you think you're playing—"

"Game?" Fury strangled my words. My breath came in shuddering waves. "You think this is a game? Did you see what those animals did to her?" I stalked closer to him, backing him up against the windows. "Because I did. They butchered her."

"Calm down," Manny told me, his eyes as cold as the glass behind him. "Getting emotional isn't going to help us win this case."

The marble hallway outside the courtroom turned the footsteps of all the people rushing in one direction or the other into a percussion melody. My finger tapped out the rhythm as I forced myself to stand still, to listen, to focus on the world beyond the hurricane of emotions that roared inside me. Manny wasn't the real target of my anger, just an easy one, I reminded myself. Making Littleton and his partners pay, that was the best justice for Tymara.

"Who told you to use *Giles*? Your ex? No way did Judge Shaw come up with it on her own."

"Jacob knew nothing about it." Although I'd asked him about the court case that had set the precedent. Months ago, long before I ever dreamed I'd need to use it.

Manny scowled, obviously not believing me. "Sure about that? Sounds like the kind of last-ditch strategy he'd use."

"He'd never compromise his own case, no matter how guilty his client is."

"A few more defendants like Littleton and he'll soon be sacrificing those sacred lambs of his, making deals to put his clients away just to dig out from under the caseload."

"I can give you references from the advocacy journals. In Ohio, they—"

"I know how to do my job." He brushed my offer aside. "Any other judge but Hippie-Dippie Shaw, and you wouldn't have even been in chambers."

"She's giving us a chance. Don't you want justice for Tymara?"

"You're missing the point. In there, I call the plays. When you're up on that witness stand, you follow my lead, understand?"

"If it nails Littleton and you convince him to roll on his partners,

I'll play any game you want."

The bailiff opened the door and called out to us. "The judge is ready to proceed."

Manny straightened, plastered on a smile that would have raised millions for any politician, and gave me a nod. "Let the games begin."

RYDER ENTERED THE courtroom and slid into the pew farthest from the jury. It had been over two decades since he'd served as an altar boy, yet he still had to fight the impulse to cross himself and genuflect. Except this was no church. He knew all too well the foibles and follies that often corrupted the profane proceedings of the criminal justice system.

The benches weren't built for a man as tall as he was. Sinking back against the polished oak, inhaling the familiar incense of lemon oil, sweat, fear, stale paper, and mildew, he stretched his legs into the aisle and crossed his ankles. His side ached a bit with the movement, but it was a good kind of ache. The *I'm alive despite being gut shot* kind of ache.

The jury was already seated, and Rossi was on the witness stand. After he'd dropped her off, he'd headed over to the jail annex in the hopes of learning something helpful from the corrections officers. It'd been a waste of time. Littleton had left little to no impression on anyone. Not affiliated with any gangs, he'd bided his time in the overcrowded facility without disturbing the equilibrium of his fellow inmates or the overworked, underpaid staff.

Ryder watched Manny Cruz efficiently walk Rossi through the medical testimony. She was lucky the judge and Manny had gone for her idea; he'd never heard of any prosecutor trying a sexual-assault case without the victim testifying. Manny tried to put a good spin on her exam findings and the history Tymara had given her, but Rossi had to tiptoe through a minefield to avoid mentioning the true causes of Tymara's brutal injuries: the men Littleton had invited to join him in Tymara's apartment after his initial attack.

Manny finished and sat, giving Ryder a few moments to observe Rossi. Despite the way her day had begun, she didn't allow her emotions to crack her professionalism. Sitting up there, waiting for her ex to begin his cross-examination, she looked damned good. Brunette hair tinted red and gold by the stained glass, a touch of color in her lips and cheeks. Her chin jutted forward, revealing the taut muscles in her neck.

No one would ever suspect she was facing a death sentence. At least, that was what his research on fatal insomnia had told him—every new report he found revealed an enemy worse than any he'd faced in Afghanistan. He wished she'd talk to him about it or let Louise, her doctor, give him details. That'd be better than the crazy shit he'd found online.

Had Rossi even told Louise about her and Ryder? He had, his one breach of Rossi's request for privacy, but he'd been going crazy with only the words "fatal insomnia" and endless, harrowing online searches. At least Louise had been able to direct him to legitimate research, scant as it was.

Ryder didn't understand Rossi's need for secrecy, but she insisted on it, and he didn't mind the mystique it added to their relationship. Hell, she wouldn't even let him call her by her first name, much less any nickname. How afraid of intimacy did a woman have to be to refuse to allow her lover to call her by her first name? His stomach clenched, and he glared across the courtroom at Jacob Voorsanger, assigning blame to the ex.

Voorsanger rose, taking his place at the podium between the prosecutor and defense tables. He stood, silent, assessing Rossi as if she were a particularly dangerous specimen trapped inside the cage that was the witness stand. Ryder looked past the defense attorney to his client, Eugene Littleton. The man was squirming, his belligerent stare vanquished by a single glance Rossi sent in his direction.

"Thank you, Dr. Rossi," Voorsanger began in the tone of a gracious host, "for taking the time to talk us through your medical findings in such precise detail."

Rossi didn't take the bait and offer any sarcasm or snark. Instead, she replied, "It's part of my job. Advocating for victims."

Voorsanger nodded, turned to his notes, but then swiveled back abruptly as if caught by her final word. "But have we established that Ms. Nelson *was* a victim of a crime? Much less one committed by my client?"

Manny looked up. "Objection."

"Sustained," the judge said. "The jury will disregard defense counsel's editorial opinions."

Voorsanger ignored the interruption and focused on Rossi. "Dr. Rossi, to the best of your knowledge, will Ms. Nelson be making an appearance here today to give us *her* account of what happened seven months ago?"

Ryder sat up straight. Asshole. Voorsanger made it sound like Tymara was too busy shopping for shoes to testify. From the stricken look that crossed Rossi's face as she glanced at Manny for guidance, he guessed the judge had ruled that no mention of the reason why Tymara wouldn't be testifying could be given. Prejudicial or some such legal bullshit.

Rossi looked up, and he locked his gaze with hers, certain she was reliving the horror of finding Tymara's body that morning. She swallowed hard, gave him a small nod, her features easing back into a mask of professionalism. Then she leaned forward to adjust her own microphone, eyeing each of the jurors in turn. "To my knowledge, Ms. Nelson is unable to testify, leaving it to me to report on the facts of her trauma."

"The medical facts?"

"Yes."

"And do your medical facts provide any *physical* evidence that the sexual intimacy between my client and Ms. Nelson was nonconsensual?"

"In the vast majority of sexual assaults, there is no physical evidence."

"Did your detailed medical examination reveal any evidence that my client assaulted Ms. Nelson?"

Rossi didn't hesitate, her voice remaining calm, confident. "Yes. My medical history indicated that Mr. Littleton sexually assaulted Tymara Nelson."

Ryder glanced at the jury. This would be the stumbling point of the case against Littleton. They had plenty of evidence showing that Littleton and Tymara had sex, but nothing except Tymara's disclosures to Rossi during her rape exam to prove it was nonconsensual. The jury was definitely paying attention, but without Tymara to tell her own story, would they buy it?

CHAPTER NINE

"HISTORY TAKEN FROM Ms. Nelson?" Jacob asked me.

"Yes."

"So basically we're talking about she said/he said. A difference of opinion." Jacob turned to the jury, his skepticism over my painstakingly recorded medical history palpable. Despite my anger at his trivialization of Tymara's assault, I marveled at the way he'd captured the jury so quickly. I'd forgotten how good an actor he was, the power of his voice, his body language. "Let's go through things from the start. See exactly how your medical history somehow proves my client assaulted Ms. Nelson in any way."

Clearing my throat, I began in a professional cadence "On May twenty-first, Tymara Nelson had a knock on her apartment door. It was the defendant, there to spray for bugs." Littleton was an exterminator whose company held the contract for the Kingston Tower.

"Ms. Nelson invited him in?" Jacob interrupted, deliberately breaking my rhythm.

"Yes. She—"

"Yes. Ms. Nelson invited him inside her apartment."

I kept my face composed, refusing to show any emotion at his cheap and all-too-common tactic. I had expected more of him.

Focus, I told myself. *Tymara's last chance at justice is riding on you.* Although, sitting there, buffeted by lawyers and their rules, I wondered why I'd been so adamant with Devon that courtroom justice was better than his street justice.

I glanced at Littleton, a totally unremarkable man if you believed his mask of normalcy. Wondered what it would take to make him feel the same terror and anguish that Tymara had at his hands and the hands of his partners. Wouldn't that be true justice?

Jacob startled me, abandoning his notes and shuffling to stand beside the podium. It was against the rules for him to approach me, but by coming out from behind the podium, it left him exposed, vulnerable.

The jury also took note. They would place added weight on the next few moments—a weight that might add up to reasonable doubt during deliberations if I wasn't careful.

I sat up straighter, the edge of the worn, wooden chair digging into my thighs, and anticipated the sparring match to come. The rest of the room faded into shimmering echoes of color accompanied by the gentle tinkle of chimes.

Not now. I couldn't risk a fugue episode *now.*

I forced my attention to center on Jacob as I massaged the pressure point between the thumb and index finger of my left hand, trying to eke additional energy and alertness from my body's diminished reserves.

Jacob took a step toward me, his stance aggressive. So unlike his usual style. A thrill vibrated through me. If only he'd been this aggressive about saving our marriage. Understated, subtle, always playing by the rules, that was Jacob.

An opposites-attract sort of thing, the rebel ER doctor and the by-the-book attorney.

But now, it was Jacob breaking the rules. My pulse revved up, buzzing beneath my skin. Something was going on here. This wasn't the way Jacob worked. What was wrong with him?

Idiot. Jacob was fine—the problem was with *me*. Hopped up on the stimulants Louise had prescribed.

Jacob squared his shoulders, facing the jury more than me.

The jurors leaned forward, entranced, waiting to see what was coming. If he disappointed them after this buildup, his client was sure to suffer the consequences. Which was exactly why Jacob seldom resorted to melodrama.

I had to work to swallow, my mouth suddenly dry. Tymara's death was my responsibility. I was the one who had persuaded her to go to the police. I was the one who had bolstered her courage, promised her that confronting her attackers was the right thing to do.

And Tymara, fool that she was, had placed her trust in me. Anger seared through me. The entire room simmered with the strength of my fury. I blinked against the image that violated my vision, more than blood, the terror on her face...

"Then Ms. Nelson led Mr. Littleton into her bedroom, correct?" Jacob said, jarring me from my morbid visions.

"She went to turn on the lights so he could see as he sprayed for roaches."

"She willingly led him to her bedroom."

I stared at him, refusing to confirm his rewording of my testimony, waiting for a question. Sweat pooled at the base of my spine, and my hands trembled. I tightened them into fists, drumming against my thighs, out of sight from the jury.

Jacob's dramatic pauses were killing me. Why didn't he just get on with it? His eyes seemed filled with sorrow and remorse. As if I was leading him somewhere he didn't want to go. Wait. Could he know? That I was sick? Once upon a time, he could read me that well.

"And then Ms. Nelson undressed for Mr. Littleton," he said.

"He was holding a knife on her."

"Did Ms. Nelson sustain any knife wounds?" Jacob countered. He rustled a stack of papers, reminding me Big Brother was watching if I detoured from the medical record.

"No." I spit out the word as if it was a spoiled piece of meat. The single syllable lingered in the air as the jury watched, mesmerized. The tension coiling between us was palpable, electricity before a lightning strike.

As if this trial needed any more drama.

Jacob consulted his notes as I waited for his next question. I risked a glance at the prosecution table and saw Manny frowning, shaking his head at me in warning.

"According to the medical history you collected from Ms. Nelson," Jacob finally said. "What happened next?"

I took a breath, trying to rein in my anger and frustration. But one glance in the direction of the defendant eroded my control. "Mr. Littleton raped her."

The jurors gaped at me. I didn't have to see Manny's scowl to know it was a mistake as soon as the words left my mouth.

Jacob took a step back behind the podium, his eyes wide at my use of the offensive verb. He glanced at his client, gave a small, regretful shrug of his shoulders. "Your Honor, permission to treat this witness as hostile?"

The judge pursed her lips, her eyes creasing, and nodded. "Granted."

Manny glared at me, half-rising from his chair before slumping back into it, resigned. By having me declared hostile, Jacob had greater latitude in his questioning, could approach me, even try to manipulate my testimony.

I'd played right into his plans. There was a good reason why this was my last case.

Below the railing, out of sight of the jury and Jacob, I shook the blood into my hands, forcing myself to concentrate, to brick up my emotions. Manny was right about one thing: If we wanted to win, I needed to get the jury to trust me as a professional, keep my emotions out of it. After all, this whole psychodrama they called a trial wasn't about me, it was about getting justice for Tymara.

Jacob wasn't making things any easier. He needed the jury to see me as flawed, emotive, weak—and therefore, not to be believed.

"You testified that Ms. Nelson told you she faked an orgasm while engaged in sexual relations with my client," Jacob said, facing me squarely. "Since she's not here for me to question her motives, I'd like your expert opinion, Dr. Rossi."

Jacob was pushing things. And getting away with it, because the jury was eating it up, leaving Manny no way to object without making things worse.

"Why? Why did Ms. Nelson do it?" he drawled, spinning to face the jury, impervious to my anger. "After all, according to your well-documented notes, she told my client she liked what he was doing to her, so much so that, and I'm quoting verbatim what Ms. Nelson told you during your medical history, she asked for 'more, please, more.' Enlighten us. If she lied to my client about how she felt in that moment of intimacy, is it possible that it could have been because she cared enough about him that she didn't want to hurt Mr. Littleton's feelings?"

Littleton had scripted her words at knifepoint. Tymara had been begging for it to stop. But I hadn't recorded her reasons for faking an orgasm verbatim as part of the medical record, so I couldn't testify to it. Which Jacob damn well knew.

If you can simmer with anger, can you boil over? I was about to. The courtroom was sweltering. If I took my jacket off, the jury would think I was shaken. They'd realize we were losing.

Manny reached for his microphone. "Objection. Calls for speculation."

Jacob dismissed him with a wave of his hand. "Withdrawn, Your Honor. I think we all know the answer without Dr. Rossi's interpretation of what a woman told her seven months ago." He pivoted to face me again. "Dr. Rossi, did you find any evidence that the sex between my client and Ms. Nelson was not consensual?"

"Ms. Nelson told me—"

"I'm not interested in hearsay, Dr. Rossi. I'm interested in the medical facts. Physical findings. Did your forensic examination reveal any physical evidence that my client used force?"

Damn him, damn him to hell. Jacob was the last person I'd expected to resort to tactics like this. But he always played by the rules—and the rules stating his client deserved the best defense he could offer trumped the simple fact that Littleton was a rapist.

I slanted a glance over at Manny, but all he could offer was a glare and a tiny shake of his head, reminding me this whole thing was my fault. The movement echoed through the air around him, shimmering in the red-gold light shining through the stained-glass windows.

Shit, not now. I pinched the flesh at the base of my thumb, hard. The pain focused my vision, and the echoes of color faded, although the chimes persisted, an aural shadow at the edge of my awareness. The echoes were a prelude to my fugues and threatened to mesmerize me, pulling me into a vortex where time stopped and I could lose myself if I wasn't careful. That's all this case needed, its star witness falling into a catatonic state, complete with drooling, right there in front of the jury.

"You seem to be having difficulty hearing me," Jacob said, marching back to the podium and the microphone there.

He left a trail of colorful ripples in his wake. I edged forward, digging my nails into my palms, and the echoes were banished. For now.

"Dr. Rossi, did your examination reveal any physical evidence that my client forced Ms. Nelson to have sex with him?"

I took a quick inventory of the jury. The only one who would meet my gaze was an older man who seemed more interested in looking down my shirt than what I had to say. No doubt about it, I'd lost them. Best to get it over with quickly.

"No."

"No what?" Jacob was relentless.

"I found no physical evidence that Mr. Littleton used force when he raped Ms. Nelson."

"Dr. Rossi," Judge Shaw said, further making Jacob's case for him, "confine your remarks to the facts presented."

"Yes, ma'am." My tone could have been more contrite, but I was having a hard time maintaining a professional facade.

"Anything else, Mr. Voorsanger?" the judge asked, glancing at her watch. We were ahead of schedule, and she liked that.

"I just have one last confirmatory question, Your Honor." Jacob glanced back over his shoulder to the spectators, then shuffled his notes as if ticking off a checklist. "Dr. Rossi, one last time for the jury. You found no evidence that Ms. Nelson was raped, correct?"

I blinked, at first certain I hadn't heard him correctly. Manny sat up so fast he knocked a pencil off his table. It hit the ground with a crack that echoed through the suddenly silent room. In the rear of the galley, Ryder straightened as well.

Jacob had his head buried in his notes. The jury had relaxed. They'd heard him ask the same question twice before already. They knew my answer.

Except they were wrong. It *wasn't* the same question, not the same question at all.

I glanced at the judge, who inclined her head in a small nod, giving me permission to answer the question Jacob had asked.

Exactly as he had asked it.

"That is not correct." My voice ricocheted off the jurors, grabbing their attention.

"Excuse me?" Jacob rocked his head up, but his face revealed no surprise. Damn the man, he knew what he was doing. Somehow he was managing to both defend his client and ensure that a group of mad-dog predators wouldn't continue to run free. Littleton picked up on it as well, frantically reaching across the defense table to yank at Jacob's sleeve.

"You asked if I found any evidence that Ms. Nelson was raped. I did find evidence. Evidence that she was both raped and physically assaulted. Multiple times. By multiple assailants." Just no evidence that *his* client had used force.

Thanks to Jacob's slip, the forensic evidence of the full extent of

Tymara's injuries could now be introduced to the jury. We'd be on the record with everything that really happened to Tymara. If it swayed the jury, it could be enough to get Littleton to give up his partners.

Thanks to Jacob, Tymara would finally have a chance to be heard. Even if it was from the grave.

Littleton's features twisted into a scowl. He pounded a fist on the tabletop. Then he focused on me, his face florid with rage.

He lunged from his seat, hands stretched toward me. "You bitch! You fucking bitch! You're not allowed to say anything and you know it!"

The judge banged her gavel, calling for silence. "Mr. Voorsanger, control your client."

Jacob stepped away from the podium and said something in a low voice. Littleton's posture stiffened, his mouth twisted with fury. The bailiff moved to stand behind Littleton, positioning himself where he could restrain him if needed.

"That's not right. She can't trick you like that," Littleton protested, whirling on Jacob. "Your fault—it's all your fault!"

Elbowing the bailiff so hard the man fell back and hit the railing, Littleton wrapped his hands around Jacob's throat. "I'll kill you, you bastard! I'll kill you!"

CHAPTER TEN

RYDER BOUNDED FROM his seat, reaching the defense table before the bailiff had time to recover. His pulse hammered so loudly in his ears he barely heard Littleton's shouts or the judge's gavel banging.

He tackled Littleton, pulling him away from Voorsanger. A wristlock and knee to the small of the back tumbled the prisoner to the ground. By that time, the bailiff was there with his cuffs.

The bailiff dragged Littleton out of reach as Ryder climbed back to his feet, his gaze scouring the courtroom, searching for any further threats. His breath had barely sped up, although his chest was tight, as if he'd run a mile. But still, for his first day back on the job, it felt pretty damn good.

The pain would hit later after the adrenaline fled, but who cared?

He blew his breath out and backed up behind the prosecutor's table as courthouse security flooded the room. It took three of them to haul out Littleton, who was screaming incoherent threats at anyone who would listen.

Ryder turned his head to check that Rossi was okay. She perched half in and half out of the witness box, a fierce expression on her face, as if she'd intended to take on Littleton herself. But she wasn't looking at him. She was focused on her ex, Jacob Voorsanger.

The judge banged her gavel once again, and a sudden silence descended over the room. Voorsanger slowly pushed himself upright, leaning heavily against the podium as he caught his breath.

"Your Honor, we request a recess to discuss options with the prosecution," Voorsanger said, his voice hoarse, his chest heaving with each word.

"Wise decision, Mr. Voorsanger. I'm declaring an immediate mistrial with no prejudice to the prosecution. Mr. Cruz, you may refile charges at your convenience, but it is my sincere hope that we do not have a repeat of this mockery of justice. At least not in my courtroom. Do I make myself clear, gentlemen?"

Both lawyers nodded, appearing sheepish. The judge turned to the jury. "Ladies and gentlemen, you are dismissed. Thank you for your time. We are adjourned."

With a regal swish of her robe, she disappeared into her chambers. Everyone else filed out, leaving only Manny Cruz, Jacob Voorsanger, Rossi, and Ryder gathered in the no-man's land between the defense and prosecution tables.

"Glad I gave up my lunch hour," Ryder said, the heel of his hand caressing the empty holster on his belt like an amputee scratching a phantom itch. Damn new rules insisted only courthouse security officers carry inside the courthouse. Those bozos weren't any better than mall rent-a-cops. "Nice show you guys put on."

"This is ridiculous." Manny wheeled on Voorsanger. "If I have to go through this shit again, I'll bury Littleton's ass deeper than the last coal they dragged out of the Cambria Mine. I swear I will."

Voorsanger was worrying at his neck, now blossoming with red marks, ignoring the other men as he stared at Rossi.

"You okay?" she asked, placing her hand on his arm, giving it a reassuring squeeze. Ryder had the feeling she wasn't talking about Voorsanger's neck. It was obvious Voorsanger's last question hadn't been a mere slip of the tongue.

Voorsanger gave her a slow nod. "I'm fine."

"So, what do you think?" Manny went on in his usual breathless way, ignorant of or ignoring the exchange, excited by his sudden reversal of fortune. His no-win case had just turned into a slam-dunk conviction. "That asswipe going to roll finally? Because now he's facing assault and attempted murder with you and Judge Shaw as my star witnesses."

"You'll need to offer his new attorney a good deal," Voorsanger said. "I don't know details, but as you know from Mr. Littleton's previous statements, the men who coerced him to assault Ms. Nelson are rich, connected, and vicious. They'll kill anyone who gets in their way or threatens them. Just like I'm assuming they killed her."

The four of them exchanged glances. Ryder shrugged. Dealing with animals was his main reason to crawl out of bed in the morning. Manny nodded, a single jerk of his chin. The three men stared at Rossi.

"I saw Tymara," Rossi reminded them. "What they did to her. We need to get them off the streets. Whatever it takes."

☽ ⚘ ☾

DEVON PRICE WAS late for his breakfast date. It was twelve thirty-eight, a few hours shy of what he considered a civilized time of day. After spending the morning trying to find a line on who killed Tymara, he wasn't moving at full speed. If it hadn't been for the trial, he'd still be in bed. But, turned out, as lousy as the morning had been, he was glad he'd taken the time to talk to the Tower residents. He hadn't learned anything new about the Brotherhood, but his conversations had raised more questions. Questions he hoped Angela would be able to answer tonight.

Always borrowing trouble. That's what the Tower women who'd raised him had told him. This time he hoped they were right, that he was seeing trouble where it didn't exist. But the itch along his spine told him otherwise.

He stood inside the entrance to the chic Pan-Asian restaurant, ostensibly to remove his sunglasses. In reality he was waiting for the pause, that micro-moment of hush when women raised their gazes to admire him while their male companions straightened to acknowledge the competition. Not that anyone here could dream to compete with Daniel Kingston's son, illegitimate or not.

It never failed. Devon wasn't used to it, but in the month since he'd returned to Cambria City and had taken over Kingston Enterprises, he'd learned to expect it. All part of the game he had to play, which was to maintain the illusion of power and control the Kingstons had cultivated for generations. He gave the other diners a lazy glance, basking in the glow. So very different from the way his father had treated his bastard son as a child. Or the way he had treated Devon's mother.

Chuckling beneath his breath at the irony, he followed the hostess in her tight silk dress. She stopped and indicated a private booth at the rear of the restaurant, dark enough that his weary eyes wouldn't be subjected to glare.

Before she left, he slipped his card into her palm. Not his business card. His personal one. She jumped, her porcelain calm shattered, her expression bordering on fear.

"Er," she stuttered, "I'm sorry, Mr. Price." He folded the card into her palm as he raised her hand to his lips, kissing the flesh immediately above her wedding ring. A promise as well as a performance for the others watching.

"Keep it," he murmured, staring her down.

"But—" She was shuffling, too polite to yank her hand free, anxious to get away.

"I'll expect you tonight." He released her, and she ran away, teetering on high heels, his card crumpled in her sweaty grip.

"Hope you're not going to torch the place if she refuses," said Gena Kravitz, his dining companion, her chopsticks waving in the air. "I like the food here."

He hid his irritation that she'd ordered and begun without him. Knew it was one of her power plays. Why was it everything in this city boiled down to a few people in power playing games? At least when he'd worked with Philly's Russian mob, they'd been honest about their brutality and the consequences of failing to meet their expectations.

"For you, I'll simply organize a kitchen-worker strike," he said with a gracious flutter of his hand. "Most of their busboys and dishwashers come from the Tower."

If it came from Kingston Tower, then Devon controlled it. As soon as he dealt with men like Eugene Littleton and his partners in crime. People needed to understand that no one trespassed on what was Devon's. No one.

Gena slurped her tea, almost dunking her outrageous blonde curls in the process. Despite being a beautiful woman with a body she loved to flaunt, Gena was a slob when it came to table manners. No appreciation for the finer things in life, she was ruled by her passions—passions that, from the rumors Devon had heard, ran to the extreme. Enough that she'd left a top-tier firm in Philly to come here and open a solo practice.

"And then you'll extract a personal payment for ending the strike, right?" she asked, her eyes gleaming. "One custom-made ego trip ready for carry-out. What will it be, Devon? A night spent with you? Will you make her husband watch?"

Without him needing to order, a young waitress appeared with a tray laden with succulent specialty items, none from the menu everyone else ordered from. Only the chef's best for Daniel Kingston's son. The chef whose wife worked as hostess.

Devon nodded to the girl as she poured tea for him, her arms moving in graceful arcs. She finished her task and left, never once making eye contact with him. He eased his elbow along the top of the bench as he watched her walk away.

"Oh," Gena said in a breathless voice that made Devon wonder about the attorney's own proclivities. "A mother-daughter double feature. Wouldn't that be sweet?"

"Need you be so crass, Gena?" He kept his tone light, maintaining the facade of boredom, hiding a frown. She had no idea what he had planned, and if Devon had his way, she never would. He cast a lazy glance around the crowded restaurant. None of them would.

"It's my nature. Besides, you like having me around, someone who sees what you do and can appreciate it without judging."

"Speaking of judges—"

"Heard about the mistrial." She made a tut-tutting sound. "So disappointing. I know you were counting on an acquittal. Especially after what happened this morning. Do the police have any leads?"

Devon scowled. "No. My men saw nothing out of the ordinary, not even the ones I had patrolling Tymara's floor."

"No cameras?"

"The original system hasn't worked in decades. I'm in the process of updating it, rewiring the entire Tower, but the work won't be done until after the New Year."

"Too bad. A mistrial means your buddy—"

"Eugene is merely a tool, a means to an end," he corrected her.

"Whatever. He gets to go through all that again. Plus facing whatever new charges the DA drums up." She jammed a wad of rice noodles into her mouth, didn't bother to swallow before speaking again. "Which means he stays behind bars. Without talking, just like he has for the last six months. My bet? He won't last long. The Brotherhood will get to him first."

He frowned at the melodramatic nickname the street had bestowed on the men he hunted. Wondered, not for the first time, if they'd christened themselves in an effort to feed their egos. "No. I want him alive."

"Good luck with that. No way in hell is he going to get bail, not after what he did today."

"You defend him. Get him released." He sipped at his tea, enjoying the faint undertones of jasmine. "Now that the public defender's office must recuse themselves, you can take it on pro bono. A service to the community, defending the rights of a poor, defenseless man victimized by the system."

"Pro bono?" Her chuckle ended abruptly when he nodded. "Do

you have any idea what I'm paid for my time?"

"You'll be well compensated."

"Damn right."

Devon smiled, letting it reach all the way to his eyes. He enjoyed her look of appraising curiosity. Time to cement their partnership. He set his cup down delicately so that the fine-boned china saucer didn't even quiver. "Of course, you do know who the prosecutor is, don't you?" He waited a beat until he was certain he had her attention. "Your new favorite plaything."

She dropped the shrimp she'd so painstakingly picked up with her chopsticks. It slid across the plate, dangling over the edge. "How did—" Her face tightened. She looked over her shoulder before returning her gaze to him and lowering her voice. "I'll do it. But you need to leave Manny out of it."

"Of course, of course. Far be it from me to interfere with true love." He smirked as he skewered the wayward shrimp and popped it into his mouth. When would she learn? It was the one thing he shared with his father: Devon always got what he wanted.

Always.

CHAPTER ELEVEN

"C'MON, DETECTIVE, LET'S get our new friend tucked in," Manny said to Ryder, walking past me.

Jacob had his back turned, shuffling his papers and files at the defense table. Ryder waited a beat, raising one eyebrow as he stared at me, his expression hungry. I couldn't help smiling in return, heat burning my cheeks.

First day back at work after getting shot and he got to tackle a guy and hopefully get a lead on Tymara's killers. Of course his hormones were raging worse than a teenage kid's. Ryder allowed his hip to nudge against my backside as he strolled past, following Manny.

Leaving Jacob and me. Our marriage had been dead and buried long enough that we could be friends without worrying too much about hurting each other. We knew each other's vulnerable spots and we both cared enough to avoid them.

I joined him at the table. The scuffle with Littleton had left his carefully organized files in a jumble. He was compulsive enough to keep his tea bags alphabetized; he wouldn't rest until the files were back in order. I arranged the ones in reach, working in silence beside him, listening to him breathe, shallow and fast, as if he were still fighting with Littleton. "You did good today."

"Did I? Did I really?" His tone was bitter and defeated. He wasn't struggling because of his wrestling match with Littleton. It was the harder fight, the one with his conscience.

Knowing that reminded me why I had fallen in love with him. If Atticus Finch had had a grandson, it would be Jacob Voorsanger.

"If you got Littleton off, you'd be condemning another woman. More than one. This way, with his help, we can nail the others. Pretty good for a day's work."

"I'm not proud of what I did." He stood, facing me, his files forgotten. "And you shouldn't be either."

For once, I was unable to read his expression. His tone implied I was at fault for his betrayal of his values. "You did this for me? I don't understand." He winced and I knew I'd hit the bull's-eye. "I didn't ask you to do this, Jacob. I never asked—"

"No, you never ask for anything, do you, Angie?"

"What's that supposed to mean?"

"Nothing. As usual, I have nothing to do with anything in your life." His focus zeroed in on an imaginary speck between his shoes as he avoided eye contact with me and shook his head, small shakes of anger and frustration.

"Exactly how is any of this my fault?" I asked. "Are you angry because of what you did? Or because I was here to see it?"

He opened his mouth, closed it again. This was the first time I could remember seeing Jacob speechless. He turned to shove the rest of the files haphazardly into his satchel. "I wish to hell I knew."

He stalked away from me.

The door opened before Jacob reached it, and Ryder reappeared. Ryder held the door as Jacob faltered, sending a last look over his shoulder to me. My stomach clenched as if something terrible and important had just happened, but I wasn't sure what.

Then Jacob was gone, leaving Ryder and me alone in the cavernous hall of justice.

Sunlight glinted through the stained-glass windows, casting red and gold diamonds on the marble floor. Ryder leaned against the heavy oak door for a long moment, staring at me, his thumbs hooked in his waistband. Appraisal laced with longing. Seconds ticked past, and he didn't blink, simply drank me in until I was surprised to find myself blushing. I couldn't remember the last time that'd happened. Funny how, with only a look, he could transform my mood. Make me forget everything.

"I've got time while they get Littleton processed." He jerked his head in the general direction of the jail wing. His expression softened. "You sure you're okay? Finding Tymara, then facing all this." His nod took in the courtroom.

I looked away to the stained-glass window where Justice always prevailed no matter what happened inside the walls she protected. Despite standing up to Jacob, I couldn't shed all my guilt. "It was my fault. She never would have agreed to testify if I hadn't talked her into it."

He stepped forward, placed his palms on my hips, and lowered his face until our foreheads touched and our gazes locked, shutting out the rest of the world. "I wasn't there for the initial case, never met Tymara, but after a decade of doing this job, I can assure you her death is not your fault. Stop feeling sorry for yourself and start thinking of anything she told you—even if it wasn't in the official medical record—that might help me catch these guys."

I straightened, annoyed at his suggestion that I might have overlooked anything that could have saved Tymara. "If there was anything, I would have told the police already."

"Then there's nothing. You're off the hook. And officially off the clock. Seems like we have some time on our hands." He slid his lips down to meet mine, in no hurry, his gaze fixed on my eyes, never wavering, waiting for me to respond. I pulled him closer, my arms wrapping around his neck. After the emotional upheaval today had brought, being in his arms was a relief.

Life with Ryder was a constant adventure. He enjoyed pushing the limits and bending the rules as much as I did. We both liked taking control, both had shadowy, soft spots best to avoid, both respected each other enough to take pleasure in the physical without probing too deeply into the feelings or the personal shit.

Just the way I wanted it. No, be honest, it was the way I *needed* it. The honorable thing to do would be to end things now before they got too messy, before anyone got hurt.

Right now, this minute, my doomsday clock ticking away the seconds, I wasn't feeling particularly honorable. Right now, I needed to forget, to block out the visions of Tymara's body, of the blood and pain that threatened to drown me.

I needed Ryder.

He slid one palm from my hip slowly up along my waist to my breast. Taking his own sweet time with the caress, the fabric of my blouse whispering against my skin. His hand was hot, searing through the silk that separated us.

I didn't care that we were in a court of law, didn't care that anyone might walk in and find us, didn't care about anything except what he had to offer. An escape from reality.

The kiss deepened, but instead of the heat I'd been expecting, it turned tender. He stroked my hair, cradling my head with a gentle caress. We broke apart, and I ended up leaning my weight against him, my face pressed against his chest, swallowing the sudden sob that ambushed me. I was a fool. We'd moved way past the point of harmless sex where no one got hurt.

"About this morning…" I started, surprised by the way my voice had grown hoarse. "We should talk—" I trembled with panic at the thought. Telling Ryder the truth of what was happening to me, it would change everything.

He traced his fingers down the back of my neck. "We will. When you're ready. I'll be here."

I blinked, trying to deny the tears his words brought. Before I could gather my strength to tell him about my diagnosis, his phone went off.

"Shit." He breathed the word, but his hands didn't release their grip on me. "Manny has a lousy sense of timing."

The phone rang again. He blew his breath out with a muffled curse. I untangled myself from his embrace and straightened my clothing, liking the way his gaze followed my every movement. It was one of the things I loved about Ryder, the way he could focus so intently, making me feel as if I was the only person in his universe. Unlike Jacob, who was always lost in clouds of intangibles like justice and ethics and morals. Ryder knew how to simply...be.

Holding the phone, he finally tore his gaze away from me to read the screen and nodded, all business now. "Manny can wait," he said. "Let me take you home first."

A stray beam of sunlight turned red by the stained glass sliced between us.

"No. I want to stay, help." I walked to the prosecution table. My ancient leather messenger's bag—a present from Jacob to carry in lieu of a doctor's bag—waited there. I opened it, revealing all of Tymara's files. Including eight-by-ten full-color glossies documenting her injuries—evidence the judge had disallowed as inadmissible, prejudicial, and irrelevant to Littleton's prosecution, but I had brought it all. None of it was irrelevant to me.

"Will these help?" I asked, offering them to Ryder.

"Absolutely. Especially if you're the one confronting Littleton. You scare the hell out of him. While you were on the stand, he was sweat-flopping like crazy, fidgeting, couldn't stop ducking his face every time you glanced his way."

I hadn't noticed. Too angry to notice. Hated to admit it, but Manny had been right about not letting my emotions take control.

"Come with me," Ryder offered. "We can nail him together." How was it he always knew what I really needed?

"And his partners," I reminded him, excited at the prospect of being able to do something concrete. I owed Tymara the chance to see the animals who'd tortured and killed her brought to justice. When I was in Ryder's arms for those few minutes, I'd been able to banish the image of her body, but now it filled my vision again, coloring my world in blood.

"And his partners," Ryder promised, taking my hand and squeezing it as we walked down the courtroom aisle. He opened the heavy oak door and held it for me.

For an instant, his form wavered, appearing translucent in the light glancing off the polished marble, as if he were glowing, some kind of mystic being or angel. I shook myself, blinked hard, forcing my vision back to normal.

Fear coiled itself around my insides, squeezing my stomach, heart, lungs. Fear of what the future might hold if I invited Ryder fully into my life. I shoved it aside, making a tight fist then releasing the fear into the air. I swear I saw it skitter across the floor, dark tendrils mimicking the mud streaking the marble, careening into the shadows where it waited in ambush.

I wanted to bellow a challenge. To fear, to fate, to my fatal insomnia.

Take your best shot.

CHAPTER TWELVE

LEAVING BEHIND THE Gothic monstrosity of the courthouse, with its drafty corridors, high ceilings, marble floors, and stained-glass windows, Ryder led Rossi across the pedestrian skyway to the modern and austere jail, all concrete and steel. They passed through two sets of guarded checkpoints before being allowed into the room where Manny waited. The jailhouse conference room was windowless, and smelled of wet paint and disinfectant.

"We need to get our shit together," Manny said as soon as he spotted Ryder. "The PD's office is replacing Jacob Voorsanger with Gena Kravitz." He prowled the perimeter with jerky steps, as if both excited and hesitant about the turn of events. "Conflict of interest for their office after the assault on Jacob."

"No shit," Ryder said. "How'd they pull that off? What she bills an hour is more than one of their guys makes in a week."

"She's doing it pro bono. But she likes the courtroom, likes grandstanding. We might be in trouble. Kravitz doesn't often deal." Manny narrowed his gaze at Rossi. "Why'd you bring her?"

Rossi leaned against the doorway and let Ryder answer. "She

brought the photos of the victim," he said, wondering at the sudden change in her. She'd been fine during the walk over, but now sweat beaded above her lip, and her pulse throbbed in her neck.

Damn, he never should have brought her. He should have sent her home to rest after everything she'd been through today. Not that she'd let him do anything to help her. Stubborn, stubborn woman. It was agony standing by, doing nothing.

He pulled out a chair for Rossi, and she sank into it, nodding her thanks. He resisted the urge to hover, and settled for taking the seat beside her. She'd bust his balls if he ever treated her as anything less than an equal.

"Typical of a power-reassurance rapist, he doesn't like being around strong women," Ryder continued, paraphrasing what Rossi had told him last week when they prepped her testimony during his convalescence. "Way she made him so nervous in court, Rossi's the best person to get him to talk."

Manny grunted his assent. "Okay, if Kravitz doesn't object."

The door banged open, and a tall, curvaceous blonde bounded in. "Object?" Gena Kravitz said, heaving a bulging briefcase onto the table. "Of course I object. I object to the trampling of my client's rights, the police brutality, and this perversion of justice that has brought us here today!"

She moved so fast that the air around her danced, as if the molecules were unable to keep up with her energy. Her laughter sliced through the room as she plopped herself into a chair. "Now that my objections are on record, what the hell are we talking about?"

"We have your client dead to rights, and you know it." Manny leaned forward on knuckled fists. Ryder remained quiet, watching the two lawyers wrangle like junkyard dogs. A sly smile played over his face as he sat back, waiting to pounce. He glanced at Rossi. Her color had returned to almost normal, and she also watched the exchange with interest.

Kravitz met Manny head-on. "I find it difficult to believe an attorney as good as Jacob Voorsanger had a simple slip of the tongue.

Besides, your victimless prosecution of the rape charges is bullshit. Can't believe Judge Shaw even allowed it to go this far."

"Who cares about the rape? Shaw's now my star witness when I charge your client with felony assault and attempted murder. Not to mention every juror, and don't forget, the entire incident was taped. I'd like to see you find reasonable doubt in that, Kravitz."

Kravitz stopped moving for a moment, her hair bouncing against her shoulders, her face crinkling with a smile as if at a private joke. Then she chuckled. "It'd be fun to try, wouldn't it?" She spun to face Manny. "Okay, what do you want?"

Ryder saw his opening and tossed Tymara's photos along the table. They skidded to a stop in front of Kravitz. "The monsters responsible for this."

Kravitz barely flicked a glance at the photos, her expression never wavering. "In exchange for?"

"We drop the rape charges," Manny said, finally settling into a chair. Kravitz waited a beat, then also took a seat.

"If he fully cooperates and testifies against the others," Rossi added, her words tight with fury. She had no patience for the games lawyers played, Ryder knew. Not with her victim caught in the middle.

Kravitz was silent, her lips pursed.

"You really don't want to haul Judge Shaw onto the witness stand and cross-examine her," Manny reminded her. "You'd be slitting your wrists any time you walked into her courtroom ever again."

"Of course, I need to put the interests of my client first," Kravitz allowed, meaning exactly the opposite.

Rossi slammed her palm down on the table in front of Kravitz, the move so sudden the noise cracked the air like a gunshot. Both Kravitz and Manny jumped. Ryder smiled. Leave it to Rossi to cut through the lawyer BS.

"Now that we've protected your ass as well as your rapist client," Rossi said, "give us the names of the men responsible for this."

She held the photo of Tymara's battered, naked body before Kravitz. Kravitz took the photo and dropped it facedown on the table, her gaze never leaving Rossi's as she gave her a smirking once-over, her fingers playing with a large emerald ring on her right hand. She took in everything, from Rossi's no-nonsense flats to the dark circles beneath her eyes. Ryder fought an urge to insert himself between the two women, but he was confident Rossi could handle Kravitz.

"I've heard of you, Dr. Rossi," Kravitz said after a long moment of consideration. "You decimated one of my former associates during the Watson case."

"I remember. He kept me on the stand for over an hour, trying to get me to agree to an alternative theory as to how a twelve-year-old's stepfather's sperm came to be found on a vaginal swab during her rape exam. Trying to imply she'd somehow artificially inseminated herself and that the stepfather wasn't involved. That he hadn't raped her weekly for the previous four years before she found the courage to speak out."

Rossi leaned forward, inserting herself into Kravitz's space, making it impossible for Kravitz to look anywhere but at her face. "We won. We got justice for that little girl, just like we will for Tymara Nelson."

"If I remember correctly, after he was convicted, the stepfather blew his brains out rather than face prison." Kravitz gazed at Rossi with another condescending look. "There's a thin line between justice and vengeance. You're taking this case much too personally."

"I take all my cases personally."

"But justice isn't personal. That's why it's blind." She shook her head. "No wonder you burned out at such a young age. Only thirty-four and taking early retirement from the ER? Makes one think there's more going on. Some kind of personal crisis, Doctor? Interfering with your work, impairing your judgment?"

Rossi kept her expression neutral, ignoring Kravitz's implied accusation. "Nice try, counselor. But my decision to take a sabbatical has no reflection on the fact your client is guilty. I have no problems at all changing my travel plans to ensure I'll be present to testify again if Mr. Cruz decides to retry him."

"A sabbatical? Is that what they're calling it these days?" Kravitz's stare was heavy, weighted with challenge and skepticism.

Rossi glared at the attorney. Beside her, Manny shifted in his seat. His ears were red, but other than that, he had his usual cocky game face on. But his gaze was riveted on Kravitz in a way that was intensely personal and more than a little possessive.

Oh shit. Kravitz and Manny? Ryder had heard rumors. A relationship between an assistant district attorney and defense attorney pretty much blew all the rules out of the water.

Kravitz dismissed Rossi with a one-shoulder shrug that sent her mass of curls rippling. Her gaze cut to Manny. "My client warns that he may not be aware of the identities of all involved in this unfortunate incident."

"No. He needs to give us names," Rossi insisted.

Kravitz deigned to glance her way. "He'll give you everything he is able to give. What you do with it is none of our concern."

It was obvious Rossi didn't like the sound of that. Neither did Ryder. Too much wiggle room. He leaned forward, his hand slipping onto her thigh, under the table, hidden. The tension that had knotted her muscles eased at his touch.

"What's it going to cost?" Manny asked. He seemed to be enjoying himself. Was it because he had a slam-dunk conviction to add to his scorecard or because of the attorney he was negotiating with?

"You tell me."

"He pleads guilty on all charges," Manny said.

"And registers as a sex offender," Ryder put in.

Manny nodded. "If his information pans out, we'll take time served."

Kravitz pursed her lips, the weight of her stare on Manny. Manny shifted in his seat, looking away first. Sensing her victory, Kravitz pushed her chair back and stood, looking down on them all. "He'll tell you everything he can, plead guilty to the assault with time served. You drop the rest. Period. None of this 'if the information pans out' bullshit. If your investigators were able to put a decent case together to start with, we wouldn't be in this mess. I'm not trusting my client's freedom to their talent," she knifed a glare at Ryder, "or lack thereof."

"No," Rossi protested. "What about Tymara?"

Manny didn't even glance in her direction. "Done," he said, getting to his feet. "Let's finalize this."

Ryder watched them leave, noticing the way Manny brushed against Kravitz's side as they went through the door. *Well, hell.*

"Did he seriously just give Littleton a walk?" Rossi's voice rose with indignation. "Just to save his conviction rate and please his girlfriend?"

So she'd seen it as well. He gave the door a pitying look. "Blondie there is going to use and abuse and grind poor Manny into the dirt with her stilettos."

"And with him, our case."

"Which do you want? Littleton in jail on assault charges or the men who killed Tymara?"

"I want them all." Her gaze was fierce. Her fists bunched on the tabletop as if ready to battle her way through the guards and concrete walls and locked doors to get to Littleton herself.

Then he noticed the tremor that quivered her hand, and it took all his strength not to gather her into his arms and carry her far away from this building filled with treacherous snakes on both sides of the law. He still refused to believe—no matter how much crepe Louise hung as she discussed the disease, but never the patient—that some microscopic, twisted strand of protein could be the end to a woman as strong and passionate and alive as Rossi.

She turned to face him, her expression earnest. "Isn't that what we're here for? Isn't that why we do this job? To nail bastards like Littleton?"

He placed his hand over hers and squeezed. The tremor fought, refusing to surrender to his touch. As stubborn as the woman. "Some of us. Yes."

How could he not try to give her everything she deserved? Ryder looked up, past Rossi, to the bright overhead lights, convincing himself that the tight burning behind his eyes came from their glare. He blinked hard. How could he not fight as hard for her as he had his squad back in Afghanistan? He'd brought them home alive. There was no way in hell he wouldn't do the same for Rossi.

No matter what it took.

CHAPTER THIRTEEN

MANNY RETURNED, A scowl on his face. "There's a small snag," he said, glaring at me. "Seems Littleton refuses to talk to us until he talks to you first."

I jerked my head up. "Me? Why's he want to talk to me?"

After what Ryder said about how Littleton acted during my testimony, I understood why Manny might want me to talk to him, but why would Littleton ask for me? What had changed in the short time since we'd faced off in the courtroom? Maybe something Gena had told him about me?

"Fuck what Littleton wants." Ryder stood, the abrupt movement fluttering the photos across the tabletop. "Let him rot here, face a new trial and new charges."

"A new trial isn't going to help. I polled the jurors. They were leaning toward acquittal," Manny said. "Without Tymara's testimony, they just weren't buying it."

"Without Littleton, we can't get the others," I said. "Besides, that's why you brought me. I make him nervous. Maybe he'll say something he'll regret."

Ryder slouched in the corner, shoulders hunched, staring at me from behind Manny's back. He gave me a wary nod, not granting me permission, more like accepting that someone had to do the dirty work. I could tell he wished he'd be the one going in to meet Littleton.

"I'll do it," I told Manny.

We had to wait while the jailers fetched Littleton and brought him to the interview room. Manny spent the time coaching me. "Remember, privilege doesn't apply, and we'll be listening through the video monitor, so anything you can get him to say—"

"I know." I gathered my photos, my fingers pausing over the last, a head shot, filled with Tymara's dark, pleading eyes.

Ryder turned away from his position at the monitor, where he'd been watching the jailers secure Littleton, now in prison orange and shackles, to the table. There was no way Littleton would be able to touch me, physically at least. "Don't let him play mind games with you."

"I won't." The door opened, and a guard beckoned. Gena Kravitz pushed in as I left, planting herself in front of the observation monitor, hands on her hips, obviously not too pleased with her client or his unorthodox demands.

Taking a deep breath outside the door to the room where Littleton waited, I shoved my nervousness aside. This was what I'd wanted, a chance to nail the men who'd killed Tymara. I pulled the vision of her brutalized body front and center in my mind, using it to fuel my adrenaline. I was walking a knife's edge—stay too calm and Littleton would grow bored, say nothing of value; reveal too much emotion and he'd slake his blood thirst with it rather than give us what we needed to find his partners.

I strode into the room and sat across the table from Littleton. Before he could speak, I snapped the photos of Tymara onto the table like a high-stakes poker player dealing aces.

"Thought you might want to take this opportunity to explain to me exactly how Tymara received these injuries and who inflicted them." Good, my voice was steady and clear.

Littleton jerked back as far as his chains would take him. "I don't want to look at that shit."

"Sure you do. Isn't that what you did while it was happening? Watch?" I lowered my voice, as if taking confession. "That's what you like to do best, isn't it, Eugene? You like to watch because you have a hard time doing anything more."

"Shut up, bitch! You don't know nothing. Tymara and me, it wasn't like that. She came on to me, messed me up, played with me until I couldn't think straight. I used to go into her place in the middle of the day, and she'd be there waiting for me, pretending to be asleep, wearing these little slips of hers, worse than if she was naked—"

"Ever stop to think that she *was* sleeping? She worked two jobs, one from three to eleven, the other overnight."

He shook his head. "No. She wanted me. Wanted me so bad. Always calling me to come spray her place extra. Said she was scared of bugs. Used to make these little screams. Once, a bunch of spiders got loose, some of them ended up in her bed. You should've seen her."

From the smirk on Littleton's face, I had a pretty good feeling how "a bunch of spiders" ended up in Tymara's bed. In his warped, narcissistic world, Littleton actually believed Tymara had been attracted to him.

"I saved her," Littleton went on, his lips curling and gaze tilting up, as if he was imagining something. "She owed me for that. She liked it rough, wanted me to do her in the worst way. Me and her, we were like this." He held up two fingers, crossed as if for luck.

"That night, that was the first time you were ever together? And the last? How does it make you feel, knowing she's gone?" If I could crack his delusion, he might give me more. Power-reassurance rapists start out stalking their victims, creating a fantasy love affair. The rape is, in their warped imagination, a much-anticipated date. Until their fairytale ending doesn't play out.

"What do you mean, how do I feel?" Littleton replied. "I loved Tymara."

He got a distant look on his face, and his hands jerked at the chains securing him to the table. Reliving his fantasy. It took everything I had to disguise my grimace of disgust.

"Loved her and lost her. That's us. Romeo and Juliet. Star-crossed lovers." Littleton opened his eyes wide and stared at the camera with a grin, playing to his unseen audience.

I tried to steer him to the information I needed. "Those other men. You trusted them with the woman you loved."

"Share and share alike. That's what brothers do."

"Brothers?"

He gave a slow nod, his gaze never leaving the monitor. "Not everyone is created equal."

I frowned, trying to follow his line of reasoning. "Tymara. She wasn't equal?"

"Got to pay to play."

"I don't understand. You loved Tymara. But you knew, somewhere deep down inside, you knew she'd never love you. That's why you let other men torture her, sodomize her, beat her, rape her. To punish her for not loving you?"

Littleton narrowed his eyes, glaring at me in silence, assessing a piece of meat: Me. My shudder was involuntary and left in its wake shimmers of color. The fugue I'd fought off earlier threatening to return at the worst possible moment.

"I don't know nothing about that." His smirk said exactly the opposite. "Besides, you're here for me to talk to, not the other way around. We just wanted to let you know there are consequences. Serious consequences, doctor. I were you, I wouldn't be going around asking more questions about Tymara. You won't like the answers that come knocking."

Littleton braced his weight on his shackled hands, leaning as close to me as he could. I was fighting my fugue, battling it for control of my body, leaving me no strength to reply.

Giving Littleton exactly what he wanted. He thought I was frozen in terror. Glee filled his eyes, making them glint in the harsh overhead light. Sparks rained down from the ceiling, showered us both, quivering and hanging in midair.

"Bet you're afraid of spiders, too, aren't you, Dr. Rossi? Might want to check under your pillow tonight."

CHAPTER FOURTEEN

BEFORE I COULD begin to process Littleton's threat, Ryder burst into the room and grabbed him, hauling him back, and forcing him back into his chair with a thud that rattled the table. I felt the opposite of an adrenaline rush. Instead of being propelled into action, I was frozen in place, my brain sluggishly struggling against my fugue as my limbs iced over.

Two guards rushed in, one helping Ryder, the other joining me. Ryder straightened and looked over his shoulder at me, his face a mix of worry and fury.

Ryder's hand grazed my arm, his fingers trailing against my skin. Tiny thrills of electricity spread through my body, warring with the frigid chill holding me hostage. Thankfully, the fugue released me and I was free to move again.

He nodded to the guard, who escorted me past him and out the door. When I looked back, Ryder took the seat opposite Littleton, an amiable smile now masking his true feelings. His game face. I'd seen it before, but it always amazed me how he could shut down his emotions faster than flicking a light switch.

"You okay, ma'am?" the guard asked as he closed the door, locking Ryder inside with Littleton.

I slumped against the wall. "I'm fine." My voice wasn't too bad, not shaky at all, so I tried it again. "Thanks."

I couldn't manage anything more, so I walked into the observation room, passing Gena as she joined Ryder and her client. Harsh institutional fluorescents beamed onto us, but every shadow seemed to radiate heat and color, shimmering into a mosaic of neon.

My meds were wearing off early. Stress of the trial, lack of exercise, skipped lunch—so many factors trying to force my body off this tightrope I walked without a net. Last thing I needed was to start gulping down pills in front of Manny.

Ryder's voice, calm, friendly even, hummed through the monitor, soothing my pulse. "The only way you get out of here, Eugene, is by talking. So go ahead, tell me everything."

Littleton began to spin a tale of his and Tymara's love affair, punctuated with fake outbursts of anger at the "bastards who hurt my lady." Never mentioning names, insisting Tymara's attack occurred after he left her, and that he had no idea who had brutalized his "girlfriend." It would look good on paper, although the video revealed his scoffing smirk. Total waste of time.

It was all for nothing. There'd be no justice served today.

My stomach rebelled at the idea. I had to get out of here, get to a safe place to take my meds before my body seized up once again.

The neurologists have a fancy name for it: an oneiric state. A fugue, in which my body becomes catatonic, while my brain keeps working on overdrive. The first time it happened, I was holding the heart of a nun who had been shot in the chest. I froze and she died. I told myself she would have died no matter what. Useless, empty words.

Breathing slow and deep, I gathered my strength. I pushed up from the chair and edged to the door.

Manny, hands shoved into his jacket pockets, shoulders slumped as he watched Gena steer her client clear of anything resembling testimony that would help build a case against Tymara's killers, didn't turn away from the monitor.

"Guess you picked a good time to go on *sabbatical*," he said, his gaze fixed forward as I fumbled for the doorknob. "Nice you won't have to see the results of your fuckup."

It was a fight to stay on my feet, but my anger trumped my physical symptoms. "You're blaming me?"

He shot me a glare lanced with disdain.

"You son of a bitch. I told you Tymara was scared for her life. I begged you to give her protection, but you wouldn't listen. You never would have gone on with the trial if it hadn't been for me insisting. Littleton would have walked anyway."

"Fat lot of good it did," he snapped. "Making me look a fool in front of Judge Shaw."

"Did you notice Littleton's choice of pronouns in there? He said *we*. Which means there will be more victims. Maybe there already have been, and we just haven't found them yet. Have you thought of that?"

"None of your business. Not anymore. Seems to me you'd best listen to his warning. Stay clear of all this. Go on vacation, your sabbatical, whatever the hell that means."

I started to leave, then turned back, my emotions getting the best of me. "How convenient for Littleton to suddenly hire a lawyer like Gena Kravitz who happens to be sleeping with the prosecution. Who's paying her, Manny? The Brotherhood? Are they paying you, too?"

The words shot out before I could think them through. With more speed than I would have imagined, Manny was across the room, shoving me back against the door.

I knew how to defend myself. Years working in the ER and hanging out with cops had taught me tricks that could put a man on the floor quickly. But I'd also learned that sometimes words were a far better weapon. Especially when I couldn't depend on my body, like now.

"How much was Tymara's life worth?" I asked him, his face mere inches from mine, his mouth open as if he were about to either scream or devour me. I wasn't even certain what I was accusing him of. All I knew was that the fury building since I discovered Tymara's body needed a target, and Manny was an easy one to hit. "How much was your honor worth?"

"You have no idea what you're talking about. Get out." Spittle sprayed my face as he hurled the words at me. His hands flew open, releasing me as his body lurched back a step. "Get out. Now."

I twisted the doorknob and yanked the door open, backing out of the room, still facing Manny. How much of our loss today was his fault? I wondered. I'd been so busy blaming myself, trying to find new options to keep Tymara's case alive, I hadn't really thought of Manny's role in all this.

Maybe he'd *never* intended to win this case.

I stumbled down the hall, back through security, to the courthouse on the other side of the pedestrian bridge. It was only after I'd locked myself into the safe tile and metal cocoon of a closet-sized women's room that I allowed myself to sag against the sink, legs wobbling, ready to collapse.

Could Manny really be working for the men who raped and killed Tymara? I'd never liked the prosecutor, didn't appreciate his idea that this was all just a game, a contest, rather than lives at stake. But helping men—no, not men...vicious animals—get away with rape and murder? Could the Brotherhood be so powerful that they could corrupt a prosecutor, taint a trial?

My entire body shook. Emotion combined with another fugue. Splashing water on my face helped a little. I fumbled through my bag. My fingers paused over my new prescription, the PXA. Two fugues coming on back-to-back. Was it worth it? Should I try it now?

No. Things weren't that bad. Not yet.

Instead, I grabbed my small makeup case. I didn't wear makeup, other than the occasional lipstick. The case was filled with plastic pillboxes containing a variety of assorted medications. They weren't labeled. I knew them all by heart.

Cupping my hand and filling it with water, I downed two Ritalins and added a longer-acting Adderall for good measure. After swallowing the pills, I sank to the floor, my back to the door. My phone vibrated, a text from Devon. *Pick you up at five, don't forget. It's important.*

Right. His urgent medical consultation. As long as it didn't involve his father, Daniel Kingston. I couldn't handle that argument, not today. I slid the phone back into my bag. The pills would start working soon. *Soon.* The word whirled through my mind, creating colors and shapes behind my eyelids, music playing with the syllables, permeations of half-lives, pharmaceutical equations, digestive process timing, pill disintegration, all coalescing in an abstract biochemical equation my mind processed with the ease of blinking. Things I couldn't do in normal time, but I had left normal time far behind.

I tried to raise the little finger of my right hand, not surprised when my body didn't obey. I'd crossed over into the fugue state, the echoes of color swallowing my awareness, my mind clearer, sharper, faster than ever—but my body beyond my control. Terror and exhilaration warred within me.

While my body was frozen, my mind rewound time with whiplash speed, dissecting every word, movement, and nuance of expression that had occurred in the courtroom and later in the interview room. The judge's perfume was an old-fashioned lilac scent, similar to the one my third-grade teacher had worn. Jacob was missing a button from his left shirtsleeve. One of the jurors had a deviated septum, giving him a slight whistle when he breathed. Details my brain overlooked at the time now flashed before me as I relived every moment.

Pupils dilating, flushes, furtive touches to lips and neck: Manny and Gena *were* involved, I was certain.

Finally, I saw what Ryder had seen while I was testifying—and more. Littleton had been waiting for a chance to act out, throw the case if it didn't go his way. But how had he known the chance would come? Did he know the judge was already leaning toward a mistrial because of Tymara being unable to testify?

Had this entire trial been orchestrated by the men behind Tymara's assault? Littleton's so-called brothers. Did they have that kind of power?

There had to be a way to stop them.

My hand twitched. Pins and needles shot through my thighs, put to sleep by the hard tile floor. I opened my eyes and slowly stretched my cramped muscles as the fugue released its grip on my body. I glanced at my watch. Twelve minutes had passed. In my mind, it felt like seconds.

To my body, it felt like days.

I grabbed on to the edge of the sink and hauled myself up. Leaning against the wall, I waited for my legs to stop shaking. I risked a glance into the mirror.

My face looked normal. How could that be? It felt like everything behind the face was so alien, so out of control. Yet, there I was, same as always.

Maybe it was good to have a reliable mask, to be able to fool the world, just like I'd fooled everyone in the courtroom this morning. Let them all think I was the same old, capable, dependable Angela, the woman with all the answers who never stopped fighting for her patients.

Fool them all into thinking I actually had a future.

CHAPTER FIFTEEN

JACOB VOORSANGER COULDN'T pinpoint the exact moment he had sold his soul. That bothered him.

If his father could talk, could form a cogent thought inside the shriveled shell of a body that refused to release its stranglehold on life, he'd be delighted to point out the moment when Jacob fell from grace and ruined everything.

For Abraham Voorsanger, that moment would probably have been the instant Jacob left his rabbinical studies and decided to practice law. Or when Jacob fell in love with Angela Rossi and asked her to marry him.

A marriage that took place inside this very courthouse before a judge in the presence of two witnesses: Angie's sister Eve and Jacob's roommate from college. The disapproving older generations from both sides had been conspicuously absent in silent protest.

Jacob paused his pacing, ignoring the late-afternoon traffic-court penitents who streamed through the courthouse's large oak doors and passed him on their way through security. If he hadn't become a lawyer, hadn't fallen in love, he wouldn't be in this situation now. He tried to follow the permutations of choice back to their roots, only to get lost in the maze of logic.

Footsteps echoed around him. Someone's heels—a woman, delicately built, he guessed from the sound—struck a perfect cadence. She laughed, short and sweet, the sound echoing against the marble floor, a tone that swirled through Jacob like rays of sunshine, making him lift his face and listen until it faded into obscurity, drowned out by the dull thuds of the rest of the crowd.

Meeting Angie, being with her, was like that sound. Pure, light, effortless.

Maybe that was where he went wrong. He should have put more effort into them, less into himself and his career. He'd let her do too much of the heavy lifting.

Idiot. Fool. Blind, stupid, fool. He shook his head, scanned the crowd. Still no sign of Angie. He resumed his pacing across the courthouse rotunda.

He may not have gone to *shul* for years, but he still studied the Talmud each week, especially the Nezikin. As well as the Christian Bible and the Quran. Often, he learned as much from the religious texts and commentaries as he did from the *Law Review* and judicial proceedings.

Long ago, Jacob had given up any hope of being a great man, or even a good man. Now, he was merely trying his best to be a just man.

Looked like he'd failed at that as well. He could almost hear Abraham's disapproval ring through his mind despite the fact that the old man hadn't spoken a coherent word in the year since the Alzheimer's swallowed him whole.

A woman's voice sang through the noise surrounding him. Angie. He spotted her at the security desk, returning her visitor's pass. She shrugged the strap of her bag onto her shoulder, one hand gripping the handle as if fearful of theft, even here in this bastion of law and order.

Her footsteps dragged. She looked tired, weary even. But despite that, she gave off an indefinable energy, a vibe that to him translated into passion, the passion she threw into everything. The passion she'd once shared with him.

He blew out his breath. It fogged in the chill, pine-scented, almost-Christmas air before drifting away. He jogged over to join her. "How'd it go?"

She didn't answer right away. Her skin was flushed, and she was sweating despite the draft in the rotunda. She turned to take a deep drink from the water fountain, and for an instant, he wondered if his actions earlier had worse consequences than he'd imagined. Had he lost her for good? But she tilted her face up to meet his gaze, and he was reassured.

"Well?" Nervous energy propelled him to take three steps and stand on her other side, where he had more room to fidget. "Did he give it up?"

"He refused to name names."

He slumped against the wall, his eyes sliding shut for a brief moment. "Damn."

"Littleton's going to walk. Time served."

"Manny let him plead out?" His sacrifice had been for nothing.

"Yes." She pursed her lips, as if holding back a secret.

He had a sinking feeling he knew what that secret was: She was disappointed in him, that he who'd lectured her so often and so freely on ethics had turned his back on his own.

She surprised him with a question rather than a recrimination. "If you can try a case without the victim, you could do it without a witness, right?"

"Depends. On the other evidence, the other witnesses, circumstances as to why they can't appear." He squinted at her. "You know all this. Why are you asking?"

"Nothing." She walked past him toward the doors.

"I'll walk you to your car."

"Didn't drive."

"Then you walk me to my car. I'll give you a lift." He was beside her, reaching for her satchel. She considered, then slipped her head free from the strap of the battered old messenger bag. He'd found it for her in a secondhand shop near their first apartment. He loved the thick leather, impervious to time or weather. Unlike their marriage.

He pulled the courthouse door open for her. Together they walked toward the attorneys' parking lot. The sun was already setting, casting a sliver of gold and red beneath the steel-gray clouds that pushed it down into the horizon.

"I was thinking, this was a rough case for everyone. Maybe I should come by tonight?" Unlike his usual careful cadence, his words emerged in the anxiety-driven rush of a schoolboy asking for a prom date. But that didn't stop him. "It's been a while." He brushed her arm with his.

"Not tonight, Jacob." Probably not ever again, her tone implied. "I have plans."

"Hmmm. I heard rumors about you and Manny." Jacob had never approved of Manny Cruz. He found the prosecutor's principles conveniently self-serving. Hah. Like he was one to talk. A rapist would soon be free because of him.

"God, no. The man despises me. Ever since I forced him into taking this case to trial. He wanted to drop it even before Tymara was killed."

"Then who?"

"What makes you think there's anyone?"

He chuckled. "I know you, Angie. You might not be able to live with a man for the long term, but you can't live without one, either."

"What happened to the court stenographer you were seeing? I thought you two were getting serious."

"So did I. Guess I was wrong." He stopped, leveled a gaze at her. "Again."

Once or twice a year, usually when the nights grew cold and long, he and Angie would reunite. More than casual sex, less than total commitment—on her side, at least. He hoped this time might be different. Last year they'd managed to make it until the day after Christmas. Angie hated the holidays, hated being alone even more.

This past Thanksgiving he'd thought, maybe…but that was the

night they'd both almost died while saving Devon's little girl. The night Matthew Ryder had saved Angie from a serial killer and gotten shot. Surely not she and Ryder? No, Ryder wasn't her type.

At least he hoped not.

"Maybe I'll just take a cab," she said as the silence grew awkward. How strange. Used to be silence didn't bother either of them. Now it was as if they barely knew each other. At least she hadn't filled the time by talking about the weather.

"No. We're here." He keyed the remote, and the lights of his silver Volvo flicked on. He opened her door for her, handed over the bag once she was seated. "Where to?"

He was surprised by her hesitation. Angie always knew where she was going, what she was doing, what happened next. She could see the ending of a movie in the opening credits and be right every time. One of many things that once irritated the hell out of him.

"Home, I guess."

Soon they were heading toward her uncle's bar. After a lengthy silence, he dared to try to breach her defenses. Damn it, someone had to. Look after her. No matter how much she despised it. "Are you all right?"

"Just because I don't want to see you tonight—"

"No. Not that. I mean really. Something seems off. Has been for a while now."

"Off, how?"

"I don't know. That's why I'm asking."

Silence.

"It's not a crime to ask for help, Angie. To need someone. What's going on?"

"Nothing. There's nothing going on. Everything's fine."

"But quitting the ER...Is it true this was your last case for the Advocacy Center?"

"I may have found a better opportunity."

"You're moving? Where? When?" It was difficult to force the words past his tightened vocal cords.

She squeezed her bag to her chest and answered, "Not sure. Yet."

He slanted a suspicious glance her way. "Sounds like—" He paused, unable to say the ugly words. Drugs. Alcohol. Addiction. It was a worry in her family, he knew. "This sabbatical—is it to rehab?"

"Rehab?" She sounded surprised. Or she was faking. At one time in his life, Jacob would have staked everything on Angie's honesty. Now he wasn't sure. That knowledge rattled him more than he cared to admit.

"Evie asked me. She was wondering if maybe something was going on. Something that made you quit the ER."

"Damn Evie. My little sister never did understand the concept of privacy."

"So is there?" He pressed. "Something wrong, I mean."

She refused to look at him, staring fixedly out her window. Which meant he'd hit a sore spot. "You know you can trust me," he tried again. "Or," he added when she knifed him a glare, "if you need a place to stay—"

"Can you just give it a rest? Please? I'm so damn tired."

That he believed. She looked a wreck. More exhausted than he'd ever seen her during the two years they were married, and that had been during her emergency medicine residency.

She leaned her head back and closed her eyes, cutting off further conversation. It was a relief when his cell phone rang. He snagged his Bluetooth ear bud. "Jacob Voorsanger."

"It's Ryder. Do you have any idea where Rossi is?" The detective's voice was clipped, tight.

"She's here with me."

"Damn her, tell her to answer her cell. Where's here?" Jacob winced as Ryder's voice thundered through the earpiece. Angie straightened beside him, twisted in her seat, gestured for the phone. He ignored her.

"I'm driving her home. What happened?"

"Didn't she tell you? Littleton threatened her. And your pal Gena Kravitz is getting him processed out tonight."

"She's no friend of mine."

"I'm setting up surveillance on Littleton, see if he'll led us to his friends, but—"

"Don't worry. I'll stay with her." He hung up before the detective could protest or question his motives.

"What the hell was that all about?" she asked.

"You didn't tell me Littleton threatened you. What was Ryder thinking, letting him anywhere near you?"

"It was the only way to get him to talk. Besides, it wasn't really a threat—he was just trying to scare me. I can take care of myself."

Of course she could. And wasn't that the problem? Hadn't it always been?

CHAPTER SIXTEEN

I WASN'T TOO surprised when Jacob parked his car in one of the employee spots beside my uncle's bar. Ever since we broke up and his father's Alzheimer's forced him into a care facility, Jacob spent most nights at Jimmy's Place. He was lonely, and my family, once they got over their initial disapproval of our marriage outside the Church, had embraced him and his musical talents, rolling both effortlessly into the ceili band my father had founded years ago.

Together we picked our way through the alley behind the bar. I wasn't about to go in through the front door and risk running into Jimmy for another uncomfortable chat. Usually, I avoided the alley. No matter how often Jimmy hosed it down, it always stank of stale beer, piss, and vomit. Plus, the past few days, a creepy homeless guy had been camped out there. But despite the shadows falling and the fact that Jimmy hadn't turned the lights on yet—saving electricity and a few dollars—I wasn't worried, not with Jacob at my side.

I opened the rear door and headed up the private staircase. To my surprise, Jacob followed. I stopped halfway up and turned to him. "Where do you think you're going?"

He surprised me with a blush. He knew full well I invited no one to my apartment. Not Jacob, not Ryder, no one. After a lifetime of having every aspect of my life dissected and aired in public by my family—what has Angela done now?—I finally set some boundaries. Well, one boundary. Maybe just a flimsy lock on a flimsy door, but it was my lock on my door.

"I told Ryder I'd keep an eye on you," he said. "Grab your fiddle. We'll play a set together before it gets busy downstairs."

An image flashed in my vision: a night last month, before everything that had happened at Thanksgiving. Jacob, beads of sweat dripping from his brow as his entire body wrestled his bow against his violin. His eyes were shut, his foot tapping in time with the beat, his entire being absorbed by the music.

When he had something on his mind, he'd pick up his violin, sit and play it for hours until he had the problem worked out. Like me, music was his solace, his safe haven—the one place he'd been able to retreat to as a child, escaping his domineering father.

"You should've kept that one," Jimmy had told me back then, setting a glass of ice water at my elbow. "Could've done a whole lot worse."

It was the truth. But I'd learned during those years with Jacob that you could love someone and still not be able to live with them.

"Angie?" he asked now, still stopped on the steep, well-worn steps.

I shook off the memory—a regular memory, thank goodness, not a fugue—and continued up to the second floor. It was strange, the only people who had any clue that I was sick, other than Louise, were two men who'd just come into my life: Devon and Ryder. The thought brought with it a twinge of guilt. Along with the reminder that I needed to tell my sister so she could be tested.

If Evie also had fatal insomnia, it would kill our mother. Patsy and I had never had a normal mother-daughter relationship after my father died and I came to live here with Jimmy's family. But she and Evie were more than family. They were each other's best friends as well.

Jacob and I reached the top of the steps. I hesitated outside my door, Jacob hovering uncomfortably close behind me. Before I could put my key into the lock, the door swung open, and I was staring into the faces of my family.

Could this day get any worse?

*   *   *

As much as he despised them, Ryder was good at stakeouts. It came from his years as a soldier, learning how to handle dragging hours of boredom, how to stalk the enemy, and learning how to develop the patience needed to wait and watch without losing focus. Right now, shivering in his car, eating a stale protein bar and washing it down with vintage water that had been stashed under the passenger seat for Lord only knew how long, he was stalking a stalker: Eugene Littleton.

So far, Littleton had led Ryder on a merry chase through the city streets. First, Gena Kravitz had driven him home. Curbside service. Only the best for her clients. Ryder wondered how the lawyer could stand being in the same vehicle as Littleton after seeing what he'd done to Tymara. Lawyers…If he'd had a partner, coming up with new adjectives or swapping bottom-dweller jokes would have chewed up a nice chunk of time, relieved the monotony.

But Ryder was alone. Sad thing was, he was actually starting to like it that way. Just as he had lost his patience with departmental politics, he'd also lost the knack for small talk. Guess that meant he was getting old. Or growing up. Some damn thing.

After being chauffeured home, Littleton left his lousy apartment building to stroll through the twilight shadows. Littleton lived a block north of the Tower, making it the second-worst neighborhood in the city. He'd gone to the corner grocery store, returning home with his arms filled with food. No side trip to the liquor store even. Ryder thought he might stay in after that, but no, Littleton surprised him, emerging a short while later, now dressed in a respectable-looking suit. Going out on the town? Picking up another "girlfriend" to terrorize? Or off to meet his partners in crime?

Littleton had hopped into a gypsy cab—real cabs didn't come to this part of town—and away they went. To, of all places, an elementary school on Second.

Nothing in Littleton's record indicated he had any ties to children. He had none of his own, had never been convicted of any crimes against children. Ryder pulled up the school's website to see if there was some kind of evening event. There was. Nothing involving children. A Narcotics Anonymous meeting being held in the school cafeteria.

Trolling an NA meeting for his next victim? Seemed like the kind of vulnerable prey a guy like Littleton might gravitate toward. Except, he didn't go inside. Instead, he waited in the cold and dark, conveniently standing beneath the spotlight over the front entrance so Ryder could see every move he made.

A bit too convenient for Ryder's taste. He scratched the back of his neck, kept checking all his mirrors, wary of an ambush. This wasn't right. A guy like Littleton, in county lockup for six months, spending his first night of freedom freezing his balls off in front of a school instead of picking up a hooker or going to a bar?

This was wrong, wrong, wrong.

Littleton seemed impervious to the cold, didn't appear anxious or impatient as he waited. Instead, he was calm, relaxed. What the hell was going on here? Every instinct that had kept Ryder and his squad alive in Afghanistan was alerted, prepared for battle.

Despite the weathermen calling for snow later tonight, the sky was clear. The temperature was falling fast, leaving Ryder facing the classic cop's stakeout dilemma. Sit in an unheated car until the windows fogged, leaving you blind? Or turn the engine on for a few minutes to thaw out and run the defogger?

Either way, you were bound to be noticed. So Ryder took the third option. He grabbed a ball cap from the back seat. People tended to fixate on details like hats, forget to notice the face below them. He wrapped his scarf up over the lower half of his face, as much for warmth as for disguise, and left the car. He had to keep his overcoat unbuttoned so he could reach his service weapon, the wind from the river pushing it open, and his gloves, thin enough to fire his weapon if need be, weren't much use. But, between Littleton acting abnormally *über*normal and the cold, he was at full alert.

People began to arrive for the meeting. Littleton, damn the man, greeted each and every one, shaking their hand and saying something to them as if he knew them. Which he couldn't. There was nothing in his case file about him ever attending NA. He sure as hell hadn't gone to any meetings held while he was in lockup. He didn't even have any drug collars on his sheet. Instead, his record consisted of several criminal trespassing charges, gross sexual imposition, terroristic threats, and one stalking charge. He'd pleaded out and entered a diversion program, receiving shock probation and intensive counseling rather than serving any jail time.

What the hell was going on here? Was this all an act for Ryder's sake? He sidled closer. Difficult to do, since the streets were empty except for the people straggling up Second to enter the school. He considered joining them. It'd be warm inside. Coffee and doughnuts as well.

He wasn't going anywhere without Littleton. Ryder took a position in a storefront doorway, out of the wind. As he watched and waited, his feet tapped out a rhythm. Not just to keep the blood flowing. It was a tune Rossi had played last night. A fiddle-playing, dying doctor. Who could have seen that one coming? But somehow, when he watched her play, the way the music came to life—and brought her to life—he forgot about the "dying" part. Forgot about everything except the woman.

If he were honest with himself, he could pinpoint the exact moment when he'd fallen for her with no hope of recovery: Three weeks ago, right after he got out of the hospital, she'd been alone onstage, the bar almost empty, and she'd played a song. Not a real song, Jimmy had told him, but something improvised there on the spot. The music was rich, complex, filled with longing and despair, yet also joyful. Her entire body had surrendered to it: head flung back, hair flying wild, her hands never ceasing movement as they coaxed the notes from her fiddle.

By the time she'd finished, tears had wet his cheeks. Jimmy's as well.

Rossi's song returned to him now. It wasn't as good as being with the woman herself, but somehow he didn't feel as vulnerable or alone. That was the magic of Rossi. Unlike the victims Ryder served now, or his squad that he'd led back in the war, he didn't feel as if he had to take care of her. Instead, each filled a void the other hadn't even realized existed.

Ryder banished his fantasies of Rossi as one last woman approached Littleton before entering the school. They spoke for a few minutes. Longer than he had with anyone else. Littleton's body language was also different. He clasped the woman's hand in his while also grasping her elbow in his other hand as they bowed their heads together, talking earnestly.

Ryder shifted position to get a good look at the woman's face. Then she vanished inside.

Littleton remained at his post outside, although now he seemed restless, casting looks at the door behind him, a little boy eager to open his Christmas presents—or at least shake them. He paced back and forth, then trailed around in a circle, obviously waiting. For what?

After almost fifteen minutes, Ryder's hands about numb from the cold, his eyes burned dry by the frigid wind, he was ready to head back to the shelter of the car. A crack like a lightning strike slammed through the night. Ryder startled. A gunshot. From inside the school.

In the gleam of the spotlight, Littleton smiled. More than a smile, a smirk. Aimed directly at Ryder as Ryder raced across the street, his weapon drawn, his phone in his other hand.

"Shots fired," he told Dispatch. "Second Avenue Elementary. Send back up."

CHAPTER SEVENTEEN

THEY WERE ALL there. Waiting inside my apartment. Jimmy, my cousins, Evie. And the queen of the clan, my mother, sitting at the head of my table. Colorful mounds of pills and capsules were arranged before her, offerings to a goddess.

"Care to explain this, young lady?" she asked before I crossed the threshold.

Jimmy held the door open. Since my door had no peephole, he must have been listening, waiting to pounce when I arrived. My cousins slouched on my couch, poorly hidden smirks dancing across their face, Ozzie on the floor between them. The dog at least bothered to stand up at my arrival, his tail thumping the floor, one person happy to see me.

It was Evie I couldn't face. She sat at my mother's side, her manicured nails sparking in the light as she clasped her hands and somehow managed to appear both elegant and worried.

Anger at the intrusion swamped me, and I shifted my stance, ready to bolt. But...Evie. She needed to know. Without my cousins gawking at her. I stepped inside and turned to face them head-on. "Jimmy, take the boys downstairs. This is no concern of yours."

My cousins were older than I am, but just as I would forever be the girl who got her father killed—no matter what Louise's tests proved—they'd always be "the boys."

Jimmy opened his mouth to protest, but my mother raised her head and nodded to him. "Go on, Jimmy. I'll handle this."

He jerked his chin at the boys, and they left. Jacob stood awkwardly at the doorway, still not stepping across the invisible barrier to my inner sanctum. His face was a question too painful for him to voice. Was he still family or not?

I sighed and reached for his arm. "Come inside. You should hear this as well."

He stepped across. I'd never seen him so frightened. I closed the door and let him hold my hand as we moved past the couch to the table where Evie and my mother waited.

"Give me one good reason why I shouldn't call the police," my mother started, waving her hand over the collection of pills, scattering a few across the table to the floor.

I resisted the urge to scramble for them. Instead, borrowing Jacob's strength, I stood quiet, focusing on controlling my fury.

"Uppers, downers, enough to choke a horse. How could you? What if the police found these? What then? Jimmy could lose everything. You're under his roof. And how would it look to Jacob's new boss? Bad enough all that mess you got twisted up in last month. I won't tolerate behavior like this. It's an embarrassment to the entire family!"

Evie kept her gaze focused down, color flushing her pale skin. She was as light as I was dark. I took after my father's Italian side of the family, but Evie mirrored the strawberry-blond, peaches-and-cream of the Kiely clan, like my mother.

"Does Ryder know?" Jacob asked in a low, serious voice when my mother paused for breath.

His question rattled me. "Yes…no…kind of."

"I knew that man was no good," Patsy screeched.

"Shut up!" My own voice surprised me. And her. She jerked, her mouth hanging open, lipstick feathering into wrinkles I'd never noticed before. "While you were sneaking through my things, did you happen to notice I have prescriptions for all of those?"

Jacob's hand tightened on mine, but it was Evie who spoke. "Prescriptions? Are you sick?"

I slid my sweat-slicked palm free of Jacob's. Stood alone and faced them all. "I'm dying."

Silence slithered through the room, an oily fog of disbelief. Patsy's body went rigid. Only Evie managed to look up and meet my gaze, her eyes wide. Jacob reached again for my hand, but I stepped farther away from him. I had to do this alone. Even Ozzie was affected, lumbering over to press his body against my legs, offering support.

I clenched my fists tight, hauled in a breath, and released it. Now came the hard part. "I have a disease called Fatal Familial Insomnia. It runs in families, mainly Italian ones. I had Louise test Dad's DNA, and he had it as well." I gave them a second to let that sink in. "It's probably what killed him."

My mother made a noise like she was choking, her hand clutching at her throat, but I pressed on. "It's always fatal. There's no cure. But the thing is, since Dad had it, there's a fifty-fifty chance Evie might as well." I wanted to hug her, but Mom got there first, wrapping Evie in her arms. "I'm sorry, Evie. You'll need to be tested."

There. It was out.

Tears slid down Evie's face as her lips pressed into a single pale line. Jacob's shoulders hunched tight, his face confused with emotions, his hands empty at his sides as I edged ever farther away from him, the dog between us. He slid over to take one of Evie's hands in both of his, someone who could accept his sympathy without crumbling.

I was barely holding on, but I had to finish this, then I could— what? Kick everyone out and retreat for a solitary pity-fest? No. That's not what I needed. Or wanted. Ryder. His face, his voice filled my mind, giving me the strength I was desperate for. As soon as I was done here, I'd find Ryder. Tell him everything. End the lies of denial. Even though I was pretty sure he already suspected the truth.

"How long?" my mother finally gasped.

"Louise isn't sure. The way my symptoms are progressing, we guess I might have less than a year." Probably way less, but they didn't need to deal with that tonight. The colorful photos of sunbaked beaches covering my refrigerator caught my eye.

Patsy shook her head. "No. I mean how long have you known? Why didn't you tell me before? How could you endanger your sister like that?"

Of course. When would I learn? Nothing ever changed, not in my family. "We weren't sure until this morning. Thank you for your concern, though."

This time it was Jacob who made a painful noise. "What can I do?" he asked.

"Nothing."

Before anyone else could say anything, the door opened, and Devon barreled through it without knocking. "Hey, doc. Jimmy said you were up here. Ready to go? They're waiting. Grab your doctor gear, and I'll meet you downstairs."

He was gracious enough to make it sound like a question instead of a command, but urgency radiated off him. Or maybe that was just me, happy to latch on to any lifeline that took me away from there.

"I'll be right down." He left, and I turned to Jacob, finally feeling strong enough to let him get close without totally crumbling. I gave him a quick hug and a kiss on the cheek. "Don't worry about me."

"Never going to happen," he said, stroking my hair back with his fingers. He glanced at the empty doorway. "Want me to come with you?"

"No. Take care of Evie. Please?" I knew my sister would need time to cry it out before she'd be able to ask any coherent questions or take in what little information I could offer her. And me being here, agitating Patsy, would only make things worse.

Jacob nodded and squeezed my shoulders. I exchanged my messenger bag for the small knapsack with my first-aid gear. Ozzie followed me, nose to my leg, refusing to stay behind, so I grabbed his leash, and we fled downstairs to the bar, where Devon waited, chatting with Jimmy.

No one else in my family seemed to notice the way Devon had insinuated himself into our lives. Despite their differences, Jacob—son of a rabbi, former assistant district attorney—and Devon—illegitimate son of real estate tycoon Daniel Kingston, former "fixer" for the Russian mob in Philly—got along so well I was surprised they weren't exchanging Christmas cookies.

Even Ryder admired the way Devon had cleaned up the gangs over at Kingston Tower, although he didn't approve of Devon's methods.

Most nights while Jacob and I played onstage, Devon would come in, lean against the bar, jawing with my uncle, and nurse a whiskey. Invariably, he'd soon have a crowd gathered around him, sharing some story that would have Jimmy and the others slapping the bar, bent over laughing. No wonder my family adored Devon.

I'd always wanted to be that person. The one who could make her family laugh and forget their problems. Like my dad could.

CHAPTER EIGHTEEN

"WHY ARE YOU handcuffing me, detective?" Littleton asked Ryder. "You're my alibi. There's no way I could have fired that shot. Shouldn't you be looking for the shooter, tending to the wounded?"

Ryder ratcheted the cuffs tight. "You're involved, Littleton. Besides, I have the right to restrain you. It's a matter of officer safety."

"If you say so. I think my lawyer's going to call it harassment."

The first squad car arrived. Ryder handed off Littleton to be secured in the back by one of the patrolmen. He nodded to the other, who opened the school's door and held it as Ryder went inside, weapon at the ready.

"One shot heard," Ryder told the officer, wishing he'd worn his vest. The adrenaline singing through his system gave him the illusion of invincibility, but the tug of his recently healed abdominal muscles reminded him of reality. Rossi would kill him if he let himself get shot again.

He focused on the empty corridor ahead. Only half of the lights were on, cost-saving measures by the school, he guessed, but no help when it came to spotting shooters hiding in dark corners. Wordlessly, he and the officer stacked up, zigzagging down the hall, checking each room for the shooter.

No one. And no sounds except his own heartbeat in his ears and the officer's heavy, ragged breathing over his shoulder.

Suddenly, footsteps pounded the floor behind them. They both whirled, weapons raised, but it was the second patrolman. "Prisoner secured, SWAT's on the way. Anything?"

Ryder shook his head and motioned him to silence, wondering where all the people were. They hadn't heard any more shots. Where were the panicked victims fleeing the scene? The silence felt heavy, lifeless, as it draped like shadows around them. What the hell had happened here?

They came to a T-intersection. The NA meeting was in the cafeteria, to the right, but the danger could come from any direction. He positioned one patrolman in the intersection to watch their backs while he led the other forward. It was slow progress, clearing each potential area of ambush before proceeding. They passed a bank of lockers and came to their first body.

It was a man, flannel shirt and jeans, face up. From the blood on his hands, it looked as if he'd tried to claw his mouth and throat open, tear his own tongue out.

"Jesus," the officer behind him breathed.

"Call it in."

"We have one down," the patrol officer radioed softly into his shoulder mic.

They stepped around the first victim. Even if he had been alive, with just the two of them, they would have kept moving forward to engage the shooter and prevent further harm. Stopping the threat was priority.

Ahead was a display case. Leading up to it was a trail of handmade Christmas decorations featuring sparkles and glitter that dusted the floor like snow. Except where it had caked in the blood of the woman who had crashed headfirst through the case's heavy plate glass.

"Is she?" the officer asked.

Ryder spared a glance. A sheet of the glass had sliced down, and the woman's head hung by a bloody string of tissue he couldn't identify. Like the first man, her face was devastated. As if she'd been trying to destroy it.

What the fuck? His belly muscles recoiled from the sight even as he and the patrolman pressed forward.

The scene reminded him of how Rossi had described Leo Kingston's victims from last month. Leo had given them a special formulation of PXA and persuaded them to torture themselves to death. Had more PXA made it onto the streets? After all, an NA meeting by definition meant junkies.

His thoughts were interrupted by more bodies, all clustered around the cafeteria entrance. Bloody gashes where eye sockets should have been, noses and mouths and throats ripped to shreds, either by hands or the cafeteria's forks and knives. The air stank of burned coffee and fresh blood.

A few of the victims appeared to be still breathing, tiny pink bubbles breaking through smears of crimson. Ryder couldn't hear any gasps, not through the adrenaline haze clouding his senses, making the scene even more surreal as the frothy bubbles burst in silence. His flesh crawling, he turned away to survey the rest of the room.

At a cleared area at the far end of the cafeteria, they found their shooter. At least, she held a pistol. She sat on a swivel office chair, her back to them. Scrawled on the tile wall above her in giant letters, the blood still dripping: I HATE YOUR FACES!

A semiautomatic dangled from her left hand, hooked by a finger. The window across from her was starred with a small hole. That's how he'd been able to hear the shot so clearly from outside. She'd shot out the window. A signal?

He and the officer approached her from opposite angles, careful not to cross their line of fire as they passed more bodies.

"Drop the gun," the officer ordered, his voice shaky.

The woman didn't move. Ryder motioned to the officer to cover him and sidled forward, knocking the gun free from the woman's hand as he approached from behind. He stepped in front of her. It was the last woman to enter the school, the one Littleton had laughed with. She'd been spared the disfiguration of the others. But he wasn't sure that was a good thing.

Her throat had been slashed. A precise cut, just deep enough to get the job done. Not much blood. The killer had cut through her airway, and she'd suffocated. It would have been a long, agonizing death.

"What the hell is that?" The officer joined Ryder. He pointed to the business card sticking out of the woman's throat as if she had been given a second mouth and was holding it in her newly formed blood-red lips.

Ryder craned his head to look at the card without touching it. It was his.

He glanced up, his gaze raking over the carnage polluting the school cafeteria. Kids played and ate here. It was supposed to be a safe place. And some butcher had turned it into a bloodbath.

His jaw tightened. He said nothing, couldn't even look at the other officer. All this. Littleton and his damn Brotherhood. They'd done this for him. A warning to Ryder.

No way Littleton would ever be charged. Hell, Ryder was his fucking alibi.

Ryder stalked away from the woman's body, his pulse beating in his ears so hard his vision vibrated in time with it. More footsteps sounded as additional officers arrived. "Clear the rest of the building. See if there's anyone living we can help," he ordered.

They found three still breathing, but the medics said it didn't look good. His rage grew. If the animals who'd done this were trying to warn Ryder away, they'd made a serious mistake.

He was going to hunt them down exactly like the beasts they were.

CHAPTER NINETEEN

"THANKS FOR COMING," Devon told me once we were in his Town Car heading toward the Tower, Ozzie poking his nose between us from the rear seat.

"Thanks for the rescue. Thought you'd be busy dealing with Eugene Littleton tonight. Isn't that why you hired Gena Kravitz to get him off?" A guess, but I was pretty sure I was right.

He did me the courtesy of not smiling. "Gena helped me with the red tape after Daniel's stroke. I figured she'd be the right person to handle Eugene's case."

"Helps that she and Manny Cruz are involved."

"Helps. But I didn't bribe Manny if that's what you're insinuating."

"Still, you got what you wanted. Littleton's free. Or is he? You don't have him locked up down in those damn tunnels, do you, Devon?" After our conversation this morning, I was only half-joking.

"Don't worry, doc. I figure the cops can handle Eugene for a night. No sense putting myself on their radar."

"Thought you didn't trust the police."

"I trust them to do their job—for the most part. I just don't trust them to get the job done."

"You mean get the job done the way you want it done. So if Ryder doesn't find Littleton's partners, what happens then? You'll take care of it?"

"Street justice is better than no justice at all."

"You make it sound so noble. Can't you see, once you start, there's no stopping? You become just as bad as they are."

"Do you really think so? Ask the women who live in the Tower and the children who now actually play in the playground instead of running past it, scared of getting killed by a stray bullet or worse."

I touched his arm. He shrugged free, his glare edged with suspicion. He'd seen how I could enter other people's minds. Even though no one else believed in my new ability, Devon did.

"No. I can't touch you and read your mind. It only works on coma patients. But why are you worried that I could? Devon, you need to let the cops do their job."

His snort of disdain fogged the icy air between us.

"Okay," I tried again. "Then work with Ryder. You trust him. Feed him information and let him work inside the law."

He hunched his shoulders and gripped the steering wheel.

"I don't want to see you get hurt." I played the one card that might have a chance of breaking through to him. "Esme needs her father." Ozzie nodded his head, as if in agreement, and made a small noise of longing at the sound of Esme's name.

"Esme deserves a father who's a better man than I can ever be. She's better off without me. But someday, maybe she'll be able to return to this place and find a city worth fighting to save instead of a cesspool sliding deeper into the sewer."

"You think by playing vigilante, you can clean up the whole city?"

"It was my father who corrupted it. Daniel twisted every level of government, funneled the hard work of honest people into shell companies run by criminals far worse than the ones I worked for in Philly. You have no idea how far it goes, Angela. It's as if the cancer inside him ate through to the city he controlled."

Devon was right about one thing: His father had warped and corrupted every life he touched. No wonder Daniel Kingston's other son, Leo, had become a sadistic serial killer. But playing vigilante, no matter how honorable his intentions, wasn't the way to cleanse the family name.

"You think you're creating a legacy for Esme," I argued, "but have you considered maybe she needs her father in her life now?"

We stopped at a red light. He turned to me, the streetlights outside the car casting a glow around him. "I don't want Esme anywhere near my kind of life. I just wish I could somehow make things easier for her."

I touched his arm again, and this time he accepted it, looked up, and met my gaze. "It takes time. And good people in her life. Maybe she needs a home, not a school filled with strangers."

"It's too risky—"

"For her? Or you? It's been a month, and the Russians haven't come after you. You're too powerful now that you control Kingston Enterprises." He was silent. "I think you're scared. Of being a father. Of letting anyone get close to you again."

"Getting close to me got Jess killed," he reminded me, a warning in the way his lips tightened.

"Jess wasn't killed because you loved her, Devon. Distancing yourself from Esme might keep you safe—you don't have to worry about what a hard job it is being a good father, you don't have to stay up nights trying to decide what's best for her future—but if your enemies want to find your weak spot, sooner or later they will find her, Flynn or no Flynn. Isn't it better she knows she has a father who loves her, a home she can find joy in, friends she can trust? Don't you want to give her everything you and Jess never had?"

I was treading on dangerous ground, and we both knew it. But he didn't flinch. Instead, he considered my words.

"I have enough money to buy her the world. But you're saying being with a man like me, a guttersnipe street runt with blood on my hands, that's what she needs?"

The light changed, and we moved forward. "I think any girl would be lucky to have you as a father," I assured Devon. "Now, want to tell me about this house call I'm making?"

He shifted in his seat as if uncertain. "The Lees—they run one of my restaurants. Their grandson is sick. None of the doctors at the clinic can figure it out, and they asked if I could help, so I thought of you."

"I'm an ER doc, not a pediatric specialist."

"I know. I thought they were just overanxious grandparents and you could reassure them." His voice trailed off.

I sat up and turned to him, my curiosity piqued. "But?"

"But today, I was talking to people in the Tower to see if anyone saw anything with Tymara. And I found there's more kids from the Tower getting sick. I'm worried it has something to do with what Daniel left behind in the tunnels." The Kingston family owned the tunnels that ran beneath the city streets from Millionaire's Row to the river. They'd been built during the Cold War as an emergency shelter, ready to evacuate the state government in case of a nuclear attack.

"What kind of symptoms?"

He frowned. "All sorts that make no sense to me. But they reminded me of what's going on with you, so—"

"What I have is inherited. And even then it's a one-in-a-hundred-million odds of getting it."

"I know. But more I look into Kingston Enterprises, more I find that makes me suspect—no, you'll think I'm crazy."

Devon and I might not share the same moral compass, but he was probably the least-crazy person I knew. "Tell me."

"Best I can decipher, Kingston Enterprises—well, one of their biotech subsidiaries—had an effective treatment for Ebola ten years ago, but never brought it to market."

"A lot of drug companies do that. It's too expensive to do all the FDA testing and get approval, so they hang on to valuable treatments until it's profitable to move forward."

"Daniel wasn't big on documenting the motives behind a lot of what he did, but—" He paused. "This is where it gets crazy. He set up what he called monitoring units all over the world. They knew about the Ebola epidemic in West Africa before any other authorities."

"You mean he didn't tell anyone?" I shouldn't have been surprised; I knew how ruthless Devon's father was, but condemning tens of thousands of people when they could have saved them? "Ryder said he was a psychopath."

"Oh, he is," Devon agreed amiably. "But I was wondering. Is there any way...Could he have somehow caused the Ebola epidemic? Because if I'm reading these records right, they went into production with their treatment almost a full year *before* the first case was documented. That's how they were able to get the WHO and CDC contracts and walk away with billions—with the CDC ushering them through the FDA application process, saving Kingston Enterprises millions of dollars."

I stared at him. "Do you have proof?"

"No. At least nothing I can interpret. You're the only person I can trust with this."

I nodded, still digesting the Machiavellian conceit behind what he'd suggested.

"But, what I'm more afraid of is what else he might have planned—plans that might already be in motion."

"You mean the PXA that Leo was working on." Leo had been working to develop PXA as the perfect torture agent to sell to the DOD or highest bidder.

PXA created the same brain-wave pattern that my fatal-insomnia-messed-up brain could communicate with. Last month I'd entered the mind of one of Leo's victims as she died from PXA. That had pretty much been the worst hell I could ever imagine. That is, until Leo had injected me with PXA.

I should have died—but I had my fatal insomnia to thank for saving my life. Not only did the PXA wear off faster than in someone with a normal brain, it had also enhanced the weird side effects from my fatal insomnia while mitigating the catatonia that left me frozen and helpless when I had a fugue spell. That combination had allowed me to save

Ryder's life and overcome Leo.

"Did you find more PXA?" I was horrified that the drug might hit the streets again.

"Not in the tunnels. Although, several Kingston subsidiaries are investigating the drug. But, I was wondering. All these sick kids live in the Tower…"

"You think Leo might have been experimenting with more than the PXA?"

He nodded grimly.

"Let's start with the basics before we go zebra-hunting," I said, using the timeworn medical theory that hoof beats most often come from horses. "You're doing a lot of renovations in the Tower. Could it be environmental? Maybe Daniel used lead paint or something like that?"

"I hadn't thought of that. Is that treatable?"

"And easy to test for. Let me see what's going on with the kids first."

He parked the car in the alley between the rear of St. Tim's and the north side of the Tower. Lazy drifts of flurries floated through the night sky, cradling the light from both buildings like silent ghosts. I got out, grabbed my bag, and turned toward the door leading into the Tower.

"No," he said, nodding instead to the church. "They're waiting at St. Tim's. In Sister Patrice's old clinic."

"Down in the tunnels?" I was glad the dark hid my shudder. I despised those damn tunnels. They had entrances scattered throughout this side of the city, including beneath St. Tim's. There was even one in the basement of Good Sam's, conveniently close to the hospital's incinerator—well, convenient if you were a serial killer like Leo Kingston.

"No. The church basement." Devon heaved open the heavy door leading into the church. He led me through the sanctuary to the side corridor where steps led down to the church basement. Here, there were rooms used for storage, two decorated for children's Sunday school, and one larger assembly area that had a silver tinsel Christmas tree in the corner, decorated with paper chains and lopsided cut-out snowflakes. About a dozen folding chairs filled the floor space, all occupied by worried parents and their children.

"Only five families could come tonight," Devon said. "I've made a list of the others."

"*Only* five?" I turned to him, aghast, praying he was wrong. After all, he had no medical training. But Devon had been raised on the streets, and the two things that had kept him alive were his instincts and his ability to see what others dismissed. I trusted him. But...I didn't want to believe him.

"How many?" I asked.

"Nineteen that I know of. All with the same symptoms."

CHAPTER TWENTY

FLYNN JERKED AWAKE, rolling silently out of bed, her knife in her hand. Crouched on the floor, she listened. Her house was still—*her* house; she was still getting used to the concept—but someone stood in the hall. She could feel it.

Normal background noise filtered through the darkness as she focused on the one wrong thing that had woken her. A floorboard creaked, followed by the tiniest whisper of breathing.

Flynn relaxed and put her knife away. *Not* a wrong thing.

Her heart had barely sped up. She almost never experienced the adrenaline rushes that normal people did, not unless she was in a fight for her life. Daniel said that was one of the reasons why she was so good at her job. Well, her old job. This new one…she wasn't at all sure she was equipped for it. What the hell did she know about taking care of a ten-year-old girl? Especially one as traumatized as Esme?

"You have to stop sneaking out of your room at night," Flynn said into the darkness beyond her open bedroom door.

"I can't sleep there," the darkness replied, separating itself from the shadows and stepping into the room as a girl, slightly on the small and skinny side, skin almost as dark as Flynn's, braids swinging above her shoulders. "Can't I stay with you?"

Flynn sighed and drew back the covers on her queen-size bed.

Daniel had taught her that power didn't come from age or brains or money. No, he'd said during one of their nightly training sessions after he'd rescued her from the street, power comes from body language. Primates are conditioned to respond to nonverbal clues. Walk in like you own the room and you don't need to say a word to get what you want.

To her surprise, he was right. It was how Flynn, despite not even being eighteen, passed for the twenty-four-year-old newly minted guardian of her "little sister," Esme, and had bullied her way past the authorities at the fancy school Devon had arranged for his daughter.

Apparently, though, Daniel had never tested his theory of power on ten-year-old girls. Esme snuggled into Flynn's bed, patting the space beside her as if she were the queen demanding an audience. Flynn obeyed, climbing back onto the bed and pulling the duvet up around them both as Esme curled up in Flynn's arms. "Tell me a story."

At first, Flynn had been concerned by how well Esme handled the trauma of seeing her mother killed and almost dying herself. She'd been prepared for tears, but Esme's grief was more insidious, taking the form of night terrors, sleepwalking, weird jerks and tremors, and insomnia. The doctors couldn't find anything wrong with her; the school psychologist said it was all normal and advised Flynn to set a routine and stick to it.

Flynn knew the girl needed to learn how to sleep in her own bed, but found it impossible to deny Esme's nightly requests. It was an unexpected weakness, this need to not just guard Esme, but also care for her. Daniel would have been extremely disappointed.

"Once school starts after Christmas break, you need to sleep in your room," Flynn said in what she wanted to be a stern voice. It emerged more like an exhausted plea. When Esme didn't sleep, neither did Flynn.

"I hate school. I'm not going back." Esme's tone reminded Flynn of Daniel. Certain. Uncompromising.

"You've only been there a few weeks. Give it time."

"No." Esme flounced on the bed, adamant. "I don't like those girls, and they don't like me. They make fun of me, call me names."

"So what?" In Flynn's world, no one gave a damn about words. It was the knives and bullets you needed to watch out for. "Call them names back."

Esme blew her breath out in frustration. "I can't. Mama said that was rude. Said I have to grow up to be a polite lady."

"There you go. You're a lady, they're not." Funny, since the girls in question came from the purebred upper tier of New England society. "Ignore them. You're above it all."

"I have." Esme's voice dropped to a sorrowful sigh. "That's why I don't have any friends."

Flynn pulled her closer, surprised that her heart sped up at Esme's words. "Don't worry. You still have me."

"I wish Mama was here. Or Ozzie. Or my daddy. Then we'd be a real family."

Devon had wanted Flynn to tell Esme he was dead, wanted his daughter as far away from him as possible, to keep her safe. But Flynn hadn't had the heart to lie to a girl who'd just lost her mother and had been uprooted from the only home she'd ever known, so she'd told Esme her father was away on business.

Big mistake, she quickly realized. But what the hell did Flynn know about little girls? Not like anyone had ever raised her properly. Before she killed her mother's boyfriend, Flynn had been used as a punching bag and sex toy. Then Daniel had taken her in, molded her from a rebellious teen who'd gotten away with murder into a stealth weapon, able to blend in with any level of society and do his bidding.

Flynn had no clue what normal was, much less a normal family. But that's what Esme needed, and she hated that she couldn't give it to her.

"Story," Esme insisted.

Before she met Esme, Flynn had no stories suitable for a little girl's ears—unless she wanted Esme to suffer even more night terrors. But Esme craved stories, they were sustenance to her, so Flynn set her imagination free, giving Esme the fairytale shoulda-coulda-woulda wistful lives neither of them had found in reality.

"Where were we?"

Esme burrowed deeper into Flynn's embrace. "Princess Rhetta was fighting the dragon to save Prince Ozzie and his kingdom." Prince Ozzie featured in all of Esme's stories, even if the princesses varied.

"Okay. How do you think Rhetta defeated a fire-breathing dragon ten times her size?" Flynn had quickly learned that when she had no clue how to twist a story, if she simply asked her audience, the answer would be supplied. Esme had very firm ideas about how a good story should be told. Princesses kicked butt and saved the day, princes rewarded them with kisses and pretty dresses, and the bad guys ended up in dungeons.

"Well..." Esme considered. "Her sword is too short for her to get close enough without getting burned by the dragon's fire, so she's going to have to trick it. I think she plays dead and waits for the dragon to open its mouth to gobble her up and—"

Esme went silent, mid-sentence.

"And then what?" Flynn prompted.

No answer. A warm wetness spread beneath the duvet and sheets. "Esme!" Flynn turned to the girl. Esme's face was slack, her eyes unblinking, staring into space. Drool slipped from the corner of her mouth, and she'd wet herself.

Flynn couldn't help herself. She shook Esme, trying to snap her out of her spell. Her breathing was okay, pulse normal. But Esme had simply vanished, leaving only her body behind.

She climbed out of bed and carefully positioned Esme on her side, away from the wet stain, head turned so she wouldn't choke on her drool. Flynn reached for the phone, then stopped, her hand hovering over it. It'd been less than a minute. Should she call an ambulance? Invite all the questions that would come with an ER visit?

Then Esme blinked. She shook herself and looked up at Flynn with mournful eyes. "It keeps happening."

"What happened? When did it start? How often?" Questions poured from Flynn as she knelt at Esme's side.

Esme sat up, one hand slipping on the wet sheets, and looked horrified. "I wet the bed?"

"That doesn't matter. Tell me what happened."

Tears slid down Esme's cheeks. "I never wet the bed. Not since I was a baby. Not even when Mama—"

Flynn bundled her into her arms and carried her from the wet bed out to the living room. At Esme's command, she'd bought them a real Christmas tree. A first for both of them. It shed needles all over the carpet, kept sagging in the tree stand, and although the pine smell was heavenly, it made Flynn's eyes itch. But they'd had fun dragging it in, setting it up, and decorating. Esme had even taught Flynn how to make a popcorn garland and the proper way to hang tinsel icicles.

Tonight, Esme ignored the tree, instead curling up on Flynn's lap, her face against Flynn's neck. "Tell me," Flynn coaxed, once the tension had fled Esme's body and her tears had stopped.

"I knew you were there—I could see, hear, feel everything." Esme's voice filled with wonder.

"Has it happened before?"

Esme nodded, her braids bouncing against Flynn's shoulder. "A few times. Once it happened in school, and I could see the answers sitting on the teacher's desk while we took a pop quiz. Not really, not with my eyes, but I'd walked past them on my way into class, and she'd turned them over before I could see. But then, when I was frozen, I could see, like I could go back in time and flip through my memories, rewind them."

Esme looked up at her, swallowed, and tried on a brave smile. "It's kind of cool. When it's not scary. I'm sorry I wet the bed. You're not mad, are you?"

Flynn's pulse buzzed, a wasp beating its way free of a spider's web. Maybe she wasn't in the fight of her life, but Esme might be. Because Flynn had seen the same kind of thing happen to one other person...the doctor who'd saved her life.

Angela Rossi.

CHAPTER TWENTY-ONE

NINETEEN KIDS FROM one apartment complex, all with the same symptoms. This was so not good.

"Let's see what we have." Somehow, I kept my voice calm, reassuring even. But my mind was whirling with the ramifications and consequences. If Devon was right, I'd have to get the Health Department involved, call the CDC, alert the staffs of all the local hospitals…except…I had no idea what to tell them.

I left Ozzie with the other families while Devon led me into a storage room that Sister Patrice had converted into an examination area. The cement-block walls were as stark white as the sheets on the cot that functioned as an exam table, but colorful, crayoned drawings and finger-painted masterpieces hanging from a bulletin board broke up the monotony. The room smelled of candle wax and antiseptic, a strange mix of faith and function.

A dark-haired boy, maybe five or six, sat on a cot, hunched over a coloring book, his back to me. A young woman, thin from worry, her cheekbones hollowed out and eyes rimmed red, held his hand and stroked his hair. She shifted to stand between me and the boy, while an older couple stood on the far side of the room, the man gray-haired with thick glasses, pressed against the wall as if hoping to melt into it, and the woman, her hair dyed black, regarding me with a fierce challenge. The grandparents.

"These are the Lees," Devon made introductions. "They run the Imperial Lotus restaurant. Randolph is their grandson, and this is his mother, Veronica." The grandparents nodded, but the mother ignored the social niceties.

"Tell me what's wrong with him, please," she pleaded.

Randolph sat cross-legged on the cot, drawing, eyes scrunched in concentration as he refused to make eye contact with me. Classic *if I can't see you, you're not there.*

"When did it start?" I asked.

"A little more than two months ago, right after school began. At first I thought it was just stress. Kindergarten, being away from me." She stroked his hair as she spoke. Randolph kept working his crayons. He gripped them with his full fist like a toddler, and his lines were shaky.

"What have you noticed?" I asked, sitting down in one of the wooden folding chairs, the kind used for funerals or bingo.

"He drops things and he falls all the time. We took him to the clinic. They said everything was fine."

"What tests did they do?"

"Blood counts, lead, something they called a chemistry panel."

Ruling out all the easy-to-treat causes, including my initial theory of lead exposure. "And then what?"

"He stopped sleeping. Began having what the doctors call night terrors." She reluctantly pulled her hand away from Randolph to reach into her purse and remove a small spiral notebook. "Here. I kept a record."

I opened the notebook. Pages after pages of detailed observations. I saw why Devon had wanted me to start with the Lees. It wasn't often I had actual data to create a diagnosis with. In the ER, finding the right reason for a patient's symptoms was more art than science. I couldn't help but think that Louise would have loved it if I'd kept a symptom journal like this for her.

According to his mother's notes, Randolph's sleep had been disturbed since September, but his night terrors were now occurring daily, and he wasn't sleeping more than two to three hours at a time. He'd also stopped eating, was choking on anything too large, and was basically subsisting on protein shakes. I kept flipping pages, the words mirroring every case report of Fatal Familial Insomnia I'd been able to find.

It could have been my own medical history, in fact. Shock ran cold through me. No. It was impossible. I glanced at the door, the other families waiting beyond, then at Devon. He nodded grimly.

Randolph's crayon slipped from his hand and fell to the floor with a clatter. I retrieved it, tried to hand it back, but he'd already moved on to a different color.

"Show her," the grandfather urged his wife. The grandmother nodded reluctantly and took a folded piece of paper from her coat pocket. She unfolded it and handed it to me, her gaze imploring.

It was a remarkably detailed freehand crayon drawing of a dinosaur. With Randolph's name carefully printed in childish block letters below it.

"He did that in August," his mother said. "Drew it all himself. Now, he can't even scribble in the lines." She sounded close to tears.

Everyone in the room went silent. Randolph's hand froze, hovering over the paper, mid-scribble. His eyes were open, unseeing, unblinking. I snapped my fingers near his ear, checked for corneal and other reflexes. Nothing.

"Has he done this before?"

The mother sniffed back her sobs and nodded. "It's new. Three times this week."

"Anything run in the family? Symptoms like this? Seizures? Anything at all?"

"Diabetes on my dad's side. But not in kids."

"And Randolph's father?"

"He was killed. Iraq. I asked his parents. The only thing that runs in their family is breast cancer on his mother's side. But she's fine."

Randolph blinked. Gave a shudder, as if shaking off a chill, then went right back to coloring as if nothing had happened.

"Randolph." I lowered myself to his eye level, although he still refused to look at me directly. "What just happened?"

"Echoes." His voice was so low I could barely hear it.

His mother wrapped her arm around his shoulders, her body shifting to cover as much of his as possible. "That's what he calls the spells. The echoes."

Like the shimmers of color and music that preceded my fugues? Or was I reading too much into it? Maybe it was a simple petit mal seizure.

Or maybe it wasn't. If it wasn't...no, how could that be possible? I forced myself to stay calm. There was already more than enough fear filling the room. "When the echoes hit, what happens? Do you see or hear anything?"

He nodded. "I see everything."

"Can you tell me something you saw?"

He thought a moment, then jerked his chin up, finally looking at me. "I want to play with the dog."

"We don't have a dog," his mother said, sounding panicked. "Randolph, there is no dog."

"Yes, there is." He twisted to point to the closed door behind him. "She brought him."

I glanced at the door, then at Devon, who stood silently in the far corner, listening. There was no way Randolph could have seen Ozzie when we came in. The door was behind him and had been open for only a few seconds.

Unless, during his fugue, he'd rewound those few seconds and noticed what had happened too fast for him to realize before. Maybe he hadn't even seen Ozzie, but with the hyperacuity the fugues brought, he'd heard or smelled the dog. At any given moment, our brain absorbs millions of data points, ninety-nine percent of which it files away as irrelevant. But in a fugue, I was able to access all of those sensory impressions, those hidden memories that the fugue allowed me to replay and slow down, analyze.

In a fugue, I truly could "see everything," just as Randolph had claimed. It was how I'd saved Esme last month.

"His name is Ozzie," I said. "Want to go out and play with him?"

For the first time, he smiled. "Yes, please."

The mother gasped. Randolph slid away from her grasp and scrambled out the door. I looked up to her anguished face as she realized her nightmare had just begun.

CHAPTER TWENTY-TWO

AFTER ENSURING THE medics didn't contaminate the crime scene as they evacuated the few victims with vital signs, Ryder had the uniforms secure the area while he returned to the patrol car where Littleton waited.

He pushed through the school's front door, the wind catching his open coat, flapping it around his knees like wings. All hell was about to break loose. He only a few minutes before the brass and press arrived along with the crime-scene techs, detectives, and for a sensational mass murder like this, any warm body with a badge. A crapstorm of blue.

This was why he preferred having no partner, why he preferred working with victims one-on-one, like he did at the Advocacy Center. Little glory, but less bullshit.

The cold felt good, cleared his head from the bloodbath inside, eased the nausea threatening to bring that stale protein bar back up again.

Animals.

Same thing he'd thought when he'd seen Tymara's body splayed open like a dissection class gone horribly wrong.

More than animals. Predators. Powerful. Using others as their tools. Manipulative. Coercive. Controlling. He glanced around the front of the building, his mind assembling and reassembling multiple versions of the crime from alternative points of view.

Had he seen them on the street? No, they would have already been inside. Watching.

The woman, the final victim. What had Littleton said to her? Some kind of message? Or a delaying tactic while his partners made sure everyone inside was dosed with whatever drug they'd used?

Why was she singled out for special treatment, forced to watch, her death delayed until after the others were gone? Wait. Victim or one of the perpetrators? A proxy, like Littleton claimed to be? He glanced at the squad car. Littleton had his face pressed against the window, eyes wide with delight. Feasting off the pain that he had helped wrought. Feeling superior.

If Littleton felt that way without even stepping inside the scene, his only role to lure Ryder here as witness, then how much more powerful did the men who controlled him feel?

He waved the officer standing guard over Littleton to him. "I've got a list for you. There are cameras on a few of the businesses across the street. Get the video for the entire day."

"The full day? But we know when—"

"The full day. Someone was here earlier, set up the drinks, coffee, brought the cookies, whatever. It's going to all be spiked, and they would have seen to it that no one at that meeting missed out." He was rambling, but it helped to think out loud. If this Brotherhood fed off the excitement that came from manipulating others to do their dirty work, maybe that someone was the final woman, the one who'd been forced to stay alive long enough to witness the results of her handiwork.

And then they'd killed her.

"Wouldn't the cameras inside the school show that better?"

Ryder shook his head. "They'll most likely be useless." The men behind this, Littleton's so-called brothers, would have seen to that. "Take a few guys and scout for cameras outside the other exits. You're going to find an exit that's open but isn't supposed to be—that's how they left. Get any security footage and secure that door for the techs to check for evidence." The last was an easy leap in logic. Someone had fired that gun and left *after* the others were dead. And they hadn't come out the front.

The officer nodded and galloped off. Ryder straightened, his gaze locked on Littleton. Fuckwad had used Ryder. Forced him to bear witness, turned Ryder into one of their goddamned proxies.

A game. That's what this was to the men pulling the strings.

It'd been seven months since Littleton raped Tymara and offered her up to his partners. No, not partners. Bosses. Hmm. That didn't feel quite right either. Maybe Littleton had nailed it the first time. Brothers. Big, bossy brothers who could persuade you to do anything.

Ryder stopped, halfway down the steps to the squad car. Brothers in blood. A fraternity hazing, taken to the extreme. The pledges so desperate to become members of the family that they'd debase themselves, sacrifice anything. He glanced back at the school.

Littleton wasn't important enough for them to stop while he'd sat in jail. In fact, Ryder guessed he was damn lucky he hadn't ended up executed like the woman inside. Maybe he'd been their first, and only after he was arrested did they realize it was safer to kill their proxies, their pledges? Hmmm...felt closer, but still not quite right.

Not quite right. That pretty much described this whole scenario. Everything felt faked, staged, from Littleton's outburst in court today to the smirk he'd given Ryder while people were dying behind the doors of the school.

He reached the patrol car, strolled around it twice before he was certain he'd reined in his anger. Then he got into the driver's seat. He didn't want anyone to have any reason to believe he'd physically intimidated Littleton—although, Lord only knew how much he wanted to.

Not tonight. Tonight, Littleton was going to be treated like a precious gem.

One of the most effective interview tools Ryder had cultivated over his years as a police officer was silence. It took no more than a minute before Littleton broke.

"What did you find inside?" Littleton asked, his voice breathless.

"Exactly what you wanted me to find," Ryder said, purposely avoiding any salacious details. "You and your brothers." He allowed Littleton to maintain the illusion that he was equal to the men who'd orchestrated tonight's atrocities. In reality, Littleton was a dead man walking. As soon as his usefulness ended, his brothers would silence him.

Littleton leaned forward, unable to mask his excitement. "Tell me."

"You're admitting to being involved?"

"Hell no. Besides, I'm technically in custody back here, so anything I say is inadmissible, even if I did. But I'm not."

Apparently, Littleton fancied himself a bit of a jailhouse lawyer. "Off the record. Hypothetically. How many other performances," he hated the word, but it was the best description he could come up with, "did your brothers stage while you were in jail? This was much too sophisticated to be their first."

Littleton leaned back, frowning. He obviously hadn't considered what his brothers had been doing while he'd been abandoned in the county lockup, protecting them. "You don't know what you're talking about."

Ryder went with the flow, changed direction. "It must have taken a lot of time and effort, convincing that woman to kill all those people. Did she know she was also condemning herself to death?"

"She's dead?" He sounded surprised.

"Throat slit." Ryder didn't mention the more personal message of his business card. "Is that what you and your brothers are running, some kind of bizarre suicide cult?"

Littleton shook his head. His eyebrows drew together in thought. Maybe he wasn't as stupid as he seemed. He opened his mouth, closed it again. Then he slumped and opened it once more. "I'm not saying anything."

Not yet, Ryder thought. But the night was young.

He settled in, letting the silence lengthen and coil itself around Littleton, strangling his resistance. Littleton glared at him in the rearview, shuffled his weight, his handcuffed wrists restricting his movement. Then, finally, he stilled.

Ryder watched and waited, giving him a few more seconds to marinate. Time to talk.

A rap on the window opposite broke the spell. It was Manny Cruz and John Marsh, the Major Case commander. Ryder left the car, closing the door on Littleton, and circled around to join them on the sidewalk. Manny's coat, unlike Ryder's, was buttoned against the cold and fit as if it'd been custom-tailored. He wore a black silk scarf around his neck and an old-fashioned fedora, like Frank Sinatra's. Marsh, despite his rank, was dressed like Ryder, an inexpensive suit beneath a wool overcoat, no hat, no gloves.

"What the hell, Manny?" Ryder said. And then to the commander, "Littleton was just getting ready to talk."

The commander answered, "It's not your case, Ryder. From my understanding, Mr. Littleton has you as his alibi. There's no way he committed this crime."

"Gena Kravitz is going to own your ass," Manny added. "She hears of this, she'll sue you and the department for harassment."

"Release Littleton," Marsh ordered. "My guys will invite him for an interview in the morning once we have more from the scene."

Ryder shook his head. "He'll be dead by then. Did you guys see what these actors did to that woman? What they had her do? They're mocking us and getting off on it."

Manny and the commander exchanged glances.

"We ID'd her," Marsh said. "Sylvie Wysycki, a pharmacist's assistant. Lost her job after abusing prescription drugs."

"The ME agreed with the medics. Looks like some new form of PXA," Manny added.

Death Head. Easy enough for a pharmacist to make or get hold of.

Damn, he'd been hoping they'd seen the last of that shit. "Those words, written on the wall—"

Manny and the commander exchanged glances again. "'I hate all your faces,'" Marsh said.

Christ. "Under the influence of PXA—"

"They all felt compelled to do something about that. Destroyed their own faces."

Ryder turned back to the patrol car. Littleton watched through the window, lips pressed so tight Ryder knew they'd never get anything out of him now. Too late, the moment had passed.

"I'm sorry," Manny said. "I've no choice. We have to let him go."

The commander wasn't as sympathetic. Of course not. He was the guy who'd transferred Ryder out of the Major Case Squad to the Advocacy Center last month. Probably hated that Ryder was caught up in one of his cases again.

"My guys will give you a call if they think of anything you can contribute." His tone suggested it was highly unlikely that he could imagine Ryder having anything to contribute to any case. Ever.

Marsh strode to the patrol car and opened the door to release Littleton. Ryder turned to Manny. "You know damn well he'll be dead by morning. They only let him live this long to set me up. They wanted me to see this, to see how powerful they are."

Manny's gaze was skeptical. "You're reading too much into this, Ryder. If the men working with Littleton were really that powerful, there'd be a string of violent offenses. Maybe they don't even exist. Maybe it's all just Littleton and a few of his buddies, making sure he'll never go back to jail or be tried again."

"No," Ryder said. "There's more going on here, I can feel it."

"Get some rest." Manny clapped his hand on Ryder's shoulder as if they were friends. They weren't. Or maybe he felt sorry for Ryder, clutching at crazy conspiracy theories—in front of the commander, no less. "You'll feel better in the morning."

Littleton stood on the sidewalk a few feet from them, rubbing his wrists now that he was free of the handcuffs. Manny left to join Marsh and the detectives. It was just Ryder and Littleton, nothing standing between them, facing each other like old-fashioned gunslingers.

Littleton regained his cocky attitude as he watched the police and crime-scene techs swarm the scene, his eyes gleaming in the bright lights of a TV crew setting up down the block. He placed his hands in his coat pockets and strolled toward Ryder.

As he came abreast, he said, "While you're wasting time here, I wonder who my brothers are calling upon next. Maybe that pretty doctor?"

It took everything Ryder had not to grind Littleton's grin into the pavement. Instead, he spun and headed for his vehicle. Trying hard not to run. Or panic.

He fumbled his phone free. Dialed Rossi.

No answer.

CHAPTER TWENTY-THREE

I SPOKE WITH the other families, one at a time, Devon watching and listening with their consent. Variations on a theme. All elementary school-age children, all fine until August or September. Some attended St. Tim's, some public school, so I couldn't blame it on that. All had the same progression of symptoms, including two more children with fugue states that their parents had witnessed. All had been cleared by the clinic or their doctors.

And none with a family history of fatal insomnia. Or seizures. Or anything that might explain their symptoms.

After the last family left, Devon and I were alone in the small exam room. "It's bad, isn't it?" he asked, pushing away from the wall he'd been leaning against.

"You have fourteen more? All from the Tower?"

"That I know of. Might be others." He hesitated, but his face said it all. "Esme?"

I wished I had better news for him. "You said she's had trouble sleeping. Do you think—"

"I don't know what to think. Was hoping you'd tell me it's nothing, but now…after hearing all that." He pulled his phone out, glanced at it, didn't see what he wanted, and returned it to his pocket. "I called and texted Flynn, told her to bring Esme home. Until we get this straightened out, I want her here, near me."

I touched his arm. His muscles were knotted with tension. "I'll do everything I can to help. But first we need to know what we're dealing with."

"Whatever it takes." He broke away from me and faced the wall, pressing one palm against it as if he needed to rest his weight. Another heaving breath, and he pushed away, spun back to me. "What's the next step?"

"Louise Mehta, my neurologist. She has a new fellow who did a rotation at the fatal insomnia research center in Venice. We should get them involved."

"I'll arrange it, pay for everything. Anything you need."

We left the room, collected Ozzie, who waited patiently by the door, and walked back to the alley where the car was parked. The wind had picked up, and the snow the weathermen had promised had begun—a wet, thick snow that left a coat of ice beneath it.

"What do you have in common with nineteen kids from the Tower?" Devon asked the question that had been hammering at me since I'd met Randolph and his family.

"I wish I knew."

We reached the car. Ozzie hopped into the back. Devon and I got in, and he started the engine, but we didn't move. I was glad for the heated seats as we waited for the air to warm up.

"It's almost as if you were all somehow targeted," Devon finally said. "I mean, there's no way in hell you have a disease that you have like one-in-a-billion chance of getting and these kids show up with the same symptoms at the same time. No fucking way."

I turned to him, horror chilling my bones. "You think Daniel did this. Part of some experiment gone wrong, like he did with the Ebola treatment."

He nodded, not looking at me as he put the engine in gear and backed out of the alley and onto the street. "There's one way to find out for sure."

I cringed, glad he couldn't see me in the darkness. "You want me to touch Daniel, enter his mind."

"I know it's not easy—"

"You have no idea," I snapped. "Try to imagine wading through another person's memories, uninvited, as they're fighting to shut you out. Imagine absorbing every living moment of their entire life into your own memories. After I found Tymara's body, want to know whose memories kept flooding over me, trying to hijack my mind?"

"Leo's," he answered grimly.

"Over and over, I have to live every sick, twisted perversion that son of a bitch enjoyed as he tortured his victims. Every single second of it, it's in my head." I tapped my temple as if trying to slap the odious memories out of my brain. "And not just his. Sister Patrice's murder—for some reason, I can't get past that, see any of the happiness the rest of her life brought her. And Alamea Syha, one of Leo's victims, I get to relive her pain and suffering."

"Echoes," Devon murmured. "That's what Randolph called it."

"He's right. Echoes of my memory and of everyone in a coma who I've touched. More than echoes—it's getting to where sometimes their memories feel more real than my own reality." I swallowed, twice, but my mouth was still parched.

"I can't do it again, Devon. I'm not sure how long I can stay sane as it is." I turned away and watched the streetlights slipping past my window. "It's just way too crowded in here. What if Leo takes over? What if I start to—"

"Wait, wait. Don't go all psychic bullshit on me. You have his memories, not his actual mind, right? I mean, we're not talking telepathic mind control here. It's Leo's memories. Not his will, his ego."

I held my breath, waited for my heart to slow, then released it. "You're right. He's not in control. But that doesn't make it any easier."

"Nothing to worry about. You're still you, doc. Always doing the right thing." His tone was almost jovial. And mostly fake. As much for him as for me. After all, everything happening to me, to the kids, maybe to Esme, it was totally uncharted territory. There *were* no answers.

Finally, he nodded, as if coming to a decision. "We'll save Daniel as a last resort. Start with your doctor friends." He glanced at me. I was part of his decision. "But, if nothing else works, I know I can rely on you to do the right thing to help those kids."

By "do the right thing" he meant enter Daniel's mind to take any answers he might have. It was blackmail, and we both knew it. But that was Devon. Once he knew what he wanted, he didn't let anything or anyone stand in his way. A lot like his father.

I remembered our earlier conversation at the Tower. "You asked me why I didn't want to take justice into my own hands, what I had to lose. That's what. Not just me, you as well. It's not enough to not let yourself be dragged down to their level, men like Daniel and Leo and Littleton. We have to rise up, be the best we can be. Not because we're better than anyone else, but because we're worse. Because you and I, we've both killed. And it would be so very easy to give in and do it again. Don't you see, Devon? Standing strong, that's our legacy. That's what you have to offer Esme."

He was silent the rest of the way back to Jimmy's Place, neither agreeing nor disagreeing with me. Devon was like that. People mistook him as unsophisticated because he never had any formal education. But he was smarter than most people I'd met. Smart enough not to make a promise he knew he couldn't keep.

CHAPTER TWENTY-FOUR

"IF YOU'RE BRINGING Esme home, you should keep Ozzie," I told Devon as he pulled up to park in front of a fire hydrant down the block from Jimmy's Place.

"Are you sure? You said he seems to know when these spells are going to hit. Your early-warning system."

"I've gotten pretty good at figuring it out for myself." I climbed out of the car, and retrieved my bag from the back, giving Ozzie a good-bye rub between the ears. "Call me tomorrow, and we'll talk to Louise, come up with a plan to check out the rest of the Tower residents."

Thank goodness money would not be a problem, because there were several hundred families who would need to be interviewed and potentially tested. Once we knew for certain if the children Devon had already identified actually had a prion disease. Maybe Tommaso, Louise's new neurofellow, could help.

Gentleman that he was, Devon insisted on walking me across the street and down the block to the bar. He kept checking his phone, but Flynn hadn't responded to his texts or voice mails.

"They're probably out Christmas shopping or something."

He frowned. "It's past Esme's bedtime."

"Flynn would have called if there was anything wrong."

"I suppose you're right." He put his phone away. "You going to play tonight? I'd stick around for that."

"No. Last thing I want is to face my family. I'm going to change clothes and head over to Ryder's."

"You two, both always trying to save the world. You deserve each other."

We turned into the alley behind the bar. The light over the rear entrance was out, leaving the alley cloaked in shadows. The dumpster that was usually on the other side of the door had been moved as well, blocking the rest of the alley from view. The homeless guy? No, why would he move the dumpster?

I tugged at Devon, pulling him back, my instincts screaming that this was all wrong.

From the shadows on the other side of the dumpster, a man moaned in pain. Devon dropped my arm, drew his gun. I reached for my phone, but before I could find it in my bag, someone grabbed me from behind, placing a gun to my temple.

I froze, my mouth half-open, any words trapped behind a wall of fear.

"Drop the gun or the girl dies," the man ordered Devon in a calm voice. He wrapped his arm around my chest, pulling me to him, both of us facing Devon.

A second man stepped out of the shadows on the other side of Devon. He wore a dark overcoat, an old-fashioned fedora, and a black stocking mask. He raised a large pistol, aiming it at Devon.

"The gun," Fedora Man told Devon. "Or the girl. Your choice."

The man holding me jammed his gun hard against the soft flesh of my cheek, so hard I couldn't stop a wince of pain. Devon didn't relinquish his gun, but he did reholster it and raise his hands, offering no resistance.

In response, Fedora Man jerked his chin in a nod of command. Two more men came out from behind the dumpster, carrying a third between them. They dropped their captive onto the pavement, and each gave him a vicious kick, rolling him over, revealing his face for the first time.

"Jacob!" I strained to run toward him, but the first man held me in place. I struggled against his grip, but he dug the pistol muzzle in deeper until my vision swam with pain. "Stop!" I shouted. I made eye contact with the man who held Devon at gunpoint, sensing he was the leader. "Please. What do you want?"

Despite the mask, I was certain he was smiling. "Nothing," Fedora Man said, his voice throaty and muffled, as if disguised. "You have nothing that we want. Not yet."

His men continued to pummel Jacob, one of them leaning over him and smashing his fist into his face so forcefully that a tooth flew free and his skull bounced against the pavement with a painful crack. Each blow rocked through me, tightening my gut. I bit my lip against a cry of agony, sensing it would only increase their pleasure and prolong Jacob's suffering.

My throat constricted so I could barely breathe. I forced my fury aside and focused instead on any detail that might help Ryder and the police hunt these animals. They had to be Littleton's so-called brothers.

"That's enough," the leader told his men, using that same conversational tone. As if he didn't need to actually order his men to do anything, a mere suggestion was enough.

Jacob's moans died. He was barely conscious, blood bubbling from his nose and mouth, eyes swollen shut, face half-caved-in. The two men bent over Jacob, doing something I couldn't see. Then they left Jacob lying in the gutter and joined the men holding us.

"You'll know what to do when it's time," the leader told me.

"Me? What do you want from me?" After Littleton got off today, I posed no threat to these men, had nothing to offer them.

"We'll be in touch."

Fedora Man strolled away, followed by the two thugs who'd beaten Jacob. Finally, the last man released me, keeping his gun sights on

Devon before he vanished as well.

As soon as I was free, I ran to Jacob. Behind me, Devon followed the men to the street. A dark sedan sped past him.

"Call 911," I shouted, my voice shredded by tears. I cradled Jacob's head between my knees, protecting his cervical spine as I examined his injuries. Blood gurgled from his mouth, his jaw hung loose—dislocated and probably broken—one eye was already swollen shut, his nose was smashed, and I hadn't even begun to check his belly or chest. More damage there as well, I was sure. Cracked ribs, maybe internal bleeding and contusions. But most frightening was what was going on inside his head. I was sure he had at the very least a skull fracture, but there could be serious bleeding and swelling along with it.

"Hang in there," I whispered, even though he was barely conscious. "Don't let them win. You're strong. You can do it."

A car screeched to a halt at the end of the alley. I whipped my head around, ready to defend Jacob if the men had returned, and saw that Devon had drawn his pistol again. But it wasn't the men who had attacked us. Instead, Ryder leapt from the driver's seat.

"What the hell happened? Are you okay?" he called as he sprinted down the alley toward me, his coat flapping around his legs. He fell to his knees beside me. "Oh, hell, no. Those bastards."

"Ambulance and paramedics are on their way," Devon said, joining us.

"Who did this?" Ryder demanded of Devon. "What did you see? Tell me every goddamned thing, and if you hold back on me—"

Devon stared at him, unflinching. Beneath my hands, Jacob moaned. Sirens echoed from between the buildings, and people began to spill out of the bar, some still holding mugs of beer.

"Not here, not now," I told them both. "Ryder, clear that crowd, let the ambulance through."

Ryder reluctantly climbed to his feet and went to the mouth of the alley.

Devon crouched beside me. "Is he going to make it?" His voice was a low, ominous whisper.

I shook my head, my hair falling into my eyes, but I couldn't free a hand to push it back. "Yes. He's strong."

I could tell he didn't believe me.

Before I could say anything more, he vanished down the other side of the alley as the ambulance pulled in from the street, police sirens wailing behind it.

CHAPTER TWENTY-FIVE

RYDER'S FIRST INSTINCT was to grab Rossi and haul her away, behind cover, where he could protect her. One look at Voorsanger's mangled face, and he knew how useless that would be. If Littleton's so-called brothers had wanted to kill Rossi, it was painfully obvious they could have easily done so already.

Shoving his fury and fear aside, Ryder did what he did best: took control, marshaled his forces—in this case the paramedics—and kept watch while they worked. After what he'd just seen at the school, he wouldn't put it past these actors to orchestrate a two-tiered attack: use Voorsanger as bait and then target the first responders.

"Oh my God, is that Jacob?" Patsy Rossi pushed her way through the crowd to grab Ryder's arm. "What did that girl do now?"

Ryder shook her free, amazed as always that he seemed to be the only person who realized Patsy never called her eldest daughter by name. No matter how many lives she saved, to her mother, Rossi would always be "that girl" who had done something wrong.

Family was family, so Rossi had to put up with Patsy's bullshit, but not Ryder. "Back up, give them room. Now!" he added when Patsy didn't obey right away.

Patsy gave him the stink eye, but Eve, Rossi's younger sister, pulled her mother back into the crowd. A second patrol car arrived, and Ryder handed over the job of crowd control to the uniforms. He returned to where the medics and Rossi were sliding Jacob Voorsanger onto a bright orange plastic backboard. The anguish on Rossi's face said it all.

Maybe Ryder couldn't help Jacob, but he could bring these bastards to justice. All he had to do was keep Littleton, his best lead, alive long enough to wring any info he could from the smug son of a bitch. Except, no way in hell would Manny bring Littleton in for questioning. The ADA didn't have the balls to go up against Gena Kravitz and face a possible harassment suit.

Ryder pulled his phone free. Why not go straight to Kravitz herself? If Kravitz was involved with Manny, the defense attorney could request protection for her client directly from Manny with a better chance of succeeding than Ryder would ever have.

"Gena Kravitz." She sounded distracted.

"Matthew Ryder here. Thought you might want to know your favorite rapist-gone-free is in danger. His so-called partners are going to do to him what they just did to Jacob Voorsanger if you don't get Littleton off the streets and into protective custody."

"Jacob?" Now he had her attention. "What happened?"

Ryder gave her a quick rundown of the events of the night, including Littleton's involvement with the massacre at the school.

"My client is an innocent bystander," came her reflex reply. "But I appreciate your warning, detective. I'll discuss it with my client and Mr. Cruz."

She hung up before Ryder could say anything more. He sighed, pocketed his phone, and jogged over to the ambulance as Jacob was being loaded. Nodded to Rossi. "I'll be right behind you." He slammed the door shut just as an alarm blared from one of the medical monitors.

As he pushed through the crowd to his car, he wondered if Devon Price didn't have the right idea. Taking justice into his own hands, avoiding the pitfalls and games that came with playing inside the rules.

If it got the job done and protected innocents like Jacob and Rossi, would that be such a bad thing?

☽ ✵ ☾

DEVON'S CAR WAS blocked in by the police and emergency vehicles, so he grabbed Ozzie and hustled the dog down back alleys to the nearest entrance to the tunnels, concealed beyond the loading doors inside the basement of a bakery owned by Kingston Enterprises. He could retrieve his car later. Faster and safer than using surface streets, he was growing fond of his new private form of transportation. Its advantages far outweighed the dark and the strange chemical smells.

Ozzie resisted, whining and sniffing the air before allowing Devon to lead him through the airtight metal door that resembled something you'd see on a bank vault or submarine. He flicked the light switch and newly installed energy-efficient LED bulbs illuminated the space. They stood at the top of two flights of metal stairs. At the bottom was another door, a twin to the one he'd just locked behind them.

As they walked down the steps, Ozzie's claws making the only noise, he considered the beating Jacob had taken. It puzzled him.

There was no passion in it, unlike most street violence. It had been delivered with an almost clinical precision, inflicting maximum damage with the least amount of effort. Not brutal or vicious, instead…businesslike. Four men. That was a lot to put at risk simply to make a point to Angela, a witness who'd already testified.

And what *was* their point? If they'd wanted to demonstrate their power over the city, why not do to Angela what they'd done to Tymara? Now, that crime, while also efficient, staged for maximum shock value, had been brutal and vicious. Someone had not only taken their time with Tymara, they had *enjoyed* it.

The men who had attacked Jacob, there had been no joy there. Why? What did they want from Angela? They said she'd know when the time came.

They reached the door at the bottom. Devon had had the locks

171

changed—employing a variety of locksmiths imported from around the tri-state region and paying them enough to ensure their silence—all coded to a master key.

He and the dog went through the door and into the tunnels, Ozzie's nose raised as he sniffed the air. The tunnels weren't the short, damp, claustrophobic stuff of horror films; they reminded Devon of shopping at a warehouse store. Maintenance scaffolding spider-webbed overhead, just below the pipes and the ceiling a good twenty-four feet above him. The lower level was divided into rooms, color-coded and separated by layers of airtight doors that created self-contained subdivisions, while the upper floor was storage.

He'd been exploring the tunnels for the past three weeks, but still hadn't covered all the territory. They extended from the Kingston family's brownstone on Millionaire's Row, traveled beneath St. Tim's and the Tower over to Good Sam's, and south to the river, where there were cleverly disguised escape hatches and a water-purification center. Despite being built in the middle of the last century, the design was advanced, able to withstand a nuclear attack. Also, Daniel had added his own special touches, including stockpiles of food, weapons, medicine, and other supplies. As if preparing for war.

He led Ozzie through the maze, heading back to the brownstone. He'd leave the dog there, where he'd be safe, then start working his street connections. Someone had to know something about this damn Brotherhood.

Cell phones didn't work in the tunnels, but as soon as they emerged, in the park across the street from the brownstone, he called Gena Kravitz. About time he got what he'd paid for: Eugene Littleton's head on a platter.

CHAPTER TWENTY-SIX

THE AMBULANCE RIDE was an ER doctor's worst nightmare. I was used to being the one giving the orders, but I'd trained these paramedics. They didn't need orders from me.

It was the hardest thing I'd ever done, watching them take care of Jacob, realizing there was nothing I could do. Earlier that night, examining the kids, I'd felt almost normal, as if I was still a doctor, still had something to contribute. But now, bouncing in the back of the ambulance, watching others take care of a man I loved, I realized how empty my future had become.

The only thing I could do was hold Jacob's hand. He somehow managed to remain conscious, clutching my fingers, squeezing them as if trying to get a message to me. With his jaw fracture and facial injuries, he couldn't speak. He was lucky he was able to still breathe on his own. The overhead exam lights flashed off metal trauma shears as the medics efficiently stripped him naked, applied their monitors, started two IVs, one in each arm, and assessed his injuries.

During the intricate choreography, I had to let go of his hand twice. Each time he moaned and stretched his fingers, searching for me.

Because the medics needed to monitor his airway, I sat at the foot of the cot, where he couldn't see me. All we had was blind touch.

The ambulance made the final turn into Good Sam's. Soon, we were rushing into the ER—my ER—with the trauma team ready and waiting. I knew everyone there, from the lab tech waiting to run the blood samples to the trauma surgeon in command. The only one who made eye contact as I was forced to release Jacob's hand and was pushed away from him was Shari, one of the ER nurses who'd also worked the Advocacy Center with me.

"He's in good hands," she said in a soothing voice as she ushered me to the door of the trauma bay. It was a tone of voice I'd often used myself, designed to break through to minds numbed with shock.

I stood in the doorway, Jacob's blood still wet on my hands, and watched. That's where Ryder found me a few minutes later.

"How's he doing?" He stood close enough that his body pressed against mine, offering comfort.

"His airway is swelling shut, so they're getting ready to intubate. Then he'll go to CAT scan, and once they have those, he'll be in surgery, probably the rest of the night." It helped to focus on the clinical details, even if they didn't answer his question.

I kept my eye on the monitor as the anesthesiologist took control of Jacob's airway. It was one of the most dangerous procedures we did in the ER, but also one of the most life saving. She did a good job, watching as the sedative took effect, using a bronchoscope, keeping his oxygen level out of the danger zone. Once the ventilator took over his breathing, his heart rate became less erratic.

As she repositioned the cervical collar around his neck, she glanced up. "Did someone try to start a central line through his jugular?"

"No," the surgeon replied. "Subclavian. Got it first stick."

"There's a puncture wound on his neck. I think he was injected with something. They must have been in a hurry, because it's left a hematoma."

I left Ryder to move closer. He followed, peering over my shoulder.

"The men who may be responsible," he said, using his professional tone, one that made me cringe because it cemented Jacob's standing as a victim, "earlier tonight, used PXA to poison a group of people."

I stepped back, one hand to my throat. PXA?

The anesthesiologist thought about that and nodded. "PXA would explain why I had to give him more sedation than I should have needed."

"I'll call the lab, add it to the tox screen," Shari said. "CT's waiting."

"Let's roll," the trauma surgeon ordered, pushing the bed rail up. "We can sort this out upstairs."

I barely heard their voices or noticed the flurry of movement as they escorted Jacob out the door. I stood frozen, Ryder's words echoing in my mind, building to a thundering crescendo that blocked out everything else.

I finally forced my lips to move. "PXA?"

Ryder was looking at me, but I couldn't meet his gaze. I glanced around the suddenly empty room, feeling trapped.

"You don't look so good. Sit down." He backed me up and settled me onto a stray examination stool. "You're shaking. He'll be okay, Rossi."

"What happened?" I asked. "You said people were poisoned with PXA?"

He crouched beside me, holding both of my hands in his, rubbing them, sharing his warmth.

"Littleton led me to a Narcotics Anonymous meeting at a school. He wanted me there. By the time I got inside, this woman, a pharmacist, looks like she poisoned everyone there with PXA. Or she might have been coerced by Littleton's Brotherhood. We're not sure yet. Told them she hated their faces. And they, they—" He broke off, swallowed hard.

"They tried to obey," I whispered, remembering the pain, the mind-shredding agony that would make anyone do whatever it took to make it stop.

"While she watched. But then someone killed her. Left my card on her body."

"What makes you think she poisoned them?" I asked. "What if she was the real victim, and they forced her to watch?" It would have been horrible to sit through, so much so that if it weren't for Leo's memories trapped in my brain, I wouldn't be able to imagine it. That's what Leo would have done. He would have chosen his intended victim and tormented them by keeping them helpless as everyone around them died.

From the grimace on Ryder's face, he was thinking the same thing. Only, of course, he didn't have the twisted memories of a serial killer floating like ghosts over his reality.

"We're not sure yet which way it went down. But Littleton said they might be coming after you next."

"Why Jacob? Was it because of what happened during the trial?" I finally found the courage to look up at him. "Or was it because of me?"

He wrapped his arms around me. "It's not your fault. I'm going to get these guys, I promise, Rossi."

A man cleared his throat behind Ryder. We broke apart. Devon stood in the doorway. "Not if I get to them first," he said, meeting Ryder's gaze with a nod that was as much a vow as it was an acknowledgment. "How's Jacob?"

Shari came into the room, holding a lab slip. "I thought you should know, Dr. Rossi. The lab confirmed it. PXA in his system."

I pushed to my feet, the world unsteady around me. "How much?" In small doses, PXA left the system within ten to twelve hours, a painful memory. But large doses overwhelmed the brain's chemical balance, leaving the patient in a coma. One for which there was no cure.

Shari's dismay broke through her professional calm. "Too much," she said. "I'm so sorry."

She left. Devon stepped into the room, ignoring the blood and debris on the floor. "They overdosed Jacob with Death Head?" Anger lanced through his voice, sharp enough that I felt Ryder tense beside me. "It wasn't enough they beat him to a pulp and made you watch, they had to—" He jerked, twisting back to the doorway as if ready to lash out at the next person he saw.

Then his shoulders slumped, and he turned back to me. He met my gaze, and I knew he'd also realized what this meant.

They'd done more than give Jacob a death sentence. PXA comas created the kind of brain waves my fatal insomnia responded to. Which meant even if Jacob made it out of the OR alive, I could never, ever touch him again.

I raised my bloody hands before my face. It was too much, the air in the room too heavy, even the light overhead felt sharp as knives. I broke, my sobs emerging in choked gasps that shook my entire body. Ryder gathered me into his arms.

"Let me take you home," he said.

I pushed free, my breath ragged. "No." The single syllable took all my energy. I grabbed on to both of Ryder's hands, clinging to his strength. "No. You go. Find who did this," I choked out. "Please."

He stepped close, our joined hands raised, pressed between our bodies. He looked down at me for a long moment, holding my gaze, kissed my forehead tenderly. We separated.

Ryder stared at his empty hands, his jaw tight. Then he looked up to meet Devon's eyes. "See her home safe."

Devon jerked his chin. "I will."

Reluctantly, I stepped away from Ryder and went with Devon.

As we stumbled out, the red lights of the Emergency sign coloring our path to Devon's car, I looked back but couldn't make out anything through the tears blinding me.

CHAPTER TWENTY-SEVEN

RYDER STARED AT the empty doorway where Rossi had stood. Usually when he was on the job, he could compartmentalize, force any random emotions behind locked doors so they wouldn't distract him. Usually. Before he'd met Rossi.

Now he stood, staring like an idiot, not even sure which emotions held him captive. Anger at the animals who'd dared to attack someone he held dear. Frustration he hadn't gotten there sooner. Fear that someday he might get there too late to save her.

He rubbed the newly formed scar on his side. She'd risked her life for him. She'd killed a man for him. Hell with feelings. He had a job to do. A promise to keep. For Rossi.

He stepped toward the door, but a woman rushed in, breathless. Louise Mehta, Rossi's best friend, neurologist, and Ryder's confidential informant when it came to all things related to fatal insomnia.

She pulled up short, her heels skidding on the linoleum. Her white lab coat was pristine, covering a colorful dress that hinted of springtime even though it was three days before Christmas.

"Matthew." She glanced around the empty room. "I was called—

another PXA overdose?"

"Jacob Voorsanger. Some guys beat him then injected him with PXA. He's with the surgeons now."

Her face crumpled with dismay. "Jacob? Oh no. Does Angie know?"

"She just left. They made her watch, Louise. I got there too late to stop it. Or catch them. The bastards are still out there."

"You think it's the same people behind the poisoning at the school?"

"Isn't it?"

She took a sheaf of papers from her coat pocket. "Maybe not. I just consulted on two survivors from the school—"

"How are they? Are they going to make it?"

"Since the overdoses last month, I've been working on a possible treatment. It's too soon to say if it will work."

"You'll try your treatment on Jacob?" he asked.

"Yes. They can start it while he's in surgery."

"How long will it be before you know if it works?" It would be great to be able to give Rossi some good news.

"I'm not sure. Every patient responds to PXA differently. There are just too many variables. Especially in the victims from the school."

Ryder did a double take. "Why?"

"They weren't solely dosed with PXA. According to their toxicology results, they were given a cocktail of PXA, Rohypnol, and scopolamine."

"PXA plus a date-rape drug? What's the last one?"

"Scopolamine. Used for motion sickness but actually quite dangerous. In South America, it's known as the zombie-maker. It can be administered by touch, orally, even by blowing the concentrated powder form into a person's face as they breathe in."

"The perfect storm if you want to convince a room full of people to tear their own faces off." Made sense. Their presumed poisoner, Wysycki—the woman who'd been executed after serving as the Brotherhood's proxy—was a pharmacy assistant. The attack tonight, timed to coincide with Littleton's release, had obviously been a long time in its planning. "Was that what they injected Jacob with? This zombie mix?"

"No. He was given pure PXA."

"That's good news, right? Means your treatment should have a better chance of working?"

She grimaced, gave a sad shake of her head. "In lower doses, maybe. But at the dose he was given—I can't make any promises. Angie really should be here when he gets out of surgery. Spend whatever time she can with him. In case…"

He blew out his breath. "I'll let her know."

"How's she doing?"

"Officially, we're still not talking about her disease. She almost told me something earlier today, then all this shit with Littleton happened. But I have to tell you, I can't take it much longer. I don't want to add to her stress with what's going on with Jacob, but—" He pivoted to the door, then back to her, hating his uncertainty. "Look, I'm not asking you to betray any confidences or mess with your doctor-patient relationship, but give me some advice here. As her friend. I just don't know what to do anymore. I want to be there for her, want to help, but how can I when she won't let me in?"

Damn, last thing he wanted was to sound like a whiny school kid with a crush. Rossi meant more to him than that. He just didn't have the right words…couldn't even begin to find them. Maybe they didn't exist; maybe there were no words for what they had. All he knew was whatever they had, he didn't want to lose it. Or her.

Louise seemed to understand. She stepped close to him, placed her palm on his arm in a motherly fashion, despite the fact that she was only a few years older than he was.

"I've known Angie for a long time. She's always been a hard read. Even worse, there's this rebel streak in her that won't let her forgive herself for her father's death, won't let her be happy, so she's always fighting. Herself more than anything else."

"You're saying I can't win here? I should just walk away?"

"Would you?"

"No. No way in hell." He wasn't abandoning Rossi. He'd seen the way her family treated her. Even Jacob took her for granted, assumed she was so strong she didn't need anything or anyone. He knew better. She *was* strong. It was the passion behind that strength that had drawn him to her. But she was also exquisitely vulnerable, even if she'd never admit it to anyone, including herself.

"Then there's your answer. Just because Angie is driven to fight against happiness, to guard herself against pain and regret, that doesn't mean she has to win."

He straightened, feeling better. "Thanks, Louise."

"What are you going to do now?" she asked.

"Exactly what I promised Rossi I'd do. I'm going to nail these bastards."

CHAPTER TWENTY-EIGHT

ANGELA SAT IN silence as Devon took the long way around to her place. He was glad he'd gone back to pick up the car after settling Ozzie in at the brownstone. He wasn't sure she'd make it the ten blocks to Jimmy's bar under her own steam.

"He's going to die," she said in a hushed voice low enough to be denied.

From what she'd told him about PXA comas, he wasn't sure that was altogether bad. In fact, if it'd been someone he loved, he might consider taking matters into his own hands, if only to end their suffering. He glanced her way. She stared out the window, her back to him.

"Jacob knows how you feel about him." It was a lie. Devon seldom lied, and never before to Angela. But the truth would only torture her. Jacob had become a friend, had shared his confusion about his ex-wife, his regret for their divorce. Said he was determined to win her back before it was too late.

Time. The greatest enemy, the ultimate victor. When he'd worked for the Russians, an *Avtorityet* in charge of their *Bratva*, or brigade, had told him that.

Angela's shoulders slumped as she shook, her forehead braced against the window. Through everything they'd seen and done together, he'd never seen her cry, not like this, losing all control. He focused on the road ahead, unsure what to do, certain she wouldn't appreciate any intercession. Like him, she was extremely private, hated being exposed as vulnerable.

The street in front of Jimmy's Place was crowded with police vehicles and a crime-scene van. He parked around the corner and circled the car to open her door, something she usually would have never allowed him do. The dome light glowed black against the dried blood that smeared her white blouse and pale skin of her hands. He helped her up out of her seat and walked with her to the bar.

Jimmy had closed the place, a handwritten sign reading Family Emergency taped to the front door. A crowd gathered beyond the crime scene tape watching the techs bustling around the alley. Angela used her keys to open the door to the bar and they made their way up to her apartment unnoticed.

Her door was unlocked. "Wait here." He drew his gun and quickly scouted the apartment, easy to do since the loft design left everything in the open except for the bathroom and a curtain drawn across the bedroom area. "Okay, it's clear."

She shambled in, her unsteady gait betraying her exhaustion. "You really think they'd come after me?"

"That guy in the alley said they wanted something from you."

She looked up at the ceiling in despair. "I don't have anything left."

Her door was a standard interior door; cheap spring lock that he could bypass in less time than it'd take to knock twice. No peephole, chain, or deadbolt. "This the only lock you have? I've seen toilets with better privacy locks."

"That's all it's there for," she said, her tone approaching robotic. "Privacy. I wasn't much worried about anything else. Jimmy takes care of the rest with the bar."

"I'll send a guy over in the morning." He spotted the mounds of pills scattered over her dining table. Stepped on several, crushing them. "Good thing Ozzie's not here. What if he ate these?"

"My mother. She loves her drama." She joined him, running her fingers through the colorful pills and capsules, picking and choosing. She gulped several down dry.

"Sure you know what you're doing with those?" Ryder would kill him if he let her overdose or do something stupid. And right now, he couldn't trust her judgment. He steered her in the direction of the bathroom. "Why don't you get cleaned up?"

Her gaze vacant, she nodded and stumbled into the bathroom. She left the door ajar, throwing her bloody clothes out, one piece at a time. "Burn those."

The water started. He gathered the clothing, shoved it into a plastic shopping bag, and set the bag outside her door in the hall. Next, he swept up the pills from the floor, washed them down the disposal, and sorted the other pills into some semblance of order.

She was still in the shower and he'd moved on to gathering the rest of the trash—he'd never have guessed her to be such a slob—when his phone rang. Gena. "Did you find Eugene Littleton?" he asked without greeting her.

"He found me. Has some idea that going on record will keep him alive. The old *if-you-kill-me, this-tape-will-be-released* ploy."

"That only works if he actually knows something."

"Exactly. Which is why I suggested we meet at your favorite restaurant."

"Perfect." There was an entrance to the tunnels below the Lees' kitchen. Once he had Eugene in private, he'd see exactly how much he knew about these brothers of his.

The water stopped. Angela emerged, wrapped in a white terrycloth robe, her skin flushed from the shower. Or her illness. He'd noticed she tended to run a fever when she was stressed. And before she entered those crazy fugues of hers.

If Littleton wouldn't talk, maybe he could persuade Angela to search his mind for the answers. They might need to dose Littleton with PXA to create the right kind of brain waves she could access. And from what she'd told him earlier when she refused to reach out to Daniel, even then it wouldn't be easy. At least not for her.

But to find the animals who killed Tymara and all those others, it would be worth any pain. He'd just have to convince her of that.

"We'll be there in twenty," he told Gena and hung up. Then he turned to Angela. "Want a chance to talk to Eugene Littleton? Maybe get some answers about who those men are?"

She answered with a smile that reminded him of the Russian *Kryshas*, the brutal enforcers who knew no compassion.

CHAPTER TWENTY-NINE

IT WASN'T RYDER'S case. Hell, technically, Ryder was a witness, therefore couldn't touch this case with a Predator drone. What were they going to do? Demote him? Again?

He left the ER and used his new passkey to enter the Advocacy Center down the hall. All he was doing was thinking. They couldn't bust him for that, much as it seemed at times that they'd like to. He unlocked the door to his office—first time he'd had his own office; detectives usually worked out of a squad room—and entered.

The overhead fluorescent light revealed a space large enough for a desk, two tall file cabinets, and a round table that seated four. Two walls were covered with whiteboards; someone had drawn *Welcome, Detective Ryder!* in colorful letters.

The desk was like any institutional desk, the only personal touch a plate of cookies with a large red bow on top. An image from tonight's crime scene flitted before him: an almost-empty plate of colorful holiday cookies right beside the shoebox holding all of the NA attendees' cell phones. Thanks, but no, thanks. He slid the plate into the garbage can. Better paranoid than dead.

He turned to survey his new domain. Computer with dedicated access to both the hospital system and the police department, as well as state and federal databases. Nice. Could come in handy, but right now it was the whiteboards he needed.

He erased the welcome note and started jotting random thoughts. Facts he listed on the left, questions on the right.

Fact: Littleton did not kill Tymara. Question: Who did?

Fact: Littleton did rape Tymara. Question: Who else did?

Fact: Littleton did not poison the people at the school. Question: Did Sylvie Wysycki?

Fact: Littleton did not kill Wysycki. Question: Who did?

He stepped back. Not much help. Yet. He grabbed a different color and began scribbling random questions.

Who were Littleton's partners? How did he contact them? How did they gain access to the school? All the people he'd seen walk in the front door were among the victims, so the killers had to be already waiting inside. Had they used the back entrance? If so, did they bribe someone to leave it open? How did they gain access to the security system? Did they work at the school? How did they know Wysycki? Why her? A random choice, or because she had access to drugs? Did they provide the drugs, or did she?

Another color. This time he focused on the crimes. Each scene felt personal; they knew the victims or, at the very least, wanted to see them suffer. There were voyeuristic and sadistic components to all the crimes, especially the PXA Jacob had been given after he'd already been beaten to a pulp. A *coup de grace*, knowing it was fatal and that he'd suffer until the minute he died.

He circled the word *personal*. Littleton or his partners had to be involved with their victims. How? Part of the NA group? Involved with Wysycki? Other cases with proxies?

That brought him up short. Before his transfer to the Advocacy Center last month, he'd worked Major Cases for years and had never seen or heard of a crime similar to this. Sure, he'd had suspects claim that someone else had done the crime or someone had made them do it, but never this weird power game of a group of men forcing someone else to act out a crime.

The level of commitment, coercion…hell, the risk. He could see it happening if they'd killed Littleton and Tymara with that first crime, but to let them both live for seven long months? It made no sense.

A third color. This time bright red. Was Tymara supposed to die seven months ago? If so, how did her not dying change things?

He read and reread his question. If Tymara had died, they'd have had nothing but a circumstantial case against Littleton. In fact, if anything, Littleton could argue that all the evidence against him—his prints, his DNA, his semen—pointed to a consensual sexual encounter. Why would he tie her up, duct-tape her mouth and eyes, and brutalize her *after* he'd already gotten what he wanted?

Not to mention the evidence that there was more than one perpetrator involved in the second assault. Evidence that came from Tymara's recounting of the event and the size of the bruises left by their hands, not evidence that could actually identify the men. Which any good defense attorney would have also used, arguing that if Littleton was smart enough not to leave evidence during that second assault on Tymara, why didn't he simply get rid of the evidence from his previous sexual encounter with her?

Soooo…Littleton *had* raped Tymara. They had her testimony that it was not consensual. Although if she had died, it would have boiled down to Littleton's word alone. But had he called in a partner or partners for the second attack?

Or was he, like he said earlier at the jail, coerced into involving his partners, this Brotherhood? What blackmail threat was strong enough to keep a man silent during seven months of jail time? If his partners were that powerful, why not just kill him? The jail was overcrowded, easy enough to get to him inside. Or post his bail and take care of business once he was released.

Why all the drama? Littleton's silence as they hammered at him to give up his partners. Tymara's murder today.

And then there was tonight. Littleton leading Ryder to the school.

Forcing him to act as his alibi witness. Thumbing his nose at Ryder and the criminal justice system like a petulant child.

Childish. That was the word. This didn't feel like the intricate, masterfully plotted scheme Littleton had suggested. Seriously? A brotherhood of power players that preyed on lesser criminals?

He'd almost believed it. Except for two things. Any "brotherhood" that would allow Littleton, the blue-collar skivvy-pervert exterminator, to join its ranks would not be the rich, powerful, well-connected elite of Cambria City. And even if this Brotherhood did exist, why had their only crimes been a botched rape-attempted murder and then today's headline-grabbing, well-orchestrated killings? If crimes had personalities, these were as different as night and day.

He stepped back from the board, rapping the marker against his teeth as his vision blurred the colors from both sides into a collage. Not a fraternity. A pair. One impulsive screw-up, Littleton. And one compulsive planner, able to patiently wait seven months and put all the moving pieces together.

They knew each other. More than that, they trusted each other.

If he was right, then who were the men who attacked Jacob? Thugs hired by Littleton or his OCD partner? What was the point after he'd already staged the massacre at the school? Could be the partner had a grudge against Jacob just like Littleton did.

Grudge. That word felt right. Petulant. Childish. Tit for tat. Winners, losers. Tag, you're it.

A game.

He wrote the words, drew a bold box around them.

Players taking turns. First, Littleton's impulses got the best of him and he attacked Tymara, called his partner to help clean up the mess, and together they'd attacked Tymara again, the game's opening move. Only they'd screwed up, leaving Tymara alive to go to the cops.

Then his partner had to wait until Littleton was freed for his turn. He'd helped things along by killing Tymara.

Were they keeping score? Ryder couldn't bring himself to write the odious question on the board. Instead, he kept following the emotional entanglement, trying to make sense of the chaos.

Littleton had chosen Tymara. Which meant Wysycki had also been handpicked. Her role in the school massacre was designed to torment her in the worst way possible, to degrade not only her life but her memory after she was killed.

Torment. Pain. Stripping her of control.

He grabbed his phone and dialed the ME. "Any results on the tox screen for Sylvie Wysycki?"

"Just preliminary. Final will take two to three weeks."

"What did it show?"

"Scopolamine, Rohypnol, and PXA, same as her victims."

"Maybe they weren't her victims." Ryder hung up. These actors wanted to take credit. That's why they hadn't been content to allow Wysycki die like the others. She'd been the true target—he needed to find out why.

Rossi's theory felt right. Someone had been there, in the room, watched the poison take effect, given the orders for the victims to rip off their own faces—probably after Wysycki had been isolated and restrained, forced to watch, powerless to do anything, writhing in pain. And once they knew there was little to no hope of anyone surviving, they'd finished Wysycki by slicing her throat and firing the shot designed to bring Ryder running.

Wysycki's name would forever be associated with the poisonings, tabloid headlines, doomed to become an urban legend.

Worse than humiliation.

Tymara's rape and murder had the same feeling of overkill. Personal.

He spun to the computer on his desk, not bothering with the chair. If they were that close, odds were Mr. No-Name Brother-In-Crime would be in the system, linked to Littleton. Known associate, arrested together. Someway, somehow, there'd be a trace. More than that, there'd be a path connecting Mr. No-Name with Wysycki, just as there was a connection between Littleton and Tymara.

Now all he had to do was find it.

CHAPTER THIRTY

DEVON DROVE US over to the restaurant the Lees managed for Kingston Enterprises. I thought of their grandson and the other sick kids from the Tower. It seemed like ages ago that I'd met them, but it'd only been a few hours. "I can go with you to the clinic, help sort things out with Louise," I offered.

"That would be helpful. A lot of these parents are uncomfortable with authority figures."

I'd noticed that tonight, but they trusted Devon, opened up with him there. He was younger than most of them, yet they treated him with the reverence of a father figure.

"We'll meet at the clinic at eight o'clock," he said.

"There's no way I can get you an appointment that soon." I was thinking maybe I could convince Louise to give up her lunch—or Tommaso's.

He said nothing, simply raised an eyebrow in my direction. "Who said anything about an appointment? I show up with a dozen kids, their distraught parents, and the Kingston checkbook, who's going to do a damn thing about it?" His grin flashed in the headlights of oncoming traffic. "I never much cared about money before, but have to admit, it's kind of fun always getting what you want just because of your father's name."

"Yeah, well, don't let it go to your head. All that money didn't do Daniel or Leo much good in the end."

"That's my point. I'm going to do a lot of good with it before it's me lying in that big old bed, waiting to die. I can promise you that, Angela." He touched my arm to emphasize his point. "Starting with nailing the bastards who did this." He meant Jacob.

We pulled to the curb. The lights in the restaurant leaked through drawn blinds, hiding the occupants waiting inside. Devon was relaxed, but I let him go first—this was his territory, his game. I was only there to help get information from Littleton. And to help ensure that no one ended up dead.

As we approached the door, Gena Kravitz opened it, the light from behind her silhouetting her body so she appeared even taller than she was. "My client has asked to speak to you in private," she told Devon, ignoring me.

The restaurant was empty, but all the lights were on, making the red leather booths and gaudy oversized paper flowers appear forlorn and abandoned. She waved to a booth halfway down the wall where Littleton sat, glaring at us like a child waiting outside the principal's office. "I'll wait here, out of earshot but ready to advise him as necessary. He will not be leaving with you, and I have the police on speed dial if you attempt to threaten him in any manner."

All this was directed at Devon. An expression flitted across his face, and I knew he wanted nothing more than to drag Littleton down into the privacy of the tunnels and beat the truth out of him. Which is exactly why he'd brought me. He knew I would never let that happen, as much as I was tempted.

We joined Littleton in his booth. I was in the corner, Devon on the end where he could quickly leave or react to any threat. Ryder always positioned himself that way as well.

Littleton bounced in his seat. "Gena told me what happened. With that lawyer and all. I just want to be clear up-front. I had nothing to do with anyone getting hurt."

How quickly he'd forgotten Tymara. And the people at the school. I dug my fingernails into my palms, wishing they were claws. "Of course not," I said, my voice sounding shrill. "It wasn't you. Just the four goons you or your so-called Brotherhood sent to beat up Jacob."

"Angela." Devon's tone was a warning. I raised my hands in surrender.

Devon sat up straighter, the table between the two men suddenly becoming inconsequential. He said nothing. Didn't have to.

"Look, you gotta understand." Littleton rushed to fill the silence. "I had no choice. I never would have done that to Tymara, let them hurt her like that, if I could've stopped it. And no way would I have hurt that lawyer. That's just asking for trouble. I'm a lover, not a fighter. Check my jacket. Ain't no collars for anything violent."

Devon's glower erased Littleton's simper. Littleton jerked his head in a nod, like a marionette, acquiescing to Devon's unspoken threat. "Right, right. I got it. You want to know about those jerks in the Brotherhood. They think they're so tough, bossing people like me around, ruining our lives."

I noticed it was solely his ruined life he was worried about. My fingers curled into fists, and I marveled at Devon's restraint. I wasn't a violent person, but it was taking everything I had not to hit Littleton, give him a small taste of what Tymara and Jacob and the others had suffered because of him.

"See," he continued, "they were watching me, knew about my girlfriends." Translation: stalking and tormenting innocent women. "They caught me with Tymara. Told me if I didn't give her to them, they'd send the video to the police. What choice did I have? I had no idea they were going to do that to her—I loved her and she loved me. But," he shook his head in sorrow, "they made me their bitch. After they were done, they said it was up to me to keep her from talking because I was the one the cops would find all the evidence on."

Littleton glanced up at us, looking at each of us in turn, his expression earnest. I glared back at him, not buying any of his oh-so-convenient story. Funny how he'd never mentioned a video before now. And what exactly had the Brotherhood caught him doing?

"I knew they wanted me to kill her," he went on, "but I couldn't, I just couldn't. So I talked to her, explained things, told her I'd protect her if she only kept quiet. She said she would." His anger broke through. Not for the first time, I wondered if he had a mood disorder, given his volatile emotions. "Bitch lied. Gave me up to the cops. I didn't kill her, but she got what she deserved."

He leaned back, crossing his arms over his chest as if daring us to argue with his impeccable logic.

"You didn't kill Tymara?" I asked, furious he couldn't see that she had died because of him. But he took my question literally.

"Nah. How could I? I was locked up, awaiting trial. It was the Brothers. Trying to help get me off. Destroy the evidence, you know."

"This Brotherhood, first they blackmailed you into letting them beat and gang-rape the woman you loved." Devon's voice sliced sharper than a scalpel. "And when you don't take care of the evidence yourself, they clean up for you, help you get free of the charges? Why would they do that?"

"They sent me a message when I was in jail. Said if I kept my mouth shut, they'd make sure I went free. That I could join them, be one of the shot-callers. When Tymara didn't show and we were winning in court, I figured that lawyer guy must have been in on it, but then," he glared at me, "all hell broke loose, and next thing I know, I'm up on charges again."

I leaned forward, furious he could have thought Jacob of all people might be working with sadistic, thrill-seeking animals like the Brotherhood. "But you're free now. Why target Jacob?"

A sly grin slid across his lips, tightening his eyes. He reached into his pocket. Devon straightened, on alert, but Littleton merely pulled out a handful of photos. "These were waiting for me when I got home. Along with instructions to be at that school, wait out front. They said it was my initiation."

He pushed the photos across the table to me, then flipped them over. Jacob's smiling face stared out at me. I shuffled through the photos with trembling hands. They had all been taken at Jimmy's Place. Images of me and Jacob playing, dancing; also Evie, Jimmy, my mom. Everyone I held dear. The date stamps ranged from weeks to over a month ago—before I met Ryder, which explained why he wasn't in any of them. I looked up at Littleton. "I don't understand."

"They blame you. You're the one who saved Tymara. You're the one got her to go to the cops. You're the one made her testify. And then when the public defender's office changed lawyers on me, guess they figured you were sleeping with the enemy."

"That's crazy. Do you have any idea the turnover at the PD's office? Lawyers get reassigned all the time. And Jacob isn't your enemy—"

Emotions overran my logic, and the photos fluttered from my suddenly numb fingers. Jacob. I shuddered at the memory of the crack that his head made when they pounded it against the curb. Even if he survived, he'd never be the same. Somehow, I found the courage to raise my face and meet Littleton's gaze. His eyes glinted with glee at my anguish. "This was all because of me?"

"Sorry, doc. Betray one brother, betray us all. You're marked for life—at least your family is." He tapped the stack of photos, drawing out one of Evie. "Your sister, she sure is pretty."

I slapped his face so hard he rocked back against the back of the booth. He raised a hand to his bloody mouth. His smile never faltered. "Take it easy, doc. I'm here to help you."

"Who are they?" I stood up in the booth. If Devon hadn't pulled me back, I would have lunged across the table and clawed that smile from Littleton's face. "Tell me!"

"Control her," Gena called from the front of the restaurant. "Or I'm leaving with my client now."

"It's cool," Littleton said, giving her a small wave. He leaned back in the booth, out of my range. "Don't know any names, didn't really see any faces. They wore masks. All I could see were their eyes."

"Were they white, black, young, old, all men? How many are there?"

Devon persisted.

"Not too young—late twenties, early thirties. I only saw two up close. One white, one black. Dressed real nice. Suits and nice shoes like yours." He nodded to Devon's Italian loafers.

"Like they had money."

"Oh yeah, they definitely had money. Don't know why they had to slum it just to get some pussy, but go figure."

I looked away in disgust, glad Devon was doing the talking, because it was taking all my willpower not to spit in Littleton's face.

"Anything else?"

"They wore gloves, but one of them, the black guy, definitely had a wedding ring on underneath, I could see."

"Distinguishing marks? Voices?"

He hesitated, his gaze narrowed, his expression that of an animal caught in a trap, deciding if it was time to chew off his own foot to escape. "Maybe. But you gotta promise me protection before I say more."

Devon's stare was heavy. I shifted my weight, half-hoping he'd refuse and let Littleton get what he deserved. But as despicable as the man was, he was our only lead to the monsters behind this.

Devon nodded. "Deal."

Littleton's smile slithered across the space between them. "Okay, then. Guy you're looking for, the main guy, I can give him to you. Heard his voice, recognized it after I got arrested." He paused, taking the time to turn and glance my way. "He'd have reason to go after your lawyer friend. Damn good reason."

I couldn't help myself. "Who? Who attacked Jacob?"

"The other lawyer. Mr. D.A. Man. Cruz."

"Manny? No way, he'd never—" I broke off, remembering how reluctant he'd been throughout Tymara's case. The way he turned every case into a game, determined to be the winner, as if he were keeping score. No. It couldn't be. Could it?

"That's the man. Leader of the pack." Littleton scooted out of the booth and stood. Gena moved forward from her position at the other side of the dining area. "Now, your end of the deal. I need cash, a lot of it. Enough to get me out of town safe and sound."

"You'll get your money. After you help us get Manny Cruz and the others."

"No way. These guys are dangerous. I'm risking my life just talking to you."

Devon slid out of the booth as well. Despite the fact that Littleton had several inches and a good twenty pounds on him, when they faced off, it was Littleton who cringed and shrank to the point where he was looking up at Devon.

"There's no man more dangerous in Cambria City than me," Devon said. "Only, I won't hurt you, Eugene."

He smoothed Littleton's collar with an intimate gesture, hand on Littleton's shoulder. "I'll do much, much worse. I'll send you back to jail and let them know what a rat you are—and you know what happens to rats in jail. But I'll make sure they won't kill you. No, you'll live a long, long life getting exactly the kind of treatment you gave Tymara Nelson. Every single day."

Littleton squirmed, the color draining from his face. Devon's fingers clamped down on the sensitive bundle of nerves running under Littleton's collarbone. Littleton yelped in pain, his arm suddenly dangling useless at his side. He glanced at me in panic. "Doc, you wouldn't let him do that, right? You couldn't. You're a doctor, you took an oath or something, right?"

I stepped back, into the shadows. "Maybe you should have thought of that before you gave Tymara to those animals. If I were you, I'd do exactly as Mr. Price says. Because one thing I can promise you, Mr. Price is a man of his word."

CHAPTER THIRTY-ONE

USUALLY, IT TOOK six hours minimum to drive from the school back to Cambria City, but Flynn was determined to make it in less. She'd debated calling Devon, letting him know of her decision to bring Esme home to see Dr. Rossi, but had to wait until she stopped for gas so Esme wouldn't overhear. By then he'd already left several text messages and voice mails telling her he was worried about Esme and to call. How'd he know? Some kind of psychic tie to his daughter? She tried to call him back, but there was no answer.

Whatever. They were on the same wavelength—Esme needed to be back home, and the sooner Flynn got her there, the better.

"Is he going to be mad at me?" Esme asked from her seat in the back of the Audi after they pulled out of the gas station. Gone was any hint of bravado or bossy princess.

"Who?" Flynn answered, focusing on the road ahead, scanning for cops as she edged her speed higher.

"Daddy. Will he be mad that I wet the bed?" She sounded scared. Flynn wished she could pull over again to give Esme a hug, some sign that she wasn't in this alone. But urgency overrode any hint of maternal instinct.

"Of course not. Your daddy loves you more than anything in the whole wide world." It was the truth, even if Devon would never admit it. Flynn had seen the way he looked at Esme, knew what he'd sacrificed for her safety.

Esme sat in silence, chewing the tip of her braid, a habit she'd begun after her first week at school.

"Ozzie will be there," Flynn promised, hoping it wasn't a lie.

Esme brightened at that. "I miss him. Can I stay there? With Ozzie and Daddy and you? We can have a family again."

Flynn glanced in the rearview, wincing at the hopeful expression on Esme's face. She desperately wanted to say yes, to promise the moon and the stars to the little girl.

Headlights glared at her as a car raced past going the other way. Flynn turned her focus back on the road. Her job wasn't to make empty promises that would end up stabbing deeper than any painful truth.

Her job was to keep Esme safe.

❄

DEVON AND I left Littleton in the booth and moved to the kitchen, where we could talk privately. Gena took her cue and rejoined her client. She seemed curiously unconcerned about whatever he'd told us—maybe because Devon and I had no official standing. Or was it because Devon was paying her bill, and all that rhetoric when we walked in was for my benefit, covering her ass? If Devon wanted Littleton, would Gena deliver him?

"Do you believe him?" I asked.

Devon leaned against the wall, his posture deceptively relaxed. His gaze never left Littleton, slouched in the corner of the booth across the restaurant. Gena sat with him, her back to us.

I didn't wait for his answer. I called Jimmy. If I called my mom, there was a good chance she'd do the opposite of anything I asked and

I didn't want to upset Evie more than she already was. "Where are you guys?"

"In the waiting room at Good Sam's," he answered. "Where the hell are you? Your mother needs you now. I haven't seen her this upset since your father."

I squeezed my eyes shut, searching for strength. "The men who did this. To Jacob. They might also be targeting the rest of the family. You, Mom, Evie, the boys."

"Not while I'm around they won't."

"Can you watch over them? Just until morning, then I can ask Devon to send some of his guys to help."

"I can take care of my own damn family. Including you. Where are you? When are you coming here?"

"Thanks, Jimmy." I hung up before he could ask more questions I couldn't answer.

Devon was on his own phone, leaving another message for Flynn. He glanced at the clock over the stove, not bothering to hide his worry.

"I'm sure they're okay," I told him.

"I think I should drive up there." He glanced toward the seating area where Littleton and Gena waited, obviously torn.

"Did you check the GPS on Flynn's car?" I suggested.

He grimaced. "I'm losing it. Should have thought of that myself." He worked with his phone. "They're halfway here. Shit, why didn't she call me back?"

"Maybe she doesn't want to talk in front of Esme. No matter, they're safe. Now, what do we do about Littleton? It makes no sense," I continued without waiting for his answer. "If Manny is involved, why take the risk? Why didn't they just kill Littleton?" My skin crawled at the thought of Manny being involved. He was Jacob's friend, and to do that to Tymara? I didn't like the man, but I never would have imagined him a sadistic killer. "It would have been so much easier than this elaborate cat-and-mouse game."

"Oh, but where's the fun in that?"

"Fun?" I stared at him.

"Sure. These guys don't get off on just the violence. They're in it for the game, the challenge. Like the way Eugene played you with those photos of your family."

"Game." Had to admit, that did sound like Manny. "Fun. Raping and torturing an innocent woman. Watching all those people claw their own faces off tonight. Beating a defenseless man into a coma. It's insane."

"No. Totally sane. I think Eugene has one thing right: These guys are intelligent, successful, and terminally bored. I used to see this kind of stupid-ass competition with the Russians. Taunting each other with dares. Only, with Eugene's Brotherhood, after they got a taste for the adrenaline rush, they escalated to torture by proxy. Have to admit, it's smart. They get their jollies with little risk. If they were ever caught, it'd probably never be prosecuted—unless you got one of them to turn on the others."

He thought about that. "Even then it might be difficult if one of them is a lawyer. Better yet, a prosecutor, in tight with the cops."

"You already suspected someone in law enforcement was involved. That's why you didn't call Ryder when you found Littleton." I let the accusation hang in the air between us.

"You know how corrupt the DA's office is. Besides, even a Boy Scout like Ryder would admit, sometimes the only way to take out the trash is to burn it yourself."

"No. Ryder would never admit that."

"Would you?" His stare was heavy.

His father was a psychopath, his half-brother a sadistic serial killer. I'd seen Devon kill, but it had been in the heat of battle. We'd been fighting for our lives. I wanted to believe he wasn't like Leo or Daniel. I'd seen true compassion in Devon, had seen how he'd sacrificed everything for those he loved.

"No," I finally answered his question. "It's wrong. Those victims deserve justice, not vengeance."

"They left Jacob for dead. Your family might be next."

I looked away, squinting into the bright lights reflecting from the stainless steel counters. "I know. But if we start randomly killing men based on Littleton's word, where does it all stop? We don't even know for sure that Manny is involved." I shook my head. "Who's to say Littleton's not setting Manny up as one of their victims and using you as the proxy this time?"

"Guess that's up to me to find out."

"How?"

"I'll pay Manny a visit myself."

It was clear that the type of visit he had in mind didn't involve hospitality gifts.

"Devon. No. What if Littleton is playing us? What if it's part of their twisted game?"

"One other way to find out." He pulled out a small plastic bottle containing pink capsules. The PXA that Louise had prescribed me. "Found this at your place. Not sure who you were planning to use it on, but why not Littleton? Then you can read his mind, find the truth. Protect your family. Get justice for Jacob and Tymara, those folks from the school. That's what you want, isn't it? Justice?"

I stared at the bottle. Pharmaceutical grade. More than enough PXA to put a man Littleton's size out for hours and induce the kind of coma I could reach. To have Littleton's memories polluting my mind? On top of the nightmare horrors that I already carried, thanks to Leo? I really would be better off dead.

"You said no one could lie when you're inside their head," Devon persisted, his voice dipping, low and insidious. "Got a better way?"

"No." I grabbed the bottle, shoved it into my pocket. "No. I won't. I can't. You don't know what you're asking."

"Same as what you're asking me. I'm taking care of what needs taking care of." He shook his head as if disappointed in me. "You know what you are, doc? A hypocrite. At least I'm honest about who I am and what I'm willing to do to stand up for what I believe in. You talk a good game about protecting the innocent, but you won't put your money where your mouth is."

"Go to hell," I snapped.

"Oh, I am." His teeth sparked as he flashed a grin. "Just want to be sure I take some company with me."

We stood in silence for a long moment.

"Why is this so important to you? That I go along with what you want?"

"You saw what they did to Jacob," he said. "What they made us watch."

"This isn't about justice. This is about your stupid wounded pride." He didn't deny it. "Jacob is the last man on earth who would want vengeance. He believes in justice, the law."

"I know," he said quietly. "Even more than Ryder. Don't get me wrong. Ryder's a good guy—good for you, especially. But Jacob...he's...decent. Probably the most honest, decent man I've ever met."

I couldn't trust my voice, so I simply nodded.

"That's why this has to be done," Devon finished. "Because a guy like Jacob—he'd never do it himself. That's why men like him need men like me, even if they don't want to admit it. Someone's gotta take out the trash."

He pushed off from the wall, his decision made. I reached for his arm. "Devon, no. You're better than this. Call Ryder. He can help. See if Littleton is telling the truth."

"I will. I promise. Once it's over. I can't take the chance they'll walk free." He pulled away from me. "Go home, Angela. Or wait here with Gena and her client. They aren't going anywhere until I check things out for myself."

"I'll go with you then." Maybe I could keep him from doing something he'd regret.

He shook his head. "No. You don't want no part of this. Call Ryder if you want. But think what these guys did to Jacob, what they could still do to him and others if we don't put an end to them. Now."

I reached for my phone, pulled up Ryder's number. My finger hovered over it, but God help me, I couldn't press it. My vision blurred, and all I could see was the alley, the men beating Jacob, his sobs of pain, his blood mixing with the dirt and grime…

I put my phone away. Devon didn't smile or meet my eyes. He wasn't triumphant, more like resigned. "We all do what we need to do."

CHAPTER THIRTY-TWO

RYDER FOCUSED FIRST on Littleton's past. He started as far back as possible. Found not only a sealed juvie record but also numerous earlier adjudications removing Littleton from his biological parents. Five times before Littleton was eleven and he was permanently placed in a group home.

The family court cases were sealed as well, but there were several social worker summaries available. They didn't make for pretty reading. Both parents were meth users and alcoholics. Mom supplemented the family income by turning tricks. A younger sibling had died under suspicious circumstances when the house burned down in a methamphetamine-related explosion. Hints of further abuse of every kind. All this before the kid was eleven.

Given his background, the fact that as an adult Littleton held a steady job and had never been convicted of anything more serious than criminal trespass should have been a testament to the success of the juvenile system—if Ryder hadn't met the rat-faced bastard in person, seen the way he enjoyed wreaking havoc with his mind games. Littleton might look like an upstanding citizen on paper, but Ryder knew the truth.

He might not have killed Tymara or the people at the school, but he was a sadistic son of a bitch just the same.

Ryder was surprised that when he searched Sylvie Wysycki's name on his computer, the first results were visits she'd made to the Advocacy Center, all for physical assaults from a partner. She'd spoken with the center's social workers but had declined to name her abuser or make an official police report.

The ninety percent of the iceberg that was domestic violence, usually invisible to law enforcement.

In Wysycki's case, she received treatment for her injuries—several times from Rossi, he noted—as well as counseling, including a referral to a safe house. After four more ER visits over ten months, she finally went. A follow-up note from the social worker said that she'd left her abuser, severing all ties.

It was dated two weeks ago. Long enough for her abuser's sadistic anger to simmer and boil over at the school tonight.

Maybe all that anger at Tymara's murder scene this morning hadn't been directed at Tymara, but rather at Wysycki? If Littleton's partner had killed Tymara in a warped tit-for-tat, it made sense he would do to his proxy victim, Tymara, everything he wished for his real-life target, Wysycki.

Talk about your co-dependent relationships. Littleton and his so-called brother were more than friends, trusted each other more than most family, the roots of their violence twisted together. Which meant time to grow and nurture that relationship. A lot of time.

He switched to the law enforcement databases. Wysycki's only offense was the prescription-drug thefts from last spring. Felony charges, but a first offense, so instead of jail time, she'd received shock probation. Then he saw the attorneys involved: Gena Kravitz for the defense; Manny Cruz for the prosecution. Figured. Talk about your friends with benefits.

Good thing he had friends in high places as well. As if just the thought of Rossi conjured her, his phone rang. "Great timing, I was just going to call you. Everything okay?"

"I'm home, safe and sound. Everything's fine," she answered, sounding rushed, as if she'd just walked in the door. Strange, because she and Price should have made it back to her apartment an hour ago. Maybe Price had been able to get her to eat something. He was good with Rossi, persuading her to take care of herself even when she didn't feel like it. "Why were you going to call me? Is Jacob—"

"Still in surgery as far as I know. Sorry, didn't mean to scare you. Can I ask a question about an Advocacy Center case you worked on? The patient is dead, if that makes a difference."

He could almost hear her frown. "Is this to help Jacob?"

"In a way, yes. The patient was Sylvie Wysycki. She's the woman the school massacre centered on. Do you remember treating her?" He gave her the dates.

After a pause, she answered. "Yes. I think so. What do you need to know?" She sounded hesitant. Worried about patient-confidentiality rules, no doubt.

"Can you tell me anything about her abuser? I'm guessing he might be Littleton's partner."

"She never gave us a name."

"Okay, it was a long shot—"

"Wait. She did say one thing." Again with the hesitation that was so unlike her. "What makes you think her abuser is working with Littleton?"

He explained his theory about Littleton and his partner trading off violent attacks. "As if it's a game or something. Anyway, just like Littleton raping Tymara started all this, I thought Wysycki leaving her abuser two weeks ago could have triggered the school attack. It would have taken that long to plan, coordinate with Littleton's trial. But I'll bet Littleton and our other actor knew each other going back a long, long time. So when I saw you'd treated Wysycki, I hoped—"

"She said her partner was an attorney," she interrupted. "Said that's why she couldn't press charges or get a restraining order."

"A lawyer?" He would have guessed another blue-collar worker like

Littleton.

"Was Manny Cruz ever involved with Littleton? I mean, have you seen any suspicion that Manny could be involved?"

"Involved in these cases?" Now he was truly surprised. "Cruz? Why would you think that?"

"Littleton said he was one of his partners. Said he helped rape Tymara."

"Was Manny one of the men who attacked Jacob tonight?" His tone was brusque, but she didn't seem to notice.

"No. They wore masks, but, no, I don't think so. But Littleton said there was a group of them, all rich, well connected. Said Manny was the only one he could identify."

"When the hell did you see Littleton?"

"Devon was the one who convinced Gena to take his case. He called her, and she arranged a meeting."

He bit down on his anger. Price was supposed to take her home, keep her safe. Not start playing vigilante. "Tell me everything."

"That's it. Really. Except, Devon's on his way to Manny's now. And after seeing what they did to Jacob, he's not exactly in a talking mood."

"Shit, Rossi, why didn't you call me?"

"I did, I am."

"I mean before you went to meet with a rapist," he snapped.

"I'm sorry. I should have. I almost did. But—"

"But you trust Price to get the job done more than you trust me."

"It's not you I don't trust. But if Manny is involved, there's a good chance others in a position of power are as well, and you already almost lost your job after what happened last month."

"This isn't about protecting my job, and you damn well know it."

"It's crazy, right? Manny couldn't be involved with a man like Littleton. Doing that to Tymara—or Jacob."

"Or the people at the school. Christ, Rossi, if you'd seen them…" He trailed off as he remembered the way Manny had interrupted just as Littleton had been ready to talk to Ryder. And the way he caved in to Gena's demands earlier today.

"You think it could be him," Rossi said.

"I think I'd better get over to Manny's before Devon Price screws up any chance of our finding out for certain." He grabbed his coat and shut down the computer. "Are you sure you're okay there?"

"Just walked in my front door, safe and sound. Seriously, don't worry about me. But Ryder—"

He winced, knowing what she was going to say before she said it. Something about taking it easy on Price, no doubt. That his heart was in the right place even if his methods crossed the line. He'd never understand how she and Price got to be so close. There was some invisible bond between the two that defied reason.

"What?" he snapped.

"Please be careful." She hung up before he could say anything more.

He slammed out the door, his anger directed as much at himself as Price and Littleton and everyone else involved in this fucked-up bloodbath of a night. How many more innocent people had to die?

*   *   *

I HUNG UP from Ryder and glanced at the kitchen clock. Eleven twenty-seven. I'd ended the day almost exactly where I'd begun it: exhausted, wide awake, and staring at Tahiti sunsets. I felt hollowed out, empty. Somewhere along the way, during this miserable, harrowing, blood-drenched day, I'd lost something.

Mechanically, lacking any appetite, I prepared a protein shake, the whir of the blender the only noise in the apartment. With the bar closed, the building was empty except for me. It was the first time I'd been alone—truly and utterly alone—in weeks.

I missed Ozzie's snoring. More than that, I missed Ryder.

I called the hospital and checked in with the OR charge nurse. Jacob was still in surgery. They'd found some additional internal bleeding, were removing his spleen. She hoped he'd be in the ICU in a few hours.

Tahiti's turquoise temptation caught my eye as I downed the shake straight from the glass container. Finished drinking, I grabbed the topmost picture and ripped it free, then crumpled it in my fist. I threw it against the window. It bounced off and landed on the dining-room table in the middle of the mounds of pills and capsules.

Tears blurred my vision. To hell with Tahiti. To hell with fighting. What good was it if the people I cared about got hurt because of me? Jacob's hands, those lovely hands that could coax beauty and passion from bow and strings and, once upon a time, my body. Who would the Brotherhood target next? Evie and my mom? Ryder? Hell, given the massacre at the school, maybe Good Sam's pediatric ward.

I couldn't do a damn thing to stop it except give them what they wanted. Whatever the hell that was. Because I had nothing left to give.

I rinsed out the blender container and left it soaking with soapy water in the sink. I wrung out the sponge, leaving what was left of my energy dribbling down the drain. Tired. I had never felt so tired.

Staring at the colorful assortment of pills Devon had so carefully organized into piles on my table, I slumped against the kitchen counter. Released from their well-ordered compartments, they appeared wild and untamed, filled with possibilities.

I dug the bottle of PXA from my pocket, tossed it onto the table with the others. I should have been furious at Devon for even suggesting that I drug Littleton in order to force the answers he held from his mind. It violated every oath I'd ever taken as a physician, was a betrayal of everything I'd worked for my entire life.

Yet, I wasn't angry.

Instead, I'd been tempted. Had actually considered the unthinkable a viable option.

I ran my fingers over the small mountains of pharmaceuticals, each containing a promise. My stomach clenched—that weird feeling, half-scared, half-excited, that you get when you stand too close to the edge of a cliff. Instead of thinking of reasons why you shouldn't jump or what would come after, you lean forward, tethered by curiosity and wondering if maybe you should jump to see how it would feel to be flying free. Wouldn't it be glorious?

A siren song, calling to me. I wasn't ready to die, nowhere near ready. And yet…a traitorous whisper slithered through my brain as I stared at the rainbow assortment of pills spread out like candy, calculating exactly which combo would do the job properly. When the time came.

It would be so easy. No more wondering, no more worrying, no more waiting.

Might even save lives. Protect my family and Ryder and everyone else I cared about from the Brotherhood. It wouldn't be a bad death, as deaths went. Like drifting off to sleep…Sleep…What a beautiful word. The idea was like heaven.

My entire body trembled as I reached for the pills. I couldn't blame it on the fatal insomnia. Except, well, I guess everything could be blamed on it. My entire life, from my dad's death to where I stood right now, contemplating an act I'd always felt was the ultimate coward's way out. How could I do this to my family? To Ryder? Leave them to clean up my mess of a life.

All my life, I'd been the one taking care of messes, whether shouldering the burden of guilt after Dad's death or wading into the chaos that was a multi-casualty trauma in the ER. Was I really about to abandon that now?

My fiddle beckoned to me from its stand beside the window. I turned away from the pills. Picked up my fiddle, tucked it under my chin, raised my bow and almost dropped it from my shaking hands. I remembered my failed attempt to play this morning, anguish bending me double. My music, the one thing left of my dad that no one could ever take from me. Except my traitorous Swiss-cheesed brain.

I set my fiddle back down. If I felt like this now, in the early stages of fatal insomnia, how in hell would I be able to function after the disease ravaged my brain and turned me into a shambling zombie, unable to care for myself or communicate with the outside world?

I'd be trapped alone inside my mind. Well, not alone. Trapped with a lifetime's worth of memories from a murdered nun, a tortured teenage girl, and a sadistic serial killer.

I closed my eyes, pressing my forehead against the icy glass of the darkened window, trying to imagine a future, any future. I wanted desperately to see a vision of Ryder. Ryder and me together. My *wish I may, wish I might* fantasy, the one I never dared admit to myself.

All I saw was black. All I felt was fear.

I turned to stare at the PXA, my genie locked inside a bottle. Could I unleash it? Should I?

A knock on my door broke my reverie. I jerked my head up, stared at the door as if I'd never laid eyes on it before. The knock repeated, an impatient tapping. Jimmy had come to drag me to the hospital where he could keep an eye on me, no doubt. Maybe if I didn't answer, he'd go away, leave me alone.

Still, old habits forged like chains dragged me to the door. I opened it. Not Jimmy. Eugene Littleton. Before I could react, he lashed out with a punch to my face that snapped my head back and sent me reeling.

Stunned, I barely registered the sound of the door slamming shut. And then he was on me.

CHAPTER THIRTY-THREE

IT WAS EXACTLY Manny Cruz's style to live in a mansion on Millionaire's Row, Ryder thought as he approached the address across the street from Kingston Park. You had to look like a winner to play a winner, he could almost hear Manny saying. He passed through the gate in the wrought-iron fence surrounding the three-story, colonial-style brick building, dialing Manny's number one more time. No answer.

Of course, the ADA couldn't afford a mansion. Ryder doubted he could afford the ground-floor condo, one of six that the former home of a steel baron had been converted into. No, the only actual millionaire still living on Cambria City's Millionaire's Row was Daniel Kingston. If you could call lying in a permanent vegetative state living.

Ryder surveyed Manny's building. The eight-foot-tall wrought-iron fence was more for looks than actual security. Not to mention the equally tall evergreens that stood just inside it. Clearly the landscaper had no knowledge of how to properly secure a perimeter. To make things worse, there was another row of evergreen shrubs directly in front of the house. A privacy hedge the landscaper would have called it, ready to provide concealment for any thief who happened by.

No lights on at this late hour except for Manny's front room, which glowed stark white through the gaps in the bay window's blinds. A man's form was silhouetted against them. From this distance, Ryder couldn't tell who it was.

He eased through the gate. Instead of following the sidewalk to the front door, he crossed the lawn to peer inside the window, concealing himself in the second row of evergreens. The blinds were open just enough for him to see Manny, face flushed, arms gesturing. Talking to whom? He sidled around to the opposite side of the wide bay window, weaving between hemlock boughs, until he found a better angle.

Devon Price. Damn it. Manny stepped forward, and for the first time, Ryder could see his right hand. Holding a semiautomatic. Price's hands were empty, held in the universal posture of surrender.

Ryder called for backup as he headed for the front door. It was designed to be accessed by a tenant's private code on a keypad. He leaned on all the buttons except Manny's until someone finally clicked the door open. He pushed into the foyer and turned right to the door leading to Manny's condo. It was ajar.

Usually, he would have waited for backup. But he knew both men inside. Honestly, it wasn't Price he was worried about, despite the fact that Ryder was certain he was carrying—the man defined cool under pressure. It was hothead Manny who was most likely to escalate the situation.

Ryder drew his weapon. The door swung open silently. He didn't go through it. Instead, he angled his body to see into the room and take aim. "Manny, it's Ryder. I've got backup on the way. Put the gun down and let me handle Price."

"What the hell?" Manny shouted, his voice pitched higher than usual. "First, this thug comes knocking, accusing me of throwing a trial, and now I have police barging in? Why can't you people just leave me the fuck alone?"

"Happy to oblige," Price said. "I'll just be leaving now. Sorry for the intrusion." He was playing it smart, not inflaming the situation.

"Want me to arrest him, Manny?" Ryder asked, also trying to placate the distraught ADA. "Put down the gun, and I'll come in. You tell me how you want him charged."

Manny bounced on his heels, his aim jerking from Price to Ryder and back. "I've got a right to protect myself in my own home. You know that, Ryder."

"Sure I do, Manny. But I can't come in and arrest Price until you put down the gun. Help me out here, one professional to another."

Ryder edged into the doorway, just enough to make eye contact with Manny.

"Right there on the table beside you would be fine, Manny. Put the gun down, and you can back up into the other room where you'll be safe. I'll take it from there, and then you can tell me what charges you want to press."

Manny nodded, his chin jerking one way then the other, jaw tight with adrenaline. Courtroom drama was one thing, but there Manny was in control. Here, with loaded weapons involved, it was a whole different story. Ryder kept a tight leash on Manny's gaze, nodding in time with him, his head gradually slowing. Manny mirrored him.

With his free hand, Ryder pantomimed placing the gun down. Manny followed suit. The semiautomatic clattered against the glass-topped table. Manny jumped back at the sound, ending up directly in front of the bay window.

Ryder shifted his attention to Price. "Join me out here. Slowly."

Price complied, backing up at an angle that wouldn't put him between Ryder and Manny, not crossing Ryder's line of fire.

"You're going away now, Price," Manny shouted, his voice still jumping with adrenaline. "Big mistake, threatening me, you asshole!"

The last was punctuated by the sound of glass breaking, followed by two more loud pops. Not the crack of a rifle. More the bass boom of a large-caliber revolver. Ryder shifted his attention to the origin of the gunshots: the window. From the corner of his eye, he saw Price draw his own weapon.

Manny staggered, a confused frown crossing his face as he patted his chest. His hand came away bloody. He held it out to Ryder, seeming to search for an explanation, when one more shot sounded, and his right eyeball exploded in a fountain of pink mist.

In the slow motion rush that came with a firefight, Ryder was already pivoting, lunging to pull Manny down, out of the line of fire, as Price ran out the door behind them. Ryder rolled Manny's body against the wall beneath the window—the closest cover—and cautiously edged his gaze over the windowsill, taking aim. No sign of the shooter.

The hemlocks rustled as if someone had pushed through them, but no one moved in the shadows of the front yard or beyond the fence. Price appeared, sprinting down the porch steps. Damn fool was a sitting duck. Ryder covered him as best he could without making himself a target.

From the distance came the sound of a car screeching away. Across the park. Shooter was smart and knew the area—you could use the park roads to gain access to half a dozen major streets.

Price reached the gate and turned to look up and then down the street, peered into the trees of the park on the other side of the street, then walked back, shrugging at Ryder as he holstered his pistol.

"Nothing," Price said through the broken window. Ryder noticed that he stayed clear of the area where the shooter had stood. "They're gone. Probably through the park."

No shit, Sherlock. Which meant they could have gone anywhere. Sirens sounded down the block.

"Get back inside. You've got some explaining to do."

Price glanced over his shoulder at the gate and freedom beyond.

"Don't make me hunt you down, Price. You know I will."

Price's smile was as fake as Manny's now-ruined knock-off designer suit. "No problem, detective. Happy to do my civic duty."

CHAPTER THIRTY-FOUR

PAIN SPIKED THROUGH my cheek from where Littleton punched me. We landed on the floor in front of the couch.

"You bitch! You wanted to see what the Brotherhood can do?" Spittle sprayed on my face. "Now's your chance."

I'd taken plenty of self-defense classes at the Advocacy Center, had learned some dirty street-fighting tricks from guys I knew, but they weren't what saved me at that moment. Instead, it was my experience growing up with my older, larger, bully-wannabe male cousins. I had one chance. If Littleton landed a few more punches like his first, I'd be finished.

As he reared over me, fists raised, I shot my hand into his groin, squeezed, and twisted as hard as I could. I felt soft tissue yield through the fabric of his pants and closed my fingers, digging in. He bellowed in pain, pushing off of me, reeling back, both hands shielding his crotch.

I scuttled away and got to my feet. He was between me and the door. No escape. I glanced at the open door to the bathroom; no, there was no window and no room to fight in there. Instead, I moved into the kitchen, placing the island between me and him.

"Get out!" I shouted.

Jimmy was gone for the night, so there was no one to hear me if I screamed for help. Phone. Where was my phone? On the table near the sofa, too far away.

Littleton staggered to his feet, shaking his head, his eyes wide with rage. "I'm going to kill you."

Music filled me, ominous bass notes of a church organ. Echoes of color shimmered around him as he seemed to move in slow motion. A fugue coming on. Once it hit, I'd be frozen, helpless. Littleton and his partners could do anything they wanted to me.

Tymara's body filled my vision. *No.* I brushed against the refrigerator, freeing two pictures of Tahiti. They floated to the floor, gold and crimson and aquamarine ribbons of light trailing behind them.

Littleton lumbered toward me, coming around the opposite end of the island, hands down at his waist, a knife in his right one. I grabbed the closest thing at hand—the glass blender container filled with soap and water—and launched it at his head.

Caught between the island and the kitchen counter, he had no room to duck. It hit his head and sprayed soapy water over his face before landing with a crash on the floor, shattering. He raised his empty hand to clear his eyes, but I didn't give him a chance.

I grabbed the top plate from the stack in the dish rack and heaved it like a discus, aiming for his arm with the knife. The heavy ceramic plate caught his wrist. He twisted, coming up against the island and leaving the side of his head exposed.

I hurled plate after plate, edge-on, hard. The blows sent him staggering back, into the puddle of water and broken glass left by the blender. He slipped, feet going out from under him, hands flailing, head cracking first the countertop and then the floor.

The sounds echoed like tympani in my brain as colors whirled around us. He was out cold, but wouldn't be for long. I grabbed on to the nearest solid object, the refrigerator, not sure if I could make it to the apartment door before the fugue overtook me. My weight bumped the refrigerator door open, its momentum carrying me back against the opposite counter. My hand grazed the drawer pull, and the drawer spilled open. The roll of duct tape on top of the other clutter sparked silver in my vision.

Suddenly, I had a plan—and it wasn't of escape, running for help, watching the justice system fail once more while lawyers like Gena Kravitz set men like Littleton free.

I knew how to get justice for Tymara and Jacob. Devon had been right all along.

My hand closed around the duct tape. My vision cleared for a moment, as if even the prions polluting my brain agreed with my insane idea.

Avoiding the broken glass that now littered my kitchen floor, I lurched forward and fell to my knees beside Littleton. He'd dropped his knife. I grabbed it. It felt so natural in my hand, as if this was meant to be.

Using the knife to cut strips off the roll, I wrapped duct tape around his wrists then wrapped more around his ankles. He moaned as I finished and stood, leaning my weight against the island, looking down on my work.

"What the fuck?" His voice was filled with incredulity and rage.

Ignoring Littleton as he writhed and struggled on the floor, I looked over at my dining table with its assortment of pills. The PXA bottle glowed as if surrounded by an angel's halo.

Shambling along the island, I headed for the table. It could have been miles away or inches—my vision was so warped I couldn't tell. As I lunged across the open space at the end of the island, I stepped on one of the fallen pictures of Tahiti.

"What the hell are you doing?" His voice held a definite quaver.

I hit the table and reached for the PXA. Could I really do this? Drug him, force my way into his brain, take what I wanted, and leave again?

"Your so-called brothers. Who are they?" I was surprised by how steady my voice was.

Rape. It would be mental rape. An absolute betrayal of everything I'd ever believed in. Of Jacob's belief in me. Of Ryder's fight for law and order.

I opened the bottle, my hands no longer shaking, counted out enough PXA to knock Littleton out for a good long Death Head trip, about ten to twelve hours. It wouldn't kill him.

As if that made what I was about to do okay.

"What did you tell yourself after you left Tymara alive?" I asked as I returned to crouch beside Littleton. Waves of purple and black poured off of him, a tribal drumbeat of color and sound filling my body as the fugue began to take over. "That what you did to her wasn't so bad because you didn't actually kill her?"

The knife blade danced across his lips. It was almost as if it wasn't my hand controlling it. Almost.

I lowered the blade. His eyes met mine. No more pretending, his fury and hatred were clear.

"Biggest mistake I ever made. I could have swore that bitch was dead. Didn't know she wasn't until the cops came to arrest me." He spat the words at me, then opened his mouth for a final epithet. "Fucking—"

I shoved the PXA down his throat, holding my hand over his mouth and nose until I was certain he'd swallowed it. The knife blade pointed at his eye was enough to keep him still.

"Relax," I told him. "You and I are going on a little trip."

I lowered the knife. He thumped his feet against the floor and tried to squirm away from me. I held his arm in a tight grip.

"You're going to tell me the truth. You're going to tell me everything."

"I ain't telling you nothing, bitch." His words were already slurring. The PXA was pharmaceutical-grade, the gel caps designed for rapid onset.

Damn. I'd forgotten. When I'd overcome Leo's defenses to force my way into his mind, I'd also been dosed with PXA. I glanced across the kitchen to the dining room table where the rest of the pills were.

The floor between here and there roiled as if the century-old pine floorboards had returned to life, bucking and churning against their imprisonment, their iron nails dancing.

Littleton slumped, eyes rolled back into his head as the PXA took control. I closed my hand tight on his, willing the fugue to release its power. But now that I'd set it free, it seemed reluctant to pounce.

"Come on, damn it!" I shouted to the heavens. "What the hell good is dying if I can't do some good before I go?" I hurled my question out into the night beyond the windows on the other side of the apartment. Each syllable crashed against the glass, shattering into infinity with a cascade of brilliant gold sparks.

My energy depleted, last remnants of adrenaline vaporized, I collapsed against Littleton. The knife clattered to the floor. As the fugue overtook me, roaring through me with the strength of a tsunami crashing down, my last words were "I'm sorry."

CHAPTER THIRTY-FIVE

As Devon and Ryder were separated, taken down to the police station, and questioned by a revolving team of detectives, Devon remembered why he avoided police. Nothing to do with his occasional skirting of the law or a fear of being arrested. Everything to do with how damn boring and predictable they were.

Hanging out with Angela and Ryder, he'd almost forgotten that. But now, with one of their own law enforcement family assassinated, they were determined to thrash through every detail as if Devon could miraculously grow X-ray vision and tell them who their shooter was.

Too bad it hadn't been Angela who'd witnessed Manny's murder. When she was in one of her fugue spells, she could dissect an event microsecond by microsecond, ferreting out every nanobyte of information her senses had absorbed, no matter how deep it was buried. If she'd been there, standing where he had, maybe she could have seen past Manny, through the slits in the blinds, and identified the shooter.

All Devon had seen was the muzzle flash. No help there. Which he told the cops repeatedly as they tag-teamed him for the next few hours.

He wasn't charged with anything. There was nothing to charge him with. He hadn't hurt Manny, and Devon's gun was legal and properly registered. It was Manny who'd held him at gunpoint. All Devon had done was knock on Manny's door and strongly insist that the prosecutor give him the truth.

As he repeated the same answers to the same questions, Devon wondered about that. Manny had been highly excitable to start with, but to react so violently to Devon's suggestion that he might know the identities of Eugene's partners suggested that maybe Eugene Littleton was not lying. Devon would never trust Eugene to tell the full truth, and Manny definitely had been involved in something less than kosher. But mass murder, rape, torture?

What didn't fit, and bothered Devon the most, was the implication that Manny had purposely thrown the case against Eugene. Devon just couldn't see that happening. Prosecutors like Manny lived and died by their conviction rate, and Manny had been especially competitive. If Manny was involved, he would have found a way to silence Eugene without letting him walk free from a trial Manny was working.

Angela was right: Killing Eugene would have been so much easier. Less mess, less risk.

"And you arrived at what time?" the current detective asked for the fourth time, sounding as bored as Devon was.

Devon's phone rang. He glanced at it, ignoring the detective's irritation. Flynn. "Where've you been? Why didn't you call me back?" he answered, not caring that the detective shamelessly listened.

"I did. We just got here," she replied, no sign of annoyance at his clipped tone. Typical Flynn. She cared even less about social niceties than Devon did.

He glanced at his phone, saw he'd missed a message from her earlier. Wait. He still had no idea why she'd left the school in the middle of the night. He stood, grabbed his coat. "What happened?"

"We're not done—" Devon shushed the detective with an impatient gesture as he walked out of the interview room, his full focus on Flynn.

"Esme. She can't sleep and has been having these spells. The doctors up there couldn't figure them out, but I know Dr. Rossi can." Flynn paused. Uncharacteristic for her. She usually never began a conversation without already having weighed and measured her words. "You know she's sick, right? I think Esme has the same thing. She's having spells like Dr. Rossi."

Devon froze in the middle of the detective squad, dozens of overworked police officers watching him, sensing something was wrong.

Esme? Having fugues like Angela? He'd halfway convinced himself that she'd be fine, that it was just a coincidence. *No, no, no...this couldn't...This can't be happening.*

He forced himself to walk at a normal pace, the detectives relaxing as he passed through the squad doors and headed to the elevators. "I'm on my way."

🌙 🔆 ☾

WAVES OF MUSIC thundered over me as my body froze. Tympani and cymbals and ponderous bass notes crashed, stirring every molecule of air surrounding me. I could sense them all, dissect each individual note. Here, a stray organophosphate molecule, garlic in tone, viridian green in color. The pesticide Littleton used at work. Despite him being in jail for months, it still seeped from his clothing. There, a whiff of too-bright artificial lemon, remnants of the soap mixed in with the water puddled on the wood floor.

And the water, oh, the water...I could see each beautiful crystal rainbow drop as it reached toward Heaven and was consumed, evaporating. I'm not sure how long I lay there, my head resting on Littleton's chest, staring transfixed and unblinking as the world pulverized into the elemental stuff life was built of. Time in a fugue was elastic, impossible to measure without some fixed point.

Littleton's breathing, rocking my head, had grown slow, erratic. The thundering echoing through my body was his heartbeat, I finally realized. I pulled my focus inward, assessing the sound like a clinician. No stethoscope necessary, not with my every sense stretched to its max.

His heart was roaring. I could feel the blood rushing through his arteries. Too fast, too hard, his blood pressure spiking. In my hyperacute state, it wasn't a difficult diagnosis to make: hypertensive crisis brought on by the PXA, leading to bleeding in his brain.

What was I thinking, giving a man with a head injury, no matter how minor, a drug like PXA? I'd as good as killed him. Recriminations roiled through me. I'd done it to save lives, but instead I'd taken one.

I could feel life slipping from him…and suddenly, I was inside him, with him, in his mind. At least I thought I was.

It wasn't at all like the other times. Then, I'd been able to reach a person, have a conversation, connect with their consciousness. Inside Littleton, I wandered in a thick fog, each tendril smoky and thick with blood, women's screams swirling the mist. I fought through the spider web of confusion, searching for something coherent.

Eugene Littleton! I called out in my mind as my body lay frozen on top of his.

No answer. But the fog around me filled with images. Horrific, brutal visions of women being raped and tortured. I recognized Tymara, Gena Kravitz, even myself among the many. Littleton's lurid fantasies.

Thunder surrounded me as I waded through the blood and screams. I lost track of the women, fought to escape, terror spiking through me as I felt him grow weaker.

Eugene! I shouted in a last effort to reach him and gain the answers I sought. *Tell me about your brothers. Who are you working with?* Laughter mixed with the crackle of fire, the mists devoured by flames that scorched everything black. A black that burned and choked and threatened to consume me in its oily stench.

She loves me best. A man's voice seared my brain. Littleton's? Or another man's? Maybe I wasn't inside Littleton at all. Maybe my fugue had allowed Leo to take control of my mind.

The thought was as frightening as the black void that surrounded me. I was trapped. Alone.

And I had no path out…

Terror spiked through me. I had no idea how long I wandered in that never-ending absence of light, sound, smell…sheer nothingness.

After what felt like infinity, gentle hands raised my body. My body! I had a body again, could feel him. It was a man, he smelled of pine and citrus. I heard the rustle of his breathing, steady and healthy. Not Ryder, I knew that instinctively.

Panic parched my mouth, burning like acid. Littleton's partners? I was helpless. They could do anything they wanted. Screams shredded my mind, but I was powerless to utter a sound. Tymara's body filled my vision.

I felt as if I was floating, my mind and body still strangely out of sync, as he carried me and then settled me, sitting up, on a leather seat. My couch.

My eyes stared straight ahead, unable to shift left or right. I couldn't see the man—couldn't see anything except my bookcases and TV, all blurred because my corneas were hopelessly dry from not blinking for so long. My mouth tasted of salt, lips and tongue parched. I stank of urine and the acrid sweat of terror.

The man caressed my hair, pulling it back from my face. My scalp itched, a strange sensation, but one I couldn't fully process, my mind reeling, the world around me collapsing and expanding as if I was trapped in a kaleidoscope.

Then he left me there. What the hell?

Behind me, I heard the man lift Littleton's body with an exhaled grunt. There was the snick of a knife blade, the scrape of duct tape being removed. More thuds as he worked on Littleton—saving him? Maybe he wasn't dead?

Finally, the man's footsteps vibrated through the floorboards. He touched my hair once more, a feathery tickle against the back of my neck, then remained out of my sight as the door creaked open and closed once more, the click echoing with finality.

I sat, still frozen in my fugue, counting dust motes as they drifted before my blurred vision, and waited. What had he done? Why leave? Had he taken Littleton with him? Why not call for help?

Who was he?

Could it be Devon? He understood my fugues. Devon would send help.

I waited and waited, still not sure how much time had passed, the world a blur around me.

Disposing of a body, destroying evidence. Things Devon also understood. He'd never abandon me.

Except...What if the man hadn't been Devon?

CHAPTER THIRTY-SIX

RYDER GLANCED AT the clock as he worked alone in the Major Case squad. Almost three thirty in the morning, and the detectives working Manny's case had finally left for the night. Not because they'd given up, simply because they were at that eye-of-the-storm stage where they'd talked to everyone they could talk to and accessed all the information they could. Now, they had to wait until the evidence at the scene was processed and business hours gave them access to more, such as private security cameras and Manny's files for the cases he was prosecuting.

Homicide investigations were like wildfires. They'd burn intense early on, stall out, then blaze again in a new direction as the wind shifted. Homicide investigators learned to get what little rest they could, when they could, because when things heated back up, they'd be running on caffeine and adrenaline.

Ryder watched them leave and felt a strange sense of ennui settle over him. He wasn't part of Manny's case, other than being a witness. He wasn't part of the team anymore. Hell, with Rossi safely tucked into her place for the night, he didn't have anyone to go home to, not even the dog. Tired, yet also too keyed up to sleep, he'd borrowed a desk and continued to ferret into Littleton's life.

Finally, he had to admit defeat. Littleton had never been arrested with anyone else. What little Ryder could access of Littleton's foster care record revealed a kid shuttled from group home to group home. The only things of interest were notations from the home administrators that, while Littleton had not shown any violent tendencies, he'd repeatedly started fires, so he was removed because of the threat to his safety and the other children at each home. That, and a stray note dated eighteen years ago from a social worker who'd been trying to locate any remaining family. She'd listed an address but no names. Ryder looked it up in the computer's reverse directory: a residence just outside of the city, no longer belonging to the Littletons. Maybe the social worker still remembered something about Littleton.

Bleary-eyed, he glanced at the clock: twelve after four. Too late to go home. Too early to call the social worker tonight, not for such a remote lead. He'd follow up later in the morning. In the meantime, the couch in the lounge was calling his name.

His phone woke him several hours later. He answered it as he wiped sleep from his eyes and inhaled the glorious scent of industrial-strength coffee. "Ryder."

"It's Louise. I need your help."

He stood up, at full alert. "Is it Rossi?"

"No. Yes." She paused, lowered her voice as if someone was listening. "It's her friend, Devon Price. Do you know him?"

"I do. What's he done now?" He pulled the phone away long enough to check the time. Only a quarter after eight. How much trouble could Price have gotten himself into in just a few hours? Answer: a helluva lot.

"He's here, at the clinic. Brought at least a dozen children with him and their parents. Said Angie was supposed to meet him here, that the children are all sick and that I'm to take care of them. He says Angie diagnosed them all with fatal insomnia."

"What? I thought you said it was hereditary."

"It is. I have my fellow Tommaso dealing with them. It's actually fortuitous. He could use more research subjects for his new nasal epithelial cell analysis—"

"Louise," he interrupted, trying to bring her back from the realms of academia, "what's this have to do with Rossi?"

"I can't find her. Mr. Price says she was supposed to be here, but she's not. She's not answering her phone. Matthew, I'm worried."

"Did you check Jacob's room? She probably held vigil at his bedside."

"No. She hasn't been back since she left the ER. Have you heard from her?"

He looked longingly at the pot of coffee before turning his back on it and grabbing his coat. "I'm headed there now. I'll call you when I hear anything."

꤫ ꙮ ꤫

RYDER HAD NEVER stepped foot inside Rossi's place. That pretty much summed up their relationship, didn't it? Sex every day in every way, but no trespassing into her safe hold. The thought added frustration and anger to the panic he already felt. He'd gone into battle with less apprehension than he had now, racing to his lover's home.

She's dead.

As he drove to her place, breaking most of the traffic laws, the thought grabbed hold of him with an iron fist, refusing to let go, filling his mind with memories of the worst death scenes he'd witnessed. He was going to kick in the door, smell the decomp, hear the flies buzzing like a black cloud over her, see her body bloated and ugly.

He braked hard, scraping a tire against the curb in front of her building.

No. She wasn't dead. She couldn't be.

He ran inside and up the stairs to her apartment. Pounded on the door so hard it shook in its frame. No response. His hand on his Glock, he found himself experiencing the same tunnel vision he'd felt during a firefight. The ambient noise receded into a dim blur. The light seemed brighter as he focused on the brass doorknob in his grip. The target zone.

He opened the unlocked door. That fact alone revved him into high alert. Rossi would have locked it. He peered inside without exposing himself. No lights on. Across the length of the apartment, a sliver of light from the open refrigerator door illuminated the space. He stopped before crossing inside. That open refrigerator bothered him. A lot.

No way in hell would Rossi have left it open. She despised waste in any form. Which meant…

The Glock was in his hand, leading him as he entered the room. "Rossi!"

His voice echoed from the timbered ceiling, taunting him. The place stank of sour sweat, urine, and blood.

The light from the hall spilled into the apartment, revealing a figure on the couch, her features sunken, relaxed like a corpse already past rigor. Her skin was ashen, her eyes open but glazed. Dried spittle caked the corner of her mouth. Her hands lay folded neatly in her lap. Not moving. *God, she's dead.* The words hammered in time with his pulse. No one living would put up with that rank odor.

He flicked the lights on. The place was trashed. He checked his urge to rush to Rossi's side when he spotted a man's foot on the floor behind the kitchen island. Weapon at the ready, he sidled over, taking aim. Littleton. Dead or near to it. He bent, checked for a pulse. No. Dead.

What the hell had happened here?

It took him only twenty-two seconds to clear the rest of the apartment and call for backup, but he couldn't help but fear those were twenty-two seconds too many.

As he raced back to Rossi, he passed the assortment of pills and tablets on the dining table. Rossi…no…No, she couldn't have, she wouldn't, not without saying good-bye.

Would she?

He sank to his knees at her side, feeling crushed.
Then he saw her chest rise.

CHAPTER THIRTY-SEVEN

RYDER RODE IN the ambulance with Rossi. The medics had tried to keep him out, but he hadn't even bothered arguing, had merely pushed past them, moving only enough to give them room to work. Between his feet sat a shopping bag filled with pills. He'd grabbed everything he could find, astonished by the array of prescriptions, vitamins, and even half a bottle of PXA.

What the hell was going on? Some kind of overdose? Was it because of Littleton? A man like that wasn't worth trying to kill yourself over.

Unless you were the doctor who'd just killed him. Especially if Littleton hadn't told her who his partners were. That would have about destroyed Rossi, the idea that because of her, more people might die at the hands of his unknown partners.

"Never seen anything like it," one of the medics was saying. He'd stabbed Rossi's arms three times, trying for a line, and had finally gotten one started in her neck. She looked like the Bride of Frankenstein, wires on her chest measuring her heartbeat, the IV in her neck with fluid rushing in, the oxygen sensor glowing red on her finger. She hadn't stirred, just lay there, not blinking...

"Can't you do something?" Ryder asked. He'd called Louise as soon as he called for the ambulance, knew she'd been in contact with them. But whatever they were doing, it wasn't working. Rossi wasn't waking up.

"Dr. Mehta said to wait," the medic said. He nodded to the bag between Ryder's feet. "Any combo of that stuff—we give her the wrong meds, and..."

Ryder grimaced. Hated how helpless he felt. Was this how Rossi felt every day, facing a disease so rare it barely had a name, much less any hope of a treatment?

They rolled into the ambulance bay, backing up to the ER entrance. Minutes later, he found himself shoved aside, even more useless once he gave up the bag of medication, while the ER staff swarmed over Rossi's body. Poking, prodding, stripping her naked, more needles, more fluids, X-rays, debates about labs, finally a big, honking tube shoved down her nose with black gunk—charcoal—poured in. Then another tube, this time in her bladder.

They kept asking him to leave. He ignored them.

Finally, Louise Mehta arrived. Most of the ER staff left. She had a nurse pull out the nasogastric tube, and at last, Ryder was able to get close enough to touch Rossi. He stroked his fingers along her arm. Her skin felt cooler now, her color less pale. They'd poured ointment in her eyes and taped her eyelids shut so she no longer gazed at him with that dead-fish stare. He squeezed her hand. It lay flaccid in his.

"She'd never kill herself. I'm sure of it." His voice betrayed him. It sounded more like he was asking Louise to convince him instead of the other way around. Maybe he was.

She flipped to the last page of the chart, nodded, then finally looked up at him. "She listed you as her emergency contact under next-of-kin."

He jerked his head up. "What? No, that's wrong. She's got a mother, a sister. I'm not related to her, I'm—" What was he? Damn sure he was closer than family, at least her family, but...

"No. It's right here. Matthew Ryder. Which means I finally have the right to discuss her case with you. I'm afraid this episode is consistent with her entering the second phase of the illness."

He stared down at Rossi. Her features were peaceful, at rest for the first time since he'd met her. "But she's sleeping now."

"No. That's the problem. This isn't sleep. More like a medically induced trance. If I attached her to an EEG, her brain waves would reveal that she's quite awake, merely unable to respond to stimuli. So her brain is going full speed, nonstop, without any of the restorative effects of sleep. In fact, in the final stage of the disease, it will literally burn itself out."

Ryder felt as if unseen bullets had ripped through him. He squinted, searching the room for a touchstone as his vision swam for an instant. Finally, he focused on Rossi's face, marred with black streaks of charcoal, red marks from tape. "You're saying her brain's fried?"

"No. Not yet. But soon. Yes. It's inevitable."

"Inevitable? You mean there's nothing you can do? You're just going to sit back and watch her die?"

Louise's smile was grim. She lowered her head, patted Rossi's hair smooth with the reflexes of a mother. "There's nothing to do. At least, nothing to stop it. We've been experimenting with a variety of vitamins, antioxidants, trying to balance stimulants and benzodiazepines, as well as some other modalities, including an experimental formulation of PXA."

"PXA? Is she going to end up like Jacob?" He clamped his lips shut. Anger hunched his shoulders. How could Rossi have not told him how bad it really was? How dare she try to face this alone?

"Her tox screen shows no sign of any in her system. This is an extreme form of the fugue state that her disease causes. It wasn't an overdose, Matthew. But you need to be prepared. These episodes are brought on by stress and extreme fatigue. It will happen again."

He turned his back on Rossi and Louise, needing a moment. He drew a breath in, smelling the antiseptic, the charcoal, and Rossi's scent, more acrid than usual. The nurses had said that to get as dehydrated as she was in the few hours since he'd last seen her, her body temperature must have been dangerously high, creating a heatstroke-like condition. Just sitting there, like a zombie, in a trance. Not moving, not even to save herself...

God, what if Littleton had found her like that? He swallowed a curse. No. They'd fought. The crime scene showed that clear enough. Rossi had won. Only to be overcome by this...fugue?

He closed his eyes, squeezed them tight, then reopened them. Nope. Not a dream. But it felt like one. Felt like he was caught in a color version of *Night of the Living Dead.*

"How long does she have?" he asked.

"Her genetic tests were indeterminate, so it's difficult to be exact..."

"How long?" he snapped, not looking up, his gaze filled with Rossi's face.

"Five months. Probably less." She shrugged. "I'm sorry, each case is different. There are only a few dozen people in the world suffering from this disease. There's just no way to know."

He puffed his chest out, ready to—to what? Take out his fury and frustration on the woman in front of him? On Rossi?

His breath escaped him, and he felt shrunken, a smaller man. He wanted to run. This wasn't his world, this world of strange diseases that could strike down a passionate woman in her prime. Now he finally understood why Rossi had locked him out of this part of her life. No amount of reading about a mysterious, rare disease could prepare him for the reality. This wasn't what he had signed up for.

Yet, Rossi had named him her next-of-kin.

"No way to know." The words circled around them, finally dying in the silence. "And this is only the second stage?" He swallowed hard. Didn't really want to hear more. Between them, Rossi's chest rose and fell. If she could bear it, he could.

Ryder turned and shuffled to the surgical sink, fumbled with the controls, grabbed a washcloth, and wet it with pink soap from the dispenser. He returned to Rossi, gently washing her face as Louise looked on.

"There have been case reports of people in the second and third stages leading functional lives," Louise said, her voice sounding dim as if she were at the end of a long tunnel, far away from him and Rossi. "It's simply not a so-called normal life. More akin to walking a tightrope, balancing medication, stress, physical activity. Her sleep-wake cycle will be chaotic. She'll feel like she's living in a world outside of our everyday reality. In many ways, she will be. Patients report having periods of extreme lucidity, allowing them to accomplish great feats. One mathematician solved a theorem no one else in the world had been able to solve while he was in one of these fugues."

Charcoal had puddled in Rossi's ear. He circled the cloth around his pinky and wiped it clean. Job finished, he finally looked up at Louise. "But she's in there all alone. That's not Rossi. She needs people."

Louise met his gaze, her expression now anything but clinical. "I expect that's why she put your name on the form, Matthew. Although she'd never admit it."

CHAPTER THIRTY-EIGHT

MY EYES WERE closed, but I knew I had to be awake—everything felt so crisp. Starched sheets sandwiching my body, icy fluid flowing in one arm. An IV?

The clatter of wheeled carts, the tones of a distant alarm, brisk footsteps on linoleum. A hospital. Felt like Good Sam. There was more. A person sat beside me, softly breathing, not quite snoring. I knew that rasp, knew his scent. Even through the sharp antiseptic perfume that bathed the air, there was no mistaking it.

I opened my eyes, squinted them shut against bright afternoon light coming from the window beside me. Everything was blurred and ringed by halos—the nurses must have put ointment in my eyes. My tongue felt sticky, my teeth wrapped in layers of lemon-flavored cotton candy. The hospital's solution for oral hygiene in an unresponsive patient. I licked my lips and swallowed. Throat hurt—NG tube? Or had they intubated me?

"How long?" My voice was scratchy, unfamiliar.

Ryder stirred beside me. He came awake instantly as he was prone to do, his right hand slipping to his hip where his gun rested. His gaze circled the room, searching out any hidden danger, then finally returned to me.

God, he looked a wreck. Stubble clouded his cheeks and chin. His eyes were sunken, clothing in disarray, as if he'd slept more than one night in them.

"How long?" I asked again. My mind was as hazy as my vision.

His face went from tight concern to wide-eyed relief. He blinked— surely those weren't tears, not from Ryder—then his mouth quirked into a halfway smile, and finally, he leaned forward and kissed me full on the lips, his palms framing my face. I responded to the kiss. Ryder was a very good kisser; it was one of my favorite ways to wake up. Didn't even mind that he tasted of stale coffee and smelled of sweat and exhaustion.

When he pulled back, he didn't go very far. He lowered the bed rail and edged his hip alongside mine, wrapping his arms around me, deftly avoiding the IV and monitor wires. "You're back."

His voice sounded worse than mine. Dark echoes shadowed it, as if he'd been the one wandering lost in a nightmare dreamscape instead of me. I remembered what I'd found inside Littleton's mind and shuddered.

"I'm the one who found you." He looked away, but I felt the tension in his body. He shook his head, itched at the stubble of his beard.

"You found me?" Which meant he'd seen Littleton. Did he know what I'd done? How could he not, finding Littleton bound by duct tape, dead on my kitchen floor? I waited apprehensively, wondering if he was here not to comfort me but to arrest me.

Then I remembered. The man who'd moved me. I thought he might have removed the duct tape, maybe even have taken the body as well. Although I had no idea why, unless he was trying to protect me from the police. I was certain it hadn't been Ryder. At least I thought I was. Confusion muddied my thoughts.

"I thought maybe it was a drug OD. I saw your stash of pills and whatnot. Scared the shit out of me, I'll tell you that—the ER docs as well. Then Dr. Mehta came along, and she put you under with drugs so that you'd really sleep. You've been asleep for," he glanced at the clock above the door; almost two in the afternoon, "thirty-one hours."

Shit. More than a day I'd lost. Shit, shit, shit. What the hell had happened?

"Some Christmas," I finally managed to croak out.

"Christmas Eve," he corrected.

"Wait." I turned to face him. "Louise told you about my condition? She had no right—"

"You listed me as your next-of-kin, your emergency contact." He stared at me as if hoping I'd have some deep, heartfelt explanation.

"No, I didn't." I'd left the space blank…Oh yeah, the anal-retentive insurance clerk at the clinic had insisted I fill it in during my last visit. Ryder's had been the first name to come to mind, the only one I trusted.

"I guess I did. List you as next-of-kin." Slowly, I raised my gaze to meet his, gave him a half smile. "Surprise."

It was a second before he returned my smile—his was clouded with doubt. "Surprise." He squeezed my hand tighter.

"Jacob?" I couldn't bring myself to finish the question, held my breath, waiting for the answer.

"Still hanging in there. Guarded, Louise said." Hospital-speak for nothing more to do except watch and wait.

I sat up straight in the bed. "I want to see him."

The world whirled like it was caught in a blender and I sank back into the pillows, eyes closed against the vertigo. Ryder hit the button to raise the head of the bed and unkinked the IV line.

"Think you're going to be sick?" he asked.

I opened my eyes and laughed. I couldn't help it, the sight: Ryder, gun on his belt, unshaven, expression on his face that of a warrior entering battle, holding a pink plastic emesis basin at the ready.

"No." I sat up again, more cautiously. No more spinning. "I'm fine." And I meant it.

He relaxed and exchanged the emesis basin for a glass of water and a straw. As I drank, it felt so good, soothing the sandpaper scratch of my throat. I finished the water and returned the glass to the bedside stand, felt strong enough to ask, "Are you here to arrest me?"

He jerked back. "God, no."

"Don't I need to talk to someone? About what happened to Littleton?"

"Louise kicked the detectives out yesterday. It was pretty clear you weren't going to be doing any talking any time soon. Told them she'd call them when you're medically cleared."

"It's not a conflict of interest for you to be here? I mean, you won't get in trouble?"

His frown was all the answer he'd give me.

"What do you remember? Before your...fugue?" He stumbled on the word.

My memory was as tumbled as pieces of a jigsaw puzzle still in the box. "Devon and I saw Littleton at the restaurant. Manny? Littleton said he was one of the leaders of the Brotherhood." That much I remembered. Devon had gone after Manny, and I'd told Ryder. "Is he talking?"

"Manny's dead. Someone shot him before either Price or I could get to him."

I sucked in my breath. I hadn't liked Manny, but that didn't mean I wanted him dead. "They didn't want him to talk."

"Because he was one of them? Or because he was innocent and Littleton was using him as a smoke screen?" He slipped away from me and began to pace the small room. Ryder did his best thinking on his feet, in motion. A lot like me that way. He reached the far wall and whirled. "I don't think there is any Brotherhood. I think all this—Tymara, the school, Manny, Jacob—I think it's all Littleton and a single partner."

I thought about that. "Tymara was blindfolded for the second attack." The violent, brutal assault that had left her near to death. "She heard voices but not close enough to identify. Said she wasn't sure how many were involved."

"When was Littleton at your place? What happened?"

I told him everything I could remember, up to the point where I duct-taped Littleton and forced the PXA down his throat. That I left out. Too ashamed at my weakness, the way I'd betrayed everything—worse, the way I'd surrendered, assuming that breaking my oath meant nothing because I was dying and there were no longer any consequences that mattered.

Ryder. He was a consequence. He mattered. I couldn't lose him.

"He collapsed, hit his head, just stunned, though. He was still alive," I finished, still uncertain about what had happened next, with the stranger in my apartment. Had that even happened? Or had it been a fugue-induced delusion? "My fugue overtook me before I could call for help."

"He couldn't have shot Manny. Timing doesn't fit." He frowned with his mouth, but after a moment smiled with his eyes. "A blender and a bunch of plates? Seriously?"

"We Rossis are known for our aim with crockery. And our tempers."

He sobered. "You must have hurt him more than you thought. Otherwise, he would have finished what he started. I found him dead on your kitchen floor. The ME said he had bleeding in his brain, along with swelling."

Littleton *was* dead. I was too confused to feel much. Had I entered his mind there at the end? Before the stranger came into my apartment? Or had it all been a hallucination?

"What about his partner? Or partners?"

"We don't know." He surprised me by framing my face between his palms and kissing me tenderly on the forehead. Then he lowered his face until his eyes became my entire world. "I just thank God he didn't hurt you worse than he did."

God, it felt so good, being with him, no matter the where or why. I gathered my strength, ready to tell him everything, when my mom barged into the room without knocking.

"About time you woke up," she said. "Did you hear about Evie?"

CHAPTER THIRTY-NINE

MY MOTHER. PERFECT timing. As usual. Ryder and I parted as Evie ran in behind Patsy. She threw her arms around me, hugging me so tight that she jostled one of the monitor leads and an alarm sounded.

"I'm so glad you're awake," Evie cried gleefully. "Dr. Mehta says I don't have it. I'm going to be all right."

Ryder turned the alarm off. He seemed much too comfortable around the medical equipment. I doubted he'd left my side the entire time I was unconscious. That would explain why he looked so awful. Same suit he'd worn at Tymara's trial two days ago, I finally noticed.

"I'm happy for you," I told Evie, meaning every word.

She stepped back, joining Patsy, who hadn't stepped more than a foot into the room. "She insisted we come tell you straightaway," she said, as if she needed an excuse to visit her dying daughter. "That nice Italian doctor—"

"Tommaso," Evie put in, making the neurofellow sound like a dreamy movie star. Evie was only two years younger than me, already finished with husband number one and looking for a suitable replacement. The expression on her face was all too familiar.

Tommaso had better watch out.

"He was able to test her without waiting for blood results," Patsy continued. "A new test using a nasal washing. Cutting-edge."

As if my old-fashioned genetic blood test that Louise had performed was second-class. Only the best for Evie.

How sick and twisted did a family have to be that wonderful news about one daughter being healthy turned into a competition?

I wasn't playing Patsy's games. Not any longer. I'd done my penance long enough. Especially since, as it turned out, I'd committed no crime. Neither had Dad. It wasn't his fault he'd inherited fatal insomnia.

Ryder slipped his hand into mine, standing by my side, saying nothing but making it clear we stood together.

"I'm glad you're going to be okay," I repeated. I took a deep breath. Faced my mother. It was more difficult than I'd imagined. "Because I won't be around much. I have a lot to do and little time. I'm leaving."

"Leaving?" Evie frowned. "Where would you go? What about Christmas? You have to at least stay for dinner tonight."

Right. The family Christmas party. I wasn't sure if any amount of rest could give me the energy to face that.

"You must be there tonight," Patsy told me, her tone stern. "You look fine. I'll talk to the doctors, make sure they release you. After all, it's only fitting you honor Jacob's memory."

Jacob? I felt the blood rush down my body, draining away. Ryder's grip tightened, keeping me anchored. "Did he—"

"He's still alive," Evie reassured me. "But the new treatment isn't working." Her expression clouded. "They're not sure how long..."

I slumped back against the pillows. Ryder tucked me in, pulling the covers over me. Not treating me as if I was a child or weak, but rather as someone he cared about.

"You should go now," he said without looking at my family, his gaze focused on me. "She needs her rest."

Patsy hesitated. Not because she wanted to stay—that much was clear—but because she hated losing a power struggle.

At least, that's what I thought. Until, for the first time in twenty-two years, she surprised me. She stepped to the other side of my bed, ignoring Ryder's protective glare, and took my hand in hers, her fingers caressing the tape around the IV in the back of my hand.

"I'm sorry," she said, her tone tentative.

Her words stunned me. Evie stood, watching, slack-jawed.

"Whatever happens," Patsy continued, not meeting my gaze, "you always have a home here. I just want you to know that." She dropped my hand and left. Evie followed after her, throwing a quick, puzzled glance over her shoulder before she closed the door behind them.

I stared after them. What had just happened? Had my mother actually finally forgiven me? Or was it all an act? I honestly could not tell.

I blinked hard, my eyes still too dry for tears. Then I realized I had none. My family had made me who I was today, and without that strength, I'd never have been able to survive what happened last month or two nights ago, much less what was still to come.

I'd never have met Ryder. I turned to him. He still held my hand, but wasn't hovering. More like he was waiting, giving me space to decide what I needed. "Tell me about Jacob," I finally said. "All of it."

Without releasing my hand, Ryder sat on the bed beside me. "Louise said they had to decide about a DNR for him."

He'd started calling Jacob by his first name. Ryder did that with victims in his cases. The rest of the world? It depended on how seriously he took them. Hence, Jacob had been Voorsanger, while Manny Cruz was always Manny. I guessed Louise was Louise and not Mehta because she'd never let anyone call her by her last name.

"Is it the PXA?"

He nodded. "Louise tried a new treatment, something called chelation? It helped a little, but not enough. Now she's trying hemofiltration. But—"

"Jacob would never want to have his life sustained if there's no hope." I stared at our joined hands, unable to look up. His hands were so different from Jacob's. Rougher, with scars and calluses.

"That's what the ethics committee decided after they reviewed his case. He's still in the ICU getting treatment, but if it fails and his heart stops…"

I could fill in the blanks. "I guess I'd better get dressed."

"What about all this?" He gestured to the IV and monitor.

"Don't need it. I feel fine." Better than fine. The enforced rest had invigorated me. I removed the monitor leads and the IV, climbed out of bed, and headed to the bathroom. After a quick shower, I changed into clean clothing someone had brought and felt worlds better. Almost human, even.

Ryder appeared in the doorway as I combed my hair, trying to avoid the bruises from where Littleton had punched me and banged my head against the floor. The left side of my face was a gorgeous palette of green, yellow, and purple, but no permanent damage. I was lucky.

I turned to Ryder, half-tempted to ask the nurses for a razor for him, but what he really needed was sleep. Ironic that I, for once, was well rested while he was exhausted.

He took me by the waist, his palms resting on my hips. "These fugues, Louise tried to explain, but I'm not sure I understand. Tell me more about them."

I hesitated, torn between wanting to share and remembering how Louise had dismissed my fugues as delusions born of seizure activity in my brain. She was the smartest person I knew. If she couldn't find a way to believe me, would Ryder?

"No more secrets," he urged.

I exhaled, pulled back, just far enough so I could meet his gaze, watch his expression. "You've read the info about fatal insomnia—"

"What little there is available. Even the case reports Louise shared sound too bizarre for words. And each patient is so radically different."

"Welcome to my world. Each symptom seems radically different—in me." I shrugged, trying to lighten the mood. "Guess I never was one for following the rules. Not even in how I die."

A wince flitted across his features at the word. "What are these fugues like for you, then?"

"They vary. I can tell they're coming. I'll get really hot, like a fever, see colors and shimmers, hear music. Oh, Ryder, the music…I could get lost in it. It's so beautiful and terrible and awe-inspiring. It fills my soul. And then I freeze. My entire body. Can't blink, can't move. But most of the time I know everything that's going on around me. I mean everything. One of my early ones happened last month when we were down in the tunnels searching for Esme. I could see the molecules of dust as they moved past me."

He frowned at that—not condemning me, trying to understand. "Like time slows down?"

"Exactly. But all my senses are taken to the Xth degree. Smells, sights, sounds. And I can rewind time, examine it for things I missed the first time around."

"That's how you found Esme."

I nodded. He seemed to accept my newfound abilities. Devon had as well, but he really had no choice since he'd witnessed them firsthand when they saved his daughter.

"These fugues, they're painful?"

"Not the kind where time slows. Except when I come out of it. Then my body feels like centuries have passed, all cramped from not moving."

"Wait. There's another kind?"

I hesitated. This was the part that could get tricky. "Yeah. The kind where I can talk with not-quite-dead people."

CHAPTER FORTY

ONE OF THE reasons why Ryder was good at his job was his ability to see beyond appearances while maintaining a healthy skepticism. He could empathize with victim or perpetrator, see their point of view, how their lives had spiraled out of control, yet also look past the self-involved picture they painted to piece together an objective reality of a crime.

From the moment he'd met her, everything about Rossi had strained those abilities to the max. "Not-quite-dead people?"

"Thanks for not laughing. Because, yes, I know how crazy it sounds. It started last month with Sister Patrice, that first night we met."

"After she'd been shot. You cracked her chest right there in the ER, tried to get her heart started."

"I was holding her heart in my hand when I heard her voice. Telling me to 'Find the girl. Save the girl.'"

"Esme…" It had been strange how Rossi had known about her being missing, seemed to know so much more about Patrice's death than she'd had any right to.

"I didn't just hear Patrice. I saw her—I *was* her, inside her mind, reliving her memories of being shot, of sending Esme to hide in the tunnels." She stopped, giving him a chance to catch up—or walk out. Her expression turned guarded; she expected him not to believe.

Ryder wanted desperately to defy those expectations. "How does it work? Has it happened with others?"

"There's a certain type of brain wave that some dying people and people who have taken PXA exhibit. Somehow, my disease, with its altered brain chemistry, responds to people with those same brain waves. PXA seems to amplify things. Both kinds of fugues, the hypersensory one where I can slow time, and the one where I can…" She searched for words. "Where I can connect with other minds."

"When you saved my life last month, shoved me out of the path of the bullet—"

"The bullet aimed at me. You threw yourself in front of me. Because of the PXA Leo gave me and my fugue, I realized where the bullet was going before it got there and was able to push you so that you only got grazed."

"But it should have hit me full-on? Your…" Now it was his turn to stumble over his words. "Your gift, it saved me. Saved Esme. Without you and what you were able to do—" He thought about it. Did it really matter how or why she'd been able to do what she did?

No. It didn't. "It *is* a gift. Rossi, how far can this go? Could you read my mind? Like when I'm sleeping or something? What about someone like Littleton, if they take PXA, could you find the truth?" God, wouldn't that be something? How many predators could he get off the street? Wouldn't be admissible in court. Hell, he could finesse his way around that.

But, there was a greater issue. He examined her face. Despite the day of rest, her skin was virtually transparent, her eyes sunken. As if she were vanishing before his eyes, eaten from the inside out by the predator prions consuming her brain. He sucked in his breath. "It's killing you, isn't it?"

She swallowed and looked away. A little nod, something she could deny if pressed. "I don't simply communicate with them. Their entire lives, all their memories, flood into me. I'm not aware of them, not all at once—seems like the dying have a focus, maybe their last wish? But after, I still have to live with them inside me." Her voice broke. "All of them."

"How many?" He was having a hard time understanding the immensity of what she was trying to describe. It was hard enough keeping track of his own thoughts and memories; he couldn't imagine having someone else inside your mind. "You said Sister Patrice. Who else?"

"Leo Kingston. Before he died. And one of his victims."

His hands balled into fists at the thought. "That savage, insane brute is living inside your head?"

"Not his consciousness. But his memories. Sometimes, they pop to the surface. It's like looking at a movie from behind the screen, trying to figure out what's my reality and what was his."

He had no words. What could he offer her? How could he spare her that burden? All he could do was circle his arms around her and bring her to him, as close as humanly possible.

Because, despite how crazy she sounded, he believed her.

"If you want to run, now's your chance," she said as she pushed back from him.

Run? Did she really think he scared that easily? Or that he would abandon her to this Hell on earth she'd found herself in? She thought she was so tough, so self-contained, so inscrutable. Not to him. He knew her, better than she knew herself. Even if only now was she finally sharing the whole truth with him.

"Where do you go when I fall asleep?" It wasn't the next question he'd intended to ask her. Wasn't even in the top one hundred. But somehow it tumbled out before he could stop it.

She jerked, a guilty look crossing her face

"We'd make love—"

"Have sex," she corrected automatically. He said nothing, simply raised an eyebrow at her. She grimaced, looked away, looked back, then, with a reluctant half smile, said, "We'd make love. You'd fall asleep—"

"But you didn't."

"No." Her eyes went wide. "No, you don't understand. *I did.* I could. Being with you was the only sleep I've had in weeks. I'm not sure why, but somehow, when I'm with you, not only can I sleep—and you have no idea what a precious gift that is—but all my symptoms improve. I don't stumble and shake. I've never had a fugue episode when it's just me and you. Everything is just…better. Lying there in your arms, able to actually shut my mind off and sleep…" Her smile turned wicked. "It was almost as good as the sex."

"But you'd leave. I'd wake up in the middle of the night, and you weren't there. I kept expecting to find a note on your pillow. Something like, *it's been fun, don't call me, I'll call you,* type of thing. Kind of hard on a man's ego." Except this had nothing to do with his ego—and they both knew it.

"This disease, the only way I can fight it is with endorphins."

"You mean like a runner's high? Is that where you went all those nights? Out running, alone in the dark?"

She nodded. He was aghast. The risk. But that was probably part of the high as well. And what did she really have to lose? That thought was more frightening than the idea of her running alone at night. Because if you started thinking like that, you could justify almost anything.

Then she looked away and asked, "Why me?"

The question startled him. "What?"

She met his gaze once more, her expression serious. "The truth. I can't stand being the damsel in distress to your Prince Charming."

"The damsel who saved my life last month—and the lives of all those other people."

"Seriously, Ryder. I'm pretty much the definition of damaged goods. Or is that it? A relationship with me is in a warped way totally risk-free. After all, you know exactly how it will end. And it won't be your fault."

"Wow, way to put the sexy into dying."

"The truth. Why me?"

He considered his words carefully. He could not afford to make a mistake. There was too much on the line. For both of them. "After the war, hell, even during the war, I guess, I lost…something. I cared about my guys, I cared about my job and doing it the best I could, but I just didn't have enough energy to really give a shit about anything else."

She nodded her understanding, and he continued. "Women came and went, but it was only sex. They'd all complain I was emotionally numb or kept my feelings walled up or bullshit like that. I'd get into trouble at work because I just didn't care about the dumbass politics. They made me see a counselor. That didn't work. It was like there was nothing left inside me to reach. And then I met this ER doctor—" He gave her a wry smile.

She returned it. "Who was just as emotionally numb. Who walls off and compartmentalizes her feelings. So we're two of a kind?"

"God, no. Excuse me, have you met yourself? Sure, you can compartmentalize when you need to. How else could you do your job or put up with your mother? But, Rossi, you are so passionate, the way you refuse to bow to anything or anyone. Not this damn disease, not a fucking serial killer."

He cupped her chin in his palm, wanting to make certain she heard every single word. "It's like you take those emotions and harness them, set them loose in the world. In your music, in the patients you care for, in the way you make love. When you refused to tell me about your illness, sure, I was frustrated, but I realized you chose *me*. Because you knew you could trust me and I will never, ever let you down. You don't need me because you're weak or dying. You need me because together we are so much stronger than either of us alone. Together we can get through this. Can't you see that?"

She squinted at him suspiciously. "I can't stand being someone's lost cause. There won't be any fairytale ending. Not with me."

Ahhh. Now they were finally at the heart of things. He wrapped his arms around her, drawing her so close her heartbeat resonated through his chest. "Anyone ever tell you you're a control freak, Rossi?"

She gave a small chuckle. "Only every man I've ever dated."

He sobered. "You brought me back to life, all of me. That's more than most men get in this world. For however long we have." God, that sounded like something from a damned soap opera. He fumbled for new words, better words, and found nothing.

Instead, he left her side and turned to his coat hanging on the back of the chair beside her bed. He'd gone home for the gift yesterday when Louise kicked him out while she did one of her tests. He should have used the time to shower, change, eat. Instead, he'd spent it checking in with the detectives handling Littleton's case. Then he called the ME's office and stopped home to get his gift for Rossi.

It was a plain cardboard box that fit into the palm of his hand, its edges worn by years and thousands of miles.

He offered it to her, wishing he'd found time to wrap it properly. "I know you have some difficult choices to make. But, whatever you decide, I want you to know I'm with you, you have a piece of me with you…" Oh hell, that sounded like a bad breakup line, which was the opposite of what he'd intended. He wanted to rewind this entire conversation, regroup, but it was too late.

She opened the box and raised the delicate silver chain with its small, circular pendant, holding it so the light shone through the amber, making it glow and bringing the silver filigree tree embedded inside the resin to life. "This didn't come from the hospital gift shop."

"It's an antique," he answered, much more comfortable with facts than feelings. "Pashtun. They drill hot needles into the amber to form the design, then fill it with silver. A tribal chief gave it to me after we saved him and his family from an ambush. Said it represented eternity. The tree of life. That no matter what a man does in this life, there is always more yet to come in the next."

He watched as she stroked the polished gold of the amber with one finger. Shifting his weight, he suddenly remembered the first time he'd asked a girl out on a date. How was it that, so many years and women later, this felt much more terrifying?

"I love it," she finally said, pulling it over her head. "Thank you."

"Have you decided?" He was pushing it, he knew. But it wasn't as if they had much time—*she* had much time. "If you'll be sticking around? Here, I mean?"

"Am I going to go off to some gorgeous tropical island to kill myself?"

The way she said the words, so frank and matter-of-fact, made him cringe. She'd obviously been thinking about doing exactly that. "Yes."

She stroked the pendant as she pursed her lips. "I was planning to. But now…" She met his gaze. "Now, I'm not so sure."

"You don't have to go alone."

"I can't ask you to do that."

"You're not. I'm volunteering. I don't need you to protect me." She buried her head against his shoulder. He drew back, just far enough to cup her chin in his palm and tilt her face up to his. "You don't need to keep running away."

"I always came back." She paused, considering, and her smile became shy, tentative. He had the feeling she and Jacob had never had talks like this. That he was the first to see how vulnerable she really was. "I always will come back."

Her words were an offering.

He accepted her promise with a kiss.

CHAPTER FORTY-ONE

"ALL OF THEM?" Devon Price asked Louise Mehta's assistant, Tommaso. "They all tested positive? Even Esme?" *Especially* Esme.

They were in Louise's private office, a windowless room on the second floor of the hospital. Her diplomas and honors were framed, covering the walls, but he cared nothing about her pedigree or credentials. All he cared about was how reliable this test was that had just condemned twenty children.

"I'm afraid so, yes," Tommaso said in a deferential tone.

"The test is wrong. You said yourself it's experimental."

"We'll confirm with the DNA testing, of course, but—"

"Devon," Louise interrupted, moving from her chair behind the desk to join him where he stood in front of it, "the test is only experimental because there are so few patients alive to try it on. I'm afraid it's quite accurate."

"Ninety-seven-point-six percent," Tommaso put in. "For the presence of prion disease. It's virtually one hundred percent accurate if it's absent."

Louise shushed him with a glance, and he took a step back, waiting in her shadow. "Which means it's virtually certain that these children, your daughter included, have a form of prion disease. What we need to focus on is treatment and identifying the cause."

"Angela told me her disease is inherited. That can't be what Esme has." He shied away from using the words *fatal insomnia*, some buried superstition that saying it aloud would make it so. If Esme didn't have what Angela had, then maybe it wasn't fatal. Maybe there was a cure. Maybe she still had hope.

"Angie's genetic testing confirmed that her father had fatal insomnia, but her own results were indeterminate. Which may indicate a new variant, or perhaps a hereditary predisposition—"

"Meaning you don't know what the hell is going on!"

"Meaning we don't know what kind of prion disease she and the children have. There are different forms, some that cross species. Scrapie in sheep, mad cow disease, chronic wasting disease in deer— they all have occasionally affected humans as well. But it's certain that, whatever they have, it is caused by prions. Tommaso's tests prove that."

"To have an outbreak like this is unheard of," Tommaso added, sounding eager at the prospect of more lab rats for his research. Devon wheeled on him, fists bunched and ready, but the younger man dipped his head in apology. "I'm sorry. I know how frustrating this must be—"

"Frustrating?" Devon asked, his tone one that would have sent his former associates with the Russian mob running for cover. "Do not talk to me about frustrations, Dr. Lazaretto." His use of the man's title and last name were not a sign of respect. Academics. Too caught up in the research possibilities, theories and hypotheses, forgetting real lives were at risk.

Anger pounded through his mind. Damn doctors were brilliant at thinking but had no idea how to get things done. But Devon did. Eight years being a fixer for the Russians had been better training than any business school. "I don't want to hear anything except answers. How do you plan to locate the source of the infection? What treatment options do we have? How are we going to find other infected children? Who is going to coordinate their care and help their families through this? Money is no object—but we need results, and we need them fast. Is that understood?"

Both Tommaso and Louise seemed taken aback by his demands.

He whirled, heading toward the door. "I expect your proposal by morning."

"Sir, you don't—" Tommaso started.

"But, Devon," Louise said, "tomorrow is Christmas."

Devon paused at the doorway. "Think of it as a present for nineteen families and their sick children."

He left, his anger and grief propelling him down the hall with staccato steps. Thank God he'd left Esme back at the brownstone with Flynn and Ozzie. He didn't want her to see him upset like this. It would frighten her too much.

But he needed answers. Not the kind that Louise and Tommaso were working on. The kind that only one person could get him.

Angela Rossi.

He took the stairs the two flights up to her room. Since her collapse, he'd checked in with her whenever he could. Every time, he'd found Ryder at her bedside and Angela still unresponsive in that eerie sleep that wasn't sleep. Passing the nurses' station without stopping, he paused to knock at her door and pushed it open without waiting for an answer.

She and Ryder stood beside the bed, embracing. Pretty clear he'd interrupted something. Too bad. As glad as he was to see her back on her feet, he couldn't help but feel resentment that she'd escaped the day and a half of worry he'd suffered through.

"Devon," she said, catching sight of him. She separated from Ryder. Her face clouded. "The children—I'm so sorry. I planned to be there. What happened?"

"Your friend Louise and her assistant used a new test that's faster than the blood one. Nineteen children from the Tower, all positive. Make that twenty."

"Twenty?"

"Esme," he said grimly. "Flynn brought her home because she has symptoms as well." He glanced at Ryder, uncertain how much he knew about Angela's illness, decided he didn't really care. "Hope you're refreshed and ready to go, doc. Because I need your help."

First time he could remember saying those words. To anyone.

She nodded, understanding.

Ryder's phone buzzed. He glanced at the number but didn't answer.

"Any luck finding Eugene Littleton's partners?" Devon asked, beating the detective to the punch.

"Not according to the Major Case detectives. They couldn't trace the drugs used at the school, and there's nothing helpful on any of the surveillance tapes. How about that fancy lawyer you bought him? Gena Kravitz. She hasn't been available for an interview, is ducking my calls."

"Gena would tell me if she knew anything." Although, come to think of it, he hadn't spoken to her since he left Littleton in her care night before last. Funny how having a sick child changed every priority.

Ryder made a noise of disbelief. "There's something about that woman. Anyway," he waved his phone, "Littleton's caseworker from when he was young is finally able to meet with me. I'm hoping the more I can trace the people from his past, maybe I can find his partner."

"You ruled out Manny Cruz?"

"As much as we can. No suspicious bank transactions. His trial record and prosecutions seem pretty solid, but it will take time to go through all of them."

"Well, good luck with that." Devon turned back to Rossi. Despite her bruises, she looked good. Almost back to normal. "Are you checked out? I want to go over what the doctors told me, get your thoughts."

Ryder bristled at that, but Rossi calmed him with a slight shake of her head. She kissed him on the cheek. "I'm fine. Honest. I'll meet you later. Think you can handle one last family party?"

"I can do that." He grabbed his overcoat, strode past Devon. Then stopped and pivoted, staring him straight in the eye. "She doesn't leave your sight, understand? Not until you deliver her to me."

Devon gave him a fake salute. "Roger, WILCO."

Ryder paused a beat.

Devon nodded, serious. With Littleton's partners still on the loose, no way in hell was he risking Angela. "She'll be fine," he promised.

Ryder sealed the pact with a jerk of his chin and left.

Angela waited a few moments, then began to bustle around the room, gathering her few belongings. While Ryder had held vigil at her bedside, Devon had brought her a change of clothing, and her coat and phone. The bare essentials.

"Doesn't the doctor need to check you out or something?" he asked.

"I'm checking myself out," she declared as she grabbed her coat and slid her phone into her pocket. "I want to see Jacob."

"I tried to see him earlier. The nurses said he's getting some kind of dialysis treatment—"

"Hemofiltration. It slows the damage from the PXA overdose."

"Whatever. They told me it would be an hour or so before anyone could see him." He assessed her. Despite her eagerness to go, she looked pale. "What happened the other night? I saw your place."

She jerked her head up at that. The look she gave him was a curious mix of fear and hope. "Did you see Littleton? While you were in my apartment? Did you do something to him?"

Devon stepped back in surprise. "Whoa, hold on there. I was in your apartment earlier *today*. After Louise said you'd be waking up. I brought you some clothing and shit. Cleaned up the mess the cops left behind. Last I saw Eugene Littleton was when I was with you."

She frowned as if she didn't believe him. "He came to my place that night. Ryder says it was about the same time Manny was killed. Littleton attacked me, but I fought back." Her voice dropped. "Please, you can't tell anyone this…"

His face flushed with rage. "Did he…Angela, did he assault you?

Are you okay?"

"No, no, nothing like that. In fact, I'm the one who assaulted him. I tied him up and forced him to take PXA. I was hoping to get answers."

"Angela, I wasn't serious—" That was a lie. But he'd never wanted her to do anything that might jeopardize her already precarious health. "What did you see?"

"Nothing helpful. And nothing I want to talk about." Her face twisted as if she'd swallowed something rotten and decayed. He could only imagine being inside a mind like Eugene Littleton's…

"What happened?" he pressed.

"That's what's so crazy. I've never had a fugue like that. Instead of being able to communicate with Littleton or having one of my hyperaware, hypersensory fugues, this one was confused, jumbled. Like being on a hallucinogenic. I swear, Littleton died—at least, I thought he did. And I thought I'd died with him. Everything was…nothing. Gone. But then a man came in. I never saw his face. He removed the duct tape from Littleton—I couldn't see him, but I heard it—then he carried me to the couch and—"

She frowned, touched her fingers to her head, as if a new memory had been released from her fog of confusion. "I know this sounds crazy, but I swear he put a hat on me. Then he took it off and left."

It did sound crazy. But Devon was used to that with Angela. "A man? Like your uncle? Then why didn't he call an ambulance? And why take the duct tape off Littleton, make it look like he collapsed while attacking you?"

Her expression was strained. She clearly had more questions and no answers. "Not my uncle. Not anyone I know. Except, I thought it might be you. Or someone you sent, following Littleton."

"I wish. I would have taken care of that bastard myself, saved you the trouble."

"Maybe I dreamed it all, part of the fugue. Louise says FFI patients have seizures that can cause delusions and confusional episodes. Maybe it wasn't even real. I just can't be sure anymore." She shook her head in small, uncertain movements.

"I couldn't tell Ryder," she continued. "I couldn't bear it if he knew how far I really went—maybe I am crazy." She cupped her temples with both hands. "Forcing myself into someone else's mind. It's almost a form of rape. Maybe that's why it didn't work and everything went so wrong."

"No," he said sternly. "You shouldn't think that. You were trying to save lives. Don't you dare compare yourself to a monster like Littleton."

She said nothing, face tilted to the floor, hair falling around it, but finally gave a nod.

Devon glanced at the clock. They still had time before they'd be able to visit Jacob. He opened the door, gestured for her to go through. "You must be starving. C'mon, dinner's on me."

They left for the hospital cafeteria. Not Devon's first choice for fine dining, but where else was he going to go?

"I'm sorry about Esme," she said as they rode down in the elevator.

His shoulders slumped as if a weight had fallen on him, and he felt anguish tense every muscle of his body. Angela said nothing, simply wrapped her arms around him, sharing his pain, offering her comfort.

CHAPTER FORTY-TWO

THE CAFETERIA SMELLED of baked ham and roasted vegetables, reminding me of how hungry I was. Contrary to popular belief, holidays at Good Samaritan meant good eating. If you were stuck working or visiting a sick family member, the kitchen staff always went all-out to make you feel at home. I loaded up my tray while Devon only got a cup of tea. He'd forgotten to bring me my wallet and laughed when I asked if he was serious about paying. Right. Sole heir to the Kingston fortune.

"With Esme home for Christmas, are you going to decorate the brownstone? Make your butler and maids dress up like elves?" I asked as we sat at a table near the windows. The sun was starting to set, and snow was falling, making the view appear magical—if you ignored the abandoned and decaying steel mill hulking along the riverbank.

"You know damn well I don't have any butlers or maids." It was the truth. He lived in the mansion alone with his comatose father, who required round-the-clock nursing. Other than that, the only staff Devon kept was a cleaning crew who came in once a week.

He smiled. "She already made Flynn go out and drag home a tree.

Monster of a thing. Had Flynn running up and down a ladder decorating it. But no Santa or elves, that kind of shit. She's too smart to fall for any of that."

"Ten's a tough age. Too old for fairytales, too young for the truth."

"Not Esme. She's already had more than her fair share of truth." Seeing Jess and Sister Patrice murdered last month had a lot to do with that. He buried his head over his steaming tea. "What kind of world do we live in where a good kid like her survives all that, only to be facing a death sentence?"

I placed my hand on his arm. "It might not be a death sentence. Maybe it's some other form of prion disease. Something new, treatable. You can't give up hope."

He glanced up at that, his expression fierce. "I'll never give up on Esme."

"I know."

"So what the hell are we up against here? An epidemic? Some kind of zombie apocalypse?"

"No. It doesn't act as if it's airborne." Not that fear of infection had stopped him from gathering those children and their families and risking his own health. Typical Devon. "More likely another form of exposure. Maybe an environmental toxin."

I stopped, puzzled. What could the kids have been exposed to that adults hadn't? Were all the cases really isolated to the Tower, or had those just been the only ones we'd found so far?

"You've got to get to the bottom of this, doc. She's all I have."

"Stop calling me that. You know I'm not a doctor, not anymore. Louise will take good care of Esme and the others."

"I call you that to remind you of who you are, not who you were. Less than a day, you figured out what was wrong with those kids. No one else could. And you'll save them. *Doctor* Rossi."

I shook my head. "I can't. I don't have the right training or the equipment. I don't even have a job—"

"There's a hell of a lot you can do. Starting with finding out why those kids got a disease you said runs in only a handful of families and is a one in a billion odds of anyone getting." His eyes narrowed to dark slits, the whites hidden, only his irises and pupils showing. "Someone's got to be behind all this. Tell me who, and I'll take care of the rest."

Back to his conspiracy theories about his father's company. "You're thinking Kingston Enterprises?"

"Why stop at Ebola? If the sick bastards will go there, what's to stop them from something worse, something there's no cure for—at least not that we know of. Yet." The gleam in his eyes told me that Kingston Enterprises was about to get the most thorough inspection tour any CEO had ever performed.

"If it is manmade and not some crazy sporadic mutation gone wild, then they must have access to a sophisticated laboratory facility, advanced techniques in genetic engineering, the same isolation protocols you'd need to handle a Level Four pathogen."

The thought of anyone playing with prions was mind-boggling. Who in their right mind would risk *that* genie escaping the bottle? Fictional depictions of a zombie apocalypse paled in comparison to what could actually happen in a world where prions were set loose. No defense, no treatment, no cure...not just in humans, in any mammal.

Talk about a horror story.

"You think Daniel might know something about this? Maybe we should go talk to him. You said no one can lie when you're inside their head. Maybe we can finally get the truth."

"I said one of his labs could be equipped to create a prion disease and turn it into a targeted weapon. Instead of looking at who could be spreading the fatal insomnia, maybe we should look at where. When Louise and I searched the CDC database, we found other clusters of prion disease. A few people, unrelated to each other. One in a small fishing village in Okinawa. Another in an ancient walled town in Umbria, Italy. A last on an island off the coast of Ireland."

"And now here?" He frowned. "That makes no sense. Unless someone is using us as guinea pigs."

I'd long since abandoned my food. He took my tray to the trash, and we returned to the elevator. As we emerged into the lobby outside the ICU, Devon said, "That's how I would do it, testing a new disease. I'd want to see how many I had to infect—" He stopped. "Wait. What if there are people out there who are infected but don't show symptoms? Couldn't we use them to create a cure? Maybe that's why it's all kids, except for you. The adults are just, I don't know, carriers. Or maybe they're immune."

"Doesn't work that way, but you're right. We need to find out how we were infected. Were the children targeted and I was accidentally exposed? Maybe Louise's original assumption was right and my dad's fatal insomnia—the genetic kind—somehow made me more susceptible." I shook my head. "Too many questions."

He jerked his chin. "Then let's start getting answers. Because if someone created this, I'm damn sure they have a cure. I'm not losing Esme. Not again."

"After I check on Jacob."

He sobered at that.

There was a women's room across the hall from the elevator bank. I'd promised Ryder I'd stay in touch. I pulled out my cell. "I'll be right back."

Of course he saw right through me. "Tell Ryder he should feed you more often."

I fingered Ryder's amber pendant. Funny thing, I didn't mind checking in with him. It felt good, knowing there was someone who cared enough to wait for my call. Plus, I wanted to know what more he'd discovered about Littleton and his partners.

So much to do. Bring the Brotherhood—or whoever Littleton's partner or partners were—to justice before they killed again. Track the fatal insomnia patients and the origin of our disease. Find a cure—or at least a treatment.

Too many questions. But first...check in with Ryder and then see Jacob.

I paused at the restroom door and swung back to Devon. He'd loved once, loved so powerfully he'd sacrificed everything, including leaving Jess and Esme behind in order to keep them safe.

If there was no cure, and if these few weeks, months, were all I had, could I ask Ryder to suffer through that with me?

I knew Ryder's answer. He'd made that clear. Just as Jess would have risked everything to go with Devon eleven years ago.

But... "When you left Jess, was it worth it? All those years apart?"

"Yes." Devon didn't appear surprised by the question. Didn't hesitate in his answer. As if it was something he thought of constantly, weighed with each passing moment. "It kept her safe. And Esme. It's the one decision I'll never regret."

His stare was heavy with the pain that decision had cost him—never seeing the woman he loved again, missing the first decade of his daughter's life. But he bore the pain, carried it until it became a part of who he was.

Eleven years Devon had lived with his choice. I'd be lucky if I had eleven months. More likely eleven weeks.

My panic must have shown.

"He's a big boy, doc. Ryder can handle it." He glanced at the ICU entrance across the lobby from the restrooms. "I'll check on Jacob, see if we can get in to see him now. Meet you in a few."

I pushed through the door to the ladies' room, glad for some privacy. Maybe Ryder could handle what was coming, but could I?

And yet, knowing that the fatal insomnia might have been manmade had awakened a small spark of hope, one I could not ignore.

Tiny, fragile hope. Was it enough to risk Ryder's future on?

CHAPTER FORTY-THREE

INSIDE THE WOMEN'S room, I called Ryder. "Just wanted to let you know that it might be a while before I make it over to Jimmy's Place," I told him. "I'm going to sit with Jacob."

"Is he doing any better?" His voice was filled with honest concern.

"I'm not sure. They were doing a procedure, so I haven't had a chance to check on him."

"You know, and I don't mean this in a bad way, but a dying ex-husband trumps a family dinner."

"Sweet of you to try to give me an excuse to avoid my family, but they love Jacob as much as I do. Tonight will be about him, honoring him. But you don't have to go—" I held my breath. Wasn't sure I could make it through the night without him.

"Of course I'll be there. He's my friend as well." He paused, and I sensed a shift in his mood from grim to playful. "Besides, that way you'll owe me."

"Owe you?" I wasn't sure I liked the sound of that. "Owe you what?"

"We do Christmas Eve with your family, then Christmas Day with mine. Well, not the whole day," he hastened to add, no doubt sensing my hesitation. "Just dinner."

"Meet your parents?" It was something I'd avoided these past three weeks.

"And my sister and brother, assorted nieces and nephews, my grandfather, and a great-uncle."

"Do they know who I am? That I'm the reason you got shot last month?"

"That you're the doctor who saved my life last month. Dinner's at four, so you've plenty of time to chicken out."

Except how could I? He'd done so much for me, tolerated my crazy family.

"I'll sweeten the deal." His voice dropped, becoming languid and sexy. "Know what we'll be doing after dinner and two servings of my mom's world-famous chocolate bourbon pecan pie?"

"Sit on the couch in a pre-diabetic stupor, watching football?"

"Oh no. I have plans for you, young lady. Testing your knowledge of the male anatomy."

That sounded promising. "Really? Want to be more specific? Is this an oral exam or practical?"

"Both. I'm going to—" His phone beeped, cutting him off. "Damn. I have to take this. I'll see you at your uncle's. Remember, you stick with Price."

"Promise." And he was gone. Despite the trauma of the past week, I felt better than I had in ages. Other people might not understand the need to joke and banter in the midst of death and destruction, but I'd needed the light Ryder cast into the darkness surrounding me.

I washed my face, the cold water sparking against my flushed skin. That man…just the sound of his voice, much less the promise of being in his arms. Despite everything, I couldn't help my smile when I caught my reflection in the mirror. Grinning like a silly schoolgirl who'd fallen in crush. In lust, was more like it.

Maybe even … in love?

Could I dare fall in love? Now?

Ryder had already seen me at my worst. And it hadn't stopped him. I circled my fingers around his pendant, caressing the amber. It was so very old and fragile, and yet still so full of life.

Maybe how many days you had left to be in love with someone wasn't as important as what you did with the time? To love so powerfully that a death sentence became meaningless. Could Ryder and I have that?

At least I'd die trying. A hopeful sigh born more of nerves and fear than joy escaped me. Focus. There were kids dying out there, kids I could maybe help. And Jacob. I had to pull myself together before seeing him.

I straightened as the door opened. A flash of black at the mirror's edge grabbed my eye. Before I could react, the man was on me, shoving me hard against the sink, pinning my face against the mirror as he leaned his weight against me.

His gloved hand circled my neck, squeezing so hard he cut off blood flow to my brain, enough so that red spots flared in my vision. His breath was hot against my ear as he whispered, "Jacob has a message for you. If you want the cure, call us after you talk with him."

Jacob was awake? There was a cure? Joy collided with my fear, a clash of emotions careening through my brain.

The man in black tossed a cell phone onto the counter, the sound a clatter of thunder as I strained to breathe, to stay conscious. Whoever he was, one of the Brotherhood, Littleton's mysterious partners, he knew his anatomy. Could a doctor be involved in their twisted games? The thought sickened me. I kicked back, my foot hitting nothing but air. He didn't react other than to squeeze harder until the world became a haze of gray.

He released me. I collapsed forward onto the sink, hitting my chin on the porcelain bowl as I slumped to the floor.

By the time my vision cleared, the door had swung shut behind him.

A moment later, Devon came rushing in. "Are you all right? When I came out of the ICU, I saw a man leaving—"

"He was one of the men who attacked Jacob." My voice was hoarse, but my mind was clearing. Devon helped me to my feet. "He gave me this phone to call him. Think you can use it to find him?"

The phone was a prepaid cell, but in addition to his street contacts, Devon had access to technology beyond the law. He grabbed the phone. "I'm on it."

We made it to the door, and he held it open for me. I stumbled to the wall beside the elevator, leaning my weight against it, still feeling shaky. "I have to check on Jacob."

"I'll take care of these bastards. I promise you won't ever have to worry about the Brotherhood again." The glare in his eyes was more dangerous than the man who'd attacked me.

"Call Ryder," I told him. "He can help."

Devon didn't answer as he turned and ran to the stairs, leaving me at the ICU doors. I rushed inside, anxious to see Jacob awake, to learn what he had to tell me that was so vital that the Brotherhood had gone to such great lengths to learn it. Had Littleton told Jacob something covered by attorney-client privilege?

Why beat him almost to death, poison him with PXA, and now two days later, tell me to play messenger? It made no sense.

The ICU was made up of several treatment areas. One pod had six special isolation rooms designed for patients at risk for infection. The main area was an open space ringed with beds for post-op patients who needed overnight monitoring but not long-term care, and in the back was a row of cubicles with walls on three sides and a privacy curtain in front. These were for the long-term patients and ones needing an advanced level of care.

Heaven's waiting room, I'd heard a medical resident call it once. The lights were always dim, the sounds hushed, even during a code. This was where I found Jacob.

The curtain around his cubicle was open, a hemofiltration unit parked at the foot of the bed. He was still on the ventilator, couldn't breathe on his own, much less talk. But the man had said...

I stopped, my pulse beating so hard in my throat I couldn't swallow. He said Jacob had a message for me. That I needed to talk to him if I wanted the cure.

I glanced over my shoulder, certain the man was there, watching me. No one except a nurse, busy charting, and Tommaso, Louise's neurology fellow, both unlucky enough to pull the Christmas Eve shift. Neither seemed to notice I was there.

My vision wavered as I realized how wrong I'd been. This wasn't about Jacob. It never had been. This was about me. Me and my damned fatal insomnia.

How could the man in black have known? My body trembled as I stepped closer to Jacob. No. It was impossible. There was no way the Brotherhood could have any idea about my ability to talk with people in comas.

Except...The PXA they'd injected Jacob with, sealing his fate, that couldn't have been intended solely to test me, could it?

Maybe he'd meant some other kind of message? I scoured the area around Jacob's bedside, looking for anything the man could have left. Nothing. Except Jacob.

He appeared shrunken—so strange for a man who always seemed larger than life. Skin pale, hair plastered to his scalp, making his face seem cadaveric. As if he'd already left this world far behind.

I sank down into the chair beside his bed, taking care not to touch him. His brain waves danced across the monitor above him, neon glows translating every nuance of consciousness. Or lack thereof. Jacob's brain-wave pattern was filled with theta spindle bursts—a pattern exhibited by patients near death or exposed to PXA. The kind of brain waves my Swiss-cheese, prion-riddled brain could communicate with.

The Brotherhood *had* put him into this specific kind of coma on purpose. The beating was just to get my attention. It was the PXA they'd used as their *coup de grace* that was the real reason behind Jacob's attack.

They wanted me to contact him inside his coma. I extended my hand toward his but pulled it back. No. I couldn't.

Worse than trespassing, it was an invasion. Every memory, every hope and dream, every sin, every guilty thought exposed. Every secret. I couldn't do that to Jacob. He deserved more from me, so much more. It would break us both.

The man in black's words hammered at me. *If you want the cure*, he'd said.

If the Brotherhood had done this to Jacob, were they now offering a chance to save him? Turning Jacob into their proxy, a performance piece in one of their sick fantasies? I didn't understand what that would accomplish. Except, if they knew of my abilities, maybe it was me they were after. Maybe I could barter my life in exchange for the cure for Jacob.

A lot of maybes.

Could I risk it?

How could I not? I placed my hand over Jacob's and let myself fall into his black dream.

CHAPTER FORTY-FOUR

THE CHILDREN, YOUTH, and Family Services offices were deserted by the time Ryder arrived. No wonder, it was almost five o'clock on Christmas Eve. But Nancy Worth, the social worker who had handled Eugene Littleton's case years ago, had said it was the only time she could meet. That gave him just enough time to shower and change.

"Nancy Worth?" he asked the gray-haired woman he found in a cubicle, typing furiously on a laptop, the keystrokes rattling through the otherwise quiet office. She was spindly thin, all angles, no curves. Except for the smile lines bracketing her lips. She waved a hand at him as she finished typing, then looked up. He saw how she'd earned those wrinkles; her smile was deep and engaging.

"If we can put men on the moon and supercomputers into the palm of our hands, why can't we find a way to eliminate paperwork?"

He smiled back at her. "Wish I had an answer to that. I'm Matthew Ryder. We spoke on the phone."

"Yes, Detective Ryder. It's so nice to meet you." She closed her laptop with one hand and gestured him into the chair beside her with the other. "You wanted to know about Eugene Littleton."

"As I told you, we haven't been able to unseal his juvenile records yet, but I was hoping for deep background. Personal insights. Nothing that would violate any confidentiality imposed by the courts."

She considered that, then gave him a nod that reminded him of his third-grade teacher. "I think we can have a conversation within those parameters. Most of the story is public record anyway."

He settled in, prepared to listen. "What can you tell me?"

"Such a tragic family. Parents both in and out of either prison or rehab, yet somehow they managed to have three children born within three years. Because of Mom's history, we were involved almost immediately."

"You were the initial caseworker?"

"Yes. Met them in the hospital. Both parents doted on their children, seemed to truly want to do right by them, but as often happens, good intentions simply aren't enough. I removed the children for neglect several times, only to have the court return them to the home. Until Edward died."

The little brother. "He was only seven, right?"

Her sigh bore the weight of the world. "Yes. Home alone with the others. Parents had been gone for days on a meth binge, leaving the children to fend for themselves."

Ryder perked up. This was a different twist than he'd read in the case summary. "I thought the fire was begun by the father cooking meth?"

"No. Although there was plenty of evidence that he had been cooking meth in the home, and certainly all the volatile chemicals turned what may have started as a small fire into a deadly blaze."

"Then what did start the fire?"

"No one could ever prove it for certain. The consensus was that one of the children turned on the gas stove in an attempt to heat the trailer."

"You sound like you don't buy that theory."

She pursed her lips, the lines around her mouth digging deep. "This is solely my opinion, but it's one based on decades of experience. I think one of the twins started the fire. On purpose."

"Wait. Twins? Littleton has a twin brother?" That would explain so much. Brotherhood—true brothers in every sense of the word.

"No. A sister."

Ryder blinked. "That's not in the case notes I saw."

"She was a pretty little thing, blond curls, the brightest blue eyes you ever saw. Was adopted as soon as the courts allowed, her records sealed. The adoptive parents didn't want to risk her natural parents tracking her down. But poor Eugene, he was a sullen, moody child. Poor social graces. There's just not much call for eleven-year-old boys suspected of arson when it comes to adoption. He stayed in the system until he was emancipated at eighteen."

"You suspect Eugene started the fire?" He could see that. Fire-starting was classic psychopath behavior. Although, Littleton seemed more anxious than psychopaths he'd dealt with before. Narcissistic would have been his bet—a follower, dependent on others to shape his identity, not a leader.

Mrs. Worth shook her head. "Not Eugene. Although he never said a word in his defense. I'm ninety percent certain it was his sister. She's a cold-hearted psychopath—lies tripped off her tongue with the prettiest, most innocent smile you could imagine. And Eugene, he would do anything she asked, totally devoted to her. Unlike Eddie. Poor baby, he had a stubborn streak, was always fighting with his sister and always paying the price."

"You think she started the fire to kill Eddie? What could a seven-year-old boy do to deserve that?"

"Once she tried to cut his eye out with a paring knife because he'd dropped one of her dolls in the mud. That girl..." Her voice trailed off, lost in the past. "I wonder what became of her."

"I don't suppose you remember the adoptive family's name?" he asked, keeping his tone nonchalant. It was a violation of confidentiality, but not like he was going to rat her out.

She stared at him appraisingly. "You think she's back in Eugene's life? Behind these crimes he's been accused of?"

"He spoke of having a partner. A boss. And until now his record has been fairly clean. Not sure what else could have escalated things so violently."

"They came from a suburb outside Philadelphia. Kravitz. That was the family name."

He sat up, startled. "The sister, her name was Gena?" Of course it was. Eugene and Gena…twins.

"That's right. Gena, with an e."

"Thank you, Mrs. Worth. I can't tell you how helpful you've been." He popped onto his feet, energized now that he had a direction. Who would have guessed the new, flamboyant rising star of Cambria City's roster of defense attorneys was a murderous psychopath?

He stopped one cubicle row away and turned back. "Can I ask? What happened to the adoptive parents? Are they still around?"

She glanced up from her computer and gave him a sad smile. "I'm afraid not. Both killed. In a fire."

Okay. He had his man—make that, woman. Sister to their main suspect. Involved with Manny Cruz. Attorney of record for their other main victim: Sylvie Wysycki.

As he headed out the door, he wondered what poor Sylvie had done to piss off Gena enough to warrant the torture and killing of all those people at the NA meeting.

He pulled up short. Sylvie had never named her abuser when she'd been seen at the Advocacy Center for domestic violence. Rossi had said it was an attorney, though. Could her romantic partner have been Gena Kravitz? Was that why Sylvie had been targeted? Because she'd dared reject Kravitz? Just like Tymara had rejected Littleton seven months ago.

It made sense, the level of violence, even the lack of any male DNA from Tymara's sexual assault except for Littleton's. Not multiple rapists; one man who had raped Tymara multiple times. And the other injuries—Tymara's beating, the assaults with foreign objects, the stab wounds—those could have been either Littleton or Kravitz.

He'd thought these crimes too intimate to be perpetrated by some anonymous "Brotherhood." He just hadn't realized how personal they truly were.

Twin brother and sister killing together. Killing *for* each other. What could be more personal than that?

CHAPTER FORTY-FIVE

DEVON SPRINTED DOWN the stairs, hoping to catch his quarry before the man exited the hospital. He got to the ground floor just in time to see the door swing shut. More footsteps sounded from the steps below leading to the parking garage. Taking a chance, he kept going down. At the very least, he might get a license plate, which would be easier for Flynn to track than a number programmed into a prepaid cell phone.

Luck wasn't with him. He chased the footsteps down to the garage, plowing through the steel door and almost toppling over a middle-aged man who was about a hundred pounds overweight. Definitely not the slim, athletic build of the man he'd glimpsed exiting the women's room.

By the time he retraced his steps to the ground floor and main lobby, there was no sign of the man in black. Eugene Littleton's partner was more elusive than Eugene had been. No surprise, Eugene obviously wasn't the brains of the operation. He pulled his phone out, debating returning to Angela. Eugene's partner could be targeting her for revenge, blaming her for Eugene's death.

But then, why hadn't he simply killed her in the women's room? Not as flashy as Tymara's murder or the killing of the folks at the school. If Eugene's partner wanted Angela here, in the ICU at Jacob's bedside, then was he planning something bigger, even more horrific than the school massacre?

He called Flynn. "I need you to track the location of a phone number."

"Hang on," she said in a whisper. "Esme finally fell asleep." A few moments later, she was back. "Okay, I'm at the computer." Daniel had trained Flynn in the ways of industrial espionage, including illegal hacking and computer surveillance. "What's the number?"

There was only one number programmed into the disposable cell the man had given Angela. Devon repeated it for Flynn and explained about the man in black. "It might be untraceable. This is a prepaid burner cell."

"Nothing's untraceable," she muttered, the click of computer keys punctuating her words. "Just give me a sec. Is Dr. Rossi okay? Need me to come over, keep an eye on her?" He knew she was reluctant to leave Esme, but the nursing staff was there.

"Good idea. She's in the ICU with Jacob, but these guys seem to be fixated on her. Who knows what they have planned next?"

"I'll leave as soon as we're done here." A mechanical chime interrupted her. "Gotcha. They thought they could hide behind a proxy, but I found them."

"You know where the owner of this number is?"

"It's not a phone number. It's a Voice Over Internet Protocol."

"Those are untraceable."

"That's what they'd like you to believe. But the DOD contracted with a subsidiary of Kingston Enterprises to create software that can trace them. Daniel, of course, sold the government a buggy beta version that was obsolete by the time they got it installed, but I have the real thing to play with." It wasn't that Flynn was any kind of computer genius. Her genius lay elsewhere, mainly in her ability for social engineering, to mold any situation to her advantage. But Daniel had provided her with cutting-edge tech and made certain she knew how to use it.

Devon stared at the burner phone. They were probably tracking its location to keep tabs on Rossi. He tucked it under the cushion of a nearby chair. Now Rossi was free to move without their knowing.

"Got them!" Flynn came back onto the line. "Supposedly condemned building. One whose neighbor is pulling about twice the electricity it should."

"Send me the address and any info you have."

"Done. Something else popped up. Interesting deliveries—from Kingston Enterprises. Seems you've outfitted these guys with pharmaceutical and lab equipment, two state-of-the-art sensory deprivation chambers, a dozen wireless EEG transmitters—those are for measuring brain waves, right? Oh, and a shitload of PXA, the good stuff, pharmaceutical grade."

Damn. He should have thought to track shipments of PXA sooner.

"Are these guys part of Kingston Enterprises? Something Daniel set up before his stroke?" Could Eugene Littleton and his partners be connected with Daniel? He doubted it. But Daniel had his fingers in a lot of pots—not all of them legal or documented.

"Nothing I ever heard of, and I'm not finding any files on them. Just invoices billed to the Almanac Care Institute. Which, other than a dummy website and some bank accounts, doesn't seem to exist."

"Okay. Get over here. Protect Angela. I'll handle the rest."

"On my way."

Feeling better, knowing Angela was protected, Devon headed back to the stairs, taking them down to the hospital's basement where there was an entrance to the tunnel system. The address Flynn sent him was a warehouse near the wharf, conveniently located near an exit from the tunnels.

Getting into the building wouldn't be a problem. He was more worried about what he was going to find once he got there. So far the Brotherhood hadn't shied away from using brute force. What he couldn't understand was the combination of violence with what sounded like a well-organized medical research facility.

Maybe the heartless violence was meant to be a smoke screen for something even more sinister. Like exposing dozens of children to a form of fatal insomnia?

◐ 🌿 ◑

RYDER CALLED THE Major Case lead detective, a guy named Holden, to let him know about Kravitz's relationship with Littleton. "We're at her place now with a search warrant," he was surprised to hear. "Your hunch that Wysycki's lover was involved was right. It was Kravitz. How's that for a kick in the pants?"

"Is she there with you?" He had a few questions for Kravitz. Starting with, did she send her brother dearest to Rossi's place two nights ago? All in all, he'd feel better if she was off the streets and safely locked up.

"Nope, gone AWOL. We're thinking she might be good for Manny Cruz as well. She has a forty-five registered in her name—same caliber that killed him."

"It's a long shot, but now that we know she's Littleton's sister, maybe she went to his place. Want me to check it out?"

Nice thing about Holden, he'd been in this job long enough not to get territorial when a fellow detective offered a helping hand. "Not like this is how we want to be spending Christmas Eve. You see her, give a shout, and maybe we can all go home."

Easier said than done, but worth a shot. Ryder drove over to Littleton's address. Definitely the last place anyone would look for a high-powered attorney like Kravitz. He made a note to ask Devon Price how exactly he'd chosen her for Littleton's defense. Dollars to doughnuts, Kravitz had inserted herself into the case, protesting in public while she secretly worked to get her brother cleared of all charges.

Quite the pair. Brother rapes a woman, calls his twin to help clean it up. And, instead of defending him in a court of law, she covers it up with a second, brutal attack. Probably told Littleton to silence Tymara for good, and when he didn't finish the job, she punished him by letting him stew in jail until his trial. But, good sister that she was, she killed Tymara while he had the perfect alibi, then got him out in time for them both to thumb their noses at the cops while they took care of her former lover, Wysycki.

He found a parking spot. The streets were already slushy from the falling snow, but luckily, most people were snugged inside their homes for the holiday. As he trudged up the unshoveled and icy steps to Littleton's apartment building, he thought about the attack on Jacob. No way could Littleton have been involved, and he was certain Kravitz had been inside the school at the time, torturing her former lover before killing her. Plus, there'd been four men in the alley with Jacob.

Friends of Littleton? Didn't seem like he actually had any. Former clients of Kravitz, hired for the night? Didn't fit, given the degree of degradation both Tymara and Wysycki had suffered, Kravitz would want to witness Jacob's downfall firsthand.

The front door of the apartment had a gaping hole where the lock should have been, so Ryder walked on in. Littleton's place was on the third floor, and there was no elevator. He started up the steps, weapon at the ready, senses on full alert.

He was pretty certain Holden was right about Kravitz being Manny's shooter. Timing fit. Probably sent her brother after Rossi while she took care of Manny herself.

No real reason for them to go after either Rossi or Manny—except sheer spite. That and the fact Littleton had set up Manny as the leader of his fictitious Brotherhood. Which meant they had to silence Manny before the ADA could defend himself.

The attack on Rossi? He gritted his teeth at the thought of just how badly that could have gone. He had no doubt at all that Littleton would have killed her the same way Tymara had been murdered. And then he would have pinned it on the mysterious Brotherhood while his lawyer gave him an alibi.

Too bad for them, Rossi fought back. He felt a hint of pride that, despite her illness, she'd been able to get the best of Littleton.

Breathing just a bit heavy, his side aching, he reached Littleton's floor. Littleton's apartment was in the rear. He braced himself on the far side of the door, gun drawn, and listened for any movement inside. The building was old enough that the doors were solid, thick enough to provide some soundproofing. He considered. Glanced down the empty corridor behind him. It was a long shot that Kravitz would come here. After all, the police had searched the place yesterday after her brother's body had been found.

Gingerly, he twisted the knob.

To his surprise, it opened. The door swung noiselessly on its hinges as Ryder stayed to the far side of the entrance. He kept his weapon aimed, remembering the scene at Manny's apartment two nights ago.

A lamp was on, its soft glow illuminating Littleton's scantily furnished living room. Brown tweed sofa, wide-screen TV, frayed braided rug.

No signs of anyone. He stepped inside. Quickly moved through the one-bedroom apartment, clearing it of any hidden dangers. At first he thought he'd been wrong. There was no sign of Kravitz. Until he arrived at the bedroom.

The mattress had been stripped. Scattered on top of it were torn and partially burned photos. He stepped closer, turned on the bedside lamp, and examined the photos without touching them. Close-ups of Rossi playing at Jimmy's Place, fiddle tucked under her chin. Photos of Rossi and Jacob together. Photos of Rossi's entire family, including her mother and Eve. All taken at Jimmy's Place.

Kravitz had been watching Rossi for a while, several weeks at least. Trial prep, knowing she'd be Manny's star witness once they killed Tymara? Or something more?

A cold, curdling feeling grabbed at his gut. Ryder holstered his weapon and turned around. On the back of the bedroom door, scrawled in red lipstick, he found Kravitz's message to him, as if what she'd left on the bed hadn't been enough to get her point across.

You should have left us alone.

Now you'll pay.

CHAPTER FORTY-SIX

ENTERING SOMEONE'S MIND was effortless—in the literal sense of the word, as in once I touched their skin, I was totally out of control, powerless. And yet I also required all my focus and concentration to avoid being sucked into the vortex of a lifetime of memories. Every other time I'd done it—except with Littleton, but I wasn't even sure if I'd been inside his mind or if I had simply dreamed the whole horrible experience—it was painful yet heart-wrenchingly beautiful, like the way hearing a Schubert sonata played with exquisite grace could bring me to tears.

As soon as I touched Jacob's hand, my entire being was suffused with music. Paganini's *Caprice*. A difficult piece, one he'd been trying to master his entire life. The music swirled in rich colors around me, silken strands creating a dream world in which only Jacob and I existed for all of eternity.

He stood at the center of waves of jewel tones, wearing a tuxedo with the bowtie undone, hanging free, his chin bent into his violin, his entire body performing the music. More than pitch-perfect—the least important part of any composition—the notes he coaxed and set free created an emotional harmony that felt as if it would resonate into the stars and across the universe, never dying, forever inspiring.

I didn't bother trying to hold back my tears. What I'd told Devon was true. There was no deception possible here in the meeting of minds. But what would have been more accurate—and what made these intrusions more painful and frightening—was that there was no hiding. I was stripped bare, everything I was and was not, my soul exposed.

To stand like that before the man I'd loved and failed...it was maybe the most humbling and terrifying experience of my life.

He finished the Paganini and lowered his violin and bow, a contented smile sharing its radiance with me. He saw me, all of me, for the first time ever, yet did not judge. Instead, he nodded to his violin. "Play with me, Angela. We were always at our best when we made music together."

My fiddle—battered and cheap compared to the gleaming instrument he held—appeared in my hand. I stepped closer, the colors swirling around my ankles.

"Remember our wedding night?" he asked.

"The wedding no one attended?"

"My father, well, he had his own way of doing things. But your family—"

"Hypocrites." The word surprised me. I'd never dare to think it, much less speak it, in the real world. But here only truth was spoken. "As soon as they heard you play, they accepted you as one of their own."

His smile grew sad.

Unable to stop the truth from flowing, I continued, "They wanted a fiddle player who worked a job with regular hours instead of my crazy shifts." It was the truth, as blunt as it was. "But they grew to love you." Also true.

"You were saving lives," he said. "It made their own seem small and inconsequential. That's why they treat you the way they do."

"That and the fact I killed my father." It was the truth as I saw it. Or had been taught my entire life to see it. Even now, knowing Dad had fatal insomnia, it still felt true. That's how deeply my guilt was etched into my soul.

His sigh was so sad the colors shifted from ruby to indigo. "You did not." His truth. "Your mother needed someone to blame. Someone other than herself. You might be the reason why your father was out on the road that night, but she's the one who sent him. Her guilt has twisted her heart, and instead of healing what was left of your family, she's been feasting on your pain."

True, all true. But a truth I'd denied for twenty-two years. The price I'd paid to keep the only family I had left. If I walked away from them, after they'd judged me unworthy of their love, I'd risk proving them right, that I was unlovable.

"I loved you," he whispered, his violin gone. The music continued as his arms wrapped around me, embracing me in a golden warmth. "I loved you with all my heart."

"Thank you." I held back, skirting my own truth.

No matter. He saw it anyway. "You loved me. I know you did. But you always guarded your heart. Afraid I'd break what was left. Scared. The bravest woman I've ever met, yet always a frightened little girl crying in the darkness."

I swiped at my tears, not that they were real, but it gave me a reason to hide my face from him. But I couldn't hide my heart. Not here.

"You need to let her go, Angela. Set that frightened child free." His words were a murmur, a counterpoint to the tones that wrapped us in rich hues. The music was unlike any I'd heard before. It burrowed into my marrow, and I hoped I could take it with me when I left.

Except, leaving Jacob—I couldn't bear to even think it. I turned to face him, anguish flooding through me as I remembered why I was here.

"You must." His voice was strong, certain. "When you return to your life, you will set that terrified girl free, and you will go to Ryder."

Our faces were touching as he whispered in my ear, his tears sliding warm down my cheek. "He loves you and you love him. You need him. Like you never needed me."

The truth hit hard. But the music continued its soothing healing.

"He's a good man. Stronger than I ever was. You can trust him."

I couldn't answer. He spoke the truth, I know he did, but it wasn't that easy. I had to force myself to look up, meet his eyes. They were stricken with grief. He knew. Of course he knew. No lies could exist here. My entire life was stripped bare here. Not just my soul.

"I'm dying." My words were a sharp counterpoint to his rich, vibrant music. They created a dissonance, leaden gray against the pure tones he'd created.

He nodded. "The men who did this to me. They had a message for you. They knew you'd be able to talk to me. They did this to me in order to reach you. It was a test."

I stepped back, stunned. His hands fell from my body, and a chill wind scattered the colors and notes. His music died. Leaving a silence deeper and darker than the coldest winter night.

"The men who killed Tymara did this to you." Even as I spoke the words, words I'd believed were true, I knew I was wrong. So very wrong.

"No. The men who did this to me were watching you. Searching for your weakness." He paused, placing his palms on my shoulders. "They found me."

I shook my head, not wanting to believe. "No. It can't be. That's impossible."

"They called you Patient Zero. Said when you came, I should tell you. There's a cure. If you cooperate, they'll give it to you." He spoke as if reciting a foreign language.

"Then there's hope. I can still save you."

He shook his head. Not sad, more like resigned. I'd seen that same expression in the others I'd visited. Right before they died.

"No!" My scream shredded the black that had crept up, surrounding us. The void. There was no return from there. "No, damn you. Jacob, you hang on. Don't you give up on me."

He cocked his head, a strange half smile playing across his lips. "I'm not. And don't you dare blame yourself. You need to go now. You need to find out who's behind this, save those children." He bent forward, kissing my forehead. "You can do it. You're the only one who can."

The void drew closer, a noose of inky black nothingness tightening around us. We were out of time.

I clung to Jacob. "I don't want to lose you."

"You haven't. But you need to go. Now. Before it's too late."

Then I realized what he'd figured out that I'd been too distracted to notice. "Devon. He's gone after the men who did this to you."

If the man in black and his cohorts truly had a cure for the fatal insomnia affecting the children... "I have to stop him."

"Go now."

But I couldn't. Black, inky sludge roiled around my feet, trapping me in its grasp. The void was Death. Not hot, not cold, not pain, just...nothing. I looked past Jacob. The void had swallowed everything except the two of us.

"Jacob, I can't find my way back."

He frowned, then nodded as if setting a tempo. Light and warm, a rich scent of springtime grass and a sound that could have been a heavenly choir—if either of us believed in Heaven—mixed with the chime of children's laughter. All emanating from Jacob. Stabbing through the blackness, revealing a path.

"Go, and remember," he commanded, his voice stronger and more powerful than I'd ever heard it before. He shoved me away from him and onto the path of shimmering light. "Love, Angela. Fear is useless. Love is everything."

His beauty shattered into a blinding cascade of music, color, perfume as he poured all that he was into holding back the void. He became life even as he faced death.

A wind, fierce yet gentle, caught me in its grip, carrying me away from him. Jacob's light, painful to look at, it was so heart-achingly pure, flared, then died.

I was falling, plummeting out of control, blackness surrounding me, grabbing for me as I twisted and careened through the void. My hand hit cold metal.

I opened my eyes as a cacophony of alarms blared, an agony of defeat. I was awake, back in my body. How long? I wondered, blinking to clear my vision, my eyes scratchy and dry from not blinking. I touched my face, felt tears dried to salt.

It had felt as if I'd spent a lifetime in Jacob's arms. But the clock said it had been only thirty-eight minutes.

A nurse ran in and silenced the alarms as she assessed Jacob. "I know he's DNR, but—" Her question hung in the air.

I pushed to my feet, still wobbly. I hung on to the bed rail, unable to wrench my gaze away from Jacob's face. He looked peaceful. More than peaceful. Radiant.

He'd chosen death in order to give me a chance at life. So typical of him, a grand gesture, impossible for me to reciprocate.

"No," I told the nurse, my words shaky yet certain. "He's gone."

CHAPTER FORTY-SEVEN

I COULDN'T BEAR to watch the routine as they prepared Jacob's corpse. He was gone; the flesh was truly empty. I asked the nurse to call his rabbi, more for Jacob's father than for him, and I left the ICU.

Devon didn't answer his phone, so I texted him, telling him the men he was after might have the key to the fatal insomnia outbreak. If he was down in the tunnels, there was no telling if he'd get the text any time soon.

Taking the stairs like I always did, I came out in the back hall of the ER, near the ambulance bay. It was empty of people but crowded with abandoned wheelchairs and gurneys. The narrow, tiled-walled hallway amplified the noise from the ER, so I wove my way through the gauntlet and stepped outside into the ambulance bay. As soon as the doors closed behind me, a gentle silence engulfed me. Past the overhang, the snow was falling, and yet the stars were visible, giving the street beyond a strange, otherworldly glow.

I tried Devon again. Still no answer. I stood, uncertain. I had no idea where Devon was. Or Ryder. Hoping I wasn't disturbing anything, I called Ryder. It went straight to voice mail. Maybe he was on another call? I wasn't sure what message to leave, so I settled for "Could you call me when you get this? Or text me and I'll meet you at your place."

There was no way I could explain about touching Jacob's mind and the men who had used him to send me a message, not over the phone. And until I heard from Devon, I had no clue where to send Ryder to help him catch the man in black and his partners. All I knew was that they'd had nothing to do with Tymara's death and that I was too exhausted to understand what they wanted from me.

As I turned to go back inside—the ER waiting room would be as safe a place to wait as anywhere—a sudden realization hit me. My apartment might have been where I lived, but it wasn't home. And the bar below it, brimming over with music and laughter, that had always been Jacob's domain, not mine. It was the music and the man I played with that had made me feel like I belonged there. Without Jacob, what was left?

I pivoted to look in the other direction, past the ER drive toward the river. The ER's blood-red sign cast a shadow over the snow. Once, I would have called the ER and the Advocacy Center my home. It was the place I lived for, where I felt in control, had some sense of power. More than that. Pride.

No more. But there was one place where I'd felt content, whole, even…at peace.

Ryder's house. I glanced around. No one watching, no one following me. Maybe I could take a cab to Ryder's? No one would ever look for me there.

Childish glee crept over me at the thought of surprising him. A Christmas celebration—the first I'd looked forward to in decades, despite Jacob's death and everything else. No. Not despite it. Because of it.

As I zipped my parka against the wind slicing off the river, my hand brushed Ryder's pendant, resting between my breasts. A part of him, he'd said. Such a small thing to ask when all he'd really wanted was to give me so much more.

Was I selfish enough to accept his gift? Could I dare to give myself to him in return?

Yesterday I would have made excuses, said no, told myself it wasn't fair to either of us. Tonight, after being with Jacob, I felt a craving for intimacy. I wanted to open my heart, no matter the risk. I didn't know how much time I'd have. But I wanted Ryder to be the man who spent it with me.

A schoolgirl giggle escaped me as I spun around on the concrete drive, snow swirling around my feet. Maybe I was dying. No maybe about it. But weren't we all?

Why the hell had I waited so long to start living?

Newly energized, I turned, deciding I should head back inside and wait for Ryder. He'd want me to stay here where I'd be safe.

"Dr. Rossi!" A man called my name. I spun around to see Tommaso, Louise's neurofellow, sprinting toward me down the drive, clutching his lab coat around him. "Wait, Dr. Rossi!"

He grabbed my arm, leaning against me as if out of breath. "I'm so glad I caught you."

Over his shoulder I saw a large black SUV approach and slow. I didn't pay it much attention. We were just down from the exit from the hospital's parking garage. But something about the way the driver intentionally steered close to the curb disturbed me.

"Where did you come from?" I asked Tommaso, trying to break free of his grasp, one hand slipping into my pocket for my phone. "Why were you outside?"

Tommaso jabbed a pistol into my spine with his free hand. "Get in," he said, his tone low and serious. He took my phone and nudged me forward toward the SUV that had come to a stop. "Now."

The passenger-window of the SUV slid down, and the driver leaned toward us, grinning. It was the man in black. "Did you get the answers you were looking for, Dr. Rossi?"

THE CLOSEST TUNNEL exit to the abandoned warehouse that the

Almanac Care people had hijacked was across the street, along the wharf.

Devon skirted the shadows of the other empty buildings—warehouses, storage facilities, light industrial, all now condemned. The warehouse he wanted was three-stories, with a worn-brick facade and faded letters painted between tall windows boarded up with graffiti-covered plywood. There were no streetlights down here and no lights from any of the buildings to allow him to read the ghostly white letters on red brick.

But the building's name wasn't what he was interested in. It was the lack of light. He glanced at his phone and the floor plans Flynn had sent, assessing his options. A loading dock around the back, a standpipe traveling from roof to basement—that would have been Flynn's choice, he was sure. She fancied herself a cat burglar. And a side door leading to the basement utilities' service area.

He didn't like the look of the front. It was too casually abandoned, the lack of light leaking when he knew damn well there were men inside. Hell, a whole medical lab. Door number three it was.

The side door was easy to pick. Maybe too easy? There was no obvious sign of surveillance measures, but button cameras were easily concealed. Nothing he could do about it now. He sidled inside the building and listened. The basement housed what appeared to be a new HVAC system, the showroom label glowing in the light of his cell phone. The air handler roared with immense power.

Good cover. But that worked both ways. He crept through the space to the stairs. At the top was a solid metal door. Unlocked. He did not like that. Not at all. He debated calling in some of his former Royales. But they were just kids, no training. They'd be cannon fodder for men like the Brotherhood. Wait for Flynn? No, he couldn't risk leaving Rossi without protection. Okay, then. Go it alone. He'd done it before, even against the Russians. These fancy-ass Brothers were no threat compared to them. He swapped his phone for his gun before opening the door.

Beyond it was a well-lit, wide-open space punctuated by several standard office cubicles and large concrete pillars. In the corner, a flight of metal stairs went up. Beside them was an area with bunk beds, beside that a glass-walled office on the front wall of the building. But what captured his attention most were the freestanding, glass-walled rooms filled with laboratory equipment. They had airlock-like doors with hazmat space suits hanging outside each unit. Shades of *The Andromeda Strain.*

Along the wall nearest to him was a stainless-steel countertop filled with notebooks and three laptops below a wall lined with whiteboards. Interesting. He used his phone to grab video of everything in sight. Then he noticed a row of bottles lined up on a shelf on the far side. A bunch of drugs he didn't recognize, PXA—that one he knew, all too well—and something with hand-printed labels: PXA-REV.

REV? For reversal? Could this be the cure the man in black had promised Angela?

He snagged a bottle, hoping she could analyze it.

"Like what you see?" a man asked from behind Devon. But that's not what made him freeze and raise his hands in surrender.

No, it was the man who emerged from behind one of the cubicles in front of him holding a shotgun aimed right at Devon's belly.

CHAPTER FORTY-EIGHT

RYDER'S FIRST CALL was to Rossi, to warn her about Gena Kravitz. No answer. Of course not. She and Price were in the ICU visiting Jacob. He left a voice mail and sent a text. His second was to the Major Case detective, Holden, letting him know about the potential threat to Rossi's family and the evidence at Littleton's apartment.

"No sign of Kravitz," he finished as he ran down the steps to his car. "I'm headed to the bar Rossi's family owns now."

"We'll meet you there. Let me get some backup rolling as well as a CSU team over to Littleton's," Holden replied. "Damn, nights like this, wish we had as many spare bodies as all those cop shows on TV. They never have to be in three places at once."

"Yeah, but we get all the glamour and glory, right?" Ryder hung up, tried Rossi again—still no answer—and headed over to Jimmy's Place. The bar wasn't far, only eight blocks, but the snow was falling more heavily and the plows hadn't been out yet—of course not, snowplow drivers got triple time for holidays, and at the end of the year like this, the city's budget was already strained to breaking.

As he grew closer to the bar, he realized there was no hope of parking within a two-block radius. Every spot illegal, legal, or not even a real parking space was filled. When he drove past the building, he saw why—it was packed full, even more so than on football Sundays or nights when Rossi's band played. The holiday wreath had been replaced with one with a black ribbon, and a banner by the door announced a tribute to Jacob Voorsanger: *One of Our Own and Beloved.*

He steered around the block and double-parked the Taurus in front of a loading dock. Then he cut through the alley to get to the bar. If Kravitz wanted revenge on Rossi for her brother's death, tonight was the night. Talk about your target-rich environment. It could be a spectacle that would be talked about for decades. Women, children, entire families at risk.

He sped up to a jog. How would she do it? Not poison again, too unpredictable with a crowd this size. Pull an active-shooter scenario? No. Jacob had plenty of friends who were cops, which meant there would definitely be armed men and women inside the bar, ready to foil her plan.

He reached the back of the bar. The rear door was blocked by the dumpster. Instincts on alert, he pulled his weapon as he searched the darkness for any sign of Kravitz. She wasn't lurking back here. He pushed his weight against the dumpster. Could barely shift it more than a few inches, it was so full. But enough to see the thick chain and padlock on the rear exit.

Fire. Of course. Her comfort zone.

He grabbed his phone as he sprinted down the alley and around to the front of the bar. "Dispatch, this is Detective Matthew Ryder. I'm at Jimmy's Place on Broad and need backup as well as EMS and fire. I have a suspected arson in progress, and the place is jam-packed with civilians."

"I'll clear a channel," she replied.

"Coordinate with Detective Holden. The suspected arsonist is also the suspect in his homicide case, Gena Kravitz. Put out a general alert to be on the lookout for her. Send that to off-duty police as well. I think there are officers present in the establishment at risk. I'm going in to evacuate the building."

"Copy that."

He hung up the phone to free his hands. A few people congregated on the sidewalk in front of the bar, glasses of beer in their hands.

"Gas leak. You all need to clear out," he told them, showing them his shield. "Any of you see a tall blonde, tons of curly blond hair?"

They shook their heads, too drunk to comment on the illogic of his requests, and meandered away. He glanced around. The front door stood open, music and laughter pouring out. No signs of any incendiary devices on the outside. Kravitz must be inside, he decided, leaving this exit for her escape. Good, that meant he still had time.

He shoved his way in, sucking in his breath to edge through the throng. The band was playing, Jacob's violin perched on an empty barstool in the place of honor at center stage, looking forlorn.

Damn, he'd never find Kravitz in this crowd. He pushed through to the bar where Jimmy and his sons were racing to keep up with demand.

"Jimmy!" he shouted.

The barkeep waved a hand in the universal *Wait, I'm busy* gesture.

Ryder didn't wait. Instead, he grabbed Jimmy's arm and hauled him closer. "I tracked an arsonist here. Sister of the man who died in Rossi's apartment. She wants revenge. You need to clear the entire place."

Jimmy frowned, Ryder's words slowly sinking in. "But it's Jacob's tribute," he protested.

"All the better. She wants Rossi to suffer. What better way than to kill everyone she loves? I don't have time to argue. Just pull the fire alarm and clear the damn bar. Now!"

The barkeep nodded. He turned to the wall behind him where a fire alarm was situated above the light switch. Pulled it.

Nothing. Shit. They were going to have to do this the hard way. "Start getting people out," Ryder said. "I'm going to try to find her."

Most arsons he'd seen had started in the lower level of a building and burned up. All the liquor and other flammables Jimmy stored would make for a helluva fire starter. "What's the fastest way to your basement?"

Jimmy pointed to the door to the private staircase leading up to Rossi's apartment. "End of the hall," he shouted.

Ryder shoved back through the crowd and made it to the basement staircase behind the one leading up to the second floor. Still no sign of Kravitz. He drew his pistol and opened the door. The basement lights were on. He looked down the steps. They were old with no risers, leaving no concealment from anyone below. Okay, if he couldn't have stealth on his side, maybe speed and surprise would work. He sprinted down, planting himself at the bottom with his back to the outside wall.

Gena Kravitz smiled at him from where she perched on a stack of whiskey cases, legs crossed as if she were a torch singer sitting on top of a piano. She blew him a kiss. In her hand she held a remote car starter. Perfect trigger for an incendiary device.

Like the propane bottles wired together and ringing the base of the oil furnace.

"Welcome to the party, Detective Ryder," she crooned. Her eyes were so wild the whites shown all around, and her hair stood on end as if she were channeling electricity. "I was just about to open my Christmas present. Or should I say Dr. Rossi's Christmas present? This is going to be a holiday she'll never forget."

CHAPTER FORTY-NINE

TOMMASO SHOVED ME into the back of the SUV, then joined me. The driver pulled away from the curb with a squeal, jostling me against Tommaso. In the enclosed space of the SUV, I smelled a scent that was strangely familiar: the same mix of evergreen and citrus I'd smelled during my fugue when the man carried me away from Littleton's body.

"It was you. You were in my apartment."

Tommaso nodded. "We've been taking turns watching you."

"We?"

"All in good time. You should be thanking me, cleaning up your amateurish attempts to use the gift we gave you."

Amateurish? Gift? As if there was precedent for what I'd done, trying to invade Littleton's mind? Then I remembered the weird sensation of something on my head. A cap. No... "You used a wireless EEG monitor."

"Of course. Easiest way to see if you were able to achieve a complete bond. If we'd known sooner, we could have saved poor Jacob quite a lot of pain."

We stopped in front of a hulking brick warehouse that stood dark against the falling snow. Tommaso got out and gestured with his gun for me to follow. I smelled the river. We were near the wharf. The wind cut through the narrow street as Tommaso and the man in black escorted me to a boarded-up entrance plastered with Condemned stickers.

As they moved the plywood aside on concealed hinges, I glanced over my shoulder and noticed another car slide to a stop up the street. Lights off, it blended totally into the night. Devon? I hoped.

They shoved me through a solid metal door, the plywood swinging back into place to hide it. There was a heavy click of a lock, but I knew that wouldn't slow Devon down much.

We were inside a glass-walled room. Security monitors and computers lined two walls. Some kind of control room? No one sat at the monitors, making me wonder if their manpower was stretched thin. If so, maybe I could use that to my advantage.

The entire first floor of the warehouse sprawled before me through a second glass door and the office's windows. I was surprised by the bright lighting. Windows that appeared covered only by plywood on the outside were completely sealed on the inside with some kind of metallic foil. To prevent both light and heat from escaping? Altering the building's thermal image, maybe?

The floor space was immaculate, the concrete floor freshly painted. There were several self-enclosed glass cubicles with airlocks at their entrances. Inside them I saw laboratory equipment. On the outside were biohazard suits.

"That's at least a Level Three biocontainment lab," I said in wonder. "What the hell are you people working on?"

Tommaso grinned. "One guess."

I whirled on him. "Prions? Are you crazy? Do you have any idea how dangerous—" I broke off. Of course they did. They were the ones who'd unleashed the fatal insomnia here in Cambria City. They'd infected all those children and who knew how many more. "What have you done? What do you want?"

"You'll see. All in good time." Tommaso nodded to the man in black, who entered a code on a keypad beside the inner door. It opened, and we entered the main floor. My ears popped with the vibration of air scrubbers. I glanced overhead. There was a sprinkler system with newer pipes extending to the biohazard labs as well as extra ventilation ducts, obviously also recently installed.

Despite the large area, I didn't see anyone else. Until they steered me around to the other side of the control room, to an area with two bunk beds and a makeshift kitchen. Leaning against a concrete support pillar in the center of the area, two men with guns flanking him, was Devon.

"Hey, doc," he said jauntily, despite the fact one eye was swollen shut and his lip was split. "Welcome to the party."

One of his guards elbowed him in the belly, hard enough to double him over, gasping.

"Stop it," I cried, flashing back to the scene of Jacob in the alley. "Tell me what you want from us."

"From you," Tommaso corrected. "First, tell me what Jacob said."

"How did you know he'd be able to talk to me?"

"What did Jacob tell you?" Tommaso repeated, his tone totally normal, making his request all the more macabre.

I focused on him, trying to search out any humanity. "Jacob said you targeted him because of me. Said he was my weakness, my vulnerable spot."

Tommaso nodded but appeared unconvinced. "Exact words. He had a message for you, yes? A name he shared with you?"

I inhaled, closed my eyes for a moment, Jacob's voice echoing in my head. "Patient Zero. He said you called me Patient Zero."

In epidemiology, Patient Zero was the first patient to show signs of a disease during an epidemic. If that was me, then…"Is this some kind of terrorist plot? To create an epidemic of fatal insomnia?"

Tommaso chuckled, as did the man in black. I turned to face the other two men, the ones guarding Devon. They were also smiling, as if my words were funny.

Before I could ask anything more, two shots sounded from above us, followed in rapid succession by two more. The men on either side of Devon fell to the ground. He sprang up, grabbing the gun from the man closest to him, and firing at the man in black beside me. But Devon's shot missed because the man in black was already running for cover and firing back at the person overhead. I glanced up. It was Flynn, leaning over the staircase railing.

Tommaso raised his gun, taking aim at Devon, but I shoved him, hard, and his shot went wide. Devon scrambled for cover behind the concrete column. Tommaso grabbed me, pulling me tight against his body as a shield, backing us up against the wall of the control room.

"Anyone makes a move, she dies," he shouted.

Flynn had already vanished from sight, and Devon was hidden behind the support beam. Tommaso kept us moving, back to the electronically controlled door, his gun jabbed into my neck.

He keyed the code into the door his movements too fast for me to see which numbers he hit, and then we were behind it, inside the control room. He released me. I ran to the exterior door, the solid metal one, and tugged at it. No luck. It was also electronically controlled.

He ignored me to work at the computers, typing with one hand while pointing his gun at me with the other. I watched as the man in black skulked behind a lab bench filled with equipment and sneaked up behind Devon. I shouted a warning as he raised his gun, but my words echoed against the glass walls.

"Soundproof," Tommaso informed me without stopping his frantic typing.

No matter. Flynn sidled from the shadows and took out the man with a shot to the back of the head. She ran to Devon, helped him to his feet. Blood covered most of his face. I was surprised he'd been able to aim at all.

Only Tommaso remained. I stepped toward him. He was quick to gesture with his gun in warning.

"What are you doing?" I asked as he returned to the computer. It was obvious I wouldn't be getting out without him unlocking the doors. Which meant I couldn't tackle him until then.

"Following protocol. No one can know what we were doing here. It's a shame to lose such a productive facility, but," he threw a smile at me that lacked any humanity, as if I was a prized possession, "I have what we came for."

"Who's we?" I repeated, trying to distract him as I moved closer. Over his shoulder, I saw that he was starting some kind of program. Something to do with the fire sprinklers, it appeared from the schematics.

"Who are we? I guess you could call us your new family." For some reason, the thought made him smile even wider. He turned to me, gesturing with the pistol. "It's done."

"What? What's done?" Past him, through the window, I saw Flynn and Devon on the move. They weren't coming to the control room. Obviously, they realized that Tommaso controlled the locks. Instead, they were headed toward the staircase Flynn had come down.

"A software virus to purge all of our data. And," his gaze moved to stare out at the containment labs, which were filling with smoke, "caustic soda to purge the rest."

Caustic soda. Also known as sodium hydroxide. Lye. The only chemical shown to eradicate prions. Which meant these people *didn't* want to cause an epidemic. What *did* they want?

I didn't have time to ask. To my horror, the sprinklers outside the containment labs began to spray a cloudy fluid. A fluid that when it hit any surface produced a corrosive smoke. He was flooding the entire floor space with lye.

"No," I yelled, lunging toward the computer.

He yanked me back, the gun pressed to my side again. "Too late, Dr. Rossi. Time to go."

The area beyond the control room window was filling with yellow-gray smoke, billowing as the ventilation system carried the lye throughout the space. I'd lost sight of Flynn and Devon. Had they made it? Or were they choking to death inside the caustic alkaline cloud, their skin and throats and eyes and airways literally melting?

CHAPTER FIFTY

"DROP THE REMOTE, Gena," Ryder told her. The music from upstairs had stopped. Jimmy taking care of business. But with only one exit, it would take time to evacuate everyone. "There's no way out."

Kravitz was no dummy. She glanced up, her expression a strange cross between dreamy apathy and bitter anger. "There was supposed to be. Before you showed up. Of course, everything was going just fine until your friend Rossi decided to meddle. Convince Tymara to talk to the cops, testify."

She held the remote up as if she was going to kiss it, her thumb poised over the buttons. "Guess she'll think twice about doing that again."

"Just tell me why," Ryder said, hoping to play to her innate narcissism. "You're a legal rock star. You could have gotten Eugene off after he raped Tymara. Why torture and leave her for dead? Why kill all those people at the school?"

The look she gave him was pitying. "Have you ever been in love, detective? If you ever had, you'd know. You never abandon the one you love. Anyone who does deserves their own special Hell. I just made certain they got it, that's all."

Ryder didn't have an answer to that. Other than it was clear Kravitz recognized no boundaries and had an unquenchable hunger for drama. Which made her particularly dangerous.

She raised her eyebrows in a seductive pout that made him want to vomit. "What do you say, lover boy? We can walk out of here together if you give me that gun of yours."

He considered stalling, giving Jimmy more time to clear the civilians and time for backup to arrive. But no way in hell was someone as sick and twisted as Kravitz going to fall for stall tactics. And no way in hell was he going to let her walk out of here with that remote.

"Well, Gena," he drawled, leaching all the adrenaline from his voice even as he shifted his weight and braced his elbows. "I'd love to take you—"

Two shots to the head, one to the chest as she rolled off her perch. The remote skittered across the floor. Ryder approached her, still aiming for a kill shot.

Too late for that. Mission accomplished.

𝔇 ⚜ ℭ

ALL I COULD think about as Tommaso dragged me out of the building and toward the SUV was Flynn and Devon. If they'd found shelter or made it up to the second floor, they might last a few minutes at most. But given the powerful ventilation system, the gas would find them, sooner rather than later.

We reached the SUV. Tommaso stopped, car keys in the hand wrapped around my body, pistol in the other. He clearly was used to his men performing thuggish jobs like kidnapping, because he seemed confused about how to proceed.

Not me. I knew exactly what to do.

In a move I'd practiced hundreds of times during the self-defense courses the Advocacy Center hosted, I dropped my weight onto his right forearm, the one with the gun, propelling it away from me as I grabbed his wrist. Using my momentum as I spun free from his grip, I twisted his hand up and in while also stepping behind him, his arm now angled in the direction opposite of what nature intended.

He squealed, falling to his knees. The pistol clattered to the pavement. I kept pushing, adrenaline fueling my movement, and felt the delicate tendons of his wrist pop. His hand flopped, useless, as he screamed again.

The whole thing happened in a blur, much faster than I'd ever practiced. I was huffing, my pulse racing, exhilarated—and a tiny bit surprised that it had worked. I reached for the gun and the car keys. Then I opened the rear door. A mesh grating separated the cargo area from the passenger seats, perfect for my needs. "Get in."

He obeyed, and I leapt into the driver's seat, fastened my seat belt, and prayed for decent air bags as I rammed the SUV into drive and floored the accelerator. I aimed for the solid brick wall away from the reinforced entrance.

Old building, soft brick, weak mortar...it should work, I told myself. But I couldn't help but close my eyes as the SUV crashed.

The sound was deafening and the recoil jolted through my entire body, but I kept my foot on the gas until we were through. The SUV skidded through the bunk beds, the air bag snapping my head back. Thunder sounded, and the SUV shook violently. I pushed the deflated air bag out of my way and hit the brakes. The SUV continued sliding across the concrete floor, a wave of collapsing bricks falling behind us.

The lye shower had ended, but smoke remained, dangerous in its own right. I turned on the SUV's headlights, realized the futility of finding Flynn and Devon in the haze. Best I could do was provide them with a clear path free from the building. The SUV responded, although sluggish. At least one tire had blown. I steered the truck to the staircase on the far side of the bunk beds, where I'd last seen Flynn and Devon. Two figures appeared through the smoke, looking more like alien astronauts than humans. Of course, the biohazard suits!

They opened the doors and jumped into the backseat, closing them before the fumes could contaminate the inside of the SUV. I gunned the engine again and steered the SUV through the rabble around the opening I'd come in through. The broken bricks had formed a small mountain at the base of the opening, more falling sporadically from above, but the SUV gamely maneuvered over it.

A minute later, we were back outside in the snow. Devon and Flynn climbed out and shucked their suits, but I sat in the driver's seat, trembling. The windshield was starred and chipped, the snow fell heavily enough to make the world outside appear as if I was trapped inside a snow globe.

Flynn opened the driver's door. "Nice timing," she said with a grin. The only time I'd ever seen Flynn smile was when either she'd just killed someone or someone was trying to kill her. The thought made me laugh. I choked it back, forcing my body to obey my commands to climb free of the SUV.

Devon held a gun on Tommaso, but it was hard to say which of them was more banged up. Tommaso cradled his right hand in his left, wincing in pain. Devon's face had blood smeared all over it, but his teeth flashed white in the night as he raised the pistol. "Let's go," he ordered. "Time for answers."

CHAPTER FIFTY-ONE

FLYNN TOOK CHARGE of Tommaso and led the way through the tunnels as I helped Devon. I hated being back inside the tunnel complex, but it was the safest place. Plus, it would give us privacy while we figured out what to do with Tommaso.

"Tommaso destroyed their computers. If he doesn't talk, we'll never know who they were or what they were up to," I told Devon as we trudged through the maze. At least this time there was light. Last time I was down here, it had been in total darkness. "What did you see?"

"I saw enough to piece together some of the puzzle. Obviously, they're behind the fatal insomnia outbreak. But who are they? And what do they have to gain from a group of children dying? From what I overheard, I'm not sure they have a cure for it. In fact, they sounded a bit desperate. To find you."

Me? I had no cure or answers. "So the cure the man told me about isn't for fatal insomnia?"

"No. Probably to reverse PXA overdoses. There was a ton of PXA there. I think it was part of their research, maybe a treatment like

Louise said?"

I was silent, thinking of Jacob. Could I have saved him if I'd called the man in black instead of letting Devon chase after them?

He followed my thoughts effortlessly. "Those guys never would have given you the PXA reversal agent in time to save Jacob. You know that."

I was silent for a long moment. I did know that. Wasn't sure if knowing could ever be the same as believing. "We should still try to find it. It could help others."

"Don't worry, I grabbed a dose. Hope it's enough for you to analyze."

Flynn was a good twenty feet ahead of us. We'd reached the area beneath Good Sam—at least, I thought we had. I didn't recognize the anonymous metal doors painted an ominous shade of red.

"Where to?" Flynn asked Devon, gesturing with the gun she aimed at Tommaso. He didn't make eye contact with us, appeared to have totally surrendered. But Flynn obviously wasn't taking anything for granted.

"Room D-22," Devon answered. Flynn nodded and disappeared around a corner. "Wait here," he told me. "I'll be right back." He followed more slowly behind Flynn.

I slumped against the concrete wall, barely able to stay on my feet. If Tommaso and his people were willing to beat Jacob nearly to death, to go to that extreme merely to test how far my fatal insomnia abilities extended, what would they do in revenge for me destroying their lab?

Who would they target next? My family? Ryder?

I shook my head. No. No one else was going to die because of me.

"We're ready." Devon beckoned me down the hall to the room where he and Flynn had taken Tommaso. "Just follow my lead."

He swung the heavy door open. Inside was a dental clinic. Most of the equipment dated back to when the tunnels had been built as a fallout shelter during the Cold War, but it was all clean, shining under the bright exam light that glared on the man strapped into the chair.

Wide leather restraints encircled Tommaso's chest, ankles, wrists, and forehead. Flynn stood behind him, watching and waiting, gun still in her hand.

Devon strode in, an aura of command surrounding him, making his injuries seem trivial. He looked at me over his shoulder as I followed him in. "There's only one way to get him to talk. I need your help to do it."

I glanced up, confused. Me? The leather straps restraining Tommaso creaked as he strained against them. Devon lifted a towel from an instrument tray. On it was a glass bottle and a syringe. He used the syringe to draw clear fluid from the bottle.

I marveled at the fact that he'd had this ready, waiting. Doubt clouded me as I wondered why Devon would be ready to host a prisoner and interrogate him. I opened my mouth to protest, but one look at the expression chiseled into Devon's face stopped me.

Esme.

He was doing this for her. He'd do anything for her—even kill a man in cold blood.

How far would I go to save her and the other children?

"You know what we call PXA on the street?" Devon asked Tommaso as he casually tapped air bubbles from the syringe. "Death Head."

Tommaso appeared frightened for the first time as he fought the thick leather restraints that held him in place. "No. Please. I have a family."

Devon sat down on the dentist's stool, wheeled it so he was in the man's field of vision, right beside him. "So do I. Her name is Esme. She's ten years old. And you're going to tell me how to cure her."

He was bluffing. I hoped. The light sparked against the shiny metal syringe.

"I don't know anything." Tommaso's words were laced with acid bitterness.

"I think you know a lot. Like which drug will save you from an overdose of PXA. Like what a drug like PXA has to do with fatal insomnia. Like who is behind all this." Devon lowered the syringe until the tip of the needle pressed against a vein in Tommaso's arm that bulged even without a tourniquet as he strained to escape. "Like how we save our children."

"No. Please. Don't." Tommaso's voice rose and broke.

Devon pierced his skin with the needle, his finger hovering over the syringe's plunger. "Tell me what you did to my daughter. Tell me how to cure her and the others."

Tommaso's eyes went wide with fear. It wasn't Devon or the syringe that he focused his gaze on, but me. "You're a doctor. You can't let him do this. You have to stop him. Please."

He was right. But oh so wrong. I'd already killed. And now I was also trying to save twenty children from the horrendous death I faced. Twenty children facing that danger because of Tommaso and his partners.

Decision made, I straightened my spine as I stared down at Tommaso. "I'm not a doctor. Not anymore. Tell him what he wants to know and this is all over."

His panicked expression softened at my words. He appeared calm, almost serene. "I can't."

"Then I'm sorry." I'd barely said the words when Devon thrust the plunger down, injecting the man.

His gaze remained locked on me. "You look so much like him."

I stepped toward him, confused. "Who?"

"Your father."

There was no way Tommaso had known my father. He would have been a child when Dad died. "Tell me what you mean," I urged. "Give us what we want, and we'll treat you with the reversal agent. Now, before the drug takes effect."

"Too late." His tone was one of regret.

He arched up, his entire body straining. The restraints gave off the creaking noise of leather being stressed to its limits, but they held. Devon pushed away with the stool and stood.

"It's barely even begun to take effect," Devon said as the man writhed below him. "Tell me, how do we cure the fatal insomnia? Save

326

my daughter. You know you can. Save all those other kids. Be a hero." His voice was hypnotic, compelling.

Devon pulled a vial from his pocket, held it up for Tommaso to see. "I stole some of your reversal agent. Tell me what I need to know and this all stops." He paused. "If you don't, then Dr. Rossi is going to take the information from you. You know she can."

Tommaso closed his eyes, jaws clenched tight, fighting the drug and the restraints. The sight made me sick, my stomach revolting at the idea that I was part of this...torture. The only word to describe it, no matter how good our intentions.

Suddenly, he began choking. His lips parted, releasing a gush of blood.

"What the hell?" Devon grabbed the man's head, forcing his jaws apart.

I rushed forward, reaching for the instrument tray. The blood was burbling like a stream, spraying us both, covering Tommaso's chest. Worse was the blood filling his airways, choking him to death.

"He bit off his tongue. Damn it. I need to clamp off the vessels." A plume of arterial blood hit me in the eye as I strained to find the blood vessels in the pool of red. I clutched at the dental suction catheter, but the vacuum wasn't engaged, so it was useless.

Tommaso stopped struggling. His eyes fluttered open, fixed on me. Fear filled them. I wasn't touching him directly, so I had no idea what he was thinking in that last second, but I do know the last thing he saw was my face.

And then he was gone. Even if we'd been in my ER instead down here in the tunnels, I probably couldn't have saved him. But still I tried. I turned the vacuum suction on high, jammed the catheter down his trachea, trying to clear it of blood. I rammed clamps into his mouth, blindly grasping at any piece of tissue that could have been a blood vessel. I did everything I could, but it was all useless.

Finally, Devon pulled me away from the man's lifeless body. I whirled on him, both of us covered in blood. "What did you do? He was our last chance!"

Flynn stepped between us, separating us. "Dr. Rossi. He didn't do anything."

I frowned, shaking my head, not understanding.

"I didn't give him any PXA," Devon explained. "It was sterile water. I couldn't risk accidentally killing him. But I figured since his people knew PXA overdoses opened a person's mind to your gifts, then all I needed was you here and the threat of the PXA."

Flynn threw a towel over Tommaso's body. "Why didn't he tell us what we want to know? Rather than go through the hell of both a PXA overdose and having a stranger invade your mind and steal your memories?"

"You used me," I accused Devon. I hated it. It was logical and perverse and was something his father or half-brother would have done.

"To save Esme, damn right I did. But I didn't kill him."

I stared down at the corpse strapped to the chair. "He bit his tongue off. He killed himself rather than expose his secrets."

"Rather than have you inside his head," Devon said. "Which means this is a lot bigger than we thought. To instill that kind of loyalty in a foot soldier—"

"Foot soldier?" The term seemed odd. Especially for someone dedicated enough to attend medical school, go through years of rigorous post-grad training. For what? To throw away his gift of healing to keep a secret that endangered dozens of children?

Who the hell were these people? What did they want? And what did my father have to do with them?

"He was just a soldier. Disposable." Devon turned to me, his face tightened into a determined mask. "Angela, don't you get it? Things are only going to get worse. We're at war. And we have no earthly idea who the enemy is or what they want."

CHAPTER FIFTY-TWO

RYDER UNLOCKED THE back door of his house and grabbed his brimming bags. "I'm home," he called out in a jovial tone, feeling like Santa Claus. He'd texted Rossi while he was wrapping things up at the station, told her the danger was over, that he'd meet her here.

"The guy who owns the health store owes me one. I got him to open up." He plopped the bags onto the counter and began unpacking them. "I've got you the best tryptophan and melatonin they make, plus organic protein powder, high-dose stress vitamins, this great berry called acai—turns everything purple but tastes good, so no more yucky green-seaweed-grass shakes. They even had vegan doggy biscuits for when Ozzie visits."

That's when it hit him. The house was silent.

Not the sleeping in on Christmas Day kind of silent. The empty, nobody lives here kind of silence.

No Ozzie racing across the hardwood floors, his claws making that funny clacking noise.

No Rossi.

He abandoned the bags and prowled through his house as if it belonged to a stranger. Finally reached the bedroom. She'd left her note on his pillow. Had she even seen the irony in that?

Ryder. We both know I suck at good-byes, but I promised you I wouldn't go without one. So here it is.

Don't try to find me. It'd break my heart—there's no way in hell I could ever give up the fight if there was any hope of salvaging one more moment with you.

Either way we both lose.

I don't regret a single moment, only that I can't give you more. But I warned you, this story can't ever have a happy ending.

Take care of yourself, stay safe, don't give up the fight—there are too many innocents who need a soldier like you keeping watch over them.

Love,

Rossi

He crumpled the paper in his fist. Sank onto the bed and ran the palm of his free hand over his face. What had she done? Where had she gone?

Was she even still alive? Was this a goodbye or a suicide note?

He smoothed the paper over his knee and read it again. And again. Until tears blurred his vision, and all he could see was her face, head thrown back, hair flying loose, fiddle tucked under her chin, her entire being suffused with joy.

The moment he had first fallen in love with her.

He set the note back on his pillow, then moved it across the bed to her side. He stood, shrugging off the heavy feeling that weighed on his shoulders like a corpse's shroud.

He prowled through the room, searching for anything she'd left behind. Nothing. Except the spare toothbrush leaning up against his on the bathroom sink. He ended up at his dresser, hoping to find a hair clip, a comb, anything valuable enough that she'd return for. Nothing.

He looked in the mirror, saw a haggard man who'd clocked too many miles and witnessed too much heartache. Nothing there, either.

Fury and frustration blossomed, billowing through his chest with each breath, racing through his veins until he could no longer contain it. He swept his arm across the dresser, sending the random detritus of his life flying to the floor, the crash of breaking glass the only sound except for his ragged breathing.

Turning back to the bed, he stared down at the note, the blue ink scrawled across white paper going in and out of focus like an abstract painting.

The morning light danced through the curtains, reminding him of a child's delight, opening presents on Christmas morning, crystalizing every pen stroke into clarity. And he realized what she hadn't left behind.

She'd left the note, but kept his pendant. That had to mean something.

She'd made her choice, and he respected that.

But it didn't mean he was going to let her go alone into the dark. Not without a fight. Definitely not without hope.

This wasn't over. They weren't over. Their story had just begun…

𝔇 ✹ ℭ

IT WAS THE hardest note I'd ever written. Even harder was waiting for Flynn to return after delivering it.

Devon and I were huddled in what appeared to be a classroom inside the underground bunker, my new home for the time being. A map of the city, including the tunnels, was spread out on the desk between us.

"I've got good news and bad." Flynn's voice startled both of us.

Devon hid it well, barely a flinch as he raised his head casually, as if he'd known she was in the room before she spoke.

Me, not so casual. After everything that had happened tonight and not having taken my meds in hours, my nerves were so brittle they felt as if they'd shatter at a high-pitched mouse squeak. I whirled and jumped, fists raised.

Flynn merely grinned. She tossed a backpack—mine—to the floor, followed it by skidding a bag of my meds across the desk to me. Then, gently, she set down my violin case.

"No one's left watching your place," she said, "except cops. There was some kind of bomb scare or something. Your family's safe. Your uncle got your message, said he'd take care of getting your mom and sister out of town."

I slumped in relief, leaning my weight on my palms braced against the desktop. It took all my strength to ask, "And Ryder?"

"Left your note. No one is watching him, not yet anyway."

My breath escaped so fast my knees buckled. I tried to hide it by sliding into one of the student desks, but knew I was fooling no one.

"What's the bad news?" Devon asked impatiently. He was coordinating his men to secure all the tunnel entrances.

"The hazmat emergency at the abandoned warehouse down at the wharf is all over the police scanner. They called in all the off-duty cops and firemen to respond."

"We expected that," I said. "It's not bad news."

"It is when I found two men watching the front and back of your doctor friend's house. And one of them was a cop. Who should have been anywhere but there."

"Louise's house?" I turned to Devon. "We need to get her and her family down here where we can protect them."

He frowned in thought. "No. She'll be safe enough for now. I'll send some men to keep an eye out. But if they're watching her, there's a good chance Tommaso had time to tell his people about the children. They come first."

"How are we going to convince nineteen families to abandon their lives and move down here? And how are we going to treat them once they are here?" They both looked at me. "I'm not a researcher. We need Louise. Her husband can help as well. He's a biostatistician, consults for the CDC."

"We have to prioritize," Devon said, sounding like a general at war. Or an ER doctor performing triage during a mass-casualty event.

"And Esme?" Flynn asked.

Devon cleared his throat, focusing on the map for a long moment. His hand tightened into a fist. "She'll move down here as well. I'll have to stay up top, keep an eye on Kingston Enterprises. Plus, that way they won't know we know they're behind the children's illness."

"They'll know someone knows," Flynn said. "Nineteen families are going to go missing."

"Not if they aren't the only ones," I said. "We can create some kind of emergency, have the Tower evacuated. Insert our people to talk to families as they leave, see if they or their children have symptoms. The ones who do can come down here."

"Merry Christmas for them," Flynn said wryly. "What do you think, Devon? Gas leak?"

"Good idea. If they're stretched thin, watching the families in the Tower, a mass evacuation will tie up their resources. Who do we have that we can trust to interview the families? My guys, they aren't equipped for that. Plus, I don't want anyone to know we're hiding people down here. Right now, all my guys know is that I'm expecting some valuable cargo I don't want the cops or the Russians to know about."

"Father Vance and the other nuns at St. Tim's," I suggested. "They can stage the evacuation area through the church. It makes sense the Tower residents would go there. And the nuns who worked with Sister Patrice have medical training, enough to interview the families and send the possible patients down into the tunnels."

He shook his head. Not naysaying my idea. There wasn't any better plan, given our limited resources and need for secrecy. More like wondering exactly how much crazier our lives were about to become. "I can get a few of my mother's old friends from the Tower involved. No one ever notices little old ladies, and they are all wizards at logistics, feeding, sheets and beds, shit like that."

"You already have all that down here, right?"

"Yep. Thanks to Daniel and his paranoia, we have supplies to last us years. It's maintaining secrecy that will be the difficult part. I'll have to think on that. Meantime, doc, here's a list of everything Tommaso's people ordered from Kingston Enterprises." He slid a sheaf of papers over to me. "I figure you can tell what was for research and what they might have used to make a cure."

"How can you be so certain there *is* a cure?" Flynn challenged him. "Tommaso never said."

"There's no way in hell anyone would let this disease loose without a treatment," I told her with more certainty than I actually possessed. But what was the use of fighting if we didn't have something to fight for? "Not unless they were trying to end the world. Prions are the closest thing we have to a zombie apocalypse scenario. There's no protection against them."

"And these guys are not madmen," Devon said. "This is an expensive operation. If they wanted to turn fatal insomnia into some kind of pandemic, they didn't need to invest so much. No, trust me, there's a profit motive here."

"How the hell can anyone profit from making a bunch of kids sick?" Flynn asked.

"Once we figure that out, we'll be halfway to figuring out who the hell these people are. In the meantime, we need to get those kids to safety, secure this facility, set up surveillance on the men watching Louise, set up a research lab and a treatment area—"

"Do you have all this equipment down here?" I tapped the list.

"Just about everything. I can get you anything else you need from up top." He took a deep breath, gathering his strength. The list of what we needed to do right away was overwhelming. "The kids come first. Guess it's time for a gas leak. Maybe a broken water main instead? More dramatic and will take longer to fix. Yeah, I like that."

He glanced at each of us in turn. Our little war council of three. Only, we had no clue who we were at war with, where they were, or what they wanted.

"I'll liaise with Father Vance and handle the families," he continued. "They'll listen to me. In the meantime, Flynn, you're in charge of securing things down here." He turned to leave. I followed him to the door.

"How can I help?" I asked. My words dragged. I needed my meds.

"I'd tell you to get some sleep, but—"

"That's not going to happen." I tried a smile, but it faltered and died. His expression turned doubtful. I was more a burden than an asset, I realized. Except for my fugues and what they could do. "Daniel," I said. "Maybe—"

I couldn't finish. The thought of having Daniel's entire life inside my head made my stomach revolt.

Devon laid his hand on my shoulder, a general acknowledging a soldier's sacrifice. "Maybe. But not until we have Louise here to monitor you. We can't risk losing you, Angela. If they want you so badly they would kill just to observe your abilities, then you're our—"

"Best bet for a hostage exchange. Trade me for the cure."

"No. It won't come to that. I won't let it."

"I'll do it. You know I will. Like you said. I'm dying anyway. What do I have to lose?" Except Ryder. But I couldn't be with him, not now when Tommaso's people could use him like they did Jacob. For the first time, I was glad we'd kept our relationship secret.

"No." Devon gripped both of my arms. Tight. I met his gaze. "What I was going to say was that you're our best hope to fight them. As soon as we have our people protected, it's our turn to go on the offensive. We find out who they are, what they want, and then you and me, doc, we're going to end them. Whatever it takes. Can you live with that?"

I didn't answer right away. Whatever it took included using me as a weapon. Like what he'd threatened Tommaso with, what I offered to do to Daniel.

Whatever it took meant me violating everything I believed in.

But that was another life, my old life, the life they'd stolen from me. I was starting a new life now. One with no rules.

Sister Patrice's voice rang through my mind. The same words that had started all this three weeks ago when I held her heart in my hand. *Save the girl,* she told me.

Save them all.

"Yes," I told Devon. "I can live with it."

THE STORY CONTINUES...

THE SLEEPLESS STARS
FATAL INSOMNIA, BOOK #3
COMING FALL, 2016

ABOUT THE AUTHOR

Pediatric ER doctor turned *New York Times* bestselling thriller writer CJ Lyons has been a storyteller all her life—something that landed her in many time-outs as a kid. She writes her Thrillers with Heart for the same reason that she became a doctor: because she believes we all have the power to change our world.

In the ER she witnessed many acts of courage by her patients and their families, learning that heroes truly are born every day. When not writing, she can be found walking the beaches near her Lowcountry home, listening to the voices in her head and plotting new and devious ways to create mayhem for her characters.

To learn more about her Thrillers with Heart go to www.CJLyons.net